# LEGEND

# TITLES BY KARINA HALLE

## DARK FANTASY, GOTHIC & HORROR ROMANCE

Darkhouse (EIT #1)

Red Fox (EIT #2)

The Benson (EIT #2.5)

Dead Sky Morning (EIT #3)

Lying Season (EIT #4)

On Demon Wings (EIT #5)

Old Blood (EIT #5.5)

The Dex Files (EIT #5.7)

Into the Hollow (EIT #6)

And with Madness Comes
the Light (EIT #6.5)

Come Alive (EIT #7)

Ashes to Ashes (EIT #8)

Dust to Dust (EIT #9)

Ghosted (EIT #9.5)

Came Back Haunted
(EIT #10)

The Devil's Metal
(The Devil's Duology #1)

The Devil's Reprise
(The Devil's Duology #2)

Veiled (Ada Palomino #1)

Song for the Dead
(Ada Palomino #2)

Black Sunshine
(The Dark Eyes Duet Book #1)

The Blood Is Love
(The Dark Eyes Duet Book #2)

Nightwolf

Blood Orange
(The Dracula Duet #1)

Black Rose (The Dracula Duet #2)

A Ship of Bones and Teeth
(Nightwind #1)

Ocean of Sin and Starlight
(Nightwind #2)

Hollow (A Gothic Shade of
Romance #1)

Legend (A Gothic Shade of
Romance #2)

Grave Matter

Death Valley

Nocturne

Realm of Thieves
(Thieves of Dragemor #1)

## Contemporary Romance

Love, in English/Love, in Spanish

Where Sea Meets Sky

Racing the Sun

Bright Midnight

The Pact

The Offer

The Play

Winter Wishes

The Lie

The Debt

Smut

Heat Wave

Before I Ever Met You

After All

Rocked Up

Wild Card (North Ridge #1)

Maverick (North Ridge #2)

Hot Shot (North Ridge #3)

Bad at Love

The Swedish Prince
   (Nordic Royals #1)

The Wild Heir (Nordic Royals #2)

A Nordic King (Nordic Royals #3)

The Royal Rogue
   (Nordic Royals #4)

Nothing Personal

My Life in Shambles

The Forbidden Man

The One That Got Away

Lovewrecked

One Hot Italian Summer

All the Love in the World
   (Anthology)

The Royals Next Door

The Royals Upstairs

## Romantic Suspense

Sins and Needles
   (The Artists Trilogy #1)

On Every Street (An Artists
   Trilogy Novella #0.5)

Shooting Scars
   (The Artists Trilogy #2)

Bold Tricks
   (The Artists Trilogy #3)

Dirty Angels (Dirty Angels #1)

Dirty Deeds (Dirty Angels #2)

Dirty Promises
   (Dirty Angels #3)

Black Hearts (Sins Duet #1)

Dirty Souls (Sins Duet #2)

Discretion (Dumonts #1)

Disarm (Dumonts #2)

Disavow (Dumonts #3)

Karina Halle

# LEGEND

ACE

NEW YORK

ACE
Published by Berkley
An imprint of Penguin Random House LLC
1745 Broadway, New York, NY 10019
penguinrandomhouse.com

Book design by Katy Riegel
Map by AS Designs

Library of Congress Cataloging-in-Publication Data

Names: Halle, Karina, author.
Title: Legend / Karina Halle.
Description: First Ace edition. | New York : Ace, 2025. |
Series: A gothic shade of romance ; 2 |
Identifiers: LCCN 2025018404 | ISBN 9780593952368 (paperback) |
ISBN 9780593952375 (ebook)
Subjects: LCGFT: Fiction | Gothic fiction | Romance fiction | Fantasy fiction | Novels
Classification: LCC PR9199.4.H356239 L44 2025
LC record available at https://lccn.loc.gov/2025018404

*Legend* was originally self-published, in different form, in 2023.

First Ace Edition: December 2025

Printed in the United States of America
1st Printing

The authorized representative in the EU for product safety and compliance is
Penguin Random House Ireland, Morrison Chambers, 32 Nassau Street,
Dublin D02 YH68, Ireland, https://eu-contact.penguin.ie.

For the grace we show ourselves,

the love that we deserve, and

the family that we find.

The old country wives, however, who are the best judges of these matters, maintain to this day that Ichabod was spirited away by supernatural means; and it is a favorite story often told about the neighborhood round the winter evening fire. The bridge became more than ever an object of superstitious awe; and that may be the reason why the road has been altered of late years, so as to approach the church by the border of the millpond. The schoolhouse being deserted soon fell to decay, and was reported to be haunted by the ghost of the unfortunate pedagogue and the plowboy, loitering homeward of a still summer evening, has often fancied his voice at a distance, chanting a melancholy psalm tune among the tranquil solitudes of Sleepy Hollow.

WASHINGTON IRVING—

"The Legend of Sleepy Hollow"

# Important Notes

Hello, it's me again! If you've read *Hollow* (and you must read *Hollow* first, this is not a standalone) then some of this will be repetitive, but it is important to pay attention to the trigger warnings here as they may have changed from the first book in this duet.

For one, please note that this book is a polyamorous/why-choose romance, with multiple sexual pairings, including M/F, M/M, and M/M/F. If those aren't up your alley, this book is not for you.

As for trigger warnings, *Legend* contains the following that may be sensitive to some readers: talk of abortion, use of possible abortion/birth control substance, recreational use of opium, knife play, blood play, breath play/choking, bondage in leather and chains, impact play, spit play, BDSM elements including dom/switch/sub dynamics, degradation kink, praise kink, primal kink (chasing and pinning down), anal sex (male and female), penetration/oral sex while menstruating, dubious consent, ritualistic sex, forced (dub con) sex, voyeurism, homophobic rhetoric and language, suicidal ideation, suicide (on page), murder, violence, and gore.

*Legend* is set in 1875, and while I did a lot of research to stay as true to the time period as possible, there may be some transgressions (and yes, *fuck* was an adjective, verb, and noun back then. It's truly always been an amazing word).

# *Playlist*

"Pleasure"—+++ (Crosses)

"New York"—The Kills

"Invisible Hand"—+++ (Crosses)

"Going to Heaven"—The Kills

"Corrupt"—Depeche Mode

"In the Air Tonight"—Natalie Taylor

"Feral Love"—Chelsea Wolfe

"Last Rites"—+++ (Crosses)

"Daffodil"—Florence + The Machine

"Built on Bones"—Emily Scott Robinson

"Werewolf Heart"—Dead Man's Bones

"Me and the Devil"—Soap&Skin

"Burn the Witch"—Queens of the Stone Age

"Bitches Brew"—+++ (Crosses)

"Phantom Bride"—Deftones

"Stripped" (single version)—Depeche Mode

"Ghost Ride"—+++ (Crosses)

"House of Metal"—Chelsea Wolfe

"Halo"—Depeche Mode

"Total Depravity"—The Veils

"The Sinner in Me"—Depeche Mode

"Dusk"—Chelsea Wolfe

"Kingdom Come"—The Kills

"In Chains"—Depeche Mode

"Runner"—+++ (Crosses)

"Bones"—Finnegan Tui

"Flatlands"—Chelsea Wolfe

"Seven Devils"—Florence + The Machine

"Crawl Home"—Desert Sessions

"Anhedonia"—Chelsea Wolfe featuring Emma Ruth Rundle

"Snake Song"—Isobel Campbell and Mark Lanegan

"Mercy in You"—Depeche Mode

"Light as a Feather"—+++ (Crosses)

Classroom

Stables

Classroom

Student Dorms

Cathedral

Classroom

Library

Classroom

Student Dorms

Faculty Dorms

Pocantico Lake

Trail to Sleepy Hollow

**SLEEPY HOLLOW INSTITUTE**
*Where Learning Goes Beyond*

# PROLOGUE

## *Brom*

*One year ago*

The creature stalks toward me.

Darkness coming out from darkness.

He's inside my head, inside my nightmare.

He's stepping out of my mind and into the hall.

The hall outside the room.

Malevolence pours under the doorway, flowing toward me like oil.

The creature forms here.

Tall, broad-shouldered, cloaked in night.

Missing a head.

He's holding something in his hand behind his back.

Something that drips onto the floor.

I see a hint of long blond hair hanging.

The color of cornsilk.

I know what it is.

I open my mouth to scream.

The headless man brings the object forward.

It's Kat's severed head, her blue eyes frozen in terror.

"Let me inside," the man says in a deeply inhuman voice that sinks into the marrow of my bones. "Let me inside and I'll put her head back on."

I sit straight up and scream. It echoes in the room and for a moment I don't remember where I am.

Then someone sits up next to me. A man.

He puts his arm around me, his skin cool against my burning body, and gives me a squeeze.

"It's a nightmare, Abe," he says in his low, rich voice. "You're all right."

I try to breathe, my lungs aching, and he runs his palm up and down my arm, soothing me.

"It's all right," he says again, resting his chin on my shoulder. "There's nothing to fear."

But there's so much to fear.

All I feel is fear.

I can't stop running from it and it can't stop coming for me.

I turn my head to glance at him from the corner of my eye.

Crane. His name is Ichabod Crane.

The mystery man at the opium den.

He had been watching me and I had been watching him.

Wondering what he wanted with me. His mannerisms were so refined despite the smoke going into his lungs. He seemed worldly.

And it seemed he wanted me.

I hated that I wanted him.

Then tonight he got up and approached me and offered me a bath and a place to stay. Anywhere was better than the slums I had been sleeping in, even though the idea of being with him both terrified and thrilled me.

So I came with him here.

I took a much-needed bath.

And then I sucked him off and reveled in his praise.

Feeling like I was good. Worthy.

I was wanted.

I was safe.

It had been such a long time since I felt any of those things.

I've been running for *so* long.

"What haunts you, Abe?" he asks, brushing the hair off my head. I close my eyes to his touch but then stop myself, pulling away and putting distance between us.

"Everything," I tell him though I know this man won't leave it at that.

"That much I know," he muses.

I lean forward and he puts his hand on my back, fingers gently brushing my spine. I hate how good it feels, hate how badly I want this man to use me again like he did earlier. That feeling of being wanted and desired so much, that urge I have inside to please.

I want to please him and keep pleasing him.

"This isn't the first time for you," he says. "Or is it?"

I shake my head no. "I don't do this often," I say, my voice raw.

There was only Pastor Ross. That man had started off as a father figure to me, someone who I turned to because my own father acted like I didn't exist. I trusted Pastor Ross. And I wanted him too. We only succumbed to our desires twice, knowing how dangerous and forbidden it was.

The first time we were together was the first time I had a man's cock in my mouth.

The second time he took my virginity.

And shortly after that, I took Kat's.

My heart squeezes at the thought of her. I left Sleepy Hollow for her. I was so afraid that the magistrate would make an example of me to the entire town, not just telling my parents that I was a product of the devil but that Kat would find out too. I truly didn't care what my parents thought of me; they already treated me like I was something they had to tolerate, as if I was thrown in their laps like a stray kitten they felt obliged to take care of.

But Kat . . . Kat was my everything. She still is. I didn't know if she'd accept me if she learned I'd been with another man. It didn't matter that Pastor Ross was twenty years older than me and I was only eighteen. There was no sparing me for being younger. I would be shamed.

Leaving her was the hardest thing I had ever done. I wanted to tell her the truth. I wanted to ask her to come with me. I should have. Sometimes I think about her alone in that house with her mother and it fills me with fear. The minute I know that the magistrate is dead, I'll head back to Sleepy Hollow and I'll rescue her, take her with me to some place far across the country where her mother can't get her.

But for now, I'm here. I'm here and I'm hiding.

Because there's something out there that wants to bring me back too.

Something dark and dangerous and evil. It wants to possess me, drag me back to Sleepy Hollow and hold me there so that I can never leave. It's hunting me down in my dreams, I see the shadows on the street, I see the eyes in every painting I pass following me, tracking my every move.

But how do I explain that to this man?

"You carry too much guilt with you," Crane says, running his fingers up and over my shoulder blades. Soft as a breeze but carried with precision.

I swallow thickly, feeling anger flare inside me. "What do you know about guilt?" I grumble.

"More than one man should, perhaps," he says gently. "I grew up with six sisters in a tiny house in Kansas, my father was the town pastor."

So maybe he does know.

"I grew up hearing that sodomy was a sin," he muses, his fingers tracing shapes on my skin. "The problem is, I'm so good at sinning." I can hear him smile. "It took time to dissect what it all meant. My attraction to men being on the same level as my attraction to women. It can be terrifying living in a world that is primed to not accept who you truly are. Isn't it?"

I find myself nodding. I want to tell him what happened with the pastor, but I want to leave Sleepy Hollow behind me for now. I want to be Abe, not Brom. I want to hide. Disappear. Become someone else entirely.

His hand trails up to my neck and wraps around it, holding me gently.

"I want you to sin with me," he whispers, his voice raw with desire.

My cock immediately hardens.

*Yes. Yes, I will sin with you, sir.*

His grip on my neck tightens and he pulls me back down into the bed.

# 1

## Crane

The ride back to Sleepy Hollow Institute is bound to be interesting.

I have Kat riding Gunpowder with me, her body snug in front of mine on the saddle as she nestles in my coat. Brom and his stallion Daredevil are in the lead. I want him where I can see him, just in case the horseman comes into possession of him again. What would happen if the Hessian in his spirit form and Brom met face-to-face? Would the ghost kill him? Or could he take over Brom completely, merging their souls until only the Hessian remained in Brom's body?

My gut churns at the thought, and Kat stiffens.

"Are you all right?" I ask Kat as she's cradled back against me. I press my lips on her neck and close my eyes to the feel of her soft skin against mine. "Cold?"

"Not with your coat," she says quietly. "I'm just exhausted. And scared." I barely hear the last part, her focus up ahead on Brom. The night is still and quiet, just the hoofbeats of our horses and the snort of their breath. Our conversation carries.

*Don't be afraid*, I say to Kat using the voice. *I've got you no matter what happens. And as long as Brom is Brom, he's got you too.*

I hope he doesn't make a liar out of me.

She doesn't answer. Instead, she leans against me, turning her face so that she looks up at me over her shoulder and meets my eyes. She's been through so much tonight. I don't know the specifics of what she did with Brom and what Brom did to her before I got there, and to be honest every time I think about it I'm tempted to reload the gun and shoot him in the other shoulder. He may remember now what happened to him, he may be the Brom that I knew, but as long as he's possessed, this isn't over.

In fact, it's only just the beginning.

*I promise*, I tell her. *I've got a hold of you and I'm not letting go. He's not going to hurt you ever again.*

The look in her eyes tells me she doesn't believe me. I want her to believe me, I need her to. I might be making promises I can't keep, but I'll die trying to be right.

I hold her tighter, leaning in to kiss her gently on the cheek. I want nothing more than to get her in my bed and make her feel safe again, erase everything that happened to her tonight, let her succumb to a gentle touch for once. I want her open and raw beneath me while I let my mouth and hands and cock bring her peace. But I don't want to impose myself when she's this vulnerable. Her heart and her body need space to heal.

Besides, when we get back to the school, I'll have to put her in Brom's room for the night where she'll be safe, and keep Brom with me in mine. If the horseman comes out through him, I foresee things turning violent between us in order to keep him in line. It should bother me that I feel my cock twitch at the thought, but it doesn't. Part of me thinks he needs real punishment. And that's something I've always been good at.

Eventually we arrive at the iron gates of the institute, and for a moment I fear they won't open for us. The emblem on them, of a snake and key, looks menacing, and the snake's eyes seem to glow red.

But then I hear the click of the lock and the gates slowly swing open.

We ride on through the wards, the cold pressure passing over us, popping our ears, and then we're in the campus. Like the outside world, it's also quiet here. All the buildings are dark except for the cathedral, faint light coming in through the stained-glass windows. We pass by the dorms, and it's then that I realize I don't want Kat in Brom's room after all.

"You're going to stay in the room next to mine," I tell Kat as we get to the stables.

"Why not Brom's?" she asks as I dismount.

I reach up and grab her waist, lifting her off the horse and placing her on the ground next to me. "Because I want you near me tonight in case the horseman's spirit shows up. He's still tied to Brom."

Brom is holding on to Daredevil, staring at us, his dark eyes unreadable.

*How long will you be with us?* I can't help but think. *How long until he takes over?*

But Brom's gaze gives no answer.

"Whose head was that anyway?" I ask him instead, gesturing to the library as I lead Gunpowder into the stable. Hours earlier the Hessian soldier strode into the library and deposited a head at my feet, as if it were an offering of some sort.

His beard bristles as he wiggles his jaw. "I'm not sure."

"The first man was Joshua Meeks," I press him. "Was this one involved with Kat as well?"

He doesn't say anything.

"There's no one else," Kat protests.

"Doesn't have to be someone you've been involved with," I say, giving her a reassuring look. "Brom's jealousy influences the horseman's actions. That's why the horseman paid me a visit and Brom did the same with you. I have no doubt the head that's in the library belongs to a man who fancied you. Isn't that right, Brom?"

He avoids my gaze, that permanent furrow shadowing his eyes. "It was a drunk man at the bonfire. He was harassing Kat." Then he looks to her and his expression is a plea. "I have no control over . . . I didn't . . ."

"I know," Kat says quietly, but she doesn't sound like she believes him.

We put the horses away and with Brom's unpredictable nature in my mind, I quickly duck into the tack room and grab a pair of reins, and straps for foreleg and hind-leg hobbling. I come out with all the leather bunched in my hands and approach Brom with an expectant look in my eyes.

"What's that for?" he asks warily, his body tensing.

"You know you can't be trusted," I tell him.

I pass the reins and hind hobbles to Kat, then stretch out the foreleg hobble until it's a loop of leather. I stop right in front of Brom and hold it above his head.

His eyes flash with resentment and he moves his head out of the way.

"Don't try my patience tonight," I warn him, an edge to my voice. "I'm afraid you won't like it."

He goes still but I know he doesn't want to obey me right now. He's fighting against it for once. Perhaps he doesn't like looking submissive in front of Kat. Perhaps he doesn't want to be submissive in general.

That would be a shame.

I slip the loop over his head, then tighten it like a collar around his neck. I take the reins from Kat and attach them to the leather strap at his throat.

"Come now," I tell him, giving the reins a tug. He broadens his stance and doesn't move.

"This isn't necessary," he says through a scowl, murder in his eyes. "You just like degrading me like this."

"And what of it?" I ask mildly. "You know very well what kind of man I am. In fact, you *liked* the kind of man I am. And at the moment I'm not about to leave you unrestrained."

I give the reins a sharper tug and he pulls back, nostrils flaring.

"It's just until we do the ritual," Kat says, putting a tentative hand on his arm.

He eyes her. "We don't even know what the ritual entails," he grumbles.

They both look to me questioningly.

"Blood magic," I tell them.

"I was expecting something more complicated," Kat muses.

"And sex magic," I add, eyeing them both. "Involving all three parties." I flash Brom a quick smile. "That's why I needed you to remember me in order to participate. Otherwise you would have been . . . harder to convince."

*I would have had fun trying though.*

I study them both. Neither looks very surprised at what the ritual entails, but I can tell Brom is hesitant. I don't think that man wants to share Kat. Perhaps he doesn't want to share me. I feel a flutter in my chest at the thought of him actually being possessive over me, but I'm not sure that's the case. I feel like we're not only back to square one, we're in the negatives.

"And the restraints are only at night," I try to assure Brom. "According to what I've read, the horseman can only take possession after nightfall."

And just because it gets me hard seeing him all bound in leather like this doesn't mean I'm not doing it for a good reason. But I keep that thought to myself.

We walk down the path to the faculty dorms, the statues seeming to follow us with their eyes as we go past. I've always felt them to be unsettling, but tonight they seem real somehow. I think about the strange school, the coven, and all the magic that lives here. I wonder if the horseman is the same as the ghostly teacher in the hallway, if there's something here, perhaps the collective magic, that's bringing things through the veil.

Suddenly an image flashes into my head. Of me walking down a winding stone staircase, descending to the darkness at the bottom. I remember the smell of damp earth and sulfur and dead flowers. A locked metal door. Leona Van Tassel standing behind me and smiling with sharp teeth, talking in a language I don't understand.

Then the image fades and I'm left with a sickly feeling that I brush away. There's no time to dwell on it now, not when I have a possessed man in my hands.

We're almost at the building. Kat is on one side of me, my coat on her shoulders, and I can't help but delight in the sight of her wearing my clothes again. On the other side of me is Brom, leather around his neck, hating every moment of this but submitting to me anyway.

The building is dark and quiet as we go up the central staircase to my floor, the air cool. It's dark but Kat gets flames to appear on her fingertips, lighting the way with a shyly confident smile. Both Brom and I seem to share the same awe at her power.

I go to the door next to my room where I hope to keep Kat and of course it's locked. There are a lot of rooms to choose from since only Daniels and the custodian are up here now that Desi has vanished, but the closer she is to me the better.

"Anyone know a spell for unlocking a door?" I whisper.

"I do," Kat says, and she reaches up into her messy hair and pulls out a hairpin. She jams it in the keyhole, twisting it around until the door unlocks with a loud click. "Ta-da. Every woman should know how to pick a lock."

She beams at me and I've never been so torn before. With her sweet proud face and then Brom's captive scowl, I want both of them at once. For a moment I want to attempt the ritual tonight, just get the books and have a go, but I have to take Kat into consideration. She needs time and sleep before we go into anything that could put her in harm's way again, and I need time to make sure I understand it properly, so that no one gets hurt in the process.

And frankly Brom deserves a little more punishment than just a gunshot wound.

The door to the room opens and it's just as barren inside as I thought, with only a single bed, a desk with an unlit candle, and an empty wardrobe. Luckily it's warm enough.

"Stay here," I tell her, leaving her in the room, with Brom following me to mine. I unlock my door and light a couple of candles at the window before I grab my pillow and an extra blanket from the foot of the bed and bring them back to Kat, Brom grumbling the whole way like an ornery dog.

"You'll be safe here," I tell her, placing the items in her arms while taking the rest of the leather straps from her. "I promise you, my *vlinder*."

I put my arm around her and bring her forward and kiss her on the top of her head. When she pulls away she looks up at me with longing in her eyes, fear, and my attention goes to the dried blood and the bruise forming on the corner of her forehead. I swallow down fire.

"I'll see you in the morning," I tell her thickly, waiting for Brom to either do something or say something. But his demeanor is no longer defensive and dark. Instead I see shame and guilt on his brow, his posture hesitant.

"Good night," she says quietly, and I notice she avoids looking at Brom.

We leave the room and go back into mine. Once inside I let go of the reins and turn my back to Brom, closing the door behind me. I take a moment, breathing in deep through my nose, resting my forehead against the door.

I'm not a man with a temper. I do fairly well keeping calm. My mind might be chaos at times—I believe the teacher at school said I had "hypermetamorphosis"—but I've gone my whole life learning to control my unstable nervous system, been able to find ways to mask my eccentric ways by burying it under academics. A lot can be excused when you're a professor.

But the rage I have building inside me is unlike anything I've ever felt.

It's all directed at Brom, unfairly or not.

I turn around and see Brom standing there in the middle of my bedroom, the loop relaxed around his throat, the reins dragging on the floor.

I feel as if I'm on fire.

I march toward him, winding up, and deck him square in the face. My knuckles explode in pain, but I ignore it and the hit is enough for him to stumble backward against the wall.

"Fuck!" he cries out, holding on to his nose.

"That's for Kat," I tell him, coming at him again and grabbing him by the throat, my fingers wrapping around the leather. I push him back against the wall, squeezing tight.

His face goes red and I know he can easily fight me off until I have him completely restrained, but he lets me do this to him. "You already shot me, isn't that enough?" he ekes out, his Adam's apple moving against my palm.

"Do *you* think it's enough?" I challenge.

He meets my eyes, trying to breathe in and out. A caged animal.

Finally I let go of him and he bends over at the waist, coughing.

"Do you want me to punish you, Brom Bones? Because I'll give you whatever punishment you think you deserve."

He looks up at me, his hair a mess, his eyes bloodshot.

"Who are *you* to punish me?" he grumbles.

Worry shoots through me. He might remember what we had together, but he might not have any interest in having that continue, no matter how attracted to me he still might be.

"I deserve whatever wrath Kat wishes to inflict on me," he goes on hoarsely. "This has nothing to do with you. How did you . . ." He shakes his head, as if trying to get sense back into him. "How is it that you're here? And with her?"

I turn over the hobbling leather in my hands, keeping an eye on him. "The universe works in mysterious ways." I pause, dragging the strap slowly between my fingers. "I've had more time to adjust to the idea of you and Kat together than you've had adjusting to the idea of she and I together. But make no mistake about it, pretty boy, that witch is mine."

His confusion turns into a scowl, his anger radiant and consuming. "I'm supposed to marry her."

I ignore the sharp spike of fear in my chest. "Are you sure about that?" I come close to him again, tugging at the straps in my hands while keeping my gaze locked on his. My goodness, this man carries such wildness inside him even when he's not possessed. "Because from what it sounds like, marrying her has never been your idea. It's been your parents'. Her parents'. It's been arranged since birth."

The line between his brows deepens. "You don't get to tell me what I want or how I feel."

"Perhaps not," I say smoothly. "But I do get to tell you how *I* feel. And as long as you're possessed, you're not to lay one fucking finger on her. You're not marrying her. You're not going to be with her. And you're certainly not going to fuck her. At least not without my permission and keen supervision."

He lets out an acidic laugh at that. "Who do you think you are?"

"Professor Ichabod Crane," I say with a smile.

His eyes narrow. "Right. And I've known Kat my whole life. You've known her, what? A month?"

"You were gone for the last four years," I say sharply.

"You know, no, you *saw* what happened to me!" he exclaims. "I had to leave!"

"And what did you do while you were gone? Tell me, Abe. Tell me. You were with me, my cock buried in that exquisite ass of yours, taking whatever I decided to give you."

His nostrils flare at that, eyes dancing wildly. "Fuck you."

"Uh-uh." I give him a quick smile, smacking his shoulder with the straps. "I believe I was the one fucking you."

That's just enough gasoline on the fire.

He lets out a roar and comes at me, teeth bared, hands open, and I duck him in the nick of time, swinging up behind him and grabbing the reins, giving them a hard yank so that they almost break. His hands fly up to his throat and I quickly yank back again, enough that he falls flat on his back, the room shaking.

I don't have time to worry if any of the teachers on this floor felt that, instead I'm getting down on the ground and taking advantage of the fact that he's got the wind knocked out of him. I flip the heavy weight of him over onto his stomach as he coughs from the damage I just inflicted to his windpipe.

I work quickly, tying his hands together behind his back with the hobbling straps and then do the same to his ankles before I straddle him so my cock is pressed against his ass.

"Here I was thinking I was out of practice," I tell him, bringing my hand down sharply against his rear until he jolts. "Guess all those years hog-tying the neighbor's calves did some good."

"Go to hell," he wheezes.

"And join you there? Don't mind if I do."

# 2

## Brom

Rage.

White-hot rage blinds me.

I attempt to fight against Crane. But the bastard is tall and heavy and I'm still trying to breathe after landing flat on my back. The pain in my shoulder returns with a vengeance, making me see spots.

The son of a bitch just laughs and I'm tied on the ground like a fucking animal.

On top of the fact that he fucking *shot* me.

"You know how this works," Crane coos at me, a hand ghosting down the middle of my back.

I don't want him touching me. I don't want him near me.

I try to buck myself off the ground and knock him off, but his thighs grip me tight and I feel his cock lengthening against the round of my ass and I hate how good that feels.

"You know I like it better when you struggle," he says. His

tone remains light and silky, like this is a game to him. It's always been a game to him.

"You're diabolical," I mumble. The more I thrash against him, the harder his cock grows until it feels like a weapon against me.

"You know I'm not," he says mildly.

I don't know anything anymore. The moment he kissed me by the covered bridge, read my mind, and brought my memories back, I was flooded with the images and feelings of us together. Nights in New York alleys. Mornings in his bed. Afternoons in the bath. Days in opium dens. I remember how I felt, how he really made me feel, and it was like seeing a light on in your house when you've been wandering in the dark for far too long.

I went straight into his arms because he'd always made me feel safe. A place to hide when you're so fucking tired from running.

But now, now that I've had some time to think, now that I've been caught by the very darkness that was hunting me, I don't know anymore. He's with Kat, thinks he has more claim to her than I do. He's not a lover anymore—he's a rival. And if I want to win Kat back after what I did to her, Crane can't be in the picture. Not with her and not with me.

"What do you want?" I manage to ask Crane, my cheek pressed against the cold floor as I try to get another breath in.

"What do I want?" he repeats. He leans forward and his lips are at my ear and I consider slamming my head back and breaking his nose. It would serve him right for shooting me, collaring me, and tying me up.

But I remember what I am.

Who I am.

Not just me.

I'm me with someone else lurking in the deep.

The devil.

I remember what I did to Kat. The way I rammed her head into her wall. How the darkness flowed over my limbs until I was just a moving shadow. How I lost every part of me that was ever good, even though I was never very good to begin with.

"I want to save you," Crane whispers against my neck, his lips moving with deliberation, his breath hot and making me shiver. "I want to save you, Brom."

*Fuck.*

"And what if you can't?" I ask. My voice comes out breathless and weak and worried but I don't care. Because Crane still has a way of wanting to put every part of me into his hands.

"I can't fail if I have your trust, the way you used to trust me," he says, his lips now brushing over the rim of my ear as he speaks. "Will you trust me?"

"Is this how you earn it? Tying me up?"

He pulls his face away from my neck, and the air that rushes in there is cold. The absence of his warmth cuts deep. "You know it's for your own good."

Then he makes a fist in my hair and yanks my head back. I gasp at the pain, such familiar pain, my eyes watering. My cock hardens underneath me, trapped between my body and the floor. "But while I'll save you, I also want to make you pay. I want to make you *hurt*," he rasps, a rumble to his voice.

Crane has always been rough with me, but I've never seen him angry. I don't know why I want to provoke him. I want to see that facade crack. I've always been hanging on by a thread, feeling seconds from snapping loose and succumbing to the chaos of my soul, while he's always been even and in control and I want to know what he's like when he lets go.

"Hurt me, then," I manage to say, my words tight in my throat as my head remains pulled back. My shoulder screams with pain. I think I feel the wound starting to bleed again.

"You know you have to ask for it nicely," he says, his fist growing tighter, making my scalp sing.

"Hurt me, please." My breath shakes.

"Such a good boy," he comments, and I hate how my heart blooms at the praise. "But this won't be a pain you'd enjoy."

He brings his mouth to my ear again. "If I licked your dick right now, would you taste like her?" Crane asks, and I'm immediately flooded with the image of him on his knees.

*Fuck.*

"Did you force yourself on her?" he goes on now, and his voice is low, so low, and it trembles with rage and I feel it now. All of this for Kat. All this anger and jealousy over her. "How much of your fucking was you and how much of it was the horseman?"

"I didn't force myself on her," I protest, wincing as he pulls my hair so tight I see stars. "I didn't. She wanted it. She wanted it, she wanted me"—that cloudy darkness starts to rise within me—"and I fucked her so good, Crane, better than you ever could, but I didn't force myself. I just made her forget who you were."

He stills at that, a sharp inhale, and the room seems to pause with him.

Then he takes my head and slams it into the floor.

White suns explode behind my eyes and the world spins and

before I can cry out his large hand slips under my face and over my mouth, holding back my garbled scream. My eyes water mercilessly.

"Shut up," he grunts, giving my mouth a painful squeeze, and then he's getting up, the pressure lifting from my back but I can't talk, I can't think. I feel darkness coming for me. Is it a concussion? Is it the horseman? Should I warn him if it is?

I decide to not.

Let the horseman fight him back.

But that doesn't matter because the darkness fades as Crane hauls me to my feet, and my vision rights itself just as he's pushing me back against the wall, his forearm against my windpipe. Blood trickles down my face from the corner of my hairline and with the deepest remorse I realize he did to me exactly what I did to Kat.

I deserve it.

I deserve so much more than this.

"Were you inside her when you did this to her?" he growls at me, nodding at the wound, this violence that vibrates through his whole body flowing onto me. I feel like he's transferring his rage onto me and he doesn't even realize it. "Was your cock inside her when you switched, when you caused her pain?"

"She likes the pain," I manage to say against his arm.

I watch as his eyes flash, the gray turning black. "I am torn, pretty boy. So very torn between wanting to fuck you and wanting to kill you, and I fear if I do one I'll end up doing the other."

"I'd rather you kill me first," I say, my throat throbbing as I try to speak. "You wouldn't even know the difference between fucking me and a corpse, would you?"

He laughs at that, a smile that shows his perfect white teeth, and I hate how my heart thumps anxiously at the sound of it.

But his eyes are still cold, the coldest fire, and they stare at me with stark intensity that seems to rummage inside me.

"That's a fair observation," he muses, his gaze dropping to my lips for a moment. "But I do love it when you fight back. Such a big strong man like you reduced to a writhing mess when I have you under my control. Is that what you do with Kat? Do you take it out on her, the things you wish you could do to me but can't because you're not man enough?"

"Fuck you," I say, and manage to get enough leverage against his arm to work my saliva up my throat and spit on him.

The spit lands on his cheek but the bastard doesn't even flinch.

"Spitting?" he questions, slowly reaching up and wiping it off with his long fingers. "That's a new one for you." He rubs my spit between his fingertips, indulgent. "Seems like a waste, doesn't it?"

Then he takes that hand and slides it down under the waist of my trousers until I feel my own spit meet the thick head of my erect cock.

I gasp but the sound is strangled with his arm on my throat and I didn't even realize how painfully hard I was until he touched me, my eyes rolling back in my head.

"That's the noise I've missed, sweet boy," he murmurs, his hand continuing down my length, pressing my shaft against my skin, the spit mixing with the beads of arousal from my crown. His hand is slick, hot, burning, or maybe it's me, and my hips buck involuntarily against his palm.

I shouldn't have done that. It brings out another laugh from him and he pulls his hand out.

"I told you I was going to punish you," he says. "Just wanted to make sure I could still make your cock weep."

Then he takes his arm off my throat and I cough, wheeze, suck in gulps of air that burn as they go down.

He eyes my neck and raises his brows. "That's going to leave a bruise," he remarks, the corner of his mouth lifting maliciously.

While I'm coughing, he reaches up and undoes the black tie at his collar and before I can question it, he's shoving the tie between my teeth, gagging me. I make a move to ram my forehead against his, but he ducks his head and slams me back against the wall again. Pain erupts at the back of my skull.

*Fight him.*

*Fuck him.*

*Kill him.*

I feel that darkness coming again. The more he hurts me, the more the horseman wants to take over, almost as if the spirit is looking out for me.

"I told you I liked the struggle," he says, fastening the tie behind my head. "I just don't like being spit on." He licks his lips and a familiar heat lowers his lids halfway as he brings his hands down over my bare chest, my shirt already torn from his emergency surgery earlier.

"You can tell me to stop," he goes on, his voice thick, "but I'm not sure I'll listen."

Cruel bastard.

I bare my teeth at him through the tie.

But I'm not about to tell him to stop.

I might hate myself for it, it might invite chaos and terror into our lives, but I'm not about to tell him to stop.

His palms are warm and my skin leaps against his touch and my cock is even harder than before, so much so that when his fingers find the buttons on my trousers and undo the first one, my stiff length practically bursts from my pants.

With a quick tug he pulls down my trousers over my thighs until my cock springs fully free, heavy, dark and full, the tip gleaming in the candlelight.

I watch as his fingers curl around the base, and the sight of my cock in his hand makes the blood thrum violently in my skull, intensifying all the pain from my shoulder, my throat, my head into a crescendo until it all but disappears.

"Let me see you stripped down to the bone," Crane whispers in my ear, giving my cock a sharp squeeze. "I want to know what you're really made of on the inside."

Then he brings his mouth to my neck and presses his lips there until I shiver. "I'm starting to think I never knew you, Abraham Van Brunt."

*Because you never knew I was the devil.* The thought rakes across my heart.

It comes from that dark place, the one that hides the horseman and all the worst parts of me.

Crane pauses at that and frowns, as if he can hear that thought.

Then he steps back. Releases his grip on my cock so that he's keeping it in place by a loose circle of his thumb and forefinger.

He bends down and I'm staring at his messy dark hair in awe of what I'm seeing, him *beneath* me. Then he runs the tip of his tongue over the slit in my crown and a helpless, ragged noise is torn from my throat, my knees threatening to buckle.

Crane throws up one arm, pressing it against my stomach to keep me from toppling over, and he lets the flat of his tongue lick all the arousal off of me with another hard pass.

"Fuck!" I cry out against the tie, jerking my hips forward.

He looks up at me, a lock of his hair falling across his forehead, and for one pitiful moment I consider begging for more. He just smiles at me and it's not a kind smile.

"Did you like that, pretty boy?" he croons, placing the back of his hand against my cheek in a faux gentle gesture. "You might not be able to speak, but I can tell you're aching for more."

His hand grips my cock again, smearing the moisture down the throbbing length before giving it a hard stroke that makes me moan loudly. I thrust up into his fist, desperation clawing through me. It's as if my body has finally clued in to this, to him, to what I've gone without for a year. It felt the same way when I was pounding into Kat and it feels the same way now in Crane's strong fist, an urge to catch up with what I've been missing, an urge to make things mine again.

But then he takes his hand away just as my balls were lifting up, an orgasm building at the thick base of me with no release, and he grabs me by the leather strap at my neck.

"I don't think you understand what your punishment is," he says, and practically drags me across his room. If my feet weren't already bound together with straps, I'd struggle from the pants gathered around my ankles, and I can barely keep my body upright. By the time he pushes me over his desk, the corner of it biting into my hips, I'm completely off-balance and at his mercy.

"I'm taking from you and not giving you a single thing in return," he goes on, and the candles that are lit along the windowsill in front of me nearly go out when I let out a strained huff of air.

He leaves me for a moment, going to his shelf stocked with jars of herbs and tinctures, and grabs a small vial of golden oil. He pours it into his hands, his eyes locked to mine in the way a hunter watches their prey, and my entire body feels alive and electric, like there is nothing else except this moment, no one else aside from the two of us here. Even Kat seems like a dream, and the horseman merely a nightmare.

Lust sullies my thoughts while faint panic courses over my body as I watch him undo his trousers, the knowing, the anticipation in every movement of his swift and skilled fingers. His lips curl into another smile, his gray gaze still cold and calculating. I expect him to pull his cock out of his pants—I *need* him to—but instead he comes around the back of me and presses an oiled hand between my shoulder blades, flattening me against the desk.

His hands go to my ass, giving each cheek a hard smack that makes my blood sing.

"Am I the last one to defile you here or have there been others?" he asks in a tight voice as his oiled finger runs slowly between my cheeks.

"Countless others," I try to say through the gag.

But that's a lie. There's only been him. I ran away from him and spent the last year trying to find him again in every man and woman I met, but it was never him and never the same.

"Mmm," he murmurs. "I'm not sure you were aware of my jealous heart."

His finger swirls in slick, smooth circles around my entrance, delicate in a way that makes me hold my breath and brace myself because I know what comes next. My erection kicks at nothing, my hands tied behind my back and unable to do anything to ease it. I can only wait.

"My very jealous, very hungry heart," he adds.

At that his finger enters me roughly, no romance, no trepidation, and I clench around him as he pushes in to the knuckle.

"Fuck!" I groan, the noise muffled through the tie.

I hear him hiss from behind me. "Jesus, Abe, I'd forgotten how damn tight you are."

He slipped up, called me by my other name, but right now it feels right, I feel like Abe to him, and he feels like the mysterious Manhattan stranger who I let use me for weeks. Then he grabs the oil again and I hear the slick sound of it, skin slapping together as he spreads it on himself, and then feel the heat of his thick crown working through my cheeks and pressing against me.

He slides his tip in and I gasp for air as the muscles at my entrance protest in shock. Pain jettisons up my spine at the invasion, followed by a bolt of pleasure that shoots right to my core. I'd forgotten how large he is.

"Oh, fuck me," I moan, my words blurred, wishing I could reach for my cock, which aches to be touched, jerking beneath me like a wild horse.

"That's what I'm doing, pretty boy," Crane chides me. "I suppose I'm not trying hard enough."

And at that he pushes all the way inside and grunts, this guttural, animal sound that ties my center in knots. He's so big and hot and slippery that I can't breathe, can't think, can't do anything but cry out, submitting to the mix of pain and pleasure as the fullness of him inside me seems to take up my entire world.

"God, you feel good." His words are a groan and a whisper, and despite the fact that I don't feel anything but him right now, I still revel in how good I'm making him feel. "So damn good. That's what I've missed."

And I've missed it too and I'm desperate, feral for more. I wish I could spread my legs wider but I can't. Wish I could touch my cock but I can't. Wish I could come from just his fucking alone but . . .

He shoves up to the hilt until I see stars and I feel the mass of his clothed body behind me, his chest pressed against my back. "The minute I think you're going to come, I'm pulling out," he grunts into my ear. "None of this is for you, Brom. You don't deserve a fucking thing."

I growl in anger, a threat of the darkness at my disposal.

"Call to your horseman," he rasps, biting the back of my wounded shoulder. "Let him come out while I'm buried inside you. I have a lesson I'd like to teach him."

I'm tempted. My hips are bruised from where he's driving me into the desk, my cock is so painfully stiff, twitching with my rapid heartbeat, electric and throbbing with pure raw need. If I called to the horseman, perhaps he'd take me away from this pain. He might end up killing Crane in the process, but at least I wouldn't be driven insane from his brutal thrusts with no release.

But before I can even think of letting the devil take over, I hear a sound from behind me, coming from the other side of the room, and a light breathy inhale.

Kat.

# 3

## Kat

The room is too cold, too empty, too dark. The lone candle flickers and even though I keep lighting my fingertips on fire to give more light, it's not enough and the use of this power drains me, making me feel more exhausted than I already am. There's an uneasy feeling in this room too, an energy that doesn't belong here. Perhaps it's because of what Crane has told me about the ghosts of his late wife and the teacher, but there's a sense of not being alone, like there are things watching me through an invisible wall, waiting for the right moment to come crawling out.

Then there are the sounds coming from the room next door, Crane's room, where he's keeping Brom. I know he told me to get some sleep, that he would take care of him, but from the floors and walls shaking, the cries and the thumps, it's impossible to.

I want to know what's happening.

Is Brom fighting off the horseman?

Has the horseman won and is he taking on Crane?

Is it Crane putting Brom in his place?

I know that Crane just saved Brom's life with his healing magic, but he's also the one who shot him and the rage he felt toward Brom was just as palpable as the sweet longing I saw between them.

Though *sweet longing* is a mild way of putting it.

The sight of my two lovers kissing and groping each other did something to me. It poked and prodded kindling inside me, stoking the flames, until what I felt for them was a mixture of jealousy, curiosity, and unrepentant desire. I don't even know what to do with these feelings, what they mean. Both men seem so worldly when compared to me and I feel so terribly naïve, young, and sheltered.

Yet it thrilled me. Turned me on. Made me yearn for them not only individually but together.

But when I pushed my arousal aside, I was left with the truth. Truth and pain and bruises on my neck and blood on my head.

Because Brom hurt me. He hunted me down to kill me. And even though it wasn't him when he said he'd put me in the grave, I still see his face over me, his dark eyes turning black. I fear him now when I shouldn't, and I would do anything for that to go away.

I really thought he was going to murder me. Rape me and slay me and I don't know when I'll be able to shake that feeling. I hope soon. Because I don't want to lose him as my friend, I don't want him to stop being Brom to me.

And yet I already feel the distance, the panic that sweeps in when I think about him touching me. It scares me, saddens me, and makes me so glad that I have Crane to protect me, even though he's protecting me against my own best friend.

There is still so much to sort through. The reason he left Sleepy Hollow to begin with. Pastor Ross? Why was Brom made to run while the pastor stayed around for at least another year? Why was the pastor not punished for his actions, an adult in that situation, when barely eighteen-year-old Brom had to leave?

And why didn't he tell me? That's what hurts most of all. He didn't trust me with his truth. I would have understood. I wouldn't have judged him. Why did he bed me, take my virginity, and then leave me to spend the next four years wondering if I was tainted goods? If I had done something to make him go?

*Did he tell you?*

I gasp and spin around on the bed, staring at the empty space behind me where I swear I heard a woman's voice. My heart beats wildly in my chest and I press my fingers there, swallowing hard. I must have imagined that.

*Did Ichabod tell you what he did?*

Now the voice, which I can only assume is Crane's late wife, is coming from in front of me. I whirl around as a cold breeze ruffles my hair, threatening to blow out the candle.

I'm not about to stay in here alone now. She might be a jealous spirit.

I get to my feet and hurry to the door, feeling this cold dark presence at my back like an oncoming storm, and I'm stepping out into the hall. It's pitch black and I light my fingertip enough for me to find Crane's door.

I open it and step inside his room.

And my mouth drops open.

Crane is behind Brom, who is bent over the desk, pants around his ankles, a tie in his mouth. Crane's jacket covers his rear, but his trousers are bunched around his thighs as he slams his hips into Brom and there is no question what he's doing to him.

Brom lifts his head to look at me and his eyes flash with pain, but whether it's a physical or emotional pain I'm unsure. Then Crane takes Brom's head in his hand and pushes it down on the desk.

"Stay down," he growls at him, and the command makes me feel like I'm unraveling. To see such a big brawny man like Brom being ravaged by Crane is mind-blowing, like every last innocent part of me has been thoroughly corrupted.

For a moment the room is filled with only the sound of Crane's animalistic grunts, the creak of the desk, the gasps escaping from Brom, the rhythmic slap of skin on skin, and I think maybe I can back out of the room without disturbing them, without disturbing *this*.

But then Crane pauses, his hands tight on Brom's hips, and his head tilts to the side, gazing at me from the corner of his eye. A strand of black hair sticks to his sweat-damp forehead.

"You don't have to leave, Kat," Crane says, his voice low and guttural, missing all that smooth silkiness that I'm used to. "Not if you don't want to. But if you want to stay, I'll ask you to shut the door."

I close the door behind me, making my choice to stay.

To watch.

To *see*.

I slowly walk toward them and Crane pulls out only to thrust back inside Brom and I'm feeling dizzy at the sight and the lewd slick sound of it all. I look at Brom and he lifts his head off the desk again to stare at me, his face flushed. Furrowed. He lets out a garbled cry against the tie as Crane pushes his head back down.

It's then that I realize it's not physical pain I'm seeing on Brom's face. He's enjoying it. From my angle I can see his cock under the desk, the long hard length of him. No, the pained expression comes from emotional pain. It comes from humiliation. Because that's what Crane is doing, isn't he? Screwing him while he's leashed and bound and bent over his desk.

"Does this turn you on, sweet witch?" Crane says in a raspy voice, and my eyes are glued to where his own cock disappears into Brom, shiny with oil, and, goodness, I might need a dip in a cold bath.

"I'm merely curious," I manage to say, but my voice betrays me with how husky it sounds.

"The way to my heart," he says through a groan.

Crane pauses again, grabbing Brom by the hair and yanking his head back. It's only then that I notice the blood under Brom's nose, a cut at the side of his head. My stomach twists knowing that Crane has hurt him, even though I know it's what he deserves for hurting me.

"Take a good look at her, Brom," Crane says. "Because a look is all you're getting."

Brom lets out another strangled roar, his eyes seeming to grow darker. The flames from the candles make it look like there's hell inside them.

*You know there is*, I remind myself. *You saw what he tried to do to you. There is hell inside that boy and you're not safe until it's gone.*

"Are you wet?" Crane asks me as he starts pumping again, the desk rattling. "Lift up your nightgown and show him."

I meet Crane's eyes, surprised at what he's asking me to do. Even though his expression is ravaged by lust, he holds my gaze with gravity. "He won't hurt you. He won't touch you. I won't touch you either, not unless you ask me to. I just want him to see what he can no longer have." He pauses. "There is more than one way to hurt a man, darling."

I swallow hard, eyeing Brom for a moment. It sounds so cruel. But it sounds perfectly cruel.

A strange jolt of power runs through me. Is this what it's like to be Crane? To be the one in charge, the one holding all the cards?

I take off Crane's coat, discarding it on the ground. Then I move over so that Brom can see me clearly. I meet Crane's stare and am delighted to see that clinical side of him is gone and instead he's staring at me with pure molten heat.

Energy buzzes inside me like I'm a beehive, my legs dripping with honey.

This power, this *power*. I can taste it on my tongue, the way that these two big men stare at me like what they're doing to each other doesn't even count, doesn't even factor.

All they see is me.

I lift up my nightgown and part my legs. My heated core is met with cool air and both Brom and Crane suck in their breath in unison.

Yes. This is the power.

Electricity curls up my spine and I bring my hand down, sliding it over my pelvic bone, parting my most sensitive area. I *am* wet—I can feel it gathered on my thighs.

I'm staring at Brom, remembering how he hurt me, feeling revenge and cruelty spike through my heart. It's not just the horseman. It's not just that he smashed my head into the wall and that he wanted to kill me. It's that he left me. I know why he left but it still doesn't stop the pain, the fact that he didn't think I was worth confiding in, that he still left me when he knew my mother never had my best interests at heart. Never once returned to Sleepy Hollow to tell me the truth, never once sent a letter to let me know he was okay.

Instead he was with this man, this man who is deep inside him, and I have to admit, I'm a little angry at Crane too, because it wasn't fair that he got to have Brom while they were in New York and I was left behind. I'm jealous that he got Brom during those lost years while I was all alone.

I look at Crane now, the lust deepening his frown, his mouth open in ragged gasps as he continues to thrust into Brom's backside. Well, if he wants to punish Brom, then I'm not going to stop him.

I'll help him.

I sidle closer to Crane, making sure Brom can still see me where it counts.

"Touch me," I say to Crane, swallowing hard. It feels like I'm acting in a play but I have to own it, own this wild energy that's running through me and claim it as mine.

His eyes flash. He clears his throat. "Ask me nicely."

This man does not let up.

"Please touch me."

He reaches out and slides his large hand up my inner thighs, making me shiver at his touch, and lets out a deep groan.

"Christ, Brom, you should feel how wet she is already," he pants. "She's dripping down her legs. Do you think it's all for you or all for me?"

Crane slows down his pace inside Brom as his hand glides up and up my thigh until it's sliding over my slick surface and I can't help the soft cry that falls from my open mouth.

"God," I breathe.

"You know I am," Crane says through a grunt, simultaneously shoving harder into Brom while starting to pleasure me with his hand. His fingers sink inside me, the movements rough even though there's barely any resistance, I'm so wet.

There's something so sinful about this. My family took me to church when I was younger but only to keep up appearances and integrate with Sleepy Hollow's society. The concept of sin didn't feel very real when you knew you were a witch, and they'd burn you at the stake if they could. But here, now, as Brom is getting defiled by Crane, while Crane has his long, skillful fingers pumping inside me, as I stand there in front of both of them, exposed and bare, I feel like this was the sin they talked about during the sermons. Something that could lead you down a wicked path from which you'd never return.

I want to go down that path and never look back.

After a life of loss and secrets, I'm choosing to be wicked.

And, my lord, it feels impossibly good.

# 4

## Kat

I let out a breathless moan, adjusting my stance so that Crane can work his fingers in deeper, the slick sound filling the room, and I start to ride his hand like he's a horse, bearing down and working my hips back and forth.

"Fuck," Crane mutters, and he suddenly straightens up. He pulls out of Brom, his cock bobbing from the release, so long, thick, and wet that another jolt of lust slams through me. Then he pulls his hand away from me and I let out a soft cry of protest, feeling cold emptiness where his hand should be.

He quickly grabs Brom by the collar and brings him off the desk and to the floor, where he slams him on his knees. He loops the reins around the legs of the desk, and while he does I'm staring down at Brom kneeling before me and avoiding my gaze, his hands tied behind his back, his shirt open and stained red, his nose swollen, the corner of his head trickling blood.

Between his legs his cock juts straight up. It looks painfully hard, the skin shiny from being stretched, the tip glistening with his arousal, the whole length darkened and twitching with his heartbeat.

There's a part of me that wants to drop to my knees and supplicate in front of him, place my lips on his cock and lick him clean until he's releasing inside my mouth.

But the other part, the one that remembers, that one makes me stay in place, keeps me back, even as Crane goes over to Brom and slides his hand over Brom's gagged mouth and under his nose.

"How does that taste, Brom Bones?" he asks, though he certainly isn't waiting for a reply. Crane then turns to me, that zealous look in his eyes, one hand on his cock, and I feel lightning in my veins, my toes curling against the floor.

"Strip," Crane says to me. It's all command. I know I don't have to, I know he would never make me do anything I didn't want to do, but the tone of his voice and the look in his eyes say otherwise.

I obey him, lifting the nightgown over my head.

"Now lie down on the floor, on your back, and spread your legs."

Oh goodness.

I stare at Crane, unsure of what he has planned, but I have a good guess. His gaze remains carnal, pinning me in place.

*You can walk away,* he says inside my head, his lips moving slightly. *I won't keep you here.*

I nod, feeling reassured, and get down on the floor, lying down on my back. The floor is cold but my body feels like it's on fire. I inhale, my chest rising, feeling energy spark and sizzle throughout me.

Crane gets down on the floor and keeps holding eye contact as he slowly runs his hands up my legs. I think he must mean to screw me, get in deep and make Brom watch, but then he runs his jaw up my inner thigh and I can feel the faint scratch of his stubble. I let out a trembling sigh, my back arching as I break our gaze.

I roll my head to the side and look at Brom.

The look in his eyes could light a thousand fires. If my body wasn't already impossibly hot, I would swear he's set me ablaze.

There's pure rage and frustration roiling through him, but underneath it all is desire. Lust. Raw need. As if his cock, stiff and thick as a tree trunk, isn't all the evidence I need to know this is arousing him.

"You can look at him all you want," Crane rasps between my thighs, his lips brushing over where I'm aching and wet, "so as long as you remember you're mine to taste and touch and fuck."

And at that his tongue makes contact, sliding down from where I'm swollen and needy until it thrusts up inside me.

I let out a whimper of pleasure, my eyes pinching shut at the intrusion, breaking eye contact with Brom. Violent need sweeps through me like a serpent, coiling at my center as Crane ravages me with his mouth. These aren't gentle kisses—I am being devoured whole.

"This is why 'sweet witch' is so apt," Crane murmurs as he suckles at me. "You're dessert on my tongue."

He continues with long, flat passes of his tongue over me until my thighs are squeezing the sides of his head, and I feel like if I don't hang on to him like this, I'll perish.

Crane groans into me and then places his warm, firm hands on the insides of my thighs and presses them apart.

"Have you tasted her before, Brom?" Crane asks him. His tone is mild but his breathing is shallow. "Have you feasted on Kat like this? Licked her out from her cunt to her clit until your face is sopping wet with her desire?"

He buries his head again and swirls his tongue around my bud before sucking it into his mouth, then fucking me with his tongue again. My back arches again and my fingernails are making grooves in the floor. I'm so close to coming and I'm whispering, "Oh God. Oh God."

But then he pauses while I'm at the edge, pulling back slightly. He lets out a huff of amusement. "I can still taste your cum inside her, pretty boy," he comments, his voice tight. "I hate to admit it, but I like the flavor of you mixed together."

Then Crane adjusts himself and presses my thigh closest to Brom flat to the cold floor. "Can you see her now?" Crane asks. "See that tight pink cunt? See how you're still dripping out of her?" Crane takes his finger and dips it inside me, making me gasp loudly, my body tightening around the tip. "It's like she's trying to get rid of you and make room for me."

Brom lets out a growl that seems to fill the room and my eyes fly open, my heart pounding, thinking he might be turning into the horseman. He's straining against the leather, his face red, sweat beading at his brow, while the slit at the top of his cock glistens with his arousal, enough that it's dripping off him.

"Finally getting to you, aren't I?" Crane surmises. "Then you should watch how a real man makes her come."

Crane dives in between my legs again, sucking me into his

hot mouth while he finger fucks me with one hand and squeezes at my breast with the other. My eyes roll back and I feel myself build and thicken to a point of no return, like I'm just peering over a ledge. Suddenly I'm frightened, hit with a nonsense fear that I'm about to die, like I'll fall forever if I let go.

I open my eyes to look at Brom, and the intensity in his gaze pushes me over the edge.

Then I'm coming, letting out muffled yelps that I try to hold back, my body convulsing around Crane's face and hands. The fear turns into starlight, something deep and bright and pure and for a moment I forget where I am, who I am. Just that one man is devouring me with his mouth and the other is doing so with his eyes and I've never felt so desired before.

Eventually I return to earth. To Crane's room in the faculty dorm. And I watch in a daze as Crane gets to his feet, slides his hand over his hard length in quick, skilled movements until he's moaning loudly and coming, his ejaculation aimed at Brom. Thick ropes of his semen lash Brom's dark red and obviously aching cock. It twitches as Crane's seed lands on him and Brom lets out a growled scream. If he wasn't gagged, I'm sure the whole building would be awoken.

Crane lets out a deep, satisfied groan as his strokes slow over his cock, and he gives Brom a lazy grin, cruelty glinting in his eyes.

"Do you think I punished you enough, pretty boy?"

Brom makes a pained sound in response, sweat beading on his forehead, his face twisted in agony. The energy created from the sexual release buzzes through my body, and if I had the strength to push through the haze in my mind and body, my limbs feeling like iron, I feel like I could create something. Push the energy out of my soul and capture it in my hands, like the fireflies I used to catch with Brom.

I stare at him for a moment, trying to reconcile the Brom I knew, the one I used to run around in the fields with at dusk, with this Brom. Even if he wasn't possessed, this side of him, raw and debased and incredibly sexual, is something to get used to.

"Up you go," Crane says to me, and before I know what's happening, he's grabbing me and hauling me to my feet. I'm unsteady, swaying, and aware that I'm completely nude while Crane is already tucked away into his pants, the only fully dressed person in the room.

"Are you all right?" he asks, peering at me curiously. He places a strong hand at the back of my neck, holding me in place, making me feel grounded.

I nod, unable to put into words exactly what I'm feeling. My knees still feel like they're going to buckle.

"Good," he says quietly, then he pulls me close and plants a kiss on my head. The tender action causes some place deep inside me to ache. How can this man be so damn devious and yet feel so safe at the same time?

"Why don't you go run a warm bath?" he asks me in a low voice. "I think we all need it."

"Sure thing," I tell him. I glance at Brom quickly before I go into the adjacent washroom and close the door behind me, assuming the two of them need privacy. Crane's fortunate that he has his own bathroom. When I move into the dorms here I won't have that luxury anymore—I'll have to share with the other girls on my floor.

And I'll have to do so tomorrow. Tomorrow I'm supposed to officially move to the institute. It seems like a lifetime ago that I had been at the bonfire with Mary, but that had only been tonight. My entire world feels like it's changed in an evening and I have no idea what to expect next. I just know that whatever is coming my way isn't going to be easy.

I try not to think about that as I light a couple of candles along the basin, the flames coming much easier now to my fingertips than they did earlier, perhaps because of the energy I still feel swirling inside me like a windstorm. I plug the large copper bathtub and turn the tap. The pipes groan from somewhere above me, the cistern probably in the dorm's attic, and lukewarm water spurts out from the faucet. I wait a bit, letting the water run over my fingers, but when it's not hot enough for my liking, I decide to do a little experiment.

I place my hand in the water and take the energy inside me and direct it out through my fingertips, focusing on heat and flame like I would usually do. Of course the flames don't appear under water but the heat does, streams of it wafting out and turning the temperature from lukewarm to hot.

I can't help but grin, feeling pride burst in my chest. Seems like I've ensured an endless number of hot baths in my future. I never thought I'd be able to take my magic and improve upon it and yet here I've been able to do just that. Whether it's my classes with Crane or, well, my other dealings with Crane, it seems he's done a lot to bring my magic to the forefront.

I'm just about to tell him this when suddenly I hear a roar

from the other room. It sounds like Brom and yet like a monster at the same time. Then all the candles in the bathroom go out at once, plunging me into near darkness, with only faint light coming from a cloud-strewn moon outside the window.

"Crane!" I yell, running for the door.

Only to find it locked.

# 5

## Crane

I should have seen it coming.

The jealousy. The rage.

I'd rattled the cage that held the devil. I shouldn't have been surprised when the devil lashed out.

But I was.

One minute I was hearing Kat running the tap in the bathroom, wondering if Brom would allow me to clean him up with a warm washcloth, the same way I used to take care of him after I'd been particularly rough or cruel.

The next Brom had burst up to his feet in one powerful jump, the reins around the desk snapping. He lunged at me with a roar, biting through the tie, and tackled me to the floor.

The wind is knocked out of me and with the faintest twinge of irony, I recall how our positions were reversed earlier. And Brom doesn't hold back.

Because it isn't Brom.

I stare up into his eyes, watching as the pupils start to bleed out into the dark brown, like black ink, until it's taking over the whites too. He looks inhuman, a monster, and he bares his teeth at me, strangely sharp. Is this what the Hessian soldier looked like before he lost his head? If so, perhaps the world was doing him a favor.

Brom leans in, jaws snapping, trying to take a bite out of my neck, and I can only hold him back, my thumb finding the half-healed wound on his shoulder. I drive it in and he screeches with his neck arched, a terrible noise, and I'm wondering how much longer I can hold him off. Brom has always been a little stronger than me, but when he's possessed, he's something else entirely.

And to think that this was the monster that was going to de-file my sweet witch.

With that rage fueling me, I let out a gruff cry to match his and somehow manage to flip him over on his back. I get my thumb inside the wound again, the noise of his flesh squelching making me nauseous, but I keep pushing it in.

Until he works through the pain and flips me back over, my head smacking the floor, and now I have no idea how I'm going to survive this. I'm unable to kill Brom, and even if I could, I wouldn't want to. If only I could get to my gun on the bed to maim him again.

"She is mine," the horseman rasps at me, his voice sounding like rusty metal, his breath smelling of rotting meat. "She has been promised to me through the ages. You will not stand in our way."

*Through the ages?* But I have no time to dwell on the words because his hand finds my throat and he's squeezing so tight that my air supply is immediately cut off and he's moments from snapping my neck in two.

*So this is how I die. Would have been nice to go out choking Brom and not the other way around.*

My vision flickers at the corners, growing gray and hazy, and I hate that the last thing I'll see isn't Brom's pretty face but one of a monster.

Then the bathroom door flies open with a bang, Kat cries out, and before I know what's happening Brom's grip on my neck is loosening. I'm staring up at those black eyes, watching as the darkness in them fades a little, no longer taking over his whole eyeball but just turning his brown eyes obsidian, and then he suddenly rolls over and to the floor, as if someone just hit him.

And then a most peculiar thing happens.

He starts sliding backward as if he's being dragged from behind, until he slams against the wall and moans in pain, his limbs contorting.

I look over at Kat.

My heart leaps.

She's holding out one of her hands toward Brom, palm out, and I can see the crackle of lightning and fire forming there, like she's birthing a thunderstorm. That same energy flows outward toward Brom, the lightning fading as it goes until it becomes invisible, but the force is apparent from the way she's holding Brom back against the wall.

Her face is growing paler, dark circles forming under her eyes, and she's growing visibly weaker as the seconds tick by. She won't be able to do this for long.

I quickly get to my feet, ignoring the pain in my throat, the tightness of my breath, like I'll never get a full lungful again, and grab the gun from the bed. I whirl around, wondering how else to keep Brom contained, but then Kat's arm drops and she wavers on her feet.

I have her in my arms before she hits the floor, my gun aimed at Brom.

But he's on his side and he's barely moving. Everything is back to normal, including his pretty face, and it's not lost on me that he's still naked and his cock is still hard, even after all that. Or, perhaps, because of all that.

The two of us are more alike than I thought.

I glance down at Kat in my arms, holding her tight. "Are you all right?" My voice is tight and ragged.

She makes a weak noise but nods. "So tired," she manages to say.

I lead her over to the bed and place her there gently, then I go over to Brom, the barrel still pointed at him just in case.

"Brom?" I ask carefully, my finger on the trigger.

He wheezes, his eyes pinched shut, but he's nodding too.

"Will you try to keep that horseman under control for the rest of the night? Because I don't think we can all keep doing this over and over again." I wince at the sight of the blood running back down his shoulder, then look over at Kat, who is lying on the bed, her eyes flickering shut.

Shame pinches my heart. I'm supposed to be the one keeping them safe. Yet both of them are spent and worse for wear and no thanks to me.

I run a hand down my face, trying to think of the next course of action. Brom is incapacitated for now, but the horseman could return and Kat needs to rest before she can try to stop him again. That was an impressive display of magic, more than I've ever seen from anyone, let alone one of my students, and as much as I want to see her use it again, I now know the cost.

A knock at the door brings me out of my thoughts.

Oh, *fuck*.

I glance at Brom and Kat, but neither of them seems to notice. Then I slip the gun into the back of my trousers and head to my door.

I open it a crack and peer out.

Daniels is dressed in his pajamas, wearing a nightcap and holding a flickering candle.

"Crane," he says in a gruff voice, eyes sleepy. "What the devil is going on in there?"

I clear my throat, trying not to grimace at the pain. "Nightmare," I tell him hoarsely.

His brow crooks up. "A nightmare? You mean to tell me all the thumping around and screaming is because of a nightmare?"

"This school plays tricks on you," I say by way of explanation.

Realization comes across his face. "Ah. Don't tell me you think you're being haunted by Vivienne Henry. Or Desi, now that he's nowhere to be found."

I need to play into this, though Vivienne Henry has become the least of my concerns tonight. "I have a susceptible mind," I tell him, tapping my temple.

"I can tell," he says gruffly. "I know your type, always ready to believe in anything."

"Well, we are witches, Daniels." I plaster an uneasy smile on my face.

"*Harrumph*," he says, squinting at me. "We are witches for sure, but we're also men. Try and keep your nightmares to yourself. I need my sleep."

He turns and I call out to him. "Daniels?"

He makes another disgruntled sound and looks at me.

"You wouldn't happen to have any chains, would you?" I ask. I'm not kidding. Chains would help immensely with keeping Brom properly restrained.

Daniels narrows his eyes at me again and gives me a dismissive wave before plodding back down the hall to his room. How I envy that man, able to sleep through the night without any headless horsemen or ghosts of dead teachers and dead wives haunting him.

I close the door behind me and turn around. Brom is sitting up now, his head in his hands, and at last his cock has subsided, though it's still delightful to look at even when flaccid. Kat is sitting up too, the blanket pulled up to her chin, covering her nudity.

I sigh and come over to her, picking up her discarded nightgown along the way.

"Here," I say to her. "Or would you rather take a bath first?"

Her eyes go wide. "Oh no, the bath!" she exclaims. She throws the covers back but I stop her, keeping her in bed with a firm grip of her arm.

"Stay," I tell her. "You need to rest. I'll go check the bath."

I get up and go to the bathroom only to see the water just about to spill over the edge of the tub. I quickly turn it off, surprised at the heat wafting off it. I gingerly brush my fingertips over the water and marvel. I haven't been able to get a hot bath since I arrived. I haven't complained about it because it's a wonder that the school has running water as it is, let alone in private bathrooms for the faculty, but the tepid water has been an annoyance on these increasingly cold days.

"Did you do that?" I ask Kat as I come back in the bedroom. Brom is still on the floor looking sorry for himself. "Did you heat up the water?"

She nods, a tiny smile on her lips. "I thought I would try and see what happened."

Brom snorts and we both look at him.

He lifts his head and eyes her warily. "Seems you now know what happens when you try."

She swallows, pain creased on her delicate brow. "I'm sorry," she whispers to him. "I didn't mean to hurt you. I didn't know what else to do."

"You meant to hurt me, Daffy," he says, and the use of his pet name for her is like a knife to the gut. "You don't need to lie about it. Don't need to pretend. The both of you wanted to hurt me." He glances at me now but his eyes look terribly empty. "The both of you did."

I let out a heavy exhale and go to my wardrobe, pulling out a shirt.

"Put this on," I say to him as I bring it over. "I can't take you seriously when you're naked."

He scowls at me, those dark brows knitting together, but swipes the shirt from my hand. "I'll only rip the seams," he notes.

"Most likely," I say, but still feel strange pride when he puts it on, keeping it unbuttoned. Both he and Kat look great in my clothes.

"So what do we do now?" Kat asks. "Will the horseman return tonight?"

Brom shrugs and leans back, the back of his head thudding against the wall. "I couldn't tell you."

"It would be rather helpful if you could," I tell him, pulling the chair from the desk out into the middle of the room, keeping myself between Brom and Kat. She may be able to protect herself—and me—from the horseman, but I don't want to put her in that position again, especially if her magic doesn't last for long.

Brom closes his eyes and swallows. "Try being nice to me for a while, even if I don't deserve it." His voice is so low, so broken and sad that I feel something fundamental inside me tear open.

"I think we can do that," I say quietly.

"What about the ritual?" Kat asks, obviously still worried. "We need to do that as soon as possible. We need to get the horseman out of him. He won't be at peace until it's gone. We won't be at peace. We can't keep doing this every single night." Her voice is rising with each sentence.

I give her a placating look, noticing how her fingers are clenching the edges of the blanket. "I need to do more research," I tell her. "This isn't as simple as casting a spell, nor is it like what we did by the lake. This involves blood and dark magic."

"And sex," she says simply.

I nod, swallowing hard. "Yes. Sex."

"I don't want Brom touching me."

It feels like all the air in the room has been sucked out. I swear the candles even flicker.

"So much for being nice," Brom comments, though he doesn't sound hurt.

"Frankly, I don't want Brom touching you either," I admit.

Brom grunts at that but doesn't say anything.

"But," I go on, "we will have to compromise somehow, whether we like it or not."

And I certainly don't like it.

"I said I don't want him touching me," Kat goes on, a look of defiance in her azure eyes, lit by candlelight. "I didn't say I won't touch him. I want to be in control. I need to be."

I'm looking at Brom now, waiting for his reaction. I'm not sure he'll like both me and Kat being dominant over him. He stares at Kat, an unreadable, dark look, but then drops his gaze. He lifts up his shoulder in a shrug but grimaces at the pain and I realize the blood is starting to seep through the shirt.

"Hold on," I say to him. I go into the bathroom, roll up my sleeve, and dunk my hand into the hot water, pulling out the plug to drain the tub enough so that someone can get in without the water spilling over. Last thing I need is for Daniels to complain that I'm flooding the dorm.

"Kat," I say to her, jerking my thumb toward the bath. "You should have a bath before Brom gets it dirty."

She shakes her head. From the worried look in her gaze I can tell what she's thinking: She doesn't want the horseman to come out when she's bathing and can't defend us.

*Are you sure?* I ask, using the voice. *It might help you sleep.*

She scoffs lightly at that. None of us will be sleeping tonight.

"All right," I say. "Then it's yours, Brom. I need to help you clean that wound. I have just enough of the poultice left for tonight. Tomorrow I'll have to make more."

"What are we going to do tomorrow?" Kat asks as I walk over to Brom and help him to his feet. His body is cold to the touch and he's quick to shrug out of my grip.

"What do you mean?" I ask her as we head to the bathroom, pausing at the door.

"Brom's been shot. How is he going to explain that? My mother will probably show up here tomorrow with a buggy full of my belongings. What am I supposed to say to her after everything that's happened?"

"Not to mention a poor man's head in the library," I muse, groaning inwardly at the mess we left the library in. "Listen, I'll make sure everything works out. Tomorrow is Saturday, I'll ensure Brom is healing nicely and I won't let you talk to your mother alone. I'll help you move."

"You really think she'll let you help?"

"I can be persuasive when I want to be. Don't worry about that. Try and get some rest," I tell her.

But I can tell she doesn't believe me. I grab the vial of leftover poultice and go into the bathroom. Brom is already fully submerged in the tub, the blood swirling in the water, looking so damn beautiful and dangerous it hurts to breathe for a moment. I leave the door open a crack and then grab the bar of soap and a washcloth.

I crouch down beside him, ready to cleanse his wound, but he's grabbing my wrist, his eyes hard as he stares at me. "I can do it myself," he says stiffly.

I give him a small smile. "I know you can. But I feel I owe you. I did shoot you and then jammed my thumb in the bullet hole."

"You also fucked me in front of Kat," he says, his brows lowering, his voice a growl. His grip becomes a vise. "Then you did the same to her in front of me." He pauses, his eyes darkening. "And you didn't let me climax."

"So perhaps I owe you more than this," I tell him. "Besides, this will hurt. Wouldn't you rather me administer the pain? You know I'm so good at it."

He sucks in his lower lip for a moment and I'm flooded with the urge to kiss him. Open his mouth with my lips, slide my tongue over his. Kiss him in a way that tells him that I'm sorry for being so cruel.

But then he drops his hand and looks away. He's conceded to let me take care of him.

So that's what I do.

I rub the washcloth on the soap and then swirl it around his wound. He lets out sharp gasps of pain, his muscles straining, his teeth grinding together, but he lets me clean him. Not just the wound, but everywhere, from head to toe, exploring his body in a way that brings me back to a year prior, the lazy days we'd have in the bath in that Manhattan hotel room.

When he's done, he steps out of the water and I wrap a towel around him and make him sit on the edge of the tub while I rub the herbs and oil onto his injury. Then I wrap him up with some gauze from behind the medicine cabinet, just in case.

"I think I hate you," he whispers to me as I tuck the ends of the gauze over his shoulder.

I go still at that, a knife between my ribs. I swallow thickly and look him in the eye, our faces mere inches away.

"Well," I say, giving him a faint smile, "at least you feel something for me."

# 6

## Kat

When dawn broke over the elm trees, turning the yellow leaves to gold, I woke up to find Crane's room empty. He'd left me a note that said he and Brom survived the night and that they'd gone to check out the damage to the library. At least that's what I thought it said—Crane's poor penmanship still amuses me.

I didn't think I'd sleep at all last night, but while they were in the bath I guess I fell into deep slumber. I didn't even hear them come back in, I'm not sure where either of them rested—I feel bad if it was the floor—but I assume they didn't sleep at all.

But even with a few hours of shut-eye, I still feel groggy.

I get up and slide open the window a crack, letting the cold morning air waft in with the sweet scent of overripe blackberries and the earthy smell of decaying leaves. Though the trees are glowing in shades of yellow, orange, and red, the morning sun is starting to fade already, obscured by a slow-moving fog. I stand there at the window and watch as it comes over the narrow finger of the dark lake, taking in the view from Crane's room until the mist has covered everything in gray.

It feels like it was only yesterday that Crane and I attempted the ritual in the veil standing by the shore of that black lake. I have to wonder if it was my fault that the horseman went after Brom. I was lost in my thoughts, thinking about Brom in the void, trying to conjure him forward but instead what I conjured was the horseman. All this time, had the horseman been looking for Brom, unable to find him, until my energy led him to me, like a hound on the scent?

I hold that thought for a moment, watching as the mist obscures the dark water. If it hadn't been for me, would Brom still be out there in New York or some other place, still on the run, still hunted? Would that have been better for him, to deal with that feeling his whole life, to never feel at peace or feel he could return home? Or is it better that he's here now, albeit under the control of a murderous spirit?

I don't have the answers. I just know that, selfishly, despite all he's done and what he's going through, I'm glad he's here with me. I know Crane and I will fix him, will expel the evil from his body. It's just a matter of when. There's a ticking clock somewhere—I just don't know what it's counting down to.

I sigh, taking in the sight of Crane's room. He doesn't have a lot to peruse, just a big doctor's-style bag filled with jars of potions and tinctures; a few more jars on a shelf along with what looks like a rat's skull, a couple of crystals, a stack of tarot cards, and some freshly cut herbs; and a stack of books on the floor that were probably on the desk until they were knocked off. But even so, I feel like I'm glimpsing parts of him that he keeps private, like it's a privilege to be here alone.

But I can't spend all morning looking around, so I go into the bathroom and draw a bath. I'm able to heat the water again, but not as hot as last night, and when I'm done I feel drained. It's like whatever energy has been built up inside me is now being rationed.

While in the tub I let my mind wander. There's too much happening at once, and it feels good to just let my thoughts go where they want. I know I have to think about facing my mother today and what I'll say to her. The questions I have about her involvement with using the Hessian to retrieve Brom, why she wants him to bed me on behalf of someone called Goruun. And I know that I'll have to start picking up the pieces of what happened between Brom and me and how my feelings about him may have changed.

But my mind goes back to Crane.

It goes back to magic.

I believe the source of this newfound power is connected to him. And if not him in particular, connected to sex. Perhaps a ritual isn't even needed for this exchange of energy. When I orgasm I can feel my body being filled with light, all that tension building up inside me finally releasing. But it doesn't just shoot out from my core, instead I feel it in my toes and my fingertips, like the energy is expelled but some is bounced back inside me.

That's the source of it all.

Sex.

I can't help the tiny smile on my face. I'd been told that witches were sexual beings, but now I know the truth. Maybe it's not the same for everyone—I have yet to make a real witch friend here and I'm not sure Paul would appreciate the conversation—but I suspect my coupling with another witch is what is creating this power.

Specifically, Crane. The fact that we can already exchange energy with each other, to a degree, must help. But is it more than just an orgasm, a biological drive, a need to release? Is there something more to it? Emotions? Deep feelings of attachment?

Is it love?

I sigh, sinking deeper into the tub, and this warm, tender spot forms inside me, akin to what I used to feel for Brom when I was younger. I just don't know what it means. I could be falling in love with Crane. Is he falling in love with me?

Sometimes the way he looks at me tells me he is, when he stares openly at me in a way that's more than just lust and desire, but some kind of hunger for my heart, my soul, for all of me. Then there's the way he acts around me, the sweetness that often catches me off-guard and hits me right in the center of my bones.

But love seems impossible right now. He is still my teacher, I'm still his student, and that's not even the biggest obstacle we're facing. There's my mother, hell-bent on making sure I marry Brom, and then there's Brom himself. Once upon a time Crane told me that he would respect my past with him, but after what happened last night, I'm not sure that's still the case.

And can I fall in love with Crane if I still love Brom?

Can I fall back in love with Brom if I'm in love with Crane?

Can I love both men?

Will they let me?

There are too many questions and my heart and body feel too exhausted to tackle any of them. I settle farther into the tub so that the water is at my chin. The bathroom window shows the gray mist flowing past, the light dulled, and I feel my eyes flutter closed. The warm of the bath slows my pulse, lulling me into a state of deep relaxation.

There's no sound at all except for the sound of my breath.

The faint beat of my heart.

The sound of the water splashing gently against the tub.

Rhythmic, constant splashing.

Why is the water in the tub still moving when I'm staying completely still?

"You let my husband touch you here," a voice hisses.

My eyes fly open to see a woman's head between my legs, dead white eyes staring right at me.

I scream but hands come up from underneath me in the tub, wrapping around my mouth and chest, and start pulling me down into the water. With sickening clarity I realize that I haven't been lying on the bottom of a copper tub but instead on a woman's spongy body.

Water goes up my nose as I'm held under the surface and I'm thrashing back and forth, pure animal panic surging through me.

She's trying to kill me.

I'm going to drown here.

With a surge of flustered power I bite the fingers she holds across my mouth. The bones snap with a sickening sound, blood flowing into the water, tasting like foul pennies as it goes past my lips.

"He read my memories and used them against me," the voice says as if she's at my ear now. "Do you know what kind of man he is? Do you know what he did to me?"

Somehow I manage to elbow her, her hand slipping away from my mouth, and then I'm scrambling over the side of the tub, water rushing over the sides, and then dropping down onto the floor in an awkward heap.

A hand reaches out and grabs my ankle, trying to pull me back in, nails digging into my skin.

I scream, twisting around to see the woman, her gray hair hanging off her in ropes, her decaying skin flayed open to show maggots underneath, the empty hole for a mouth and white eyes that seem to consume me whole.

"You cannot love a man like that," she hisses. "Ichabod will never let you leave!"

"Marie?" I manage to say, remembering Crane's late wife's name.

She drops my ankle in surprise.

Then smiles, that gaping black hole spreading across her face until all her features are swallowed by it.

She slowly stands up and starts stepping out of the tub.

Heaven help me.

Just then I hear the door in the bedroom open and Crane's faint voice, "Kat?"

"Crane!" I scream. "Help me!" I get to my feet just as the door opens and Crane and Brom come running inside. I collapse into

Crane's arms and look over my shoulder but the bathroom is empty. The bathtub is still. The water on the floor is the only sign there's been any disturbance.

"What happened?" Crane asks.

"Th-there was a woman," I stutter, unable to catch my breath. "A dead woman. She was right there, I swear to you."

"I believe you," he says, running his hand down my back. "I believe you."

I stare up at him in horror. "It was your late wife."

Crane's jaw flexes.

"You were married?" Brom asks incredulously, a hint of betrayal in his voice.

"It's a long story," he says, his eyes glimmering darkly.

"And a story I think we ought to hear," I tell him, straightening up. I'm suddenly aware that I'm naked once more around these two, but Crane grabs a towel and wraps it around me.

"And you will," Crane says, holding my hand and giving it a squeeze. But I don't find any comfort in it. "Both of you will. I promise you that. But right now we need to get you dressed and out onto the grounds. It may be the weekend, but soon everyone will be up and your mother will be here and the last thing we need is trouble from the coven. We have our own shit to figure out first."

I can barely think, my heart is still beating too fast, and I feel like I can't breathe. I close my eyes and try to take in a deep breath while Crane whispers, "I'm sorry we left you alone for so long. We had to go to the library first thing, and you looked so peaceful sleeping."

"Did you find the head?" I ask warily. I've been trying not to think about that head, knowing it was the drunken fellow who was pawing at me at the bonfire. Mary did a good enough job getting him to leave me alone, there was no need to murder him in cold blood. I suppress a shiver at that, knowing his murderer is standing in the room with me.

"The head is gone." Crane says this so easily, as if we're discussing something trivial. "I cleaned up the mess we left in our tussle but the head is gone. And no, Brom has no idea where it went."

I glance at Brom but he seems lost in thought, that hurt expression in his eyes, and I know he's still thinking about the fact that he didn't know Crane was married before.

I swallow uneasily and look up at Crane. "I think your wife was trying to kill me."

He gives me a tight smile. "I'm sure she was. She has a lot to be angry about."

I squint at him. *What did you do to her?*

But I know that question will have to wait for later. I tuck it away with the million other questions I have, knowing it's probably futile to expect answers anytime soon.

# 7

## Kat

After the incident with Crane's dead wife, I dressed in his shirt and coat and made my way over to the women's side of the faculty dormitories. Since I arrived at school in just my nightgown, the only way to get proper clothes would be to go back to my house. But I don't want to go back there. I don't even know what time my mother and Famke got back last night from the bonfire—or if they did at all—but my gut instinct is telling me that going back to my house wouldn't be safe.

Of course we're only assuming that my mother is coming here today with my belongings to move me into the dorm. One would think she would have come here as soon as she returned home last night and realized I wasn't there. Or perhaps she thinks I'm still in my room sleeping. It's early enough in the morning.

Though I'm hit with the memory of trying to escape from my bedroom and finding the door locked. Did that really happen? Had someone locked me in my bedroom with Brom? Had she been home at that time while I was struggling? Or had it been Brom himself who somehow locked the door when he shut it?

Either way, my mother was determined that I move to the institute.

But since none of us are ready to discuss with her—or anyone for that matter—what really happened last night, I can't be walking around campus in a nightgown, with bare feet, and covered in bruises. Thus it's up to me to try and wrangle clothes from one of the teachers. I don't know any of the female students well enough, but at least the teachers will feel obliged to help, given that my family runs the school.

Brom and Crane stay behind in their area as I go down the women's hallway and knock on the first door I see. Ms. Peek, my alchemy teacher, answers it.

"Katrina," she says, gripping her dressing gown around her, her black hair swept up under a bonnet. "Good heavens, what are you doing here? Come in, come in."

She ushers me into her warm room, smelling of incense. Thankfully she's always been welcoming to me and supportive in my classes with her, even though I'm not as good at alchemy as I want to be.

"What happened, dear?" she asks. She's probably the same age as my mother but appears much younger in some ways, with beautiful porcelain skin and bright brown eyes that seem to never miss a thing.

I give her a quivering smile and launch into the story I concocted in my head. "I went for a walk by the lake this morning with my friend to try out a dawn spell and I tripped over some roots. So embarrassing. I fell right into the lake. He was kind enough to give me his clothes but my nightgown and boots are all soaked and I don't have anything else to wear at the moment."

She purses her lips as she listens, studying me closely. I can tell she doesn't quite believe me.

"Are you all right?" she eventually says, her gaze going to the corner of my head now. "You hit your head?"

"I'm fine," I tell her quickly, pasting on a smile. "Just smacked it on a rock when I fell, but I feel fine. Just embarrassed, that's all. You wouldn't happen to have clothes you could lend me for the day, would you? I'll return them to you tonight. I won't get them dirty, I promise."

She folds her arms, still focused on the wound on my head, and I'm glad I did up Crane's collar high enough so that it covers the bruises on my neck. "You really should see the nurse. She's an excellent healer."

"I will. But I can't go like this," I say, gesturing to Crane's oversized clothes. I hold out my arms in emphasis and his scent wafts up toward my nose, warm spices and fire, and my stomach does summersaults. I'm amazed that after all we've done and been through, just his smell is enough to make my knees weak.

Crane says he's under my spell but I think I'm the one under his.

"I don't have a large selection," she says with a reluctant sigh, heading toward her wardrobe and throwing open the doors. "Teacher's budget, you know."

I take a look around the room while she does this, noticing more than the incense wafting from her desk: the smell of tobacco.

"Oh," she says, catching me staring at a burning cigarette in a mortar. "I hope you don't mind. I know smoking is frowned upon, but it's a habit I picked up on my travels. It's from Egypt. Not that I've been there, but I know people who have. I cleared it with Sister Leona, in case you're worried."

I shake my head. "I'm not worried. I've never met a woman who smokes."

"Some of us do," she says, going through her clothes again. "In private." She pauses. "I also have some opium, if you're interested."

My brows shoot up at the mention of Crane's weakness, ignoring the fact that my teacher is offering me drugs. "You have opium? How did you get it here? Did you manage to leave the institute?"

"Of course," she says, coming over to me holding out a plain navy blue skirt and bodice I've seen her wear a few times before. "I don't have a corset that will hold your, well, ample attributes, but I think you should still fit this. I'm sorry it's not as nice as what you're used to."

"No, it's perfect," I say absently, taking the items from her, my mind still tripping over what she just said.

"Hmm, you need shoes and stockings," she says as she eyes my feet. "My boots might be too small for you but they should do for now. Oh and you'll need a chemise as well. As for drawers . . ."

"I'll go without," I say quickly, and she doesn't bat an eye at how scandalous that sounds. Instead she goes to her armoire and opens the drawers. "Ms. Peek," I begin.

"Please, call me Narae," she says. "We should be on a first-name basis if you are wearing my clothes."

"Of course, Narae. You said you left the school. When? How?"

"This summer," she says, bringing out a chemise from the drawer. "I was gone until the end of August. Took the riverboat down to Manhattan, and then the train to Boston."

"And they let you leave?" I ask, holding the chemise along with the skirt and bodice.

She gives me a funny look. "Of course. Many teachers stay but I like to travel. I don't remember a thing about the school while I'm gone, just that I teach here and that's it."

"But when you're gone you still know you're a witch . . ."

"I do," she says with a slow nod. "But it doesn't feel as important when I'm out there. It's as if all my magic stays here at the school. I'm barely a witch at all when I leave." A worrying expression comes over her as she gives her head a shake. "But I did have a note from your aunt with me. It said to bring back as much opium as possible. She'd given me money too. I'd forgotten, but it was there in my pocketbook."

"Leona wanted you to bring back opium?" I ask, thinking I'd heard her wrong.

"Yes."

"What for?"

She shrugs. "I didn't ask. Or if I did, I don't remember. Why don't you go into the bathroom and put those on? I can help you with your boots after."

In a daze I walk into the bathroom and put on the chemise, skirt, and bodice. It's a little tight but thankfully it fits because I'm not using a bustle at my rear. The bodice only does up at the front because it has a ribbon closure instead of hook and eye.

When I emerge I feel out of sorts but passable, and I sit down in her chair as she brings out stockings and boots.

"I can do that myself," I tell her as she starts to roll the stocking up over my foot, and despite what happened in the bath earlier, I'm glad I'm freshly clean.

"You are used to a housemaid," she says. "And I was a housemaid before I became a teacher. It's not a problem for me."

Ms. Peek—*Narae*—finishes up with the stockings, securing them below the knee with matching navy ribbons, and then the cream-colored boots that are too tight and pinch my toes together, doing them up with a button hook, and I can't help but think about Famke and the way she always assisted me. My mother never did. It feels good, even if for a moment, and I wonder if I'll eventually make any girlfriends in the dorms where we might help each other with things like this.

I'll miss Famke. I know I'll have to find a way to go back into Sleepy Hollow to visit her. There's still so much we need to discuss.

In the end, Famke said she was loyal to my father and to me. Maybe when I graduate from this school I can bring her with me, wherever I end up going, though it feels a little pathetic that the only way I'll have any sense of family is by paying her to be my housemaid.

And all at once I'm hit with the intensely hollow feeling I get when I miss my father out of the blue, the profound shock of his absence mingling with the present.

"Are you in pain?" Narae asks me, and I glance at her in surprise. She's finished doing up my boots and is holding out her hand for me to stand up. I quickly reach up under my eyes to find my cheeks wet—I've been crying.

"I suppose I am," I say hoarsely, swallowing the lump in my throat before taking her hand as she helps me to my feet.

"Your feet are too big for my shoes," she points out, thinking that's why I'm crying. "It might be painful for a bit. Try not to walk too much today until you get your clothes." She drops my hand and then starts fixing my hair, bringing out a few pins from under her bonnet and putting my strands up in a loose bun, letting a few strands hang loose.

"There," she says. "Now you look less like you've fallen into a lake." Her gaze hardens. "You know you can talk to me about anything, Katrina," she says in a low, steady voice. "You're a special witch and I think you know it. Perhaps alchemy isn't your strong suit yet, but with your bloodlines, you have the ability to go far. You can do anything." Her look softens. "You'll find your place here, with the right people. Sometimes it just takes time to find the right path to take you there."

She pats my cheek gently and then takes me by the arm and leads me to the door.

I wonder how much of what I feel is visible on my face. She can't possibly know everything I'm going through. Then again, she could be an empath witch. Either way, when I thank her for her help and I step out into the hall, I feel lighter than I did when I first entered. In fact I barely feel the pain from her boots when I shuffle down the hall and back to the men's wing.

There are Crane and Brom together, waiting for me outside Crane's room.

My men.

My people.

They're what's waiting at the end of the right path.

God, I hope this is the right path.

Crane is leaning against the wall, fiddling with his watch, but straightens up when I approach, his storm-cloud eyes pinned to my every move. Brom is beside him, brooding in an ever-present state of tension, but his shoulders relax when he sees me. And for the first time today, I really see Brom. Because the horseman won't be inside him until dark. I see my old friend, the one I used to trust more than anything. It gives me a dash of hope.

"You look nice," Crane says, clearing his throat as he looks me up and down, taking his clothes from my arms.

"Ms. Peek was kind enough to lend me her things," I tell him. "She also gave me some information that I think you'll want to hear."

"Do tell," Crane says, unlocking his door and tossing the clothes inside so they land on a heap on the floor, not even bothering to hang them up.

This man is such an enigma sometimes.

Then he locks the door and puts his hand at my lower back. I can feel the heat of his palm through the fabric, and my eyes close for a moment at his touch.

"I'll tell you when you feel like telling us about your late wife," I say, using the information as leverage.

He lets out a huff of amusement, the corner of his sculpted lips rising.

"Well played, little witch," he says. Then he sighs. "But all must wait because first you have to see your mother."

I balk. "She's here already?"

Brom nods toward the windows at the end of the hall that face onto the courtyard. "I just saw your mother's horse and cart go down the path toward the women's dorm."

I make a face as my heart sinks. I don't know why I'm so scared but I am.

"We'll go with you," Crane says as he gently prods me down the hall. I notice he said *we* as in him and Brom and not just him, for once.

I sigh heavily, squaring my shoulders, the tight bodice pulling at my back as I do so. "I want you both there, but . . . I need to do this alone. And I don't think she'll let either of you in the girls' dorm."

"Not even your future fiancé?" Brom asks flatly, which makes Crane's fingers press into my back, his breath a sharp inhale.

"No," I say, trying to weigh my words so that I don't hurt Brom, knowing what he said to me last night. "They can think what they want to think about us getting married, but the both of us know that's not going to happen, not when they want it to happen for reasons we don't understand."

Crane's grip relaxes slightly, but I can't ignore the pinch of rejection on Brom's brow and I instantly feel bad. Why does everything have to be so damn complicated all the time?

They lead me down to the first floor, but before I walk out the door, Crane pulls me aside and lets his thumb hover above the wound on my forehead. "I should have done this earlier. This might hurt a little."

I go still as he gently presses his thumb to my skin. It stings and I grit my teeth. "How you seem to love causing pain," I manage to comment.

"I happen to be very good at it," he says before closing his eyes and chanting a few words that I barely hear and can't decipher. Slowly the pain melts into something warm and soft, like honey, and then he's removing his hand. "There. That should take care of that."

That warm softness spreads from my head and down the rest of my body and I feel the urge to fall into his arms and give in to it, just succumb to his strength, let it wrap me up in golden chains.

But Crane seems a little drained from what he just did, and I realize he did more than heal me. I think he gave me some of his own energy so that I can survive the next ordeal.

"Thank you," I whisper.

He gives me a quick kiss on the forehead and spins me around to the door. "You're welcome."

With newfound verve, I give them a wave goodbye as I gather up my courage and walk down the curved path toward the women's dorms, my gait awkward thanks to Ms. Peek's boots. It's still early and everyone here seems to sleep in on the weekends, so the grounds are quiet except for the birds chirping about, small flocks of sparrows and finches that land on the heads of the statues like jaunty hats, coupled with the sound of the breeze rustling the dead and dying leaves of the surrounding woods. The mist from earlier has started to infiltrate the campus, like a phantom's translucent fingers wrapping around a neck.

A chill runs through me and I look back to see Crane and Brom still standing in the doorway to the faculty dorms, watching me until the fog moves in and makes them blurry.

I gulp and turn around in time to see my mother emerging

from her buggy holding a box of my things, heading to my new dorm, the door to the building propped open. Her back is to me but she senses me anyway because she comes to a dead stop and whirls around to look me dead in the eyes.

"Kat!" she says sharply, and for once in my life I see relief in her face, as if she's actually been worried about me, even though it does nothing to hide how frail and awful she looks. "Goodness gracious, where have you been?" She adjusts the box in her hands as I approach her, and she looks me up and down. "And what on earth are you wearing?"

Time for another lie, but this one is one she'll want to hear.

I perfect a sheepish grin. "I had to borrow clothes from one of my teachers."

She shakes her head. "Why? I don't understand? When I woke up this morning and you weren't there, I was afraid the worst had happened."

"And what would the worst be?" I ask curiously.

She frowns. "That you were murdered or abducted by the headless horseman."

Funny. She didn't seem that concerned about it before.

"Oh," I say. "No. I met up with Brom at the bonfire and we came back here to his room for the night. My clothes, uh, they got damaged in the process."

She seems to transform before my eyes. The whites of her yellowing bloodshot eyes growing brighter, her cheeks turning pink, a smile broadening.

"You were with Brom?" she says, excitement palpable in every word.

I keep the shy smile on my face.

"Yes." I say. And I shouldn't say the next part but I do. "That's what you wanted, isn't it?"

Her expression falters for a moment. "It's what everyone wants. And it's what you want too."

I nod slowly, keeping up the appearance of the daughter who doesn't want to discuss such intimate things with her mother. "Yes, well, I would like to get some of that special tea from you."

Her eyes narrow. "Tea? What do you mean?"

"I just started school, Mother," I tell her. "I don't want any children, not yet."

She scoffs loudly at that. "Gracious me, Katrina. Your studies aren't as important as your future husband and family. Just who do you think you are, expecting to choose an education before all else?"

My head spins with whiplash, but I don't have the energy to get into why my mother wanted me to marry Brom my whole life, then forced me to go to this damn school once he disappeared, and now wants me to marry Brom again as if the school no longer matters. If I questioned her about it she would just give me a bunch of lies stacked on top of lies.

"Still, I'd like the tea," I tell her in a measured voice.

Her eyes narrow further and for a moment I feel suction, as if I'm looking into an airless void.

God. What kind of witch is my mother?

"I will not make you any such tea. You were born to carry Brom's baby, Katrina. That is your purpose. That is your fate." She gestures to the school. "All of this is just . . . filling the time."

My teeth grind together and I can't keep the words to myself. "And what if Brom isn't the only man I'm still sleeping with?"

She reaches out and snatches my wrist, her grip hurting me until I cry out and try to twist away but she doesn't let go. "Don't tell me you're still with Crane? What kind of whore are you?"

Turns out I only like being called a whore when Brom says it.

Rage explodes inside me and I growl at her, pushing all my fiery energy onto her until she yelps and lets go, the force causing her to tumble backward onto the ground, dropping the box, my books spilling out onto the cobblestone.

She stares up at me and I expect her to get back up and come at me, fueled by anger, or perhaps back away out of fear of her own daughter, but instead she's staring at me with awe, her mouth open, while my hand prickles with electricity.

"Sarah," Famke calls out, and to my surprise I see her coming out of the building, hurrying over to us. "Kat!" she exclaims when she notices me. "Where have you been, child? What happened here?"

I feel a rush of relief at seeing Famke, though it's a little jarring given that she's not a witch and yet has somehow been allowed on campus. Then again, there's a lot I don't know about her. Or this school.

"I—I'm fine, I lost my balance," my mother says, her disbelieving eyes still on me as Famke helps her to her feet. Famke then crouches down to start gathering up the books.

My mother stares at me, wobbling slightly.

I lift my chin to let my mother know I'm not to be reckoned with.

But my mother only smiles in return.

A cunning smile.

The one a fox would have before it corners its prey.

With cold clarity, as if being doused with ice water, I realize I've made a huge mistake.

*Promise me that when you feel the call to magic, to the strange and the unusual, to power, that you ignore it.* My father's words ring in my ears.

*That you will never show it or tell anyone about it . . . including your mother.*

"I knew you had it in you, Katrina," my mother says in a low voice. "All this time your father made me believe you didn't have power, but I knew he was lying. I knew this school would bring it out."

Famke looks up at my mother with concern, and I can feel her eyes on me but I can't look away from my mother's gaze, the way she's staring at me like I'm her next meal.

"Look at you, my dear daughter," my mother goes on. "You're ripe for the picking."

# 8

## Crane

Such a foul mood Mother Nature is in," Daniels says as he sidles up behind me. He clamps a hand on my shoulder as he always does, but this time it makes me jump. "Looks like you're in a mood too."

I glance at him. I'm standing at the front of the school's herb garden. I'm supposed to be finding some yarrow to make another poultice for Brom's almost healed shoulder. I had left Brom in his dorm room since there's no need for him to be under my supervision until after nightfall. He's still in some discomfort from being shot, and while opium would go a long way, a healing poultice will have to do.

He doesn't like me taking care of him like this. It's like when we first met all over again. In need and hating it, hating that I'm the one to do it. He's ornery and grumpy and has every right to be, considering what's been happening to him. But it doesn't matter how many times he tells me to take a hike, I'm still going to help him heal. After all, I am the one who put a bullet in him. It's the least that I can do.

But instead of finding the herbs, I'm staring off into the distance. To Daniels it probably looks like I'm observing the weather, the fine drizzle, the dark clouds above the treetops, hovering above the stone buildings like an ominous hand, the patchy line of fog that travels through the gardens.

I'm not looking at the weather though, nor am I looking for the plants. Instead I'm staring at the female students' dorm, knowing that Kat is in there with her mother. I should be in there with her. I should be watching over her and I can't. Kat didn't want me there and I know Sarah wouldn't have let me. If she were any other woman I would chalk it up to protective motherly instincts, but I know that's not the case with her. She's protective over Kat the way a breeder is protective over their prize broodmare.

"I guess I'm a little tired," I tell Daniels, forcing a quick smile. "You know, the nightmares and all. Any news about Desi?"

Daniels rubs at his mustache. "Not a word." Then he shrugs. "Apparently they're bringing a new linguistics teacher. From Greece. A man again, which is nice. Feels like it's just you, me, and the custodian against the world sometimes." He gestures to the school.

"Well, you know witches," I say, absently plucking some damp sage with my fingers, releasing the scent into the air. "It's a woman's world. Male witches seem to be in short supply."

"It's probably for the best," he concedes. "I have a feeling this institute would be chaos if male witches were in charge. You know how Jeremias would run it."

Jeremias is a dark mage, a male witch who has done some questionable things with his powers, according to the rumors. But at this point anyone would be better than the sisters.

Then, as if I conjured her up from my own thoughts, I hear a voice call out.

"Ichabod Crane?"

I turn around to see Leona Van Tassel come out of the mist, hood up, face in shadow, cloaks floating around her like black ink.

"Sounds like you're in trouble," Daniels says under his breath. He seems like he's joking but from the uneasy look in his eyes and the way he quickly nods at Leona and hurries away, I don't think he is.

"Ah," Leona says, lowering back her hood, her all-seeing eyes following Daniels as he scurries off. "I'm starting to get the feeling that Mr. Daniels is afraid of me." Then she turns her sharp eyes to me. "But not you, Ichabod. You seem able to handle all sorts of things."

I don't want to ask what she means by *all sorts of things*.

I lift my chin as I peer down at her. "You know I can."

She gives me a tight, fleeting smile, not intimidated by me in the slightest. I could be seven feet tall like the horseman and it wouldn't matter to a witch like her because no matter what, her magic will always be stronger than mine.

For now, at least.

Her thin brows come together as she studies me with a discerning eye.

"You've learned something new," she says warily.

"And what's that?"

"You've learned to block your thoughts," she says, tapping the side of her graying temple.

Now my smile is genuine. "Yes. A vampire once taught me how to do that. I just didn't think I would need to use it with anyone." She's been reading my thoughts ever since the day she stalked me outside the opium joint.

"Vampire," she says sourly. "I'm surprised you were able to get close to one."

"Oh, I think I'd be able to surprise you with a lot of things," I tell her, an edge coming to my voice. I clasp my hands behind my back. "Now, I can tell you have something on your mind."

"I do," she says. "A lot, as it is. Will you accompany me to my office?"

Hmm. Perhaps Daniels was right about me being in trouble.

But I have no choice but to follow. I don't think telling her I need herbs for a student I shot last night would be a good idea. Besides, now I want to know what's on her mind, though I worry that Leona might distract me from Kat when she might need me.

She turns and gestures back to the cathedral. The mist is obscuring most of it, making the sharp spires look like nails suspended in air.

We walk down the path and I let the sage drift down from my fingers as I go.

I haven't been inside the cathedral other than the first day I arrived at school and even then I was in Sister Margaret's office. The only time I was in the cathedral itself was for the initiation tests, of which I still remember very little.

But here Leona leads me straight through the gargantuan iron doors, which swing open for us with a heavy creak, aided only by magic, and she takes me past the glass display cases that showcase crystals, gemstones, and esoteric relics, past the first few offices and into the cathedral proper.

Memories of the tests come back, falling on me like snow. Or perhaps like ash. I remember all the candles being lit, flickering like a rapid heartbeat and throwing soot into the air. The statues that I see now that line the edges of the space seemed bigger back then. I remember thinking they had eyes, though now they're just blank and still. The stained-glass windows threw a multitude of colors on the stone floor, even though my test took place at night. Right now the colors are muted from the fog.

"I'm assuming you're remembering some of the tests," she says, glancing at me over her shoulder as we walk down the center of the aisle. On either side of us are a few rows of church pews and then it opens up to big empty space. My footsteps echo loudly as we walk, but hers don't seem to make a sound at all.

It's damp in here and I can't help but shiver underneath my wool coat, as if it's colder than outside, and it smells like hot wax and incense and damp earth.

Finally we approach the altar made of bones, with feathers and candles and chicken feet spread across a wooden slab, and she beckons with her finger for me to follow her even though I don't know where we could possibly go.

But we go behind the altar and there I see a door in the ground and steps leading to a well-lit basement.

Fear shudders through me for a moment as I remember a fragment of the dream I had. Being in the basement, being with Leona, and suddenly it's as if my gut is screaming at me to not follow her, that it's a trap.

*We're all just flies in a web.*

But my feet keep moving thanks to my own curiosity and I'm going down the steps, ducking as I go.

"You'll have to forgive the low ceilings, Mr. Crane," she notes. "Humans were shorter back then."

"I'm used to it," I tell her, relieved to see that the area underneath the cathedral is just a short stone-lined passage lit by sconces with two doors across from each other, *Sister Leona Van Tassel* etched on one with *Sister Ana Van Tassel* on the other.

She opens her door, with a sinister creak, and we step inside. With a flourish of her hands all the candles in the room are lit, as is the fireplace in the corner.

"Take a seat," she says, taking hers behind the teak desk.

I sit down on the old velvet chair across from her, my body a bit too tall for it, my long legs splayed awkwardly.

"Why do I feel like I'm about to be fired?" I say, hoping that lands as a joke.

But from the tepid smile on Leona's face, I don't think I stuck the landing.

"Not quite, Ichabod," she says, folding her hands on the desk. "Or I guess it all depends on what you have to say to the accusations."

My brows rise at the same time that my stomach sinks. "Accusations?"

"Yes," she says sharply. "It has come to our attention that you are having sexual relations with one of your students. Katrina Van Tassel."

I suppose it should be a relief that she didn't say *two* of my students.

"Was that wrong?"

She blinks at me. "I beg your pardon?"

I splay my hands in defense. "I didn't know that was frowned upon. I don't remember seeing any rules regarding teacher and student relations here."

"It's a given, Mr. Crane," she admonishes me.

"I see," I say. "Well then, I'm sorry I didn't know."

She gives me a contemptuous look. "You honestly expect me to believe . . . Oh, it doesn't matter. The point is, you must call off your relationship at once."

"Or?"

"Or you'll be fired."

I narrow my eyes as I study her. At the moment she looks relatively normal, that strangely ageless yet not unattractive older woman, but every now and then her face will shift, like the more angry she gets, the more her magic starts to slip. She's covering something up under there.

She's covering up her real face.

I close my eyes for a moment, refusing to let my imagination run away on me as it is apt to do. The last thing I need is to start picturing what she might really look like.

"Can I ask you a question?" I say, opening my eyes and daring another glance at her.

"What?" she says with a tired sigh.

"How old are you?"

Her pointy chin jerks inward. "I'm not sure that's an appropriate question," she says, her tone haughty.

"I mean no offense by it, I'm just curious. You seem like you're much older than you look."

"Well, I appreciate the compliment," she says, folding and re-folding her hands, and for a moment it looks like she has an extra knuckle. "But I'm old enough to run a school and run it well. And that means laying down the law when it comes to errant teachers such as yourself."

"One hundred years?" I press on. "Two hundred years?"

She lets out a bark of a laugh. "Mr. Crane, I am not immortal."

I lean forward in my seat, my elbows on my thighs as I stare her right in the eyes. "No. But you wish you were."

Her back straightens. "Don't we all?"

"No," I say with a shake of my head. "I don't. I told you I've been with a vampire. This particular one had to watch his love die while he could only live on, still pining for her hundreds of years later. I wouldn't wish that on anyone."

Leona tilts her head to study me for a moment. I hate the way her eyes feel on my skin, like buzzing flies landing and then taking off before you can swat them.

"I don't believe you," she surmises. "You're too curious to just submit and die. You want to know what happens to everything and everyone, don't you? You want to watch what happens to the world. But I can tell you what happens to the world, Mr. Crane. This world burns. Eventually this world will burn and all that's left will be ash . . . and us witches."

I stare at her for a moment before I smack my knee. "I'd like to stick to my original answer."

She gives me an acidic grin. "Very well, Mr. Crane. You're lucky that such immortality will never be thrust upon you anyway. You're slated to die, just like everyone else."

The skin prickles at the back of my neck. I take a chance.

"Who is Goruun?"

Her body stiffens. "I'm sorry?"

"Goruun," I repeat with a smile. "I've heard that name thrown around here. I've tried to do research at the library about it but I can't find anything." Which is a half-truth. I haven't had time today to do any research, but I figured it's better to hear it from her anyway and see if it matches with what I find in the future.

She stares at me blankly for a moment and I feel that pinch of intrusion at my temple, like she's trying to read my thoughts again. I remain steady in blocking her. I don't even flinch.

"I don't . . . ," she begins. Then she clears her throat and gives me a hard look. "I mentioned Goruun to you on the first night we met."

The memory slides into place. I knew I had heard it somewhere the moment that Brom mentioned it.

"I wasn't put on this earth by Goruun to blend in," I say softly.

"That's right," Leona says. "And it's still true."

I fix my eyes on her. "And so Goruun is . . . God?"

She rubs her thin lips together, her eyes seeking the ceiling in thought. "Goruun is . . . divine. He is not God. He is the deity of our coven. So, *a* god if you will."

*More likely a demon*, I think.

"And you believe your coven's deity has something to do with me?"

"Oh, he has something to do with everyone who crosses my path," she says brightly. "Think of this school as a web."

I swallow hard, my nails digging into my knee. "And we're all just flies in it?"

"You don't have to be a fly, Ichabod," she says. "You can be a spider instead. Your long legs, your black hair, your dark nature—I think you'd be a very apt arachnid, wouldn't you agree?"

"I don't have a dark nature," I say, wishing I didn't sound so defensive.

"But you do," she says. A pause follows, heavy enough to fill the entire room. "I know you killed your wife."

I bare my teeth at her, anger turning my hands into fists. "It was an accident. You know it was an accident."

"Was it?" she asks. "Or is that what you've told yourself so many times that you've come to believe it? You were involved with that other man, the one she had the affair with. She caught the two of you fucking. She threatened to divorce you, tell the school, and you couldn't have that so you killed her."

My eyes pinch shut, blocking out the memories. "No, no, no."

"You killed her and coerced that man, what was his name? The witness report said it was Ray. You coerced him to cover up for you, to tell the police it was an accident. You were going to blackmail him too."

My heart is beating so hard in my head that I can't even think.

"How would Katrina feel if she knew her lover killed his wife?" she goes on.

I glare at her. "She wouldn't care because I'd tell the truth, I was going to tell her the truth."

"No, you weren't," she says. "You wouldn't risk it. You're afraid that she'll find out the truth anyway, perhaps by getting inside your head, or perhaps just by looking at you. You wear guilt so well."

"It was an accident!" I shout, the chair toppling over as I spring to my feet. "It was an accident, that's the fucking truth!" I lean over the desk and shove my finger in her face. "You're trying to place false memories in my mind, I know what you're doing, you witch!"

She stares at my finger, so calm, so poised, and for one horrible second I want to jam my finger straight into her eye, press it into her brain and make her stop, make her just fucking *stop*.

"That rage inside you will break you until you face it, until you let it out," she says smoothly. "And you're already a broken man, Ichabod. You want to lash out, but the person you truly wish to hurt the most is yourself."

"Fuck you," I growl, turning around and striding to the door.

"Let me be clear here," she says loudly.

But I don't want to listen to any more of this. I put my hand on the knob and try to turn it. It won't open. Of course I'm locked in here.

I pivot to face her but she's already on the other side of the desk, hovering several inches above the damn floor.

"This is my school," Leona says, and I can't stop staring at where her feet don't touch the ground. "It always has been and it always will be. My coven has more power in our fingertips than you'll know in your sad, angry little life. You're saying to yourself that you don't want to give up Kat, that you'll quit and give up being a teacher, because she's worth it and this school is dangerous anyway. You would be right about that last part, of course, but you won't quit. Because you can't. Because you're needed here. The students need you to teach them, to take care of them, and that's what you want more than anything, anything to soothe that guilt in your soul. You need to be here to protect them, isn't that right?"

I try to swallow but can't.

She goes on. "So you won't quit. You will stay and you will teach and you will protect and you will keep your students safe in order to absolve your sins. And as for Katrina, you were going to tell me you'd break it off, but both of us know you'd be lying. So I'm going to tell you this instead: There is destiny in the works, Ichabod, something bigger and greater than you'll ever be witness to. Katrina Van Tassel belongs to Brom Bones—it is written in the stars, scored in the earth, burned in the ashes, and the more you get involved, the more your life will be at stake."

My muscles tense. "Are you threatening me?" I ask gruffly.

"Yes," she says. "This is a threat. And it's not the only threat. If you don't comply, we are telling Katrina that you killed your wife and meant it. Don't think you can bluff your way out of it when changing police records is an easy thing to do. It would be so embarrassing for a school to have unknowingly hired a fugitive from justice, but I'm sure the world would move on pretty quickly. You, however, would lose her . . . and go straight to jail."

"And so that's why you hired me," I say slowly, becoming sick with the realization. "Not because I'm a brilliant teacher but because you had something on me. Something you could use and bend to your will."

She smiles and lowers several inches until she's back on the ground. "We call it collateral. It's what smart businesses do to protect themselves in this day and age. So be a good boy, Mr. Crane, and stay and teach and keep away from those who aren't meant to be yours."

At that, the doorknob clicks and I turn to see it open by itself.

"You are a brilliant teacher, by the way," she says as I step outside. "You're doing what you're meant to do. So keep doing it and don't mess things up."

Then the door slams shut behind me.

# 9

## Brom

Insistent rapping at my door brings me out of my dark thoughts. Thoughts I'm not sure belong to me or someone else. The *other*.

I get up and hurry over to the door, the knocking continuing, assuming it's Crane, hoping it's Kat.

I open it to see Crane on the other side, fist raised to knock again, his face contorted, hair wet and sticking to his neck.

I've never seen this man look like this before. Haunted, broken and wild, an animal torn between being predator and prey, and for the first time I see what it must be like to be him looking at *me*.

"Crane?" I ask, wondering what's happened. "Has the horseman—"

He bursts into the room, kicking the door shut with his foot as he grabs my face hard and kisses me even harder before I can finish the sentence. His mouth is lush and wet and warm but there's no tenderness here, there rarely is these days, and he fucks me with his tongue like he's taking complete ownership.

My beard scratches against the stubble on his face, and his skin is hot to touch.

He tastes like rain.

We both stumble backward until I'm pressed against the wooden wardrobe, the handle digging into the soft flesh by my kidneys but the pain only feels right. His fists go to my shirt, holding on as the kiss deepens, becomes violent, and I moan against his lips, unable to contain myself. I haven't felt this wanted and desired in such a long time. Last night was punishment, this is something else entirely.

"Hit me," he rasps, his eyes like flint as he pulls back. "Hit me, Abe."

I blink at him rapidly, at the sound of my old name, at the oddity of his request.

"Sir?" My old moniker for him slipping out as well.

"I said fucking hit me," he growls. "Hurt me."

I shake my head, licking the taste of him from my lips. I've been full of such hatred and anger toward him, but now seeing him like this, wounded and lashing out, I can't do it. The turmoil I've felt about him seems to evaporate.

"No, I—"

"I'm not asking, I'm ordering you to," he says, grabbing me by the throat and spinning me around so that his back is against the wardrobe. "You fought back so well last night."

"Crane . . ."

"Want me to get you in the mood, is that it? Get you to hate me again? You seem to do it so easily, you slippery fucker." He says this all with a sneer on his upper lip, his eyes flickering between madness and desire, if desire was a fever he needed to be cured of. "How about all the times I fucked your fiancée and made her come screaming my name? How I made her forget you even existed? How I told her she belonged to me and only to me and she wanted it, she wanted, needed, to be with me, not you, *never* you, you missed your fucking chance, you—"

I unleash.

I strike him right across his sharp cheekbone, my knuckles feeling like fire.

The back of his head smacks against the wardrobe.

Then he raises his head, his damp black hair flopping across his forehead, and his eyes search mine in the same way that Pastor Ross's did when he was praying to God. "Do it again." My fist shakes, I hesitate, and his hand is still on my throat. "Do it again or I'll tell you how I used a riding crop on her ass and a ruler on her cunt and I dominated that sweet witch until she was puffy and pink and slick with—"

Pure jealousy slams into me and I punch him again, this time getting his jaw until I hear his teeth clank together, and his grip on my throat loosens, his chin dipping down.

"Crane," I say, breathing hard, my knuckles burning, my shoulder hurting from the action, and somewhere deep inside me I feel the horseman stir in that darkness. "Please don't make me do it again. I don't want the Hessian to come out. He might break the rules and come out during the day."

Crane lifts his head, his hair obscuring most of his haunted eyes. "Maybe that's what I deserve. Maybe that's what I want."

I swallow hard, not liking any of this, how quickly our roles have reversed. I'd always wanted to see Crane snap, to see that flippant mask slip, to know what it's like to punish him for a change, but I don't want any of it. Not like this.

"Well, I don't want it," I say gruffly. "I don't want it, Crane. This isn't safe."

I knew that word would get his attention.

He nods slowly, my words sinking in. His gaze drops and his hands go down to my trousers, pressing the heel of his palm against my erection, which I hadn't given much thought to until now.

"Then I just want to fuck," he says, his voice low and husky, sounding more normal again, and when he gazes at me, I see his pupils blacken in lust. "I want to fuck. I want to come inside you and make you come too."

He presses harder against my length and I gasp. The foolish little noises I make when I'm with him embarrass me and I feel my cheeks already going hot.

"There's that color I like to see," he murmurs before he grabs me by the back of my neck and gives me a possessive kiss that makes my fingers curl at my sides. "My pretty boy," he adds as he breaks away with a smirk.

Then he reaches up and grabs my hair in his hands and gives it a sharp tug, making my mouth drop open, the pain causing my dick to twitch with blood, with need. It's fucking beautiful.

"Yes," he hisses, leaning in to lick the rim of my open mouth. "Oh damn it, Brom, I'm going to fuck your seed right out of you."

With another tug that makes my eyes water, he leads me over to my bed and orders me to get undressed, and then undress him when I'm done.

I work as fast as I can with shaking hands, shucking off my clothes and his, my dick already so thick and swollen that I feel the faintest breath on it will make me climax. Then, when I'm nude, and his naked body is standing before me, those extra inches on him seeming to have that same effect on his cock, I stare openly at him. Last night I never saw a thing, but now he's raw and open and right in front of me.

Crane looks like a god. Perhaps a fallen one at the moment, but still a fucking god. His lean, long, yet defined body, his skin pale as the moon, smooth as silk, only a dusting of black hair under his arms and the trail running from his stomach to his cock that stands up like a heavy, darkened pole between his muscular legs.

It thrums through me, this want, it fills up every crevice and hollow until I can't see straight, can't think straight.

Then Crane pushes me so I'm on my back and on the bed and he comes over me, the heat of him overpowering and even though it's the afternoon and gray light is coming in through the window, it feels like the whole world goes black and is whittled down to just him, like he's standing at the end of a tunnel.

"Can I be your savior?" he murmurs, running the tip of his nose over mine.

I can only swallow in response, hoping my eyes tell him the rest.

Except he's not the only one who needs saving in this bed.

I hope he knows that too.

He kisses me, hot, deep, violent, and my breath catches in my lungs, wrung out, and it's so easy to succumb to this man. I reach up, running my fingers over the defined bones of his clavicles, his shoulders, then down over the hard planes of his chest and the chiseled grooves of his abdomen. I'm trying to remember this, the way he feels, in case it doesn't happen again. In case there might be a day soon, too fucking soon, where the horseman takes over and doesn't give me back.

That day is coming, isn't it?

And soon?

How much time do I have?

"Do you have any oil?" Crane says gruffly, biting at my neck and bringing me back to the present. His teeth pinch and hurt but then he soothes it with flat sweeps of his tongue. I'm trembling with need now, hard as stone, all my blood gathered in my cock, leaving the rest of me to feel empty.

"No," I say through a disappointed gasp as I let my hands trail over his lean hips to his thick cock that juts out between us. He feels like fiery iron in my hands, veiny and rigid, all of this for me. I run my thumb over the flared tip, gliding along the slit and pushing the beads of arousal down his length until he lets out a low groan that shakes the bed and gets me even harder.

"Touching me without my permission?" Crane muses, though the tremor in his voice betrays his easy tone. "I'll allow it."

Then he lays his entire body over mine, his weight taking my breath away, and then pulls back enough to spit into his palm. He brings that hand down to his cock, his wrist rubbing against mine as he does so and causing me to press my hips up into him in a desperate need to fuck.

"Open your mouth, sweetheart," he says to me, and I obey as he dips his head down and licks the inside of my lips, tasting, savoring, so wet, wet, wet, before he presses his hips down against mine, rubbing his cock against mine.

"Fuck," I cry out, my eyes rolling back and spine bowing toward him as the sensations threaten to destroy me. There's enough moisture from our arousal and his spit to make the rutting silky smooth and I feel myself let go, lost to the sensation of this man above me, taking what he wants from me and keeping me safe at the same time.

He might not be able to save me but at least, in this moment, he's all mine and I'm all his.

"God, you're handsome when you're beneath me," he says in a throaty, lust-choked voice that makes my blood run even hotter. "I'm going to have to keep you for life."

I hate the way my heart jumps at those words, the lightness inside me, like I haven't seen the sun in years.

But that hate melts into pleasure as he begins to move his hips against mine, our cocks rubbing and fucking against each other, our stomachs taut, hard and growing slicker by the second. The feeling of him above me is like nothing else and I'm reaching up, my nails making half-moon grooves into his shoulder blades as they work, his elbows planted on either side of my shoulders as he braces himself.

Sweat begins to drip off him and onto my chest, pooling to my stomach as he works me, his lower body grinding and flexing, the bed creaking, our ragged breath and grunts filling the space of this small room.

"Sir," I say through a gasp, unable to keep myself from slipping back into a year ago.

"Mmm?" he says, his voice rumbling, breath shallow and tight as he presses a sweat-damp forehead against mine.

"Can I come?" I whisper.

*I'm going to come* is what I mean to say, the muscles in my thighs tensing as I try to hold my orgasm back. But it's too good, it's too good like this, with him.

Like this, with him.

Too good.

He pulls back enough to stare me in the eyes, his pupils black and frenzied, the control on his face is being held together by a thread.

"Yes," he whispers back.

He drives his hips against me hard, unrepentant thrusts that make my back arch, my mouth fall open in a rough cry as I come, my orgasm a sharp, venomous monster that claws through my body after being teased for so long last night. My cock jerks alongside my convulsing limbs, thick streams of semen spurting out between our stomachs.

"Oh, Jesus," Crane murmurs through a strained gasp and I know him, I know his body, how he's unable to hold himself back whenever I come. He ruts against my body faster and harder now, his cock lubricated by my own hot seed, and then his neck is bending back, showing me his perfect long throat and he's releasing between us, warmth and stickiness spreading.

Then he stills and his head is buried in the crook of my neck and as he collapses his full weight on me, I wrap my arms around his back and hold him. I want to ask him what's wrong, what happened today, but I don't want to rush him. He needed to get that out of him first.

We just remain as we are, breathing hard, our hearts nearly colliding as they beat wildly against our rib cages. Somewhere in my darkened depths I know that the Hessian is still there, waiting for nightfall. But at this moment, it's just me.

And for once I let myself just enjoy this.

No shame.

No hate.

Finally Crane pulls back and reaches up, smoothing my hair off my forehead with his long, delicate fingers, and I'd forgotten how much I missed this part, the after, the peace and softness that follow. Our fucking wasn't rough this time but even so, this quiet, it's needed.

"I want you for myself, Brom," Crane says softly, his gray eyes flitting over my lips, my nose, my brows. "I want you for myself and I want Kat for myself and I'm not sure I want you to have each other."

My chest tightens with a stab of possessiveness. "I don't think you get to decide that."

"Perhaps not," he muses after a moment, giving me a fleeting smile. "But it's what I want."

"To have us both but not to share."

"Something like that."

"I shouldn't be surprised."

"Yes, well, I have an uphill battle," he says with a weary sigh. He puts his long thigh over mine, the hair of his legs tickling my balls, and rests his head beside mine on the pillow, his body too tall and large to fit fully beside me on the single bed. "After all, you're the golden boy, Brom."

I snort. "They wouldn't think that if they knew the Hessian was still inside me. None of my supposed betrothal to Kat is because of me, of who I am. It's not that I came from a better family or that my parents wanted something good for me, or that they all think I'm a good, worthy person at all." The pain digs a deep hole when I admit this. "I see the way they look at me, like I'm not even fucking there, like I'm just seed to be used. It's a transaction, isn't it? I'm the golden boy to those witches because it's what someone called Goruun dictates."

He stiffens at that.

I swallow uneasily. "Did you find out what Goruun is?"

He nods, licking his lips. "I did. I found out a lot of things today and none of them are good."

I turn my head on the pillow to look at him, the pained expression held in the groove between his black brows. "No matter what it involves, or if you don't want to tell Kat, you can tell me. I can handle it. I need to be able to protect her too."

He stares at me for a moment, his lips moving as he runs his tongue over his teeth.

*Damn it, Crane, what the hell do you know?*

"I was called into Sister Leona's office today," he begins, and I wasn't expecting to hear that.

"What for?"

"For fucking Kat," he says bluntly. "She wants me to put a stop to it."

Raw pride and ownership flare inside me, like I've won her hand in jousting.

"Yes, I know," he says, reading me, "not a bad deal for you. But it is for me. I'll be fired otherwise."

"Something tells me you'd rather lose your job than lose Kat," I say begrudgingly.

"You know I'm nothing if not loyal, Brom," he concedes. "And nothing if not possessive." He pauses. "But while I don't intend to stop with Kat, I do think it's worth keeping it a secret and continuing to work here. There's something terrible happening at this school, something I can't even wrap my head around. But I feel like the students are at risk."

"You feel or you know?"

"Both," he says slowly. "Leona told me I'm needed to protect them. From what, I don't know and she didn't say. But it did lead to talk of Goruun. Who, it turns out, is a deity linked to their coven."

"A fucking deity?" I repeat. I close my eyes and try to remember exactly what Sarah had said to me when I was still half-possessed. *"Help us bring Goruun's wishes to life."* I repeat her words quietly. *"Help us usher in a new age."*

"Does this new age have anything to do with the end of the world?" Crane ventures.

My eyes fly open. "Not that I know of. Sarah only said I had to take what was owed to me and go get her daughter. Perhaps I read into that wrong. Maybe I'm not meant to marry Kat on behalf of this Goruun."

"Or maybe you're meant to get her pregnant," Crane says, his voice like iron. "And the marriage is ceremonial. I don't know. But I can tell you this much: Regardless of whether we exile the Hessian from you sooner or later, I still don't think your cock should go anywhere near her. Not for the sake of Kat's safety but because this is what *they* want. And you have to wonder why that is."

He's right. I fucking hate that he's right, but he is.

"I'll be careful," I tell him.

He grabs my face and gives my jaw a sharp, painful squeeze as his eyes bore into mine. "You are not to fucking touch her," he growls at me, holding me tight. "Not unless it's for the ritual, not unless it's under my supervision. Understood?"

I can't even talk against the pressure in his fingers. I manage to nod.

But I never verbally agree.

# 10

==

## *Kat*

I spend the rest of the afternoon staring out my new window, waiting and hoping to catch a glimpse of Crane or Brom. I'm on the first floor, which makes it easy for me to sneak out my window at a later hour, but I don't think I'm allowed to wander over to their dorms as it is.

After my mother told me I was ripe for the picking, which she then clarified by saying I was ready for my magic to be fully useful—something that seemed to please her to no end—I let her usher me into the dorm to set up my room. There was no chance for me to talk to Famke about what I really wanted to (mainly, if she knew who or what on earth Goruun was). My mother watched me the whole time. It's like her eyes were drinking me in and by the time they finally left, I felt completely drained, as if she'd taken back whatever energy Crane had given to me. It couldn't have been my imagination that she seemed brighter and stronger than earlier.

Finally they left and while I was sad to see Famke go, I felt nothing but relief the minute my mother left me alone in my new bedroom. There had been no more talk of tea but she did say she wanted Brom and me to come for dinner next weekend. I said I would depending on the weather but she gave me a look that told me she wasn't going to take no for an answer. Well, she would have to come and drag me there.

Now that I'm back into my regular clothes and there isn't much more to do, I need to find Crane and Brom. But out there in the halls I can hear my fellow students laughing and chatting and I suddenly feel lonely.

*This isn't the time to make friends*, I remind myself, trying to feel stronger. *Your focus is Brom and Crane and that's it right now.*

Finally, when the drizzle that had started earlier seems to let up, I gather up Ms. Peek's clothes and boots, planning to go to the faculty dorm and give them to her. That way I can quickly swing by the men's wing and see if Crane is there.

The hall is empty of students when I step out and lock my door, slipping the key into one of my tiny pockets on the bodice where I keep my button hook. I exit the building through the main doors and into the cold air. The sun is still up somewhere but the fog and clouds have swallowed up almost all light, plunging the campus into a hazy darkness. It's strangely still and quiet, only the faint dripping from the eaves and onto the cobblestone, and for one terrifying moment I feel like I'm the only person left in the world. Like this is all there is left, just me, the stillness.

And something dark and sinister that lurks in the shadows.

Something that wants to eat me.

Then a breeze ruffles my hair and I hear the call of crows as a flock of them take flight from the trees, and everything seems normal again.

A violent shiver rocks through me and I hurry over to the faculty dorm, careful not to slip on the slick path, and then head up the stairs to the mezzanine. I think about going to Ms. Peek's first to drop off her clothes, but I'm pulled toward the men's wing, the need to see Crane too strong to ignore.

I turn the corner of the hall and then come to a stop when I find Sister Sophie standing outside his door, as if she just knocked and is waiting for him to answer.

Her head swivels toward me. "Katrina?" she asks, sounding surprised and yet uneasy at the same time, as if I caught her doing something wrong. Then she squares her shoulders and walks toward me, chin raised, that haughty coldness that all the sisters seem to share corrupting her eyes.

"What are you doing here?" she asks suspiciously.

"I was returning some clothes to Ms. Peek," I tell her, raising the items. "Were you seeing Professor Crane?"

Her eyes flick over me. "Yes," she says after a moment. "I had something I wanted to discuss with him. And you were only going to see Ms. Peek?" She raises a thin brow. Even with her hood down, she still seems shrouded by shadows.

"I sensed someone was down here," I lie. "I was curious."

Her lips wrinkle. "You and the professor are very much alike, aren't you? Always so curious."

"You make it sound like that's a bad thing."

"It can be," she says, her eyes narrowing slightly. "Katrina, I know the two of us don't talk very often, so while you're here, let me offer you a word of advice." She leans in closer to me and in her pupils I see strange pinpricks of light, the scent of sulfur filling my nose. "Don't make trouble for yourself. You won't be able to handle the repercussions."

I stare at her, dread filling my chest. "What do you mean?"

"You're meant to be with Brom," she says, her voice lowering. "They brought him back for you."

"But why? Why him? Why did everyone decide this when I was born? What do you get out of it?"

She looks away for a moment, as if listening to something I can't hear, before returning her steady gaze back to mine. "Did you know your mother was never supposed to marry your father?"

"Actually," I say, finally knowing something, "my mother said something akin to that. That none of her sisters approved of her marriage to my father."

"That's right. They didn't. Neither did I." She pauses, wiggling her jaw. "You know I am not related to you, Katrina, but I am related to Brom."

My mouth drops. This is news to me.

"How?" I ask.

She ignores me. "And your mother was supposed to marry Liam Van Brunt," she adds.

"My mother was supposed to marry Brom's father?"

What on earth?

Sister Sophie gives me a tight smile. "But she didn't, did she? She chose your father instead."

"Because she fell in love with him," I say feebly.

She lets out an acidic laugh. "She never loved your father. Oh, you are such a naïve girl, Katrina, even after all you've been through. To think either of our families have anything to do with love."

A sinking feeling creeps through me and I press Ms. Peek's clothes to my chest. "Why are you telling me all of this?"

"Consider it a warning," she says gravely.

"But what if I don't marry Brom? What if . . ."

*What if I marry Crane instead?*

But I don't dare say it.

"As I said," she says, brushing past me. The contact of her shoulder against mine makes me feel dizzy. "It would be wise for you not to make trouble for yourself. You have no idea what you're dealing with here. Good day, Katrina. If you see Professor Crane, and I'm sure you will, please tell him I was looking for him."

She walks off down the hall, her cloak rustling behind her as she goes.

I stand there for a few moments, feeling absolutely dumbfounded by what she said. I want to run after her and demand she tell me more, but I have a feeling that whatever she just told me, she wasn't supposed to.

So why tell me at all?

I mull it all over as I go over to Ms. Peek's hall and knock on her door.

"Katrina," Ms. Peek says as she opens it. "Oh, I'm sorry. You prefer Kat, don't you?"

"Thank you, Narae," I say to her with a grateful nod, handing her the clothes. "I really appreciate your generosity."

"It was my pleasure," she says, taking the clothes from me.

She reaches out and touches the top of my forehead, causing me to flinch.

I smile awkwardly. "Sorry."

"Your wound is all healed," she marvels, taking her hand away. "You went to the nurse?"

"I got someone to heal me," I tell her.

"They did a marvelous job," she muses. Then she opens the door wider. "Here, why don't you come inside? We can have a chat. Get to know each other a little better." She gives me a sly smile. "I'll let you try a cigarette."

Even though it sounds really lovely to sit with her and watch her smoke cigarettes and talk about her travels and her life, my mind can't sit still.

"I have to go, but I would love to visit with you another time," I tell her.

"Of course," she says. "I'll see you in class. Take care of yourself, all right?"

I promise I will and as she shuts the door, I hear heavy steps down at the mezzanine and my skin prickles with goose bumps at the sound of his distinctive gait.

I hurry around the corner to see Crane striding toward his wing.

"Crane!" I whisper as loud as I can, and as he turns I start running toward him.

At first his face lights up when he sees me, like he has candles within him, but the closer I get something inside him shifts, an awareness, and he's taking a step back from me. Perhaps I am being a little too bold in my approach.

"Kat," he says, my name sounding caught in his throat. He

reaches out and takes my hand, giving it a squeeze before quickly dropping it. "I don't think you should be here."

"Why not?" I ask. "I need to talk to you."

It's then that I notice his face looks a little beat up, a bruise at his jaw and his cheekbone. "What happened to you, are you okay?"

I reach up to touch him but he moves his face out of the way.

"Clearly I'm fine," he says, giving me a quick smile. "Just a little scuffle with Brom, nothing out of the ordinary."

"Is Brom okay?"

"He's more than fine," he says with a private smile.

"Well, I still need to talk to you."

He looks around him, even though the hall is empty. "And I need to talk to you but now is not the time." He pauses. "At the moment, for now, I can't be seen with you."

It feels like he's kicked me in the ribs and my breath hitches. "Why not?"

"Because I'll get fired if I'm with you, Kat," he says, and the admission stuns me. "And while I'm prepared to lose my job for you, just . . . I need time to figure this out."

"Fired? What happened?" Oh God. "Do you not want to be with me anymore?"

I hate how pathetic I sound, how quickly my lip pouts, how the tears rush to my eyes without warning.

"Oh, heavens, my *vlinder*," he says, his expression crumbling as he cups my face in his warm hands, a single tear rolling down my cheek. He stares down at me with burning intensity that I feel in my toes. "I want to be with you every single moment of every day. You're all I think about, all I dream about, all I want, and I promise you, I promise you, nothing is going to stand in the way of that. Everything I am doing, I am doing for you, Kat. I'm doing it for us."

He slowly runs his thumb over my cheek, wiping away the tear as his eyes trail over my face. "But for now, we need to meet in secret. Just like before. We were getting careless and now we can't afford to be."

I feel slightly more assured, enough to let out a deep breath. "Who told you they would fire you?"

"Your aunt Leona."

"Really? Because I just saw Sister Sophie here. She was knocking on your door. Wanted to talk to you about something."

He sighs, letting go of my face, and it feels so cold without his contact. He runs a hand through his hair. "She probably wanted to tell me the same thing that Leona did."

I shake my head. "No. I don't think so. She knew I was going to see you and she didn't seem to care. But she did tell me I needed to be careful or I would face repercussions."

"And that's what I'm talking about," he says in gruff annoyance.

"Then she told me that she's a Van Brunt."

Crane does a double take. "Come again?"

I'm nodding. "Sister Sophie is related to Brom. She wouldn't say how. Which, I suppose, means that Sister Margaret is too. And she said that my mother was supposed to marry Brom's father, Liam, but obviously that never happened. And now I'm supposed to marry Brom because . . . because . . ."

"Because Goruun said so," he says.

"I didn't get that far," I say warily.

"But I did." He gives his head a shake and then looks off with a pained expression. "We need to talk. But not here. Not tonight when I know they'll be watching closely."

"So then you're going to leave Brom on his own tonight?"

"No. He'll be with me. They never said I had to stay away from Brom, only you, and if they make me explain why I have Brom chained up in my room, then I'll be quick to tell them it's either that or he's going to be unleashing the headless horseman on campus."

"Chains?"

He looks chagrined as he brushes a strand of his hair behind his ear. "The custodian lent me some."

Why does the idea of Brom in chains make my core grow hot?

"So what am I supposed to do?" I say, trying not to whine but failing, hating how powerless I feel. I'm seconds away from stomping my foot like a child. "You can't just leave me."

"My, you're stunning when you're being a brat," Crane muses.

"A brat?" I repeat in shock.

He grins at me. "Yes. Impatient and petulant. Not used to it when things don't go your way."

I glare at him. "I don't think I deserve that."

"You deserve my ruler on your pretty pink cunt, that's what you deserve," he murmurs, his eyes darkening. "Swatting you until you come so hard you're spraying me with it."

Heat floods through me, flaming my cheeks and gathering between my legs. "You're not being fair," I manage to say.

"I never said I was a fair man, did I?" he says, clearly enjoying this. "Not to worry, darling, it's just for tonight. Tomorrow morning come meet me in the library. Nine o'clock. It should be quiet then and there's no rules about a teacher tutoring his student in public."

"Will Brom be there too?"

"If he wants to be," he says begrudgingly. Then he leans in, placing a fast kiss on my forehead. "I'll see you then. In the meantime, try to make some friends."

He turns and walks off toward his door. "Oh, and," he says over his shoulder, giving me a cold smile, "stay away from Brom."

# 11

## Crane

*One year ago*

W hat are these?" comes Abe's groggy voice.

I step out of the bathroom, completely naked, to see him standing by my desk, already dressed, and fingering the stack of tarot cards beside the glass of water I left out for him this morning while I was in the bath. I'd wondered when he'd notice since I made no attempt to hide them, but I guess we've been doing nothing but fucking for the last few days, ever since he came home with me from the opium joint.

"Tarot cards," I tell him.

"That's what I thought," he says, about to pick one up and then thinking better of it.

"Does it bother you that I have them?" I ask carefully. I reach out and take the deck, shuffling it between my fingers as I do so.

He seems to puzzle over them before shooting me a furtive glance. "No. I knew someone who used to use these."

"Another lover?" I ask. "Were they as handsome as me?"

He laughs. He so rarely laughs and I feel a surge of pride every time I make him do it. It's a beautiful sound, deep and boisterous, the only time he doesn't seem like he's haunted.

"It was a woman. A neighbor," Abe says, grinning at me and looking so damn gorgeous it takes my breath away with his straight white teeth, the way the tip of his nose dips down when he smiles, his dimples hidden by his beard, the deep lines that form at the corners of his eyes, making him look older than he is.

Oh, he is so damn pretty.

He nods at the stack in my hands. "Will you do a reading for me?"

He sounds both shy and hopeful and fuck it if that doesn't make my cock immediately stiffen. He notices, his gaze going to my half-hard dick. He raises a brow. "Is this turning you on?"

"What doesn't fucking turn me on?" I ask him gruffly. "Feels unfair that I'm naked and you're already dressed. Hoping to go somewhere?"

The lightness in his expression fades. "No," he says, a defensive edge to his voice, like I'd caught him out in something.

I've learned that his moods are mercurial and it's best to roll with them. "Good," I tell him. "Sit down and I'll tell you your fortune."

He sits dutifully on the edge of my bed, staring up at me expectantly while I shuffle. Every now and then he'll glance at my cock and swallow hard and I can read the hunger in his eyes. It will have to wait.

"What do you know about the arcana?" I ask him.

"Not much," he admits.

"All right," I say. Abe doesn't know of my magic and I intend to keep it that way. If I tell him too much, he may think of me differently and after what happened in San Francisco, I'm not willing to risk that. "Tell me, then, what would you like me to focus on? Is there a specific question you want answered? In what area of your life do you need the most insight?"

He worries a lip between his teeth as he thinks.

I keep shuffling, trying to wake up the cards to his plight. The more I shuffle, the more my energy influences the draw, the more I feel tapped into the veil and the future beyond. It's the same feeling the air gets right before a thunderstorm, when everything is dark and alive and electric.

Finally he says, "I want to know where I should go."

I freeze, about to repeat his question back to him. The cards seem to buzz at my fingertips, like a hummingbird caught in my hands, and I quickly start shuffling again.

Where should he go? Why does he have to go anywhere? Why can't he stay here?

"All right," I say, clearing my throat. I close my eyes and ignore my own feelings on the matter and look in deep, past the dark spaces inside me and out the other side to the beyond, where things are darker still. "Where should Abe go?" I ask the ether.

I stop shuffling and wait. A constricting feeling wraps around my rib cage, something painful, like a snake is inside me, trying to put its fangs in my heart.

"What is it?" Abe whispers.

I open my eyes and notice that my hands are trembling. I quickly lay the cards out on the desk like an accordion and clear my throat. "Pick one," I say hoarsely, that tight feeling not letting go of me. It feels like heartbreak.

Abe stares at me for a moment, his dark brows furrowed, then he looks to the deck. His black-brown eyes sweep over them, reflecting the faint morning light, until he taps one of them.

"This one," he says.

I glance at the card, still face down.

*Yes*, something inside me buzzes. *That's the one.*

I reach over and gingerly pick it up, afraid of what I'll see.

It's The Tower.

On the card it's an image of a castle's tower on fire, being struck by lightning, with two men falling out of it, presumably to their doom.

In my head, I see the same thing come to life. A dark spired cathedral shrouded by fog, a fire burning it up from the inside, and the two men falling through the air are me and Abe. We land in the mud, stagger to our feet, and though we try to run away from the burning church, we can't. That constricting feeling around my ribs deepens and, in the vision, it pulls me back to the building. I'm yelling something at Abe, how we can't leave without . . . without . . .

And then the image fades and before I know it I've collapsed to my knees in front of Abe. He reaches out and presses my head against his thigh, stroking my head in such a way that my eyes roll back.

"What happened?" he whispers, his voice pitching.

"I don't know," I say, trying to calm my heart. I'd get up but I rather like where my head is, like how doting Abe is being. It's a nice change. "I think perhaps it's been too long since I've eaten anything. I got faint."

I'm not about to tell him that using divination can literally drain me.

"What did the card say?"

I take in a long breath through my nose as the vision fully fades away. "It's The Tower," I eventually say.

"That sounds okay."

"Yes." I nod against his leg. "It seems innocuous enough. It indicates a sudden change or release. It could be anything from uncovering a hidden truth to having a revelation that changes the course of your whole life."

The muscles in his thighs tense up. "So what do you read it as? Where am I going?"

"I don't know where you are going," I say carefully, lifting my head to look up at him. "But I know you're going there because of what has happened to you. An upheaval has already occurred. Where you are going is a direct response to that."

He stares down at me and scrunches up his nose. "None of this is helpful."

"Sometimes we don't want to know our future," I hedge, not wanting him to know my vision.

"These cards don't tell you what *will* happen though," Abe says. "They tell you what might happen. At least that's what my, uh, neighbor said."

I nod. I can't tell him that what I see almost always does happen.

At that, I get back to my feet and start attending to the deck, shuffling it back neatly.

*The session is complete*, I chant to myself, putting the deck back where it was and placing a stick of selenite on top to seal it closed.

But while my back is to Abe, I can't help the faint smile I feel tugging my lips.

Because even though that card was dark, that future was dark, I was there. *I* was in his future. I've only known this man one week and in that week he's turned my world upside down, given me something to hold on to when I've been grasping at straws. He's given me something to wake up to each morning instead of that endless need to smoke and escape and forget.

My cock, which never fully went back down, is hard again and raring to go.

I turn around and his gaze immediately goes to it.

"On your knees, pretty boy," I tell him.

His eyes go heavy with lust. "Yes, sir."

He drops to his knees and opens his mouth.

And while I push the head of my cock past his sweet lips, over his flat tongue, and down his tight throat, I feel sated in knowing that we'll be together, in whatever darkness the future holds.

*One week later* I wake up in my bed to find it empty.

I spend the day with my heart in my hands, waiting for him to return.

He never does.

# 12

## Kat

I have a bad habit that when someone tells me I can't do something, say something, see someone, it makes me want to do it even more. I don't know who taught me to be so rebellious in a world where rebellion is so often punished. But perhaps I like the punishment. I certainly do when Crane is doling it out.

So when Crane told me I couldn't see him until tomorrow and also had to stay away from Brom, naturally it made me want to see them both. When I left the faculty dorm I was already plotting how to sneak out through my window to visit him and Brom in the night. I wanted to see what Brom looked like naked and covered in chains. I was assuming he'd be naked, anyway. In my mind he was.

But when night had fallen and I was in bed, wondering when I should attempt my escape, I remembered the anguish in Crane's face. He was trying to be strong, his face a blasé mask, but I saw it slip when he held my face in his hands and told me that everything he was doing, he was doing for me.

And I trust Crane, deeply. I know I am at the forefront of his actions and desires—perhaps side-by-side with Brom, but still at the front. As much as I don't like being apart from him, especially now when the world seems so precarious, I also don't want him to lose his job. If he does, it means he has to leave and he'll never be allowed back in through those gates.

But then of course, I would leave too. The more that happens the more I think there's no point in staying at the school as it is. I'm an adult, I can make my own decisions. If it comes to it, I can leave this school, leave Sleepy Hollow, and never look back, as long as I have Crane and Brom at my side.

I'm not leaving either one behind.

So instead of sneaking out my window and paying my men a visit, I fall asleep.

A deep, dark sleep.

So deep that the next morning I wake up not knowing where I am for a moment. I sit up in bed, my heart beating rapidly, until I look around the room, barely lit by the gray morning light, and realize I'm someplace entirely new.

I exhale loudly, feeling utmost relief. My mother isn't in the same house as me anymore. There's a gate and magic wards and a long trail through a dark woods between us now. I finally have broken free from her in the way I always yearned to.

Granted, her influence is everywhere since I'm now stuck with her sisters, but even though I fear my aunts (and Sisters Margaret and Sophie, to a degree), I still feel like I'm one step closer to truly spreading my wings. I close my eyes and I think of blue butterflies taking flight into the sky, my fingertips tingling.

But instead of taking flight, I get up and get ready for the day.

I'm up early enough on this Sunday that the bathroom and toilets are available, so I do my business and take a quick bath before the rest of the girls in this dorm get up. Then I take my time getting dressed, taking extra care to make sure my clothes are particularly flattering and that my hair looks nice—all for Crane, including not wearing any drawers—and forgo breakfast in the dining hall so that I can get to the library by nine.

The library is a short walk away and while the morning mist is damp on my face, the rain holds off. The librarian, Ms. Albarez, gives me a courteous yet distant nod as I enter, and I'm relieved to find it completely empty except for one very tall, dark-haired gentleman at the very back of the hall, silhouetted by the morning light at the windows, sitting with his back to me.

My stomach does a little flip as I walk toward him and he raises his head, sensing my presence.

I'm about to throw my arms around him, kiss him on the cheek, but I remember where we are and the roles we have to play. He is the teacher, I am the student. Nothing more.

I walk around the desk and stand primly on the other side, my back to the large Gothic windows that look out onto the woods.

"Good morning, Professor Crane," I say to him.

He stares up at me with a feverish glint in his eyes, his full mouth curved, taking me in like I'm some sort of tonic he's been deprived of for weeks on end. If I could bottle this look and carry it around with me, I would. I want him to gaze at me like this forever.

"Good morning, Kat," he purrs, and then gestures with a quick tap of his elegant fingers. "Have a seat."

I dutifully sit down across from him, glancing at all the books he has strewn across the table in haphazard piles. "What are these?" I ask.

"*Many a quaint and curious volume of forgotten lore,*" he says, to which I frown. "You haven't read any Poe?" he asks.

I shake my head.

"What a shame," says Crane. "Now there's a fellow I would have liked to have a drink with." He clears his throat. "But there will be other times to read his works. These are books I found that should help us with performing the ritual. I want to get it right before we even attempt it."

I take the nearest one to me, a dusty old thing with a plain leather cover, and open it. The text is in Latin, but my grasp of it is rubbish. *Tenebrae veniam.* Something about the dark. The darkness will come?

*How are you?* Crane asks, his warm voice sliding into my head.

I glance up at him, wishing I could learn the same technique.

"I'm fine," I say quietly, my attention back down on the page as I flip it. "I take it last night went well."

*Well enough,* he says, still using the voice. *At least I know I'm no longer going insane. Vivienne Henry showed up.*

I look at him sharply.

*Brom saw her,* he goes on. *I couldn't risk following her with him in chains—we'd wake up the entire faculty—but once I heard her outside the door, I opened it to show him. Sure enough she was dragging her bloody body around the corner. Brom took it in stride, of course, but he saw her too.*

I shiver. I want to make a comment about the chains but I

can't, especially not since Ms. Albarez is a few aisles down putting books away, so I don't say anything at all. To her it looks like the two of us are flipping through the books in silence.

After several minutes, however, she finally moves on out of earshot.

"Where is Brom now?" I whisper, keeping my eyes on her as she takes her place near the door and a couple of older students walk in.

"Asleep," Crane says, licking his thumb as he turns the page.

I would love to be that thumb.

"Still in chains?"

He nods, a wry, knowing smile on his lips, a dreamy look passing over his eyes.

Despite everything, my gut twists with a mixture of desire and jealousy.

"Did you punish him?" I whisper as I lean forward across the desk.

Crane eyes me in surprise. *Kat,* he says inside my head. *We don't need to talk about what Brom and I—*

"I want to talk about it," I say softly. "I want to hear about it."

He stares at me for a moment and then looks over his shoulder as the students disappear into the aisles closest to the door, the librarian busy cataloging. My gaze catches on the definition of his fine jaw, the fading bruises left there by Brom, the faint stubble coming in above his lip and on his chin since I don't think he's shaved in a few days.

What a ridiculously handsome man he is. So refined in many ways and yet depraved in others. And it only makes me want to be depraved in return.

*You want to know what happened with us last night?* he asks, molten heat coming over his gaze as his eyes meet mine. I nod eagerly.

"Please," I whisper, knowing what effect that word has on him.

*I fucked him*, he says, and the sound of that in my head makes me swallow hard.

"How?"

The corner of his mouth lifts. *I got him naked first. Then I had him in chains, around his ankles and his wrists. The chains at his ankles were pulled to keep his legs apart as I bent him over the bed. He offered his ass up to me like a gift, Kat. You should have seen it.*

My mind goes to the other night when I did see exactly that.

*Is this making you jealous or turning you on?*

"Both," I whisper.

*Do you want me to tell you exactly what it's like to fuck Brom Bones?*

I nod.

*Then put your hand down your skirt and start playing with yourself. I know just how swollen and wet you already are.*

This man knows too much about me.

But I do as he says, carefully, making sure no one in the library can see. I didn't wear drawers for a reason and the feel of my hand sliding over my mound and between my legs in front of Crane, let alone in public, is thrilling. The moment I dip between my thighs and discover how wet and hot I am, I have to bite my lip from groaning.

Crane inhales sharply.

*Oh, Kat,* he says, voice lowering. *I can hear how wet you are. You're making it hard for me to sit here.*

"Keep talking," I whisper, my eyes falling closed as I let my fingers explore my most secret parts in a most public setting.

I hear him adjust himself in his seat and I open my eyes to see him reaching down into his trousers.

*Brom was just as needy as you are right now,* he goes on. *So I ran my hands over his ass, marveling at how muscular it is, the power he has. He's such a fine specimen of a man, it's hard not to admire him. Hard not to bite him, hurt him. I spanked him a few times, hard, just to wake him up, and each time I did so he started to shake. I know his cock must have been weeping, twitching for my touch, and I was feeling merciful, so I reached down and slid my hand over it. He has a beautiful cock, doesn't he, sweet witch? Big, long, and thick. So easy to please. And to my delight he was wet, his seed already leaking from the tip. I did him another favor by spreading it down his length, then I let go and he let out a desperate cry in return, the kind you feel in your bones. Those cries, they are music to my ears. So I took my sticky hand and spread his cheeks apart. Took a look at that pretty asshole.*

Oh goodness. Oh God.

I can't tell what's bringing me to the edge faster, my fingers or Crane's description in my head.

*I kept him spread and put my mouth on it. He tasted like soap from the bath we just had, and he tasted like him. I ran the tip of my tongue around the pucker, teasing and savoring and then he was crying. Crying real tears because he wanted to be fucked so bad. By my tongue, by my cock. I wrapped my hand around his throat and pulled his head back and licked the tears from his cheeks before releasing him. Then I grabbed the oil and slathered it along my own cock and it was so hard now I wasn't sure how I'd survive it. But I did. Fuck . . .*

He trails off and I look to see his wrist moving faster under the desk, his eyes heavy with lust as they stare at me.

*Do you know how tight Brom's ass is, Kat? Sometimes I think it's tighter than your cunt. It takes a lot of effort to open him up wide and push the head of my cock past that first ring of muscle, even when we're both slick and slippery. Even just the flared crown of my cock is enough to make Brom start losing control. He started to jerk beneath me, desperate for purchase, for his own release, but I shoved his head down on the bed, held him down with my arm as I jammed the rest of my cock into him.*

He licks his lips. *Shove your fingers in your cunt, sweet witch. Shove them in deep.*

I do as he says, my legs spreading under the desk as I clench around my fingers.

*Good girl*, he says. *You are such a good girl, my* vlinder. *And Brom, he was such a good boy. Brom was whimpering. He was needy. He was a writhing mess beneath me. Do you know what it's like to have a big strong man like that reduced to someone who pleads and begs under your power and is completely at your mercy? There's nothing else quite like it. I fucked him until I couldn't see straight, couldn't breathe, and all the while Brom was crying, begging for my clemency and I held that power in my hand knowing I was the only one to grant it to him. To set him free.*

Crane suddenly lets out a sharp gasp as he works himself and

I'm already on the path of no return as I do the same to myself, both of us pleasuring ourselves under the desk while the rest of the library has no idea.

*You know what happens when someone comes when you're deep inside them?* Crane rasps. *Their whole body constricts. All of it. I couldn't wait a moment longer, I reached down and found Brom's heavy, hot cock and I started stroking it. He couldn't hold back. He came immediately, shooting his thick, hot seed onto the bed, his body squeezing my own cock until . . . until . . .*

Oh God.

I'm coming.

I try to hold back my cry but it's like trying to cage a wild animal. The sound claws through me, set loose by the orgasm that makes me buck in my chair, but mercifully gets caught in my throat before I can alert the entire library to what I'm doing.

I choke on it, writhing, my boots sliding against the floor as my legs move, trying to ride it out.

When I lift my head, my neck feeling boneless, I see Crane staring at me with such a dark, carnal look burning in his eyes that I think I might burst into flames on the spot.

"Fuck," he mutters under his breath.

Then he's up on his feet and coming around the desk to me, tucking his cock hastily back inside his trousers as he takes a quick cursory glance around the library, then pulls me up. I can barely walk, my legs shaking like jelly, but he quickly pulls me back into a row of books, until we're half-hidden by shadow.

"I can't wait," he says gruffly as he pushes me back against the books. He reaches down and bunches up my gown while he lifts me up at the same time, his mouth going to my neck, biting beneath my ear. His hands go to his trousers, pulling them down and I feel the hot hard length of him against my bare thigh.

I think my body is still pulsing when he shoves inside me, his cock so stiff and hard and long that it wrings the air from my lungs, despite how wet and open I am.

"God," I cry out, but Crane covers my mouth with his hand and fucks me.

*I don't care what I just told you about Brom*, he says inside my head, his hand still over my mouth. *You belong with me, sweet witch. You belong with me.*

He nips at my earlobe, his breath hot and ragged, and from the whimper he lets out, I know he's unable to hold back any longer. His thrusts get quicker, deeper, more frenzied, the books at my back taking a beating.

*Going to come*, he rasps. *Oh, sweetheart, I'm coming.*

His hips jerk up into me, his hands sliding down from my mouth to reach my clit, and when he pulls back I see the determination on his brow, the need to make me come again, contort into pure animalistic pleasure as the orgasm takes hold of him.

"Fuck." He breaks off in a ragged gasp, biting my hair to keep from yelling, while his finger glides over where I'm hard and pouting, enough to make me come with him.

My body explodes again as we come in unison, both of us hanging on to each other like if we don't, we'll be lost forever.

"Crane," I whisper, my nails digging into his jacket, secret words on the tip of my tongue, emotions uncovered by our union and the energy flowing through me. "Crane, I . . . I . . ."

But I hear students talking from somewhere in the library, and the realization of where we are hits me. We can't stay away from each other, even in public. Our bodies, our energy, will always be tethered to each other in this way.

He quickly pulls out of me, tucking himself back in his trousers, while quickly smoothing over my skirt before brushing a strand of hair off my face.

"My beautiful, sweet Kat," he whispers to me, his eyes wild and burning as they gaze deep into mine. "You are an obsession that borders on psychosis."

Then he kisses me on the forehead and takes hold of my hand briefly, leading me to the end of the stacks before he finally lets go.

# 13

## Kat

After we disentangle ourselves from each other, Crane has the nerve to head straight to Ms. Alvarez and check out a couple of the books he'd selected. But if she senses that anything funny went down in the stacks, she doesn't show it, even though I'm frantically patting down my hair to make sure it looks tidy.

"I shall walk you back to your dorm," Crane says to me, making sure the librarian hears it, as we step out into the morning. Just like it always does after sex, everything seems brighter, hopeful even, energy radiating through me. The rain is still held at bay and there's even a hint of sunlight trying to burn through the morning fog, and I like to think I brought that sunshine on.

We walk down the path and I'm surprised to see how many students have come outside during the time we've been in the library. Though the grounds are damp from rain, groups of them are clustered around talking, taking advantage of the break in the weather. One group has even set up a lively game of croquet.

Most of them don't pay us any attention as we pass them by—probably because they're used to seeing us together by now—though they're still in earshot.

*I can't risk talking to you in private,* he says inside my head as we slowly stroll down the path side-by-side, his hands behind his back. *But I think walking next to you in silence will be permitted by the coven.*

I make a small noise of agreement.

*First things first, is my seed dripping down your leg?*

I blink at him, my mouth dropping open. Now that he mentions it, it's pooling at the top of my stockings. I'll need to wash them right away.

*I was just curious,* he goes on smoothly. *If only we were alone I'd be dropping to my knees and shoving it back inside your cunt.*

"Crane!" I admonish him, clamping my lips together as soon as we pass a pair of teachers who are discussing something in a low voice. I can't stop my cheeks from burning though.

*Sorry,* he says. *I should get to the pressing matter at hand.*

I give him an imploring look to say, *Yes, please do.*

I can't survive his filthy mouth in public.

Again.

We walk to the center courtyard and pause by one of the benches underneath the statue of a skeleton with angel wings.

*Yesterday I found out a few things that affect all of us,* he says, his tone growing grave as he surveys the campus. *You and Brom in particular. Your aunt Leona brought me into her office. Not only did she threaten to fire me if I continued to see you, but I now suspect that the witches here are on a quest to become immortal and I think you and Brom are the key to it.*

I go still, sickly fingers squeezing my chest. "What?" I say through a gasp.

It's enough for the students standing nearby to look my way. I avert my eyes, my heart pounding in my head, and keep walking.

*Careful, sweet witch,* he warns in step beside me. *This is all a theory and conjecture. I have no concrete evidence. But I do think that your aunt is much older than she looks. I think she's been performing ceremonies and rituals for a long time to keep herself alive. It explains why her face is often moving. Do you know of Jeremias? He is the head witch of an old order that worshipped a demon called the Dark One. He too has a moving face, though his is composed of all the sacrifices he's done over the centuries. Or so they say, anyway.* His look darkens. *I believe the Dark One and Goruun might be one and the same.*

*Goruun is a demon?* I ask inside my head, hoping he can hear me and, if he can't, at least read the question on my face.

He stares at me for a moment but I am unsure if he heard me. *Or maybe they're not. Leona says he's a deity to their coven, but I think that's another word for demon to them. They believe that Goruun does everything for them, including manipulating our lives to put us on their path. Catch us in their web.*

His gaze goes to the cathedral by the woods.

*To what end, I don't know,* he goes on. *But they worship him. With all that I've gathered from your conversation with Sister Sophie, and from what Brom has said about your mother, I have reason to think that your marriage to Brom is part of some . . . ritual, or ceremony, something that involves Goruun. Something that will benefit their coven, which is why I mentioned the immor-*

*tal part. Your aunt said that the only things that will be left at the end of the world will be ashes and witches.*

I swallow hard, having a hard time processing any of this. The world seems to slide away, my vision growing hazy.

He clears his throat, bringing my attention back to him, his gaze steady on me.

*We will get to the bottom of this, Kat,* he says. *Trust me. I know you have feelings for Brom and it's very clear he has feelings for you, but the both of you must understand that until we figure this out, the two of you cannot be together. Certainly not in any way that could result in your pregnancy.*

I glance at him, eyes wide.

He gives me an uneasy smile. *There's a chance that they have a sacrifice in mind. Perhaps they promised Goruun your future child with Brom.*

I stop and shake my head, feeling sick. "No," I whisper. "They wouldn't."

But the look he gives me in return says that they would.

*I know you don't want to think about it,* he says softly, his lips barely moving. *You don't need to think about it. No matter what the truth is, no matter what they hope to happen, they aren't touching you. They aren't taking you. They can't force the two of you to marry and they can't force Brom to get you pregnant. I've discussed this with him too, he knows what might be at stake.*

He starts walking off and I follow, the sick feeling not leaving me. I wait until we're out of earshot of people before I whisper, "But they're witches. They can force us to do many things."

"And we are witches too," he whispers back, eyes blazing. "Don't you forget that. We aren't defenseless and we aren't helpless. The more that you and I work together on your magic, on my magic, the more—"

"How is that going to happen? How are you supposed to teach me? We can barely talk to each other now."

"I am still your teacher," he says to me starkly. "You are still my student. In class I will teach you, right in front of their prying eyes. But before we can even begin to tackle what the coven wants from the both of you, we have to focus on getting that spirit out of Brom before . . ."

He doesn't need to finish that thought.

Before the horseman takes over him.

Before he becomes a weapon that the coven can control.

Before they make him come after me.

Now I know for sure that the horseman was never meant to kill me.

He was meant to put Brom's seed in me.

"I think we should leave," I tell him. "Leave the school. Go beyond Sleepy Hollow. Somewhere, anywhere."

He exhales and I hear the weight of the world in his breath. "I agree with you. But the best chance of fixing Brom is here. This is a nexus of energy. There's a reason the school is built here, why so many ghosts are drawn here. This place gives us the extra power we need to make the ritual work. Not to mention with the horseman still in him, they'll be able to track him down and use him wherever he goes. Brom won't get very far."

Shoot. I forgot about that. "So once we save Brom, we're going?"

He gnaws on his lip for a moment. "I feel I need to protect the students."

"From what?"

"I don't know," he says tiredly. "You just have to trust me on that. I wouldn't be much of a man if I turned my back on them." He glances at me, his brow contorting. "But I wouldn't be much of a man if I didn't get you and Brom out of here either. I promise you, as soon as he is free from the horseman, we'll go. Even if I'm not with you, I'll make sure you and Brom get out."

I balk, horror flaring in my chest. "I'm not going anywhere without you."

"I appreciate the loyalty, darling," he says with a grateful smile. "But there might come a time when—"

"I said I am not going anywhere without you. And I'm not going anywhere without Brom either. I'm not leaving my men behind."

He just nods at that, though he looks a little pleased at my devotion.

I sigh; whatever light I felt earlier has disappeared, and Crane leads me to the herb garden, which thankfully is also devoid of people.

"I need to make more of that poultice, just in case I end up shooting Brom again," he says, gesturing to the plants, and I can't tell if he's joking or not. "Didn't you say you needed something from here?"

I nod. God, do I need it more than ever.

"If you tell me what you need, I can help you," he goes on.

I glance around, making sure again that no one is in listening distance and lean forward to pick a few chamomile flowers.

Despite it being October, everything in the garden is growing and healthy, albeit drooping over because of the overnight rain.

"I need . . . ," I whisper, barely moving my lips. "I need something to prevent pregnancy. Especially after all you've just told me."

He goes silent for a moment.

"I see," he says uneasily. "I'm going to assume you . . . I mean, are you worried about me, or . . ."

I swallow the brick in my throat as I eye him. "Either way," I whisper.

He flinches, just a little, and anxiously runs his hand through his hair. "Did he come inside you the other night?" He pauses, a hard look coming over his eyes. "Before he assaulted you?"

I nod. I don't feel ashamed for having slept with Brom that night, but Crane's words have weight.

"There's a chance that I already got you pregnant," Crane adds, sounding strangely hopeful. "Then you have nothing to worry about."

I almost laugh, then give him an incredulous look. His face is totally grave.

He's serious.

"You mean to say that you getting me pregnant is nothing to worry about?" I ask.

"It would solve a lot of problems," he says with a shrug.

"It would *create* a lot of problems."

He gives me a shy smile. "Would it?" he asks, his voice soft.

His sincerity scares me. "Crane . . ."

"Right," he says with a sigh, frowning at the garden. "Where were we?"

I can't help but stare at him for a moment as he starts rifling through the herbs. Was he serious about wanting to get me pregnant? Does Crane want to become a father? Goodness, we aren't even married. We aren't even in love.

But that last thought has my heart twisted in knots.

"This should help," Crane says, picking what I recognize as feverfew and yarrow and a few other herbs and flowers that I don't know.

"You don't even have to consult a book?" I ask him.

His face lengthens. "I already did. Soon as I guessed what the coven's plan might be. Only in a witch's text would this be found. The rest of the world doesn't want women to have that sort of power."

I stare at the plants in his hand. "I wouldn't be surprised if those books disappear, if the coven ever catches on to what we're doing."

He nods, sticking the plants inside his coat. "Then these are safest with me. I'll make you a tincture and bring it to your class tomorrow."

Then he puts his hand on my lower back, and for all that just happened in the library, for his seed that is still wet between my thighs, the feeling of his slightly possessive grip at my waist almost unravels me.

He steers me away from the garden and toward my dorm, though he doesn't walk me all the way there.

"I'll see you in class tomorrow," he says to me when we're halfway across the yard, giving me a polite wave that I know is just for show.

"I'll make sure I do my homework," I answer before turning my back to him and hurrying back to my room.

*The next morning* I forced myself to go to the dining hall to have breakfast. I missed out on dinner because I was too busy in the library trying to read the rest of the ritual and spell books that Crane had selected, and when I was done I was able to grab a piece of the leftover pastry that the cooks leave out each day. Also, I was too afraid to go and sit by myself, thinking no one would want me at their table.

But this morning my stomach decided I didn't have time to be shy and feel sorry for myself and thankfully the moment I stepped inside the dining hall, Paul waved me over to sit with him and a few of his friends. I looked around for Crane and Brom but didn't see them (another twist of jealousy when I imagined the two of them still lazing in bed together), so I was able to be a simple student on campus for a moment.

If being a simple student means you're secretly part of some sacrifice or ritual that involves the coven that runs the school.

"Mind if I walk you to Professor Crane's class?" Paul asks as we exit the dining hall, nibbling on a cheese Danish.

"I appreciate the offer but I left my books back in my room," I tell him, patting him on the arm.

"I'll wait for you here," he says with a smile.

"All right, won't be a moment," I tell him, hurrying around the corner to my dorm. I'm actually touched that Paul wants to walk me. I'm sure he knows that there's something going on between Crane and me, which means he just wants to be friends and I could use a real friend.

I gather my books from my room and am stepping out of the front doors when someone grabs my arm roughly and pulls me to the side of the building in a flurry of black hair and black clothes.

"Brom," I gasp, his grip tight around my bicep as he presses me against the wall. "What are you doing here?"

Brom just stares at me with those wild black eyes of his. He looks better than he has lately, his dark hair off his face, his beard neatly trimmed, his clothes clean and tailored. Even though my heart is going fast at his intrusion, I relax when I remember that it's the daytime and I don't have to worry about the horseman coming out. There's only Brom right now, the Brom I've always known and trusted.

He doesn't let go of my arm though.

"I wanted to see you before class," he says roughly, taking a step closer until he's boxed me in against the stone. "I haven't had a chance to talk to you alone. I need to talk to you. I need to be with you."

"Can you let go of my arm?" I ask firmly.

He looks down at where he's gripping me and his forehead crinkles, as if surprised. He drops his hand. "Sorry." He glances up at me, a lost look in his eyes that makes me want to touch him. I manage to refrain, my fingers curling around my books instead.

"You think differently of me now," he says in a low voice. Though he is no longer holding on to me, he's still close, so close, his face inches from mine. His eyes are so dark and soulful that I feel myself falling into them like I used to.

"What do you mean?" I ask cautiously.

"I mean everything, Daffy," he says, and my heart trips over my nickname. "When I first came back to Sleepy Hollow, you looked at me like I was your world. Now you look at me and all I see is fear."

"Can you blame me? You know what you did to me."

"It wasn't me," he snaps. "Honey, I wouldn't do anything to hurt you, not unless you wanted it."

"Honey?" I repeat. Since when has he ever used that word for me before? "I'm not your *honey*, Brom. You know we shouldn't even be this close, nor should we be alone."

"Why?" he asks, leaning in even further, as if I challenged him. His mouth is so close now that if I moved at all it would brush against mine. "Don't say it's because of Crane. Tell me it's because of the coven, but don't you dare say it's because of Crane. He doesn't get to come here to Sleepy Hollow and fuck things up for us."

"He's not messing anything up, I just can't be with you, you know I can't, I—"

He leans in, his mouth on mine in one hard, deep kiss. With one hand on my books, the other goes to his chest to push him off, but I don't. I just keep my hand there, feeling the pure power beneath my fingers, and sink into the heat of his kiss. He kisses deeply, slowly, like he's trying to fuse me to him, his tongue owning every inch of my mouth.

"Let me fuck you right here," he says against my lips, voice both hoarse and soft, and his hand goes to the front of my skirt and between my legs, cupping me there where I'm already hot. "No one has to know."

I let out a moan at the pressure of his hand, bearing down on it, and his mouth goes to my neck and my head goes back against the wall, succumbing, clutching my books to my chest as if they are a shield to protect me from the devil that is Brom Bones.

"It's just you and me, Kat, like it always should have been," he murmurs.

Goodness. I feel every shred of resistance fade as he licks up my neck, sucking in my skin, his beard scratching me. I want to know what that beard feels like between my legs.

"No one is going to keep me away from you," he groans, pulling me into another deep, lingering kiss as his hands start gathering up my skirt and his erection is pressed into my hip and everything rolling off him is hot, dark energy, like I'm being enveloped by a living, breathing tornado that I want to destroy me and—

"Kat?"

The sound of Paul's voice makes me gasp and I immediately spring into action, breaking away from Brom's mouth and shoving him back from me as hard as I can. He stumbles back a few steps, looking completely bewildered, like even he wasn't sure what just happened.

"No," I whisper to Brom, all my resolve coming back into me. "This isn't happening and you know exactly why."

"Even though you want it?" he asks, his voice breaking slightly, brows creating shadows over his eyes.

"Even though I want it," I admit. I can at least give him that much.

Then I brush past him toward the sound of Paul's voice that came from around the corner.

But Brom is right on my tail and ends up walking beside me as we see Paul approaching the dorm.

"Sorry," I tell Paul, clutching my books to my chest and pasting a smile on my face. "I got stuck talking with Brom. You know Paul, don't you, Brom?"

Brom just nods and Paul gives him a faint smile that borders on suspicion. I suppose that tornado energy is palpable to more people than just me.

"Lucky we all have the same class," Paul says flatly as the three of us walk down the path toward the building that houses Crane's classroom. To say that it's an awkward journey would be an understatement. I know that Paul suspects there is something going on between Crane and me but he must wonder about the degree of my friendship with Brom. If he only knew the truth.

# 14

## Brom

*Eleven years ago*

Where do you want to live when we get married?" I ask Kat.

We're sitting on a log under the Hollow Creek bridge playing troll and princess, a game that is starting to feel too young for me, now that I've just turned twelve and my father says I should start acting like a man, but Kat was insistent. As usual. We always do things her way.

"I suppose my house," she says, her long blond hair falling over her shoulder, reminding me of the silk that comes off the corn at harvest time. "My house is bigger," she adds brightly before throwing a stone into the creek.

"No," I say to her, picking up an even bigger rock and chucking it into the fast-moving stream. "I mean, what town? City? Where do you want to go?"

She stares up at me, puzzled. "Why would we leave? My father and mother are here."

"Mine are here too," I point out, but I don't say anything else.

She just gives me a nod, because she knows. She goes into deep thought, rubbing her lips together as she does so.

"I think I'd like to stay in Sleepy Hollow," she eventually says. "I like it here."

"You've never been anywhere else."

"Neither have you," she says, poking me in the arm.

"But I read about other places, in books," I say. "And I've been on the riverboat once and I've been to Tarrytown."

"Everyone has been to Tarrytown," she says with a roll of her eyes. "I'm not moving there."

"So then pick a place. Any place. How about London? I like the idea of moving to England. And what type of house? Do you want horses?"

"Of course I want horses," she says excitedly. "I want horses and goats and chickens and pigs and cows. I'll make them all be my friends. I'll be a mama too, so we'll have lots of babies running around. It will be fun."

"Well, I'm going to buy you the nicest carriage that you can ride around in," I tell her. "And all the ladies will look at you in envy. They'll go, *There goes Brom Van Brunt's wife. Isn't she the luckiest girl in town?*"

"That would be nice," she says shyly. Then she grows serious, her lip pouting. "Do you promise to take care of me?"

"Of course I'll take care of you," I say imploringly. "I'll be your husband. That's what husbands do. They take care of their wives."

"And you'll protect me?"

I put my arm around her and hold her to me and her hair smells like meadow flowers. "I will always protect you, Kat."

She rests her head on my shoulder and I feel like I'm melting on the inside. "Because my father once told me that he won't always be here to keep me safe," she says quietly. "And my mother won't be either."

I feel darkness at the mention of her mother, like a cloud over the sun. I've never liked her mother, never trusted her. She's one of the reasons I want to take Kat away from Sleepy Hollow, even though I don't understand why.

"I told my father you would protect me though," she adds, sounding small.

I swallow. "Did he agree?"

She nods.

"I'll protect you, Daffy," I tell her. "I'll keep you safe."

Even though I've never felt safe a day in my life.

She lifts her head to look at me, smiling so broadly. "Really?"

"Really."

I can't help myself.

I lean down and I press my lips to hers.

I kiss her.

It's soft and strange and she goes completely still and I'm not sure if I'm supposed to do anything else, but nothing else in this world has ever felt so nice.

But it's nice and it's scary at the same time.

My body is doing strange things. I feel dizzy. Like I'm going to be sick but in a good way.

The sudden trundle of a carriage over the bridge breaks us apart and I'm breathing hard, eyes wide, my lips tingling where hers were pressed against mine.

But Kat doesn't look surprised at all. She just smiles at me and looks away, picking up another stone from beside her and throwing it into the creek, like nothing happened.

How can that be? My whole world feels like it's been turned upside down.

I get to my feet, staggering down to the creek, and quickly crouch down to splash the cold, clear water on my face to try and feel normal again. My first kiss. I kissed Kat and it feels like nothing will ever be the same again. I won't be the same again.

I glance at her over my shoulder and she's sitting there with her skirt neatly around her, a pebble in her hand, staring at me curiously.

"I should go home," I tell her, my heart beating hard. "My parents said I had to come home straight after school."

"Why are you lying?" she asks, getting to her feet and shuffling toward me. "Your parents have never said that before."

"I just have to go, okay?" I tell her, grabbing my books by the book belt and walking out from under the bridge. Down the road toward Sleepy Hollow, dust rises from behind the carriage that passed moments earlier.

I can't be here with her right now. I have to go think. I need to be alone.

"Okay," she says in a soft voice as I walk up the bank to the road. "Did I do something wrong?"

I stop, trying to take a deep breath.

"No, Daffodil," I say to her, glancing at her over my shoulder. "I just have to go home. I'll see you tomorrow before school."

"Okay," she says brightly, her voice as sweet as sugar, as pretty as a flower.

I feel bad leaving her there but she doesn't live too far from the bridge and I know when I'm not with her, she's often wandering about the fields by herself; at least that's what her father jokes about. Katrina constantly communicating with Mother Nature, calling to the birds. I've seen some pretty special things happen around my best friend.

Nothing as special as that kiss though. I run my hand down my face, trying to get some sense back into me. It was like when I kissed her I saw my future with her. And it wasn't here in Sleepy Hollow, it was somewhere far away and we were happy.

That means she and I are really meant to be with each other.

I better start learning how to act like a man so I can provide for her one day, be a good husband and run a good farm. I have to learn how to be brave and tough, how to protect her from harm.

I think about that the entire walk home, every single thought revolving around Kat, about how I'm going to make sure she's happy for the rest of her life, how she'll need only me, until I'm right outside my front door, a wayward chicken running past that I'll have to deal with later.

I step into the house and am met with silence. My mother and father are both sitting by the fire, my father reading a book and puffing on an awful-smelling pipe, my mother knitting something as always. Neither of them says a word, neither of them looks toward me.

"I'm home," I say loudly, putting my books on the table.

They still don't stir. It's like I'm a ghost in my own house.

"I said I'm home!" I yell, the anger snapping through me like a mangy dog. I bang my fists, making my books jump.

"Heavens, Abraham," my father says around his pipe. "We heard you the first time."

"Try and use your manners, dear," my mother says to me, looking at me only briefly before going back to her needles.

I stand there and I suddenly think, *These aren't my parents.*

*These aren't my parents!*

They are just people pretending to be my parents.

Playing a role, just like the performance I did at school last week when I was in the background of *A Midsummer Night's Dream*. It's all acting, all make-believe, made by somebody else.

But I have to shake that thought out of my head. It's pure nonsense. Of course they are my parents.

They just don't care about me, that's all.

And it doesn't matter in the long run.

I don't need my parents to love me.

I'm going to marry Katrina Van Tassel.

# 15

## Crane

Good morning, Professor Crane," Paul says to me as he walks into my classroom. His voice has a knowing tone to it, and when I look up from my books, he's smirking to himself as he goes over to his desk.

Then I see Kat in the doorway, and my heart blooms in my chest at the sight of her sweet, beautiful face, a halo of blond hair around it, an angel descending to my domain.

Until I see Brom close behind, towering over her, his eyes meeting mine. And though I also feel something soft inside for my beautiful boy, it's getting tangled up in a tight knot of jealousy, because why are they together? I thought I told him to stay away from her?

But with that dark look in his eyes, the way he lifts his broad chin, he's telling me he's going to do what he wants, regardless of what I say.

White-hot anger flares inside me but I remember where I am and I swiftly swallow it down.

Bastard. He just loves punishment, doesn't he?

They take their seats, and it takes me a moment to get sense back into my head. I open my desk drawer for chalk and see the tincture I made for Kat in the corner. After our visit to the herb garden yesterday, I spent the evening making this tincture for her. Brom was with me after nightfall—a miracle he still willingly lets me bind him in chains—but when he asked what I was making, I just said it was for Kat and didn't explain what it was. It's not an abortifacient per se, though I'm sure it could have those effects, rather it prevents pregnancy from taking place.

I can't help the pinch in my chest. It must be done to keep her from becoming pregnant with Brom's child, and if that's what the coven really wants from their union. But if I happen to get her pregnant and we . . . No, I don't want to think about that potential loss.

Either way, I'm hoping to hell that the two of them didn't just fuck on the way over here because Kat does look a little guilty as she sits in the front, and that defiant look in Brom's eyes is telling me he at least wants me to think that, and if it's true, I'm going to rip his fucking head off.

I take in a deep breath, and as the last student comes in, I motion for them to close the door.

"I hope you all had a nice weekend," I say to the class, though I have to admit I have no idea what the students get up to here when they aren't in class. It's not as if they can go into town for a change of pace. "Did anything interesting happen?"

"Someone was murdered in Sleepy Hollow," Martha says, looking a tad too excited for the subject matter. "*Again.*"

"Headless horseman cut a man's head off and left his body outside the bonfire," adds Josephine. "They never found the head."

"Oh?" I say. "I hadn't heard about that. That *is* interesting." I meet Kat's and Brom's eyes for a moment and then clap my hands together. "All right, so we have a murderer on the loose. Anything else? Anyone pick up any magic or spells?"

No one says anything for a moment.

Then Martha says, "Who do you think the headless horseman is?"

"Yes, Professor Crane, is he real?" asks Mark.

"You know what, class, I'm not sure," I say, pressing my palms together. "But if there's been a murder, I am sure the police in Sleepy Hollow are dealing with it."

"Yeah," speaks up Matilda. "We're safe here at the institute. The wards will keep the horseman out."

A nervous laugh escapes my lips. I can't help it.

"All right, time to get on with today's lesson," I say, turning around and writing the words *ENERGY AUGMENTATION* on the chalkboard.

I turn back around, and everyone squints at it.

"What does that say?" Paul asks, pointing at the board.

"It says 'energy augmentation,'" I snap, looking over my shoulder at the board. Clearly that's what it says. "And what is energy augmentation when it comes to magic? Good question. Energy augmentation differs from bestowal and absorption, because it's about the ability to weaken or enhance someone else's powers. Why, you ask, would we want to know how to do that, especially the latter? Well, let's take the headless horseman for a moment."

Now I seem to have their attention, though both Kat and Brom shift uneasily in their seats.

"What would happen to this school if the headless horseman were to break through the wards?" I go on, pacing back and forth. "Wouldn't you want to know how to defend yourself? Or say it's not the headless horseman, but another witch, or coven, or some leader of the dark arts, coming here to hurt you and your friends. Wouldn't you want to know how to defend yourselves?"

"Yes," Paul says, a determined look on his face.

"Yes," Martha says. "Please teach us."

The rest of the students nod eagerly.

I can't help but smile at their enthusiasm. A classroom full of students who know how to fight back goes a long way when I know I have to protect them from whatever the future holds.

"I need a volunteer," I say.

Paul is first to raise his hand, and I wave him over onto the platform in front of the class. Paul's always been dependable for any demonstrations.

"Hold out your hand," I say to him. "Palm up."

He does as I ask.

I take my hand and place it above his, hovering just a few inches. I focus my concentration on the empty space between our hands, willing it to fill with energy and light. At first, heat begins to pool in my hand and then radiate downward toward Paul, then light begins to build, like a firefly is caught between our hands.

The class oohs and aahs and Paul lets out an impressed chuckle.

"Keep your hand still," I tell him, slowly taking my hand away. "And concentrate on hanging on to that energy. Visualize it going into your skin, into your muscle, your veins, your bones, and hold it there inside you."

I step back, and though my hand still gives off warmth and light, it's fading, while the rest seems to sink into Paul's skin.

"Now that isn't augmentation, that's just a very visual representation of bestowal," I announce to the class. "But, for demonstration purposes, I have to give Paul magic that you'll be able to witness when he augments it."

I face Paul again. "Now, I'm going to try and use something called the voice on you. With the voice, I'm going to try and talk to you inside your head. You'll notice my lips barely moving, but you, and only you, Paul, will hear me. When you hear my voice, I want you to use the power I gave you and try and pull the voice from my throat so that the whole class can hear it. That will be a good example of augmenting another's power."

"All right," Paul says, looking nervous.

*Hello, Paul,* I say to him in his head.

His eyes widen.

"H-hello," he says.

*You can tell the class that you hear me.*

He gives the class an anxious look. "I can hear him in my head."

More impressed murmurs abound.

*Now, I'm going to keep talking to you and I want you to take that magic I just gave you and try to pull this voice from my throat. Keep visualizing that heat and light that you saw that went in you. Make sure it goes back out of your palm.*

He nods. "Okay." He looks at the class again. "He's telling me to take his voice."

I stare into Paul's dark eyes. *Are you ready? I'll keep my voice going, but I need you to start visualizing and manifesting this to happen.* His pupils go large as he frowns in concentration. *Focus on my voice, focus on taking it, focus on that golden light, that pure energy and life force and using it to—*

Golden streams sprout out from Paul's hand and come for my throat. I try to keep using the voice, but already I feel it being taken from me.

I watch as the gold twists in the air and then suddenly:

*IT WORKED!*

Paul's voice blows through the room, enough to make me stumble backward against the desk, my hands over my ears.

Then the light goes out, and he rushes over to me. "I'm so sorry, are you all right?" he asks, sounding panicked.

I laugh, straightening up. "I'm fine. I'm fine. You were just a little loud, that's all."

"So it really worked?" he asks. "How long do I have it for? Will it ever go back to you?"

"I hope so," I admit, since I've never actually had it taken away from me. "Energy is renewable. My voice is earned by magic I've practiced so it should come back. But for now, I'm depleted of it. As for you, it depends." I look at the class, feeling a burst of pride at how enraptured they all are. This is why I am here. This is what I was meant to do.

"I don't expect this exact scenario to ever come up," I tell them, "because all it will end up being is a shouting match, but now you know that if you are in a situation, where perhaps someone is attacking you with fire, you can take that fire from them and either use it for yourself or disable it within the person, at least for a period of time."

"Can we have another demonstration?" Matilda asks. "Something that would hold back the headless horseman?"

"Of course," I say, but I don't ask for a volunteer. I pick on Kat all the damn time so I decide to pick on Brom for a change.

Brom, who has shown zero magical ability.

But if he's related to Sisters Sophie and Margaret, there is potentially a lot of power lying in those bulky veins of his. After all, there must be some reason why he's the one chosen to be with Kat. What does it say about me that I'm a little disappointed that I was never the chosen one that Kat was supposed to marry?

"Brom Bones," I say to him with a flourish of my hand. "Care to step up here, help me demonstrate how to defend yourself against the headless horseman?"

Oh, if looks could kill, I would be a dead man.

But Brom gets to his feet, and I'm honestly surprised he's doing this at all, considering, well, *everything*. It also gets me hot under the collar to know that even in this setting, he obeys me like the good boy that he is. It takes all my self-control to keep from praising him like that as he stands in front of me on the platform.

I'm still grinning at him like a fool, though.

"Brom," I say to him, standing much closer to him than I was to Paul.

"Professor Crane," he says slowly, his jaw flexing.

"Tell me," I say, tapping my finger on my chin, "let's pretend you're the horseman for a moment. What kind of power would you have, what kind of magic would you use to try to hurt me?"

He stares. "I'd probably use my ax and chop your damn head off."

Students burst out laughing. Even I find it funny, though a little unsettling at how much he seems to mean it. Perhaps I should tread more carefully with him and his moods.

"So," I go on, "let's pretend for a moment that the horseman is an evil spirit. What would be one way someone like me could disable such a spirit?"

And if the actual horseman could give Brom some real insight right now, that would be lovely.

"You would have to disable the source," Brom says, surprising me, and I'm not sure if he just came up with that or if he knows something.

"The source?" I ask. "You mean—"

"Professor Crane?" one of the students says.

I squint at Brom, trying to figure him out, then look over at the student. They're standing by the window along with a few others, staring outside.

"What is it?" I ask testily, wanting their full attention, wanting Brom to keep talking.

"There's a woman standing on the roof of the cathedral," Josephine says, staring at me with saucer-wide eyes.

"What?" I say, running off the platform and over to the window, putting my face close to the glass. Sure enough, on the top of the Gothic cathedral, in between two of the spires, is a girl.

Not just any girl though. She's as thin as a beanpole, with long dark hair, and is dressed in a dirty white gown, torn at the seams.

She looks exactly like the girl I had seen dancing by the lake one night before the sisters came and took her away.

"That's Lotte," someone else says. "She was in my history class the first week of school and then never came back."

Suddenly Kat is beside me and I move over to make room for her, Brom coming behind me. "Oh my God," Kat whispers. "She's going to jump."

"Are you sure?" I ask her, and sure enough the girl starts looking over the edge and dangling one foot off it.

"Jesus," I swear, and run out of the classroom and down the hall, bursting through the doors and outside. I hear all the students following me as we run into the light rain, yelling at the girl not to jump, and in seconds Brom is running beside me as we sprint across the wet lawn to the cathedral.

"Do we try and catch her?" he asks, legs pumping effortlessly with pure athleticism.

"We have to try something," I say. "Lotte!" I yell up at the roof as we get closer, hoping that really is her name. "Stay where you are, don't jump!"

But Lotte starts laughing. "Stay where I am?" she yells back. "And let them continue to eat me alive? We're all just flies in a web."

And then, before Brom and I can reach her, she throws her arms up in the air, as if she's doing a ballerina spin, letting herself fall off the cathedral. I scream, running as if through a bad dream, watching as her body dances on the way down, before landing on the stone path with a sickening splat.

I stop dead in my tracks, unsure of what to do.

Flashbacks of Marie keep coming into my vision, mixing with the girl on the ground.

I see Marie's head hitting the wooden floor in the living room, blood pooling around her like a cape of death. If the rug had been a few inches longer, she would have lived, it would have softened the blow.

But it hadn't been longer, and Marie died.

I see Marie's eyes staring up at the ceiling and watch as the light goes out of them.

I was screaming then, and I'm screaming now.

The girl lying on the stones, the blood slowly pooling out of the back of her head, the way her limbs are broken and splayed at unnatural angles—the girl blinks at the gray sky.

She isn't dead, not yet.

It's enough to make me move, stumble to my knees beside her.

"Lotte," I say to her, my voice a quiver, placing my hand at her cheek.

Her eyes look at me, a light green, and though I don't know this girl, I feel like I do. She is hovering in that space between here and the veil, about to leave, but still present. The light is going out of her eyes like it did with Marie, but it's leaving slower. She wants to stay.

*May you find peace*, I say to her using the voice, and I'm surprised to find my magic comes back to me.

She stares right into my eyes, and I think she hears me.

I reach down and I grab her hand, her cold, frail hand, letting her know she's not alone when she goes. It's what I wish I could have done with Marie instead of what actually happened. All around us I hear crying and screaming and yelling and more and more people rushing to the scene, but right now it's just this girl and me on the damp stone and a spreading lake of blood.

It would be selfish to ask this dying girl what she meant. It would be selfish to ask her what happened to her. It would be selfish to ask her what caused her to take her life.

But I am a selfish man.

*Who did this to you?* I ask, because someone has done this to her. Someone has led her here, to jump off the roof, to end her short life surrounded by strangers such as myself.

Someone has thrown her into a misery from which this is the only escape.

The girl stares at me, her mouth moving slightly.

*Everything here is built on bones*, she says inside my head. *Save yourself.*

Then I see the life leave her.

It moves out of her like strands of gold, out of the crown of her head and twisting toward the sky until it's carried away in the breeze, pushed toward the lake.

In a second, she is gone, and her eyes don't see me anymore.

"No," I cry out in desperation, in that wild, panicked feeling of trying to hang on to life when it's already left. "No. No. *No.*"

Tears rush to my eyes, and I keep squeezing this girl's hand as if it will bring her back.

"No," I whisper.

I feel hands on my shoulders, pulling me back while someone else brushes past me, the school nurse, as if a bandage would fix anything, and then I'm pulled away from the dead girl, from the crowd, and I realize it's Brom who has me. I rest my forehead against his chest, trying to breathe.

"Crane," he says, his voice low. "I'm here."

Such simple words, and yet they mean everything to me.

He keeps his hands on my shoulders, massaging me gently.

"Okay," I say through a faint gasp. "Okay."

Because I just saw a girl die in front of me, and it's the second time someone has died right in front of me. And maybe that means nothing, but it feels like something.

At least I knew enough this time around to not make the same mistake again.

At least I didn't try to bring her back to life.

No one should ever be brought back to life.

"What a strange thing it is to cry," I mutter, watching as a teardrop falls from my face and down to the ground between us. "What a strange thing to have our hearts bleed in such a way that it comes out from our eyes."

I lift up my head and meet Brom's gaze.

It holds me in place, and for once I let him be my strength.

I put my hand at the back of his head and hold him there for a moment.

"Thank you," I whisper, hoping my eyes tell him more than my words ever could. "Thank you."

His face remains impassive, a rock, so unlike the usual Brom who shows everything with the tilt of his eyes, the shift of his brows, the angle of his mouth. But now he's being what he thinks I need, someone who can weather the storm, not be the storm.

And yet, in the depths of those black-brown eyes, I see him soften for me.

I raise my head, taking in a deep steadying breath, and then look back over the scene. Classmates have their arms around each other, crying, teachers are standing around in shock. Then there's Kat, between us and the scene of travesty, staring at me solemnly, and beyond her are Sisters Sophie and Margaret. Sister Margaret is chanting something up to the sky.

Sister Sophie is staring right at me with a look in her eyes that I can't quite decipher.

But it feels like a warning.

# 16

## Kat

The entire campus has been upended. Classes have been canceled. Everyone has been shuttered away in these little pockets of grief and shock. The church bells of the cathedral ring and ring and ring until I can't stand it anymore, and I'm on my bed, covering my ears.

Sister Margaret has been going around to the dorms and letting students know that there will be an assembly in the cathedral at nine this evening for all of us to mourn and discuss what happened to Lotte.

But I can't spend my day stumbling around in a daze, and I can't find empty solace in the arms of others who don't care for me. I saw someone die in front of me for the second time, and though it wasn't my father, though it wasn't someone I loved more than anything else, it was still traumatic to witness. To see that poor girl on top of the roof and know, know that no matter what we did, she would jump and we wouldn't reach her in time.

A few hours after the incident, after I've been in my room unsure of what to do next, I hear my name being called outside my window, so softly it takes me a moment to realize it, and when I get up, I see both Crane and Brom outside, two tall dark figures in the mist. They both gesture in the direction of the stable and start walking toward it.

I quickly grab my coat and put it on before hurrying out of my room and out into the quiet, foggy afternoon.

Crane and Brom are at the stable by the time I catch up to them.

"What are you two doing?" I ask as they both head to the tack room.

"We're going to Sleepy Hollow," Crane says as he brings Gunpowder's saddle and bridle off the wall. "And you're coming with us."

"Sleepy Hollow? Why?" I follow him to the horse's stall.

"To see the constable," Crane explains, his eyes turning dark. "A girl just died before our eyes, and I have a feeling the school is in no hurry to tell the rest of the world about it. We need to beat them to it, before the sisters have a chance to either lie or sweep it under the rug. Her family deserves to be notified."

"You think they would do that?" I ask. "Hide her death?"

Brom snorts from over in Daredevil's stall, and I hear the slap of the tack going on the horse. "It's awfully convenient that the students' memories are wiped clean once they leave the school," he says. "Who would be able to talk about it, except us?"

I think about that as Crane quickly finishes tacking Gunpowder and leads him out of the stall. Gunpowder's ears are flicking back and forth, picking up on our tumultuous energy, so I try to give him a few soothing pats to let him know everything is okay.

It doesn't work. He doesn't believe it, probably because I don't either.

"Well, if we're going into town, I might as well drop by the house and get Snowdrop," I say as Crane leads Gunpowder out of the stall. "That way I don't have to keep sharing a horse with you."

Crane gives me an incredulous look as he holds the reins. "You have a problem sharing a horse with me?"

"You ride a little slow for my liking," I say with a smirk. "Perhaps you better ride with Brom, and I'll take Gunpowder. Show the old horse a thing or two."

"He is *not* riding with me," Brom says, quickly mounting Daredevil.

"Are you sure, Brom?" Crane asks. "I promise to be gentle."

"That will be the day," Brom says under his breath, gathering the reins and circling his black stallion around us.

"Fine. Up you go," Crane says to me, grabbing me by the waist and lifting me up on Gunpowder's back. The strength this man possess always catches me off-guard because I'm definitely not a light and dainty girl.

He swings up after me, and I'm settled snugly against him, his arms on either side of me while he holds the reins. There's no place where I feel as safe and, despite the circumstances, I immediately relax.

"See, this isn't so bad, is it?" his rich voice murmurs into my ear.

But, though Crane sounds like his normal self, there's something off in his tone.

When Lotte had jumped from the roof, I was running behind Crane and Brom, trying to catch up, and cursing my little legs for being so slow. The scream that Crane let out when she fell was something I'll never forget. It was a scream from his past, and I can only imagine it had to do with his late wife. How did she die? What did he witness? Did he blame himself for any of it? Because Marie, even in death, sure seems to blame him.

And then, when I saw him with Lotte as she lay dying, I was transfixed by how hard Crane was taking it. It seemed to go beyond the traumatic and horrific sight of a poor girl dying at her own hand, it seemed personal, and Crane seemed close to losing it. He's always been so composed, so to see Brom take him away from the scene and comfort him nearly broke my heart.

Now there's a heaviness in Crane that I can feel, his energy twisting into sorrow, his eyes melancholy. For once I wish I could give him the same feeling of safety that he gives me.

"We need to be quick about this," Crane says as we ride through the center of campus. "As soon as we're past the gates, we won't stop until we get to town. Kat, we'll get Snowdrop on the way back, after we've talked to the constable. I don't want to be out there after the sun goes down."

He doesn't have to elaborate on what that means.

Once again, I fear the gate won't open and the wards will hold us back, but luckily, they let us pass, and the moment we're through, Crane urges Gunpowder into a gallop, with Daredevil, being younger and faster, taking the lead easily.

Crane is silent while we gallop down the fog-shrouded trail, the trees whizzing past us and mist clawing at our faces like fingers, the sound of thundering hooves filling the air as we follow Brom and Daredevil. By the time we're passing Wiley's Swamp, the weather shifts and the mist dissipates. The afternoon sunshine comes through the trees and I blink at it, as if I've never seen light before.

Once we pass through the Hollow Creek bridge it's like we've entered a whole new land. The sky is a piercing blue with high white clouds, the fields soggy and golden with a murmuration of starlings over them. In the distance, the Hudson River sparkles enough to hurt my eyes. I see Mary's house and I feel a calling to her, to see how she is. What happened after the bonfire? Did she ever hear me knocking at her door and yelling for help? Did her horse ever return?

But that has to wait. We gallop past her house and then past mine. I can't look away from my front door, thinking my mother will throw it open at any moment to stop us, but nothing happens and in seconds we're gone.

We ride fast and hard all the way to the start of town, where Crane and Brom pull the horses back to a trot, then a walk as we hit Main Street, ensuring Gunpowder and Daredevil have enough time to cool down before we come to a stop. The police station is located on the other end of town, so we spend a bit going past the shops and buildings.

Despite having been here last week for the bonfire, it's a little jarring to see civilization again, especially in the daytime. All the whitewashed buildings gleaming extra bright in the sunshine, the festive autumnal displays of carved gourds and pumpkins and stalks of corn, the perfectly pruned bright red and orange foliage of the trees around the square.

As I expected, the townspeople are staring at us as they go about their day, some whispering to each other as we pass them on the street. I'm sure everyone recognizes me, but Crane is a stranger to them, and from the snippets of conversation I hear, Brom is the talk of the town, the boy who disappeared and returned to Sleepy Hollow.

"Considering a school for witches is just outside their doorstep, they seem to be an awfully judgmental bunch," Crane muses under his breath. "Have they never seen two people sharing a horse before?"

"They're probably wondering why I'm with you and not with Brom," I point out quietly.

"Ah, so they've noticed the golden boy has returned," he says.

We dismount and tie the horses up outside the station, and then step inside.

Constable Kirkbride is sitting at his desk, puffing on a pipe and looking over some papers. He looks up in surprise, raising a bushy gray brow.

"Can I help you?" he says in his Bostonian accent, putting the pipe down.

"Yes, we would like to report a suicide," Crane says bluntly, leaning with his hands on the constable's desk.

"Good heavens," the constable says. He eyes me and Brom and looks back to Crane, frowning. "What happened?"

"A young girl named Lotte," Crane says. "She jumped from the roof. There are many witnesses who saw it happen."

"Dear God," he says, making the sign of the cross and bringing out his quill and ink and a piece of paper. "What did you say her name was? Lotte?"

"Yes," Crane goes on, hesitating. "I don't know her last name, but I believe you can find that out. Her parents or family need to be informed."

"Of course, of course," he says, writing it down. "Where and when did this happen?"

A pause. I can hear Crane swallow. "It happened this morning around nine thirty. At the school where I teach. Sleepy Hollow Institute."

At the mention of the school, the constable stiffens and then slowly puts down the quill, taking a moment to sit back in his chair. "I see."

"You see what? Why didn't you write that down?" Crane reaches over and taps the paper impatiently.

The constable glares at him. "I didn't write it down because it's none of my business."

"What do you mean?" I ask, standing beside Crane.

"A suicide is none of my business," he says, folding his arms. "If you don't think any foul play was involved, then it's out of my hands."

"But you seemed to make it your business until he mentioned the school," Brom speaks up.

The constable squints at Brom. "*You.* You know, when I saw you a couple of weeks ago, I didn't put two and two together. But you're Abraham Van Brunt. You know we turned this whole town over looking for you years ago. We thought you'd been murdered. Taken. Beaten by marauders. And here you are just waltzing back into Sleepy Hollow like you had only left for an evening stroll."

"You should be happy that one of your beloved citizens is back," Crane snipes at him. "Or would you have preferred him to turn up dead?"

"Easy there . . . ," the constable says, raising his hands. "What did you say your name was?"

"I didn't," Crane says, staring down his nose at him with disdain. "Professor Ichabod Crane."

The constable leans back farther in his chair. "Well, Mr. Crane, what do you suppose I do about this girl's death?"

"Lotte," I tell him, hating how blasé he's being. "Her name was Lotte."

"Go to the school and collect the body," Crane says. "Run an autopsy."

"An autopsy," the constable laughs, getting to his feet. "For a suicide with witnesses?"

"She may have been drugged or poisoned," Crane explains.

"*May have* isn't good enough for me," he says. "Besides, that's a matter for the school. What goes on at the institute doesn't involve me unless the sisters bring it to my attention. Until then, I stay out of their hair."

"But they're just going to sweep this under the rug," I say. "You watch, I bet they won't come into town and tell you about it."

"And that would be their prerogative, Ms. Van Tassel. Now, if you don't mind, there's a murderer on the loose. The three of you don't seem too concerned about that."

"Should we be?" Crane asks, egging him on. "What are you doing to keep Sleepy Hollow safe from another attack from the horseman?"

The constable rolls his eyes. "Enough with the ghost stories. The headless horseman is just the legend of Sleepy Hollow, nothing more. This is a murderer, a sick human. I expected more from a teacher, quite frankly." He tilts his head. "Then again, you do teach at *that* school. You're a queer bunch up there, that's all I'll say."

"Please, just pay the school a visit," I say, putting my hands together. "Look around. What if this happens again?"

"Another suicide?" he laughs. "Is your academic schedule really so difficult? No. I know my place, and my place is protecting the citizens of Sleepy Hollow. That school is legally outside the town's boundaries and my jurisdiction as it is. If you really want to take it up with someone, take it up with Pleasantville police. Pay a visit to the pickle factory while you're there." He comes around the desk and gestures to the door. "Now if you'll excuse me, I have a murderer to catch."

"Well, he was very rude," I mutter as we leave the station and step back onto the street, the door swinging closed behind us. Normally the constable is fairly even-keeled and friendly.

"Rude and as useless as tits on a bull," Crane says, putting his hand on my lower back. "But he's probably right about the school being out of his jurisdiction. Perhaps we should take it up with the police in Pleasantville. Perhaps they're not as intimidated by the sisters as the constable seems to be. If we get Snowdrop another day, we could make it back to campus before dark."

I nod as I mount Gunpowder, noticing how Brom is standing still and staring at the constable through the front window of the police station.

"Brom?" I ask as Crane gets on the horse behind me.

Brom keeps staring straight ahead until he finally looks up at me. His eyes are dark and shadowed, but there's a chilling twist to his lips as he meets my gaze.

"Brom?" I say again, feeling uneasy this time.

He just nods at me and unties Daredevil, swinging up on the stallion's back. "Let's go."

We trot down Main Street with Brom in the lead until the road curves and leaves the town behind. By the old manor house it splits, with one road leading south to Tarrytown and the other going north to Pleasantville.

We're cantering on the road north, going past carriages and other riders, until the road enters a forest of orange and yellow maples, and there's a large coach up ahead turning around, the horses pulling it looking agitated as they try to navigate the narrow road.

"What seems to be the problem?" Brom yells up ahead at the coach.

The driver in a top hat shakes his head. "Road is blocked. Can't get past."

He maneuvers the coach around and toward us by going into a ditch briefly, and then we see the problem. A massive sycamore tree has fallen across the road, blocking it completely.

"When did this happen?" Crane asks.

The driver shrugs. "Must have just fallen. I had taken folks to Pleasantville earlier today and it was fine. I better go tell the constable."

He cracks his whip at his team of horses and the coach takes off, leaving us in the dust, the passengers staring at us out the windows as they go.

"Curious," Crane muses as his gaze goes over the tree. "How does a tree that large just fall out of the blue with no wind?"

"Too much rain in the roots?" Brom suggests as Daredevil throws up his head, snorting wildly. "Whoa there, what's gotten into you?" he chides his horse as he dances around, the whites of his eyes showing.

"I should investigate," Crane says, clucking for Gunpowder to go closer to the fallen tree, but Gunpowder's ears flatten back and he starts swishing his tail vigorously, moving forward a few feet and then reversing.

*Gunpowder*, I tell him, trying to communicate. *It's all right. We just want a closer look at the tree.*

But Gunpowder won't go, and when Crane kicks his side, the old horse suddenly rears, almost throwing the both of us off. We both manage to hold on.

"Jesus," Crane swears. "What's wrong with them?"

"It doesn't matter," says Brom, bringing Daredevil over to us. "The tree is down; we can't get through to town."

"There are other ways to Pleasantville," I tell them as Gunpowder spins around and starts heading back to Sleepy Hollow. "There's another road farther east, some trails . . ."

"Those take longer," Brom says. "Didn't you want me back in chains before nightfall?" he asks Crane, a razor edge to his voice.

"You like the chains, don't kid yourself," Crane says under his breath. He clears his throat. "All right, we'll head back to Kat's, collect her horse, and hopefully not have to deal with her mother, and then back to the school. Save Pleasantville for another day."

We start riding back the way we came, and Crane says into my ear, "I guess it's true what they say."

"What?" I say back, looking over my shoulder at him to meet his sharp gaze.

"Welcome to Sleepy Hollow," he says gravely. "May you never leave."

# 17

## Crane

I'm not a huge believer in coincidences. Life isn't as random as people make it out to be, I suppose that's why I do tarot and have a gift for divinity. Things happen because they are supposed to, because it is ordained, because there is order to life. Are we all flies in a web? Perhaps. But are we all cogs in a wheel? Most definitely.

The fact that our way out of Sleepy Hollow was blocked by a giant, healthy-looking tree wasn't a coincidence to me. It was there for a reason. To prevent us from leaving. And if we had more time, perhaps to venture on another route to Pleasantville, or the road to Tarrytown, or on a riverboat down the Hudson, each of those attempts would have been thwarted in some way. The prickling feeling on the back of my neck, that kick in the gut that I've come to trust as instinct, all of those things are telling me that there is no escape now, at least not for today.

I don't voice this to Kat or Brom, of course. They don't need to hear my wild theories, especially ones so demoralizing and based on nothing but a gut feeling. But I know it. Witchcraft and magic go beyond what you can see, and often beyond what you understand. The sisters have been at this game for a very, very long time. They are in charge of the chessboard, seeing the moves ahead of time. The wards protect the school; does something similar protect Sleepy Hollow when they want it to?

All the more reason to get the damn horseman out of Brom, to start working on our magic so in the event we are being kept from leaving town, we can learn to break through it. I'll admit my defenses, as I demonstrated in class earlier this morning, aren't the strongest, but I also know I have the ability to change that.

"We'll do the ritual tomorrow night," I shout as we're cantering down the road to Kat's house, loud enough that Brom hears me. "It's the dark moon. The energy will be perfect for shadow magic too. If it doesn't work, then we only have two weeks until the full moon ritual. And if that fails, it's just a couple of days until Samhain."

And if *that* doesn't work, on the day of the year where the veil is at its thinnest, well . . .

Both Kat and Brom nod. I'm still a little worried about how they'll do during the ritual. Brom because I don't want him to get funny when it comes to Kat. I take control when it comes to the both of them, but he's used to being the dominant with her. He's going to struggle with having to obey me in this case. Luckily, I like it when he struggles.

Kat, I worry about more. She seems a little looser around Brom now, she doesn't freeze up when he's close, which is good for their relationship, bad for my possessiveness and my need to keep them apart. Still, I need to make sure she feels safe and protected throughout the whole ritual. She's our most important piece, the one both of us love dearly, the key to bonding the three of us together.

The ritual will get intense, as well. I'll need her complete trust in order to have the whole thing go off without a hitch, because the last thing we need is the ritual being broken. There will be pain, there will be blood drawn (all superficial wounds that I will quickly heal), and Kat might be terrified in the process, especially when dealing with shadow work, but she will need to commit to the ceremony one hundred percent or it won't work.

Then, after, if we are successful in driving the horseman's spirit from Brom's body and back into the spirit world, we can think about leaving Sleepy Hollow.

All I know is that when the time comes, a fallen tree isn't going to stop me.

*And the students?* the voice in the back of my head nags. *What will you do to protect them?*

To that I don't have an answer yet. I don't even know what the truth is, what the true purpose of the school is. I'm starting to think it's not about education at all, that's just a ruse. If I could find out exactly what the sisters are up to, then I can at least warn the students and help them leave if they need to. I could tell the outside world the truth.

But Kat and Brom come first. Everything else is second. And my conscience will have to live with that.

It's not long before we're approaching Kat's house. In the sunshine it looks like a perfectly bucolic scene—the stately farmhouse, the fallow fields, the river in the distance—but I know inside that house there is one very wicked witch, and I'm doubtful that we'll be able to get Snowdrop without calling attention to ourselves.

Still, we all fall silent, taking the horses straight to the stable, where Kat slips off Gunpowder and runs in to get her tack for Snowdrop. I have to admit, I'll miss having her pressed up against me.

It isn't until she's mounted on her horse and we're riding past the house, about to take off at a gallop back to the school, that the front door swings open and Sarah comes striding out, her shawl floating behind her. She's more gaunt than usual, her eyes sunken.

"What the heavens is going on here?" Sarah says to us. Though she looks frail, her voice and temperament remain sharp. Behind her, the housemaid Famke peeks her head through the door, then disappears back into the shadows of the house.

"I wanted to get Snowdrop," Kat says, squaring her shoulders. I can feel her energy, how intimidated she is by her mother, and yet her voice doesn't quaver. "She's my horse, she should be with me at the school."

"Of course," Sarah says, her gaze going to Brom, where it softens. She doesn't even look my way. She doesn't need to. She knows I'm right there, staring at her from atop her dead husband's horse.

"Brom," she says as she approaches him. "Did Kat tell you I invited you both over for supper?"

"Uhhh," Brom says. "Yes. She did." Clearly lying.

"And? Will you be able to make it? I can't imagine having any big plans up at the school. You know, now that you'll be marrying into the family, we're going to be spending a lot more time together."

"Of course," Brom says in resignation.

"So you'll be there. Great. Come at three." Her hands clap together, and then she finally brings her attention to me. "Mr. Crane. I hope you won't be too offended to know you won't be invited. And if I see you dare set foot on this land again, I won't have any qualms grabbing my shotgun and putting it to use."

"No offense taken," I tell her with a jaunty tip of my head. "Sometimes we have to take drastic measures to protect our property." But while my tone is polite, my eyes are not, and I hold her gaze until I see her falter.

She looks away, giving Kat an uneasy smile, and I bask in my minor triumph.

"You should hurry back to class, dear," she says. "Not very smart to come get Snowdrop in the middle of a school day."

The front door opens and Famke comes out, holding something wrapped in a cloth.

"Katrina," she says, bustling toward her. "Here, I made some *banketstaaf*, your favorite. Practicing for Christmas already." She hands Kat the bundle. "There's enough for everyone." She nods at Brom and then me, and there's something in her eyes that I can't seem to read.

I stare at her, trying to get a hold of her aura, her energy. She's warning me about something, but I don't know what it is. It's not coming from a malicious place, it's coming from her need to protect Kat, something we both can agree on.

I give her a slight nod so she sees that I'm on her side, then give Gunpowder a nudge. "Mrs. Van Tassel is right," I announce.

"We should go back to the school. Especially before dark. Can't be too careful with the headless horseman about."

Brom is first to go, nodding his goodbye to the women before Daredevil takes off at a gallop, with Kat following and me bringing up the rear. Gunpowder is already tired from all the exertion earlier, so I take it easy on him. The only time I catch up is at the end of the trail when Kat and Brom are waiting by the school gates, their horses huffing.

"Oh, I see how it's going to be now," I comment, bringing Gunpowder between them. "Leaving the old man in the dust."

Kat and Brom exchange a glance, and she laughs as he bites back a smile.

"Try to keep up, Crane," Brom says as the gates swing open toward us.

After we pass through the wards, the atmosphere back on school grounds is more of an adjustment than ever. While you can hear the occasional bird, it's quiet compared to how the woods outside sang with calls from wrens and thrushes, the way the sunlight had filtered through the autumnal trees, but here there's nothing but low fog and gray gloom. This truly is a land of harbored secrets and I'm starting to suspect the fog works in the way that the sisters' moving faces do.

It keeps you from looking too closely.

We bring the horses to the stable and dismount, giving them a quick groom before putting them away.

"Are you going to the assembly tonight in the cathedral?" I ask Kat as I stop by her stall. I would go out of curiosity, but I'm not leaving Brom unattended.

She shakes her head. "I would feel too strange about it."

"Then I guess I'll see you in class tomorrow, unless those are also canceled," I say. I'm about to tell her to read up on the rituals if she can so she can get a better picture of what tomorrow night will bring, but I'm distracted by a movement out of the corner of my eye.

"Excuse me," I say to her, and march down the stable aisle to the feed room at the end.

I peer inside and see the peculiar stable boy standing by a bag of oats, looking as if he's been caught doing something he shouldn't.

"What is your name?" I ask him as Brom and Kat come behind me, hovering in the doorway.

The boy seems most scared of Brom, his eyes widening at the sight of him, and I have to look over my shoulder to make sure Brom still has a head. He does, as handsome and surly as ever.

"Don't worry, you're not in any trouble," I try to assure the boy, bending at the waist so I'm not so tall. "I'm just curious to know your name. We've never officially met. I'm Professor Ichabod Crane. That lovely lady over there is Katrina Van Tassel, and that disagreeable-looking fellow is Brom Bones."

"S-Simon," the boy says.

"And, Simon, you've been taking such great care of our horses," I tell him, hoping to put him at ease. "How long have you been the master of the stables?"

"A couple of years," he says, his eyes flicking to each of us.

"Do you live here?"

He nods, his blond hair flopping back and forth.

"Where do you live? Do you live with your family? The sisters?" I ask.

"I live with my mother," he says. "She lives in the basement."

"You live in the basement?" Kat asks incredulously. "Here at the school?"

Simon is breathing hard, his eyes looking wild. "No. Yes. My mother, she lives in the basement, I live in the dorms. I have my own room."

"Who is your mother?" I ask Simon. "What is her name? Is she a teacher here?"

He stares at me with large, rounded eyes. He's terrified.

"I have to go now," he says. He moves around me, quick as a wink, and then he's running past Kat and Brom who make no effort to stop him, and it's probably for the best.

"What a peculiar child," I comment, glancing at the both of them. "What do you make of him?"

"I wasn't even aware the school had a basement," Kat says.

"Any of the buildings could," Brom says. "Crane, you said when you met with Sister Leona in her office, that was underground, underneath the cathedral."

"That's right," I say slowly. "But from what I saw, it was just two rooms down there. Leona's and Ana's offices. Nothing else."

"Then that means the same things could exist under the rest of the buildings," Kat points out. "Perhaps there are tunnels connecting them. Maybe a lot of the staff live there. We have the school nurse, the cooks. Crane, you said you only have two other men in your wing. Professor Daniels and the custodian. But some of the cooks are men. Where do they live?"

I can't believe I never questioned that before. "I suppose I thought they lived in Sleepy Hollow. Quite obviously they don't," I grumble.

"Then that settles it for now," Kat says. "His mother might be a teacher, might be a nurse. I'm not sure it's worth thinking about."

But she gives me a look that tells me she knows I'm going to be thinking about it anyway.

"We better get going," I concede with a nod. "The dark is starting to fall faster these days. Like a blade." I demonstrate by running my finger across my throat, staring at Brom as I do so.

The three of us head across the misty school grounds, Kat going her own way, Brom and I going the other. I want to be selfish and ask her to spend the night with us, but with Brom the way he is, I don't want to put her at risk. She also deserves a good night of sleep, something I won't be getting. Not tonight, not ever, not until Brom is free.

"*Crane?*" *Brom whispers* to me.

I wake up slowly, blinking at the near dark, at the faint candle in the corner nearly melted in a puddle of wax. I realize I must have fallen asleep, after all that talk about never sleeping again. I feel Brom squished beside me on my bed, his chest at my back, the cold feeling of the chains on my skin. I'd been sleep-deprived for too many days trying to keep my eye on Brom, and I guess it finally caught up to me.

"I fell asleep," I manage to say, my head too groggy for my liking.

"I know," Brom says. "You were snoring."

"Oh."

"But listen . . . ," he whispers.

I hold my breath, straining.

I hear nothing except Brom's breathing at my ear.

"What?" I say after a moment.

"It was the woman," Brom says. "The dead teacher. She went past the door."

I shiver and get out of bed. "I have to admit, I don't mind that I slept through that."

I go to the door and unlock it, poking my head out into the hall. A trail of blood gleams along the floor, and I can't help but think about the stable boy for some reason. There's a memory deep inside my mind that wants to surface, something about what he said that feels like a grave about to be unearthed. But the more I try to focus on it, the more it stays buried.

I hear the clink of Brom's chains and my heart skips and I whirl around, prepared to see him rushing toward me, the Hessian in full effect. But instead, he's standing at my desk, naked, and staring out the window.

"Brom?" I say, closing the door quietly and locking it. "Don't tell me that she scares you too. We need one of us to be brave when it comes to ghosts, and I'm not sure I'm cut out for it."

He doesn't say anything. Doesn't move.

My heart thumps uneasily.

I slowly move toward him, my hand outstretched for his shoulder.

"Brom?" I say again, more forcefully.

I place my hand on his shoulder and he doesn't flinch, still facing the window.

I walk around him and see that his eyes are completely black, swirling in inky shadows, like they had when he was possessed. I gasp, quickly looking around for my gun, not wanting to take my eyes off him for long.

But he doesn't move a muscle.

And when the blackness in his eyes fades, they reveal the fluttering whites of his eyeballs rolled back in his head.

"Brom!" I yell at him, shaking him now by both shoulders. Is he suffering from falling sickness? Is this possession?

I don't like to hurt him without his permission and not when he doesn't deserve it, but I wind up and slap him across the face so hard that my palm stings, and the impact would have knocked anyone off-balance.

But not him.

Oh shit.

*Shit.*

Then finally, finally, he closes his eyes and his chin dips down for a moment.

"Abe!" I try, shaking him again in panic. "Abraham Van Brunt!"

His head tilts back and forth for a moment and then he looks up at me. His eyes are normal, black in this dim light.

I place my hands on either side of his face, his beard rough against my palms. "It's me." I swallow hard, staring deep into his eyes, willing him to come back to me. "It's Ichabod."

"Ichabod," he repeats, blinking. Then gives his head a shake as he steps back, running his hand over his face, the chains clinking. "What the devil just happened?"

"I was hoping you would know," I say, my fingers closing over his wrist and holding him. "I went to go look in the hall, and when I turned around you were staring out the window like this.

Your eyes . . . they'd gone black at first, then they rolled back in your head. What happened to you? Where did you go?"

His jaw tenses, his brows coming together, and I can't tell what he's thinking. It's only because I'm looking at him so closely that I see the dimple appear in his beard, just for a moment. The quickest, faintest smile.

Then he turns his head to mine, his gaze impassive.

"I don't know what happened," he says blankly. "I don't remember."

And I know he's lying.

# 18

---

## *Kat*

The next day went slowly. Classes had been canceled for an official day of mourning over Lotte, so I didn't see Crane or Brom until I ran into them in the library. It was busy in there since the students didn't have much else to do, but I managed to sit with the two of them for an hour. We didn't discuss the ritual because Crane's voice only works one way and there were too many people around us, but when we left he did tell me that we would meet in a glen in the woods at 3:00 a.m., wearing a robe with nothing underneath, and in order to prepare I was to cleanse myself thoroughly. In his words, my cunt and my asshole should be clean enough to eat off of.

Naturally, that night I didn't sleep a wink. I kept my eye on the clock, watching as the minutes and hours ticked down to three. I'd had an extra bath as Crane so crudely instructed me to do, but that did nothing to relax me. All I could think of was what was going to happen tonight.

I know blood magic involves blood, so that part has me a little squeamish.

I know sex magic involves sex, and even though I'm fairly certain I'm open to anything, my inexperience might get in the way. I know by now that my trysts with Crane and Brom, and even poor Joshua Meeks, have been varied, but sex magic with two partners at once is beyond anything I've ever thought about.

All right, I suppose that's a lie. I've thought about it. I've fantasized about it until I was hot under the collar. And, of course, I was partially involved in one last week. But Brom never touched me and he had been restrained. What will happen when he's free to do what he wants?

*Crane is in charge*, I remind myself, *he'll keep Brom in his place.*

But a sick part of me wonders what would happen if Brom broke free?

At ten to three, I take off my nightgown and drawers so that I am completely nude, then wrap the dark ceremonial robe that students all have around me. Boots are too fussy, but I don't want to go through the woods barefoot, so I put on my slippers, knowing I am going to damage them, open my window, and steal away into the night.

The damp grass kicks up on my calves as I run across the campus toward the library. Crane had said to go behind the building where the Gothic windows are and walk straight into the woods from there, but with no moon in the sky, it's hard to see the library itself, and I'm too afraid to light my fingertips in case of calling attention to myself.

But even though I'm entering the woods in the pitch dark, I

can sense Brom and Crane ahead of me. I don't see the light from their candles yet, nor do I hear them, but my body is pulled forward anyway, their energy calling to mine.

I stumble through the brush, nearly losing my slippers on the bramble and slippery roots, and by the time I see a faint glow up ahead, I know the boys have heard me coming.

Finally, I step out of the thicket and into the mystical clearing.

The glen isn't very large, an oval shape of grass and weeds surrounded by tall maples and firs, and there's a circle drawn around the perimeter with white salt. A few candles are set into the grass, flickering at the nexus points of the circle, with Crane's leather bag open, displaying some books, tiny vials of herbs and oil, selenite and quartz crystals, and two paring knives.

Standing inside the circle, cloaked in the same black robes as I am, are Crane and Brom. With their hoods up and faces in shadow, the only way I know who is whom is because of Crane's excessive height. Both of them radiate such powerful, dark energy that I feel a chill run down my spine.

"For a moment I was afraid you wouldn't come," Crane says in a deep voice, stepping toward me, and in the candlelight, I see the sharp cut of his jaw, the hollow under his cheekbones, though his eyes remain in the dark. "No one saw you, I take it?"

I shake my head. "Not that I could tell. I was very careful." I look at Brom. "You're not being restrained," I note.

"In the circle of protection, he should be safe from the horseman," Crane explains.

"So you could have drawn a circle of salt around me this whole time instead of keeping me in chains?" Brom grinds out.

A charming smile flashes across Crane's face as he glances at

Brom over his shoulder. "I suppose, but chains are more fun, aren't they?"

Brom lets out a huff of air, his fingers flexing and unflexing.

"Brom," Crane chides him. "Put your temper away for tonight. Take my hand." He holds out his hand for him.

Brom sighs and steps forward, his strong bearded jaw and full lips coming into the candlelight. He reaches for Crane's hand, and such a simple gesture has my heart doing summersaults.

"The only way this is going to work is if the three of us are a united front," Crane says, holding out his other hand to me now. "Kat, take both our hands."

I place mine in Crane's, and he curls his long fingers around me, holding me tight. I glance up at Brom, and he gives me a nod, taking my other hand in his. Both of their hands are warm and large, their grip strong, and it immediately gives me a sense of peace, like I'm being anchored to the spot.

"Kat, this evening is all about you," Crane says. Even though his eyes are in shadows, I can still feel them burning on my skin. "We can't exorcise the horseman from Brom without your help. We will need you to be the vessel for us, the one who contains and creates the energy that will bond us together. That means all of our, well, desire will be channeled into you. So to speak. You are the key to making this work. Does that sound like something you're willing to do?"

I nod, gnawing on my lip, my anxiety rising. "Of course."

"Say yes or no," he clarifies. "We need a definitive answer."

"Yes," I say, though I hate how the word trembles.

Crane gives me a kind smile. "Very good. Now, there are some things you need to understand about tonight. We are going to be playing with black magic, especially when it comes time to try and expel the horseman. Things are going to get dangerous. There is going to be a lot of trust required between the three of us, but especially with you. There will be times where you will be scared, and that's a good thing. Terror can heighten sex, tighten those bonds, expand that energy. But you need to know we will never put you in harm's way, and that you are safe."

"What kind of danger?" I ask warily.

He tilts his head toward Brom, but I can't see their exchange. He looks back to me. "There are two parts to tonight. First is where we solely worship you, make sure you feel safe and desired. It's all about your pleasure, not ours." My heart beats louder at that. "The more ready for us your body is, the better it will be."

He pauses, his voice growing grave. "The second part will involve the exchange of fluids, blood and otherwise. For this part we will all be partaking in a potion that will enhance our ability to communicate through the veil. Now, this is where things might get scary. We're going to have to cut you—it won't be deep, and you'll be healed after. You will see things around us that might terrify you. You might be terrified of us. We might not look like ourselves. But you have to trust that it's us all the same."

Now my heart is really galloping. "All right," I say in a small voice.

Both men squeeze my hands in unison.

"Kat," Crane says solemnly. "It's not too late to back out."

I lift my chin, trying to feel brave. "I won't back out."

"You have to trust us completely. Not just me, but Brom too."

I glance at Brom out of the corner of my eye, wishing I could see his eyes. "I suppose I'm worried about the horseman."

"I will do all I can to keep him at bay," Brom assures me, though I don't feel all that assured. He didn't seem able to stop him before. Unless he *wanted* him to come out those other times . . .

"And I will do everything to keep you safe," Crane says, lifting my hand to his mouth and kissing my knuckles. "This I promise you. I will keep you safe from harm, no matter what it is." He licks his lips. "But you have to consent to this now. You have to consent to the danger, to the terror. You must not break the circle. You must not leave the ritual once it's in motion. Doing so will have deadly consequences. When we begin the second part, there will be no escape for you, and you must finish the whole thing, even if that means us having to pin you down. Do you understand?"

My eyes widen. "Pin me down?"

"You can't break the ritual once it is in motion," Crane says, his voice hard. "Even if you decide you have had enough, we won't let you leave, and we will force you to finish it. So now, while you can still consent to this, I need to know that you *will* consent to it."

I try and swallow the brick in my throat. "I need to see your eyes while you tell me I will be safe this entire time."

Crane gives me an apologetic smile and lets go of Brom's hand while he pulls his hood back. Brom takes the opportunity to do the same. "Of course," Crane says, and I see the sincerity in those beautiful eyes. "I will keep you safe the entire time, *vlinder*. No harm will come to you. I will die before anyone hurts you."

"And I would kill anyone who did the same," Brom says, and I'm captured by his dark gaze.

"All right," I say, knowing that I have two knights to watch over me, and even if one is compromised, the other is still there. I also have my own magic, which isn't to be discounted considering I'm the one who disarmed the horseman last time. "I consent to the ritual. Even if I try to break the circle, I submit to what you need to do to keep me there."

"Good girl," Crane says, and I can't help but flush at his praise. Then he looks at Brom. "And you, I need you to consent too. That you will obey me without question. I know you're usually very good at that, but we've never shared Kat before in this way. I have to be the one in charge or it doesn't work."

Brom lets out a low rumble.

"What was that?" Crane says, leaning in, hand at his ear.

"I said I consent," Brom says sharply. "Doesn't mean I'm happy about it."

"Trust me, pretty boy, you'll be a very happy man by the end of this." He pauses, smiles. "Getting your cock sucked dry by our sweet witch."

"And there he goes," Brom says under his breath with a shake of his head.

Meanwhile my face is burning now. Despite the chill this October night and being naked under my robe, my body is already overheating.

"Shall we begin?" Crane says, ignoring Brom. "Please step over the circle, Kat."

They both reach back to take my hands as I step over the salt, careful not to disturb it, and they lead me to the middle beside the candles. Then they let go of my hands and step back.

"Disrobe," Crane commands me.

I gulp. I undo the robe and let it slide off my shoulders, pooling at the ground. I stand there completely naked and cold, Brom on one side of me, Crane on the other.

"Jesus," Crane murmurs as he stares at me.

Brom takes in a sharp inhale.

I feel both their eyes coasting all over my body, leaving no spot unseen. It feels like butterfly wings all over my skin. Outside the circle, the surrounding trees seem to whisper, their leaves shaking from a breeze that coasts over my body, tightening my nipples and creating goose bumps in its wake.

"Let down your hair," Crane murmurs to me, his voice already thick with lust. "Every part of you should be free."

I have my hair pinned into a low bun, so I reach up and take out the pins, tossing them to the side. My long hair tumbles over my shoulders in silken waves, catching the candlelight.

"You've always had the most beautiful hair," Brom whispers, and I blush again.

"Now take off your slippers and lie down on your back on the ground," Crane says, his hands going to the front of his robe.

I take off my slippers, tossing them to the side, and run my bare foot over the grass. "But it's cold and damp."

"You need the earth's energy to ground you," he explains with a wave of his hand. "It won't stay cold for long, I can promise you that."

I nod, my scalp tingling with what's about to happen.

*This is only the first part*, I remind myself. *This is the part for your pleasure.*

I take in a deep breath.

Get down on my knees, sinking into the cool, wet grass.

Then I lie back, shivering as my body makes contact with the earth.

"Brom, come over here," Crane says in a low voice.

I lift my head slightly, watching as Brom walks around to where Crane is standing near the base of my feet. Both of them stare down at me, and I've never felt more on display in my whole life.

Then Crane says, "Open your legs and show Brom what a pretty cunt you have."

And *now* I've never felt more on display.

I swallow hard and do as I'm told, widening my legs.

Brom's breath hitches, his eyes burning, and in both men I notice the bulge at the front of their robes, the fabric twitching over their growing cocks.

"I normally wouldn't do you the courtesy of asking," Crane begins, leaning in to Brom, his gaze flicking over his face. "But do you want to make her come first, or should I?"

Brom meets his eyes, glaring at him. "What do you think?"

Crane grabs him by the back of the neck, bringing his face close to his own, his mouth twisted in a sneer. "I think that's the last time I give you an option."

Then, with his hand still around Brom's neck, Crane looks to me. "Do you want Brom to eat out that sweet cunt of yours?"

*Do* you *want that?* I want to say.

But I can't even form words. I just nod.

"He promises to keep his cock to himself," Crane says, giving Brom a push as he releases him, holding back his robe so that he's naked. "Get on your knees, pretty boy, and crawl to her. I want our witch sopping wet."

Brom stumbles to his knees in front of my spread legs, my heart leaping against my ribs as I take in the sight of him, his cock thick and throbbing. My thighs are starting to shake in anticipation, my nerves on fire, as Brom meets my eyes and crawls forward. I've never had him down there before, never known what his mouth might feel like. Will he ravage me the same way he kisses me? Will he devour me with his dark energy?

Brom's gaze stays on mine as he reaches out, wrapping his large, calloused hands around my hips, holding me in place, his head dipping down. I stare right back at him, feeling the connection between us growing. There's something unsaid here, that this is him and this is me and we are stepping into new territory together.

And in this moment, I must trust him.

I give him the slightest nod, because I think that's what he's checking in on, to see if I really want this, and I catch the faintest dimple before he dives his head down, his tongue sweeping over my clit with a powerful stroke that makes my head fly back against the ground.

"Hell," I swear, my back arching up, as he continues to lick at me with the apex of his tongue, his beard scratching the sides of my sensitive skin, adding to the sensation. My eyes flutter closed, surrendering to every second.

"I thought about this moment," comes Crane's voice, sounding far away. "I thought it would eat me alive with jealousy to see him between your legs. And it does make me jealous. I just didn't know how badly it would affect me." I hear Crane let out a slow, shaking breath. "I want the both of you so much that I can hardly stand it."

I hear him take off his robe, hear his footsteps as they come closer. I open my eyes and stare up at the fog above the trees and Crane's face as he peers down at me, as naked as the rest of us. "Sweet witch," he says softly. I hold Crane's gaze even as Brom's fingers make a wide V against my skin, separating my folds and stretching me while his tongue flicks my clit harder.

"Oh God," I say through a choked cry, my eyes falling closed again, and then I feel Crane lying beside me on the grass, his mouth at my ear, breath hot.

"I'm your god, Kat, don't you forget it," Crane murmurs, taking my lobe between his teeth and giving it a sharp tug. "I'm your god and he's your devil."

Then he's running his hands over my breasts, his head lowering and licking around the nipple at the same time that Brom is sucking my clit between his lips.

"Oh heavens," I cry out, my hands going into Brom's hair now and making fists.

Crane chuckles against my breast, biting my skin hard enough that I cry out, that I see stars, before he soothes the marks with his lips. Then he starts kissing up my chest, licking up my throat with abandon.

"Doesn't it feel nice to have Brom's head between your legs?" he asks, sucking and biting on my neck, making my back bow from the mix of pleasure and pain. "I know what it feels like, the roughness of his beard on my legs when he's choking on my cock, when I'm sitting on his face, putting his tongue to good use. Such a talented tongue he has. Perfect for fucking."

He raises his head off my neck, placing a tender kiss on my clavicle. "Look how handsome he is when he's giving you pleasure."

At that, I open my eyes and follow Crane's gaze. Brom lifts his head from between my thighs, his beard glistening in the candlelight, eyes simmering with desire, eyeing the both of us before his mouth ravages me again.

"Look at how he adores you," Crane breathes in my ear, and I let out a fluttering moan. "Look at how badly he wants you to come. How badly *he* wants to come. See his hips moving, he's so needy and desperate that he's trying to fuck the grass, trying to get some release. But he's not allowed, not yet. He's saving it all for you."

I roll my head to the side to look at Crane beside me on the ground, his body so long and lean, every muscle tense, his cock looking impossibly large and dark.

"And what about you?" I whisper, keeping one hand fisted in Brom's hair, the other reaching down for Crane's cock. He inches his hips away, out of reach. "Are you saving it for me too? Or can I make you come now?"

He breaks into a grin that lights up his face, even though his eyes are still heavy with need. "Where did I even find you, my sweet girl? How did I ever get so lucky?"

Then his expression grows somber, his eyes darkening, and I don't know what he's thinking, but Brom's fingers are now stroking circles around my entrance before plunging roughly inside me.

I open my mouth to gasp at the intrusion, and then Crane's covering mine with his, pulling me into a deep kiss while Brom adds another finger, then another. Crane moans into my mouth, his tongue fucking me with long, wide strokes, just as Brom does the same to me below with his fingers, and I'm starting to tremble, feeling a heated knot in my belly grow tighter and tighter, being slowly driven mad by mindless need.

"Oh, Kat," Crane says against my lips, his breath hitching. He kisses me like he's drowning and I'm the only thing keeping him afloat, but the truth is he's pulling me down with him. We're both sinking into each other. My hands are in Crane's hair now, holding on, and he's doing the same to mine, and maybe it's Brom who's anchoring us so we don't slide off into the void together.

"Make her come, pretty boy," Crane commands as he pulls his mouth away from mine without breaking my gaze. His eyes are searing, his pupils so wide and black that I feel I'm still falling headfirst into the abyss. He lets go of my hair and holds my chin between his fingers, his other hand pinching my nipple hard, Brom still licking me over and over again.

"I love you," Crane whispers to me, voice shaking, and his words, those words, it's like I can't breathe and even Brom pauses between my legs for just a moment.

"I love you, Kat," Crane goes on, impassioned. "And I love him. I love both of you, want both of you, *need* both of you. I think I'll die otherwise."

I feel my chest tighten, like it's growing too small for my heart, and I can no longer tell if it's because Brom's tongue is pushing me to the edge of an orgasm or Crane's words are pushing me to the edge of love, but I'm ready to submit, I'm ready to surrender to both of them.

And then Brom's rough mouth pushes me over the edge, and I come like a gunshot. I open my mouth to scream, but then Crane's covering my mouth with his and I'm whimpering against his lips, my sounds swallowed. I'm thrusting my hips up against Brom's face, my thighs smashing against either side of his head, his beard burning my skin. The orgasm rolls through me like a herd of horses. I'm being trampled alive, and I never want it to stop.

"You're doing so well, Brom," Crane croons to him. "Look at how hard you're making her come."

I moan louder against Crane, and he pulls away, resting his forehead against mine, his hand at my cheek. "And you're such a good witch," he says to me, with such affection and tenderness it makes my head spin. "And now it's my turn."

# 19

## Kat

While I'm lying on the grass in a daze, the orgasm still making my thighs quiver, Brom gets out from between my legs, and Crane goes down to take Brom's place. I can only stare up at the sky, my heart thudding in my ears, and it feels like we're the only people left in the entire planet, like this small clearing in the dark woods is our only world. I've never felt so connected to both of these men, nor the earth before, like we're all one being, and we haven't officially started the ritual yet.

Crane is saying something to Brom in a low voice, and then Brom is kneeling beside me, stroking the hair off my forehead.

"Hello," I manage to say to him, my mind swimming. I give him a lazy smile, feeling drugged.

His eyes are still dark, but there's a lightness about him that wasn't there earlier. I feel it too, this new, bright energy between us that's banishing the shadows and tension from before.

"Are you all right?" he asks me softly as his eyes search mine, and oh, how my heart soars at the tenderness in his words. This is Brom. This is the man I have missed.

"Yes," I say, reaching up and putting my hand at his beard. "Yes, I'm all right. Are you?"

He gives me a faint smile before turning and kissing my wrist. "I would be better if I were allowed to fucking come."

I can't help but laugh.

"Patience," Crane chides him, and suddenly he's grabbing my thighs and spreading them wide.

I gasp and look down to see Crane's dark hair, the slight curl at the ends, the backs of my thighs resting on his wide shoulders.

Without hesitation Crane's slick, wet mouth dives in to where I'm already open and drenched, nose rubbing against my clit, his strong tongue pushing up into my cunt. My hips jerk involuntarily, squeezing around his head. His teeth gently nip at me, sending more pleasure-pain through my body until my toes are curling.

I moan breathlessly and look up at Brom. He's watching Crane ravage me, his jaw tight and flexed, a line between his dark low brows.

"Are you jealous?" I whisper to Brom, running a hand through his hair and making a fist when Crane makes my body turn into an inferno.

Brom glances at me quickly. "Yes."

"Do you want him to be doing that to you as well?" I ask, pausing as my back bows off the damp grass, Crane giving my clit a fluttering suck. "Or do you want to be down there with him?" I manage to finish, ending it with another moan.

"Both," he says, a hint of shame on his face. Then the shame burns, melts, turns to raw lust. "I want to lick you from behind. Is that all right?"

Crane makes a noise of agreement against me, having heard Brom, the vibrations sinking deep into my core. I gulp, my heart skipping at the thought, the tightness in my belly building to the heights it was earlier. "Yes."

Then Brom moves down toward Crane, who, without removing his face from my cunt, twists my hips to the side while I keep my back as flat as possible to the earth, bending at the waist. Brom goes down across from Crane, and my body jerks at the intrusion of his face at my rear. I can understand why Crane was adamant I have such a thorough bath.

And then both men lick, suck, and ravage me from both sides. I'm immediately swept up into a hurricane of raw hunger, both their mouths feeding me at once in a most dirty and depraved way, and my hands are grabbing their hair, grabbing the grass, doing what I can to not float away.

But I am very much caught between them. It's not just their mouths that work at me in tandem—they both wrap their strong hands around my waist, my hips, my thighs. Even if I wanted to escape them, I wouldn't be able to, and they give no quarter.

I glance down and that's enough to make me feel wild, the sight of both of their dark heads, their muscular shoulders, their strong tongues and soft mouths on my most private places. I feel like I'm being eaten alive as they pin down my hips, as they fill the night air with the wet, messy sounds of their hunger.

When the orgasm comes for me this time, it's like it's coming from someplace else. From Brom, from Crane, and from the depths of the earth, and from another world. It shoots through me like a comet, my body set ablaze, burning under the night sky, soaring high above the trees. I erupt, biting back my cries, my body convulsing and shaking until my mind is scrambled, held in place by these two men, the constant firm pressure of their hands and mouths keeping me secure, keeping me safe.

Inside me, something tender breaks, and I feel a rush of tears coming to my eyes, because it's too good, all of this, them, us. I love them. I love Crane. I love Brom. I never want to be without either. I want, *need*, this ritual to work so that Brom can return to us fully and we can leave this place and never look back.

"Oh God," I whisper, my words broken, my heart full.

I feel them break away from me, and I'm so cold and empty and scared, but then their hands stay on my body, keeping the connection, and they move up on either side of me, touching me. Holding me, letting me know that they have me.

Crane tilts my chin toward him, and I'm still so dizzy from the orgasm and my roiling emotions that I have a hard time even focusing on his beautiful, austere face. Then he leans in and kisses the tears away from my eyes, savoring them.

"Tears of pleasure taste the same as tears of pain," he murmurs, almost to himself, as if it's another fact to file away, and I can't help but break into a smile because even in the midst of all of this, he's still curious. He's still Professor Crane.

He meets my eyes. "I think we got you wet enough to handle anything."

I clear my throat. "I would say so." Though I am starting to get nervous about what's next to come.

Brom gently trails his fingers over my stomach, resting his

head on my shoulder. "Are you all right?" he asks, and my skin tingles at how attentive and gentle he's being.

I nod. "I am. Are you still needing to come?"

"What do you think?" Brom asks, moving his hips so the stiff length of his erection is pressed against my side. It's so hot it feels like it's branding me.

I reach down and wrap my hand around his thick, blunt head, sliding my thumb over the pearly beads of arousal, and he pinches his eyes shut, letting out a hiss.

I go to do the same to Crane on the other side of me, but like before, he moves his hips out of the way. "I don't need extra encouragement. And you should probably let go of his dick because he looks seconds from coming right on your face. There will be plenty of time for that later." He leans in and kisses my shoulder. "The most important part is that we made you feel loved and cherished."

"You did."

"Good," he says, placing a soft kiss beside my lips. "Because now we need to move on to the ritual before it gets too late."

And at that he gets up.

The energy in the glen shifts.

Sobriety settles in, clearing my head.

Brom gets up next and then they both reach down and pull me to my feet. It's really hard not to notice their cocks, how heavy and thick and engorged they are, obviously aching to be touched, to find release. "Are you sure I can't help you?" I whisper, wanting to touch them, wanting to watch their eyes roll back in their heads for a change.

"Trust me, darling, you will," Crane says. They lead me closer to the bag at the edge of the circle, where Crane brings out several vials.

"This," Crane says to me, holding up one of oil with a yellow tinge, "is sunflower oil. You'll figure out what that's for soon." Then he holds up a greenish one with herbs in it. "This is the poultice to heal any of our wounds. All the cuts for the blood magic will be superficial, but this will still go a long way." He puts them back in the bag and then pulls out three more vials, purple in color. "And these are the elixirs that will help us be more perceptive to the veil—and help those in the veil be more perceptive to us."

He hands a vial to me and Brom, and I stare down at the liquid as it seems to move around in the glass, making the skin of my palm glow mauve.

"So what's the plan?" I ask quietly. "What do we do?"

"First we take the elixir," he says.

"We take it first?" I exclaim. "I thought we would take it at the end! Why open us up to the veil now?"

"Because we need to draw on that energy too," Crane explains. "You recall when you were in the void? You were drawing things to you because of your energy. This school draws things to it because of its energy. Blood magic will bond us, sex magic will intensify that bond, which is needed to act as a united front. But those two things combined together will draw even more energy toward us. Dark magic from the spirit world is needed to exorcise the horseman. Our bond will push him out, the spirits will pull him the rest of the way. They want to take. They will take the horseman."

"You sound so certain," I say.

"Have you even done this before?" Brom asks him.

"What do you think?" Crane says.

Brom shakes his head and shrugs. "I honestly don't know, Crane, you're *you*. You could have had séance orgies every Sunday night for all we know."

Crane lifts his chin slightly and sniffs. "Well, I haven't. There's a first time for everything." He gives me a steady look. "We take the elixir now. You will get on the ground. I will cut you, and we will cut ourselves, and the blood will flow. Then I will fuck the hell out of you, and you're going to suck Brom's cock, and we're both going to come inside you."

"Christ," Brom swears, his voice thick as he reaches a hand down over his bulge.

Crane quickly grabs Brom's hand and snatches it away, twisting it to the side, enough to make Brom grunt in pain. "*And* as we're coming, I'm going to recite the lines of a spell to invite the spirits in and take the horseman out. If it doesn't work, if we have to do it again tonight, we will."

I feel delirious just listening to this. "But if we invite the spirits in . . ."

"They can't stay," Crane says adamantly. "The three of us will be fused to each other, there won't be any room inside us. All of our energy will be inside each other."

"You do realize I'm not a witch," Brom glowers.

"It's in your blood, whether you want it to be or not," Crane says. "And besides, this should still work even if one of us isn't magically inclined." He places a leveling gaze on me and then back to Brom. "Do we all understand? Are we all in agreement? Kat, this is your last chance to back out. We can leave it to us just fucking in the woods and that's that."

"As if that's trivial," I say under my breath, then I straighten up. "I'm not backing out."

Crane gives me a quick smile. "Brave girl," he says. "Bottoms up."

He uncorks the top of his bottle and drinks the elixir down. Brom and I do the same in unison. Ugh. I can't help but make a face. It tastes awful, like strong bitters mixed with too much salt, but I manage to swallow it down.

"Now I will officially start the ritual," Crane says.

He goes around the circle, placing the quartz and selenite crystals at certain intervals, then walks around clockwise and then counterclockwise, chanting something under his breath. Because he's doing this all naked, with an erection, it looks very primitive indeed.

"The ritual has begun," he says, tilting his head up to the sky. "The circle may not be broken."

"When do we know it's working?" I ask Crane as he comes back and takes the bottles from us and places them beside his bag.

"You'll know," he says to me, his brows lowering. "Go to the middle of the circle and get on your hands and knees."

I swallow hard at his direction, but do as he says. I go to the middle of the clearing, then drop down to my knees, then my hands, my rear facing them. I hear Crane whisper something to Brom, and whatever it is sounds detailed and I can't help but shiver, but whether it's from anticipation or fear, I can't tell. So far, I don't feel anything from the elixir. I had hoped it at least had a tranquilizing or calming effect.

I see their shadows cast by candlelight as they walk over to me. Brom goes in front of me, dropping to his knees, his cock right in front of my face, crying tears of arousal. My mouth automatically salivates, and I make a move for it, but then Crane is grabbing my hips tightly.

"Stay still," he whispers to me. "This will hurt."

At that warning I freeze, the air hitching in my throat, and Brom reaches down and places his fingers under my chin, making me look up to meet his eyes.

"I've got you, Daffy," he says to me.

Then my back explodes in pain. I cry out as the knife runs between my shoulder blades and down beside my spine, mixing together with a spike of pleasure.

"Look at me, look at me," Brom commands, his grip tighter on my chin. "Hey, Kat, look at me."

I manage to open my eyes, wincing hard as the blade continues to run down my back.

"Breathe," he says to me, his dark eyes piercing. "You're not breathing, it hurts more when you don't breathe. You need to breathe. Breathe in. Breathe in. Come on."

I open my mouth and try to take in a breath, the knife still trailing toward my tailbone, and now I'm gritting my teeth at the pain as it envelops me, and I have to close my eyes again, trying to concentrate on the part of it that feels strangely good.

"I'm sorry," Crane says softly. "I can't do this fast or I'll make a mistake. Almost done. You're being such a good girl."

Then he removes the knife from my back, and the pain stops, and my head drops down, my hair flowing over Brom's cock.

"Oh, fuck," Brom swears. "I don't know how much of this I can take. I could come right in your hair, Kat."

"You're going to take as much as I tell you to," Crane snaps at him. "Pick up your knife and cut your palm."

I don't know if it's the elixir taking effect but suddenly all the pain vanishes. The sharp stinging sensation from the blade is gone, and instead I feel more aroused than ever. I raise my head to look up at Brom as he glides the knife over his palm, blood dripping down onto his cock.

I'm overcome with a most perverted urge, something that seems to come from the darkest, most primal reaches of my soul. I grab Brom's cock, holding the hot, velvet length in my hand, then slide it into my mouth, the taste of his arousal mixed with the blood from his palm hitting my tongue and making me moan.

"Fuck!" Brom calls out, his hips jerking his cock deeper into my mouth. "Oh, fuck, Kat."

"Getting ahead of ourselves?" Crane grumbles, sounding petulant. "At least put your hand on her back."

Brom leans forward and presses his hand over the cut along my spine, and I feel the hot sticky warmth of his blood mixing with mine. It doesn't hurt anymore, instead it feels like I'm stepping into a hot bath, made all the better by his beautiful dick in my mouth. I feel like I'm transforming, turning into an animal that only has mindless sex on her mind, who wants to be utterly defiled by these two powerful and virile men.

Then I feel Crane's hand do the same, sliding down my spine, and then he's nudging my legs apart with his knee and I feel the kiss of his cock at my entrance.

"Still wet," he rasps. "That's my girl."

With this angle Crane feels so large and wide that I brace myself, sucking harder on Brom as Crane shoves in an inch.

I let out a choked cry, and their hands are everywhere—Brom's gathering my hair in his fist, his other hand smoothing down my back, Crane's hand coasting up my back to meet Brom's, his other a bruising grip on my hips.

"Jesus, you're too tight," Crane manages to eke out, making slow progress until finally he forces himself in to the hilt. "Your cunt is trying to kill me, darling. *Fuck.*"

I can't even respond. I truly feel like a vessel for their seed tonight, being penetrated on both ends, and my body seems to grow mad with the desire for more. More of them, more of this, more of us. I want them to unleash inside me, fill me up until I'm drowning in it.

"Look at her, Brom," Crane muses through a ragged groan. "Look at our desperate, greedy little witch. Have you ever seen someone so hungry for our cocks? God, Kat, you're taking us both so well."

Brom only grunts, his hips pushing in harder and faster as he holds my head in place.

"She might even suck your cock better than you suck mine," Crane says, his own hips slamming against me harder, driving deeper with each thrust until his thick crown starts pressing on some place inside me, a spot that makes me want to explode. "You're growing even wetter by the second, sweetheart, you're dripping on the ground, and I've barely even touched you."

I groan over Brom's length, which causes another hiss from him, his fist tightening in my hair and yanking on it, but there's no pain now, only pleasure. There's only this, only us.

"I can't hold back much longer," Brom says, his fingers desperate and wild as they try to grab my face, pressing into my skin, my tonsils being rubbed raw from his blunt head.

"You're not coming yet," Crane warns, and suddenly I feel him lean over me. I look up, careful not to let Brom's cock slip from my mouth, and watch as Crane grabs Brom by the throat. "You're not coming until I say you do. Same goes for you, Kat, or I'm choking you too."

I let my teeth gently graze over Brom's hard ridge, watching as Crane continues to choke Brom until Brom's face starts to darken from lack of oxygen, his lips raised in a sneer. Then Crane pulls his head forward, and even though I can't see them above me anymore, not from this angle, I can hear them kissing. Wet and hungry, coupled with shallow breaths and fluttering moans, and even with the two of them pounding deep inside me, I'm struck with jealousy.

Then they break apart. Crane releases Brom and begins to chant something under his breath, the words fast and unintelligible, but they feel sacred, feel like they mean something. He repeats these words over and over, and then he groans.

"I'm going to come," Crane breathes, and he reaches down and runs his fingers over my clit as he pushes in deeper, and Brom drives himself so far down my throat that I choke. He pulses inside my mouth, and at first he's so far back I don't taste his seed as it spills down, but then I'm hit with the salt of it and I'm swallowing and swallowing, just as I feel Crane shooting inside me, letting out a garbled cry, his grip painful.

And then I'm coming too, a violent and wonderfully terrifying feeling amid all their groans and their ragged breathing and the wet, lewd slap of skin. There's a moment when I feel I should hold back, temper my orgasm somehow, it's that fear of falling, the fear of the unknown.

But then I let go. My body becomes not my own. It surprises me, yanking my insides around, burning me up like a fire before the flames slowly go out.

I'm crying again, tears that try to express all the things I'm feeling but don't have words for, and I suppose that's everything. My cunt squeezes and pulses around Crane's throbbing cock, and Brom is pulling out from my mouth, my jaw aching in response.

My head hangs down and I collapse to my elbows, trying to breathe, trying to ground myself with my forehead pressed against the cool grass, my eyes closed.

"Did it work?" Crane asks, his hand gently running down my back in a soothing manner as he pulls out of me, making me feel hollow.

"I don't know," Brom says, clearing his throat. "I don't think so. I still . . . I still feel connected to him. And I don't see any spirits."

"Perhaps we were supposed to take our time," Crane ponders, his voice still thick from sex. "Maybe it needs to work through our systems first."

"Her cut is already healing," Brom points out.

"Then we'll do it to her on the other side."

Those words seem to bring me back to the moment. I slowly push myself up on my hands, prickles of fear breaking through the satisfied haze.

"You're going to cut me again?" I ask, lifting up my head, though I can't see either of them with my hair in my face.

"We have to try again while we can," Crane explains softly. "We can't close the ritual yet, not when the elixir hasn't fully worked. It . . ."

He trails off.

"Brom," he whispers, an edge to his voice. "Do you see that?"

I hear Brom swallow loudly.

"Yes. I do."

His tone makes my blood run cold.

I quickly brush my hair out of my face and follow their gaze to the edge of the circle.

Where several shadowy figures have gathered.

Watching us.

# 20

## Kat

"Oh my God," I cry out at the figures standing in the woods, standing there, facing us and not moving. "Who are they?" *What are they?*

I start to panic, straightening up, but then Crane is grabbing me around the waist and holding me back against his chest. Somehow his cock is hard again, the hot, slick length of him pressed along my bottom.

"We're supposed to see them," he says into my ear. "It means it's working. The ritual is still in play."

I gape at the figures in horror. Some of them are clearly human, ghosts, perhaps, with chest wounds, some with their heads caved in, others looking intact except for black eyes and mouths stretched open in a silent scream. Others are dark and shadowy with red eyes and sharp teeth and . . .

I look down at where Crane is holding on to me across my waist.

His arm is just shadow now.

"Crane?" I cry out, and I try to look at him over my shoulder.

His face is gone. Instead, he's just darkness personified, a moving, smoking abyss with two crimson dots for eyes. "Kat," the shadow monster says in an inhuman voice.

"Help! Brom, he's—" I cry out, twisting around to face Brom, to get him to save me, but Brom isn't there anymore.

Instead, it's the headless horseman kneeling in front of me, in his black leather armor and cape and that festering wound that used to hold a head.

"No!" I scream. "No, no!"

"Kat," the shadow hisses in my ear. "I told you this would happen, you're fine, we've got you."

"He's the horseman," I manage to say. "He's the horseman!"

The horseman reaches for me with his black gloved hands, and I scream again. I bring my elbow back and jab it into the shadow's ribs. I don't even feel it make contact, but it lets go of me and I get to my feet, trying to run.

"Grab her!" the shadow yells. "Don't let her break the circle!"

I'm screaming, running toward the edge of the clearing, away from the gathered ghouls, my feet slipping under me on the wet grass, but I'm almost there, I'm almost—

I yelp as powerful arms wrap around my calves, slamming me down to the ground, my hands breaking my fall.

"Pin her down," the shadow commands, and I'm kicking, trying to get away, but then the horseman is turning me over on my back, holding my arms above my head and pinning my wrists in place. The shadow man comes at me with a knife raised, his thighs on top of mine, the weight keeping me from bucking. "Easy, Kat, we're trying not to hurt you."

"Kat, Katrina," the thing with no head says. "It's okay. It's okay. It's Brom and it's Crane."

"No, no," I cry, tears spilling out as I shake my head, my heart feeling like it will burst from my chest and run away because I can't. "You're not them, you're not them."

"We are us," the shadow says. "Sweet witch, please, you have to choose to see us for what we are. We are not what you're seeing, that's fear. There are a lot of creatures around us right now sending you this fear, playing with your mind, because they love the way your fear tastes. You know us, you feel us."

I struggle beneath them, but they're too big and strong.

I am their captive.

I will die at their hands.

"Daffy," the horseman says. "I'm not the horseman right now. I'm just Brom. I'm *your* Brom. Choose to see me. Look past it and see me. *Please*, Daffodil, do this for me."

The last *please* sounds so desperate that something inside me cracks.

And suddenly the image of the horseman starts to fade. Brom, my moody, dark Brom comes back into view, his head where there wasn't a head before.

"Do you see me?" he asks, his face upside down as he peers over me. I nod frantically. "Do you see Crane now?"

I swallow and raise my head to see Crane pinning down my legs. It doesn't help that he's holding a knife in his hands, but at least there's no shadow at all, just his pale, toned body lit by candles.

"I see you," I whisper to Crane, relief flooding through me, trying to sweep away the terror. It's him. It's Crane, my teacher, my lover, with his thick black hair, his high cheekbones, that downturned mouth.

"Good," Crane says, giving me a soft smile.

But the smile is fleeting.

"Now we're going to keep you pinned down because this next part is going to hurt again, and I don't want you running from the pain. We need to keep going. All right?"

I nod, sucking in my breath and trying not to squirm despite what he just told me, watching as he takes the knife and presses it right between my clavicles and runs it down between my breasts.

"Ah!" I cry out, the pain even worse than before, and when I roll my head to the side to look away, I'm staring at all the dark spirits hovering on the other side of the salt circle.

Waiting for us to slip up.

Feeding on my pain.

"I'm sorry," Crane says, the knife now going over my stomach, making me try and move, to escape the pain. "Please, try—"

The knife feels like it's cutting deep, blood spilling over my stomach. I try to shift, to get up and run from it, but they keep me pinned down, and I'm bucking beneath them, the agony unbearable, taking over every part of my body.

I let out a scream, the sound echoing through the forest before Brom clamps his hand over my mouth. "We can't call attention to ourselves," he reminds me, and so I bite his hand instead.

He grimaces, but he doesn't let up, even when I bite harder as Crane drags the sharp tip of the knife over my belly button where he finally stops.

The pain stops.

I close my eyes and exhale into Brom's palm as my body lets go, turning into a rag doll beneath them. I sink into the grass, my heart rate spiking, a buzzing sensation inside me like I've been struck by lightning. The energy inside me roils and thunders, a storm of creation, a deluge of power there for the taking.

Brom takes his hand away and I hear him grunt, feel wet drops on my breasts as I realize he's cut open his palm again.

I open my eyes to look at him and see his hand in Crane's, clasped in a bleeding handshake over my body, the blood dripping down. They're both looking into each other's eyes with feverish intensity, a mix of pain and longing and love and history, and again I'm hit with the sting of jealousy. These men share something I don't, they share secrets, they connect in shadows, their attraction to each other forbidden, their love even more so. There is a bond between them I can't even begin to become a part of, but I want it all the same.

As if hearing me, Crane breaks away from Brom's gaze, his eyes finding mine as they let go of each other's bloodied hands.

And his eyes widen.

"Kat," Crane says through a gasp. "Your eyes."

Brom looks down at me and frowns. "They're gold," he whispers.

"Gold?" I ask, my heart jumping, feeling unnerved. "Why are my eyes gold? What does that mean?"

"The energy," Crane says in awe. Then his expression hardens with determination. "We can't waste it."

He reaches down and runs his palm down my body, right over the bleeding cut, and then Brom does the same from the opposite direction before he brings his other hand over and starts cupping my breasts, bloody thumbs brushing over my nipples, hardening them into little furls.

I let out a raw gasp, my hips bucking up even though Crane is still pinning me down.

"At least you're learning to embrace your fear, sweet witch," Crane murmurs as he gets off me, my legs tingling without his weight. "Now get on your side."

He grabs my hips and rolls me over so that I'm facing the dark figures at the edge of the forest, more of them now crowding around. I close my eyes to them, feeling the blood roll off my body and onto the grass.

"Brom, get down there and push my seed back into her cunt," he demands.

Brom grunts and positions himself with his head between my legs and starts sliding his tongue up the sides of my thighs while I hear Crane walk away. I open my eyes and look back to see Crane approach with the small vial of pale-yellow oil, pouring it into his hands and then smearing it over his cock. It gleams menacingly in the dim light, and from the heated look in his gray eyes I know exactly how he plans to claim me.

He drops to his knees beside me, running an oiled palm over my hip, hissing at the pain from his cut, then brings his fingers down over my rear.

"Brom, lift her leg up," Crane says hoarsely. Brom obeys and grabs my thigh, pushing it up while he thrusts his fingers inside my cunt. I let out a choked cry as his fingers slide in deep, my entrance still so wet from both Crane's seed and my own arousal. Then I feel Crane from behind me positioning the flat head of his cock against my most secret place.

"This will feel different," Crane whispers, pushing my hair off my shoulders. "It should feel good. Any discomfort will disappear in time, I promise, so long as you submit yourself to me."

With his other hand I feel him make a fist around his cock, pressing in firmly against the pleated entrance of my rear. "I'll be the first man to fuck you here," Crane says, his words shaking with impatience, making me shake in return. "The first man to spill my seed inside your tight little ass. Pretty boy may have taken your virginity, but I'm taking this for myself."

Crane doesn't thrust in all at once like I expect him to. Instead, he works himself in, shoving in inch by inch, his thick hot crown, slick with oil and arousal, pushing past my entrance, then farther in, and I can't breathe, I can't think. I start squirming, trying to deal with the intrusion. Because he's big, he feels too big for my body, and it hurts—it does, and yet I want more of it. It feels too foreign and strange, but also so full. Pain catches in the depth of my core, and I don't know how to let go of it. I don't know anything right now, I'm a mess of feelings and sensations with nowhere to go.

"Make her open for me, pretty boy," Crane says through a ragged gasp as he pushes in further. "Help her relax."

Brom attacks my cunt with gusto, his tongue assaulting while his lips soothe and, yes, yes, now I feel myself opening up, wanting more, the pain sliding away until Crane's cock is pushed all the way in. I'm still breathless, like the air has been wrung from my lungs, and yet I want to laugh at how good and strange it feels. These two men are all I feel.

"Are you getting her wet?" Crane manages to say to him, his voice thick, and he makes a fist in my hair, yanking my head back until my eyes water.

Brom makes a noise of agreement against me, the vibrations nearly sending me over the edge, while Crane is swearing quietly from behind me as he continues to thrust inside me.

"God, she's tight, Brom," Crane groans through clenched teeth. "You should feel her like this. I can't even see straight; she's trying to strangle me."

Brom moans in response and I try to clamp my thighs over his head.

"Fuck," Crane says through a harsh inhale. "I won't last long. Lie down on your back, Brom. Get each other to come while I finish here."

Suddenly Crane pulls out, an empty, scooped-out feeling chasing his absence, and then he's moving me so that I'm on my hands and knees, planted over Brom, Brom's cock now near my mouth, my cunt at his.

Without hesitating I take Brom's weeping and rigid length in my mouth again, his velvet skin burning hot, and I relish the salty hit of his arousal on my tongue, as he reaches up with his mouth, doing the same to me. We both let out a breathless noise of want, in unison, making me feel like we are one being, captive to lust.

Crane, meanwhile, remains in charge of us. He grabs my hips, and this time he doesn't hesitate. He spears me with his cock in one hard shove and I gasp around Brom's length while Brom pushes his hips up, driving himself deeper into my throat. Like before I feel swept away and unmoored, lost to the feeling of having these men deep inside me, but now with Brom suckling my clit into his mouth, it takes this to another level.

"You should see what I see," Crane rasps, pulling out again to the tip before pushing back in until I'm breathless again, and I'm driven wild by the most subtle feeling of all, the softness of his testicles pressed against my swollen entrance, the contact making me ache.

"Both of you beneath me, both of you so beautiful in your need, so stunning in your wildness. You are such dark and vibrant creatures: a fallen angel, a risen devil, coming together as one and belonging to me, only me, your god."

Then he lets out a trembling exhale and starts reciting those words again, a low, guttural chant that sounds like it's coming from some place deep inside Crane, a place dark and unknown from where magic is drawn and spells are born. It brings the thrill of terror through me, the only feeling able to penetrate the twisted knot of want and sex and desire that we've become.

"I'm going to come again," Crane whispers, his fingers digging into my hips, letting go only to give my rear a painful smack with his palm. I jolt, Brom's cock driving in deeper into my throat, his own tongue thrusting deeper inside me. What happens to one of us affects the rest of us. We truly are joined now and the energy inside me seems to grow brighter, hotter, as if Crane's chanting has coaxed it up like a snake charmer.

"You belong to me in heart, body, and soul now. Together, just like this," Crane says before breaking off into a low, shuddering groan. "Oh, you are mine. There's no room for anyone else but us." He gives my rear another hard smack. "I'm going to come. You better come too. Give me one more, sweet witch, one more."

He doesn't have to tell me twice. My cunt is so taut it hurts.

Brom's tongue and lips flick at my clit until I'm pushed to the point of no return, his cock starts to jerk and swell inside my mouth, and Crane's pace grows wild and uneven, as if he's no longer in control.

The three of us come at once, and I'm swallowing Brom's seed, and I'm the vessel for Crane's, and in the back of my mind I'm aware that there are monsters around us, spirits that want what we have, that are dying to taste what we have, and though they can't have us, they can have the horseman.

*Take him*, I think to them, hoping they can hear me, even as the orgasm is plucking my thoughts out of my head as I succumb to the undertow. *Take the Hessian from Brom. He's what you want, he's what . . .*

I can't finish the wish. I yelp, moaning loudly and uncontrollably as I continue to come hard, the white-hot energy inside me filling every vein, bouncing around my soul like fireflies in a jar.

In this moment I am no longer a witch.

I am a goddess.

And I'm being consumed by two dark gods.

Then the lights go out. I collapse on top of Brom, careful not to crush his still-pulsing cock, and roll over beside him, causing Crane to pull out of me. I can't think, can't breathe, can't talk. I am just here, and that's all there is. There's just us.

I close my eyes and feel my body drift away, as if floating on a dark current, taken somewhere safe, and I don't know how long I lie like that for, but it isn't until I feel Crane's arms wrap around me, kissing the back of my head, that I realize we're still in the middle of the circle, in the middle of the glen, in the middle of the woods, and I'm in the middle of these men.

They're talking too, their voices low and hushed.

"It didn't work," Brom says. There's no disappointment in his voice, just fact.

I open my eyes to see Brom sitting up beside me, his knees drawn to his chest, staring out at the woods.

"Do you know for sure?" Crane asks cagily.

Brom nods. "We're still connected. He's not here right now, but . . . we're connected. The ritual didn't work."

Crane exhales and presses his mouth against my head again. "All right," he says quietly. "All right." He lifts his head and brushes my hair off my face, his actions so soft and tender. "We knew that this might not work on the first go. The horseman has been bound to you by a spell cast by the sisters, so of course it will be harder to break. We will have better luck on the full moon, and if not then, Samhain. I will keep reading and learning. I won't give up on you, Brom. *We* won't."

Brom looks at us, his brows lowered, casting his black eyes into shadow. "Maybe keeping the horseman inside me wouldn't be so bad, if it has to be that way."

I gasp and sit up. "Are you being serious? No, Brom. You can't go around the rest of your life being possessed by the Hessian soldier. We will get him out of you. No matter what."

He looks at Crane. "Maybe I could learn to live with him."

"Out of the question," Crane says stiffly. "You want to spend the rest of your nights in chains?"

"I'm sure you wouldn't have a problem with that," he mumbles, looking away.

"I like my sleep," Crane says indignantly. "Don't be such a misanthrope. This ritual is new to all of us. In time we will get better. Perhaps the dark moon was working against us. We don't know. But we will try again, and none of us are giving up hope, including you. Do you hear me?"

"Yes, sir," he says flatly. He looks around the clearing. "What do we do about the ghosts?"

I follow his gaze, the shadows still gathering at the edge of the circle, their hunger palpable.

"We wait until the elixir wears off," Crane says. "Should be soon. And then I'll close the ceremony and open the circle." He sighs. "And then, we'll go back to our beds and try to get some sleep if we can."

Crane sounds so tired as he says that, and I can't help but feel for him, the burden of having to make sure Brom doesn't go around harming those on campus. But it's necessary, especially since, so far, Brom being under restraint has meant the actual spirit of the Hessian hasn't gone around killing people either.

For now, that is.

# 21

## Brom

*In the darkness, I will do thy bidding.*
 *In the darkness, I will wait.*
 *For you to awake.*
*To let me in.*
*Use me, Abraham Van Brunt.*
*Let me rule you. Let me be your power.*
*You never have to feel alone again.*

I dream of a black wood. I am a raven in the trees. I look down on the three writhing, naked bodies. I see myself, and Kat, and Crane. I see us as what we really are—heathens. We are no longer civilized people, no longer humans; we are animals, succumbing to the most basic, mindless desires to rut, to mate, to make and take pleasure. To use, to be abused. To want, and crave, and hunger.

I watch us from above, Kat in the center, the vessel for our seed, for our power. She glows golden from within, her hair shining like cornsilk, her body sun fire, and she revels in it, in this creation of her true self. A witch, a goddess, the love of my life. Crane and I are just two heathens in her orbit, sharp enough to provide the spark. She is the flame. She will always be the flame.

I flap my wings and take off, flying through the darkness and the mist until it clears and I'm soaring over Sleepy Hollow. I pass by my old house, where my parents are—or the people pretending to be my parents. I know they're not. I can't prove it, I've never been able to, but I know they're not. They're just minders. They had a job, and that was to raise me. It was never to love me or save me or protect me. It was to raise me like my father's prize bull. When my purpose is over, I'll be sent to the slaughter. It's around the corner, waiting for me. My body will be sliced into chunks and fed to the pigs.

I keep flying straight to town, circling over the police station.

I have been pulled here in the dream, but now I'm starting to think this isn't a dream at all.

Because I saw this on the ground, through my own eyes.

Through *his* eyes.

At the back of the station is a small house.

That's where he enters.

It's where I enter.

It's where the blood flows down through the floorboards.

Where a man loses his life.

Loses his head.

I don't regret a thing.

*I wake up* to Crane snoring again. I know he gets embarrassed when I mention it, which is why I do mention it. To see shame on Crane's usually nonchalant face is a gift. To see color on those pale cheeks is a novelty. But the truth is, his snoring comforts me. It means he's at rest, something he so rarely seems to be. It means he trusts me enough to let go, even when his whole goal is to watch over me. It might be the only time I've seen him truly surrender.

Sometimes that's all I want from him. For him to submit and surrender to me.

Just once.

Just so he can truly be mine.

So I lie there beside him, caught between the wall and Crane. Barely any space, but there's no place I would rather be than pressed up against his firm back, his taut ass.

Pale morning light starts to fill the window. The candles have burned out in the night. I move my hand, and the cut on my palm stings a little despite Crane rubbing on the healing oil. I'm not sure what time we got back to the dorm. We had to wait in the clearing until the drugs wore off. Kat fell asleep for some of it, and I even nodded off for a bit. Then Crane said it was time to leave. He closed the ritual when the ghosts were gone.

We dropped off Kat at her room, helped her go in through the window. There's a chance the sisters spotted us, since they seem to be watching Kat so closely, but it's hard to know if Crane will get in trouble if I'm there. I suppose we'll hear about it if that's the case.

Then we collapsed into Crane's bed, our bodies spent by all the sex and blood and magic.

Crane didn't even remember to put me in chains.

But it's okay.

He doesn't have to do that anymore.

We have an agreement, the horseman and I.

His appetite can be quenched.

He can be controlled.

I just have to give him things in return.

I have to do what I can to keep him satisfied.

Crane lets out a deep sigh and stirs. My arm is around him and he reaches up tentatively, his fingers around my bare wrist.

"Brom?" he asks warily, voice rich with sleep.

"Yes?" I mumble into the back of his head. His hair smells like bonfire even though we didn't have a fire last night. I think I might smell like that too. The scent of heathens.

"You're not in chains," he comments.

"No, sir," I tell him, moving my hand so that I'm grasping on to his fingers. "You didn't do your due diligence," I add, knowing how that will hurt his pride.

I hear him swallow. "You were here the whole night?"

"If by 'whole night' you mean the couple of hours of sleep we got, then yes. Don't you think you would have noticed if I left?"

He groans, running his hand over his face. "I don't know anymore. I could sleep for weeks. Do you think they'd care if I didn't show up to teach today?"

"It would probably make the sisters suspicious, if that's what you want."

He sighs again and then turns over slightly, looking over his shoulder to meet my eyes. "There you are. And you didn't run away. Good boy."

While I didn't run away, I don't deserve his praise. Not now.

"How are you feeling?" I ask, running my fingers through his hair. "Other than wanting to sleep for weeks?"

He mulls that over, dark gray eyes flicking over my face. "Disappointed. With myself. The ritual should have worked. We did everything right. It should have expelled the horseman."

Truth wants to bubble to the surface, this incessant need to be honest with him, but I manage to swallow it down. I can't ruin this, not yet.

"We will try again," I assure him.

He turns around, the covers being pulled off me as he does, and I'm pressed against the wall. Both our cocks are hard as they push against each other. "You seem different," he says to me, putting his arm around me, his hand possessive at the back of my neck.

"How so?" I whisper, unable to look away from his penetrating gaze.

"Happier, perhaps? Though I'd never go as far as to describe you as happy. That's too pedantic a word. You seem"—he sucks at his teeth in thought—"a little less burdened. Which surprises me. Because I feel burdened in knowing the horseman is still with us. I can't imagine how you must be feeling."

"I think I'm getting used to it," I admit carefully.

His eyes narrow imperceptibly.

"You think you can hide under that brooding exterior, keep your secrets under that beard, but I know you, Brom. I can read you like a book. I know what you're thinking."

"What am I thinking?" I challenge, my pulse quickening.

He searches my eyes for a long moment.

"That you're in love with me." He says this so simply that I can't help but laugh. "Don't laugh," he chides me. "You know it's true. I'm not saying you do love me, but rather you think you do."

"You have quite the way of getting to the point," I manage to say. I'm grateful he didn't say what I thought he was going to, but even so, I'm not sure how to deal with this. I don't know what my feelings for Crane are. One minute I hate him, the next I envy him, the next I feel safe with him, and in the next I love him. On top of it all I deeply desire him in a way that makes me mad, both angry and driven to insanity. But none of it is a conscious choice. I succumb to him like I succumb to breathing oxygen.

"Don't feel pressured to refute me," he says. "Let me go on dreaming."

But I heard what he said last night to Kat. I heard what he said to me.

*I love him. I love both of you, want both of you, need both of you. I think I'll die otherwise.*

Crane melted my heart last night whether I wanted him to or not.

As I said, whatever my feelings for him are, I don't have a choice in the matter.

"Were you jealous of me with Kat last night?" he then asks, the look in his eyes growing dark with lust.

"Yes," I say, and the image of his cock inside her makes my stomach twist in knots. "Were you jealous of me with her?"

"Yes," he answers dourly. "She belongs to me. The possession I feel for her isn't something to be trifled with. It's consuming."

He took the words right out of my mouth.

"So what does that mean? What do we do about it?"

"We don't do anything about it. It's jealousy. It's only a feeling, and one that means and feels like a lot of different things. It doesn't have to be bad. We just feel it, and we deal with it, and in this situation I think we need to accept that as long as we are sharing her, it's going to be there. Like another person in the room with us."

"Another person," I mutter. "I can barely deal with three."

He pauses, a small smile curling his lips. "If it helps, I think Kat was jealous of us."

"How so?" It does actually help a little.

"How could she not be?" Crane explains. "She hasn't been in my bed for the past week, but *you* have. You're with me every night, and she's not. I'm sure all she wants is to join us."

"We must correct this injustice," I say, unable to keep from smiling.

Crane notices, puts his hand on my cheek, gazing at me with mournful eyes.

"Are you sure you're not in love with me, pretty boy?"

But before I can say anything he kisses me so deeply that I feel it in my soul.

And my soul starts to burn.

*Despite Crane wanting* to sleep for weeks, after we made each other come and took a bath together, we went on with our day. He used just a bit of his magic to speed up the healing process on our palms, not wanting to attract any attention with our identical scars, and then we were off to our morning classes.

My first class is history, so I won't see Crane or Kat until the afternoon. I can't even try to pay attention. While the teacher—I can never remember her name—drones on and on about the Salem witch trials, all I can think about is last night. The sight of Kat's voluptuous, soft body covered in our blood, how deeply she took me down her throat, how ruthlessly Crane pounded into her. I want that again. I don't care about the ritual part, I just want that debased fucking in the forest. I want to feel free.

And truth be told, I want to come inside Kat. I want to pin her down, impale her with my cock, and spread my seed deep inside her cunt. I know it's forbidden because of what the sisters have planned for us, I know that's why I need to stay away from her in that way, why I was only allowed to come inside her mouth, and any deviance from this might lead to tragic consequences.

But I can't help what I want. It's what I've always wanted.

I love Kat, even more now than I did yesterday.

I want to marry her despite everything.

I want to get her pregnant, no matter what Crane says.

I want her soul and her love just as much as he does.

It isn't fair that I don't get to have that just because the sisters and her mother have arranged it from day one. Why do I have to suffer because of it?

*You don't have to suffer*, the horseman says to me. His voice is so loud that I stiffen, I think everyone in class can hear it. I look around, and no one is paying me any attention.

*You don't have to suffer, Abraham Van Brunt.*

*You can take what's owed to you, what's promised to you.*

*And if you don't, then I will.*

*It might be harder than you think to keep me satisfied.*

"No!" I cry out, pushing my chair back from the desk with a loud scrape.

I look up to see the entire class looking at me now.

The teacher gives me a curious frown.

"You might say no, Brom, but in 1694, the witches didn't have a choice," the teacher goes on, turning back to the chalkboard. "The only two covens to escape were the Devotus and the Erusians. Both of these covens were enemies who turned each other in to the authorities."

I give my head a shake. The horseman doesn't usually talk to me in the day, and he's never been so loud before.

He's never . . . read my thoughts like that before.

Or perhaps that's all he's been doing.

"Brom," the teacher says again, and I look at her.

"Yes?"

"Are you all right? Your hand?"

I look down to see the cut on my hand open again, blood smeared on the desk.

"Oh," I say uneasily. "It's just a paper cut."

I wipe my hand on my pant leg, then swipe my arm across the blood on the desk to clean it off.

"You'd better go to the nurse and have that looked at," she tells me. "You're excused." She makes a sour face and then looks to the class. "Now, these covens aren't said to exist anymore, but rumor has it that both might have settled around Sleepy Hollow."

I get up, feeling the eyes of my classmates on me as I stride quickly toward the door.

"And an even greater rumor is that the Devotus and Erusian covens may have both survived thanks to a bargain made with a demon, a bargain to bring in what some would consider the anti-Christ."

I stop dead in my tracks, one hand on the doorknob.

I slowly turn around to look at my teacher. "Can you repeat that?"

The teacher puts a hand on her hip. "Aren't you going to the nurse's office?"

"I am." I glower at her. "Now what is this about the anti-Christ in Sleepy Hollow?"

She laughs nervously. "It's a rumor, Brom." She faces the class again. "There are no records of either the Devotus or Erusian covens past 1705. It's as if they disappeared off the map. So many perished during the trials, it's hard to say how many members actually survived in the end."

A student raises his hand. "But what is this deal with the devil?"

"As I said, a rumor. A fun tidbit. Fun tidbits make history class more interesting, wouldn't you say?" The student just stares at her to go on. She lets out a tired sigh. "All right. The *rumor* is that the remaining members of the two warring covens were granted safe passage from the trials because they agreed to let a child, born of both sides, become a vessel for the demon. They would be granted immortality, their covens would be united in power, and in exchange the demon would be given possession of the child."

"To bring about the end of the world," I mumble.

"Perhaps," the teacher says carefully, narrowing her eyes at me. "Or perhaps it's just another legend of Sleepy Hollow. There do seem to be a lot of them."

"Yeah, like the headless horseman," another student says. "Did you hear that another person was found murdered?"

And at that I leave the classroom and close the door.

I need to speak to Crane and Kat.

# 22

## Crane

Ms. Van Tassel, may I have a word?"

Kat meets my gaze as she gathers her books, her eyes glimmering with amusement.

"Of course," she says, as the other students exit the classroom. I can hear their scoffs, see them rolling their eyes. There is no hiding it with us but, even so, I can't be reprimanded by the sisters for wanting to talk to a student after class. It's one of my rights as a professor. They may have told me to stop fucking Kat, but they can't expect me to let her flounder in her studies, can they?

Kat comes over to me and stands by the desk, staring down at me expectantly as she clutches her books to her chest. I feel the need to pinch myself, to remind me this stunning, special young witch is mine.

"How are you?" I ask in a low voice after I'm sure the last student has gone out the door. "I've been thinking about you all morning. It's been torture not to talk to you."

"I'm fine," she says quietly, giving her shoulder a shrug. "A little tired, a little out of sorts. I slept hard and didn't want to wake up this morning."

"And your wounds?" I ask, my heart pinching slightly as I remember Brom and me rubbing the poultice down her front and back before we left the circle. I applied a bit of my healing magic but not enough, since I was already in a state of exhaustion.

"They hurt a little," she says, and that pinch increases.

"If you close the door and lock it I can help heal you more," I tell her, handing her the key to the classroom. "I can do a lot of things to make you feel better."

She plucks the key from my hand. "I have to be honest with you, Crane, I'm a little worn out from last night." Then she grimaces. "And I just, uh . . ."

"Uh what?" I coax.

She wiggles her lips. "I am experiencing that woman's time of the month."

"You're menstruating?" I ask bluntly.

She nods shyly, averting her eyes. "Yes."

"But that's good news, Kat. It means, well . . ." It means she's not pregnant with my child, but she's certainly not pregnant with Brom's. "It means you're in the clear, for now."

"Which is a relief. It's just a hindrance when it comes to . . ."

I grin at her. "If you think I'll find a little blood a hindrance, clearly you weren't paying attention last night." I nod at the key. "Now, be a good girl and go lock that door."

Kat gives me a quiet smile and turns, walking toward the door in time for loud footsteps to ring out from the hall. She freezes just as Brom appears in the doorway, then she sighs with relief.

"I need to talk to you," Brom says, looking at me, then at Kat. He walks over to her first, puts his arm around her and kisses the top of her head, and then comes over to my desk. "I learned something in class today."

"You mean to tell me you've been learning in everyone else's class except mine?" I ask, leaning back in my chair and folding my hands across my chest.

He fixes me with his glare. God, I love my moody boy.

"What is it?" Kat asks him.

He breaks his stare to look at her. "In history, my teacher was talking about the Salem witch trials. She had said that there were two covens that had escaped and might have settled in Sleepy Hollow, the . . . Devotus? And the . . . I can't remember the other one. Starts with an *E*. She said they were enemies, but they had made a bargain with a demon to get them out, *if* they gave the demon one of their heirs. Meaning, the child of the two covens. That demon would bring about the end of the world while the covens would be granted immortality."

I stare at him grimly, a sinking feeling in my chest. It's not that what he's saying doesn't make sense. It's that it makes perfect sense. And I wasn't able to figure it out. A damn history teacher at the school did instead.

"Who is your teacher?" I ask.

How does she know more than I do?

"I don't know her name, I never pay attention," Brom says.

"I need to speak to her," I tell him, getting to my feet. "I need to find out where she's heard this, where she's read this."

"Do you think it's true?" Kat asks, wringing her hands together.

"It could be," I tell her.

"She kept saying it was a rumor," Brom says. "She didn't seem to believe it herself. Said it was . . ."

"Was what?" Kat asks.

"Another legend," he says, his voice growing quiet.

"Well, the only way to figure out the truth is to do my own research, after I talk to the teacher. Brom, can you take me to your classroom? Perhaps she's still there."

"Sure." He nods.

"I'm coming too," Kat says.

"Of course you are," I tell her, putting my hand at her lower back. "This involves you more than anyone."

We leave the classroom and head out the doors of the building and into the damp afternoon, when Daniels passes me heading inside.

"Crane," Daniels says, looking bothered, his mustache bristling. "Have you heard the news?"

"What news?" I ask.

"Another body has been found in Sleepy Hollow. Head sliced clean off, hasn't been found yet. It's said to be Constable Kirkbride."

Both Kat and I look immediately at Brom.

He doesn't say anything, just looks down, shadows casting over his eyes and making them unreadable. My blood goes cold.

"That's terrible," I manage to say to Daniels. "Hey, listen, while I have you here, what's the name of the history teacher?"

"Joy," he says. "Ms. Joy Wiltern. And don't bother making any advances toward her, she's not interested," he says with a huff, walking into the building.

The door closes behind him, and I spin around to face Brom.

"What did you do?" I ask him.

He holds up his hands. "I didn't do anything. It was the horseman."

"When? Last night when you weren't in chains? Is that when you snuck out and did it?"

His gaze hardens, blackens, turns into the gaze of a would-be killer. "I didn't leave your side. It was the horseman. You know I can't control him."

"That's funny, because I could have sworn you said something last night about being able to control him one day."

"So I was wrong," he snaps.

"Boys," Kat says, putting her hands on both our chests. "It's quite obvious the horseman did it, whether you wanted him to or not, Brom." She eyes me. "We can't keep blaming him every time someone loses a head."

"Oh really?"

"Crane, be kind," she admonishes me. "You know . . ."

She trails off and a flush of embarrassment comes across her cheeks as she shifts slightly.

"What?" I ask.

"I, uh, have to go. I'll find you later," she says and starts walking off quickly toward her dorm.

"What's wrong with her?" Brom asks.

"Lady problems," I surmise, watching her go. Then I reach out and grab Brom by the arm and yank him back toward the building. I practically drag him down the hall until we're back in the classroom and I have the door shut and him pressed up against it, my forearm at his throat.

"You want to tell me again, now that Kat's not around, that you had nothing to do with the constable's death?"

He just stares at me, his mouth a hard line.

Finally, I let him go and he sucks in a greedy gulp of air.

"Be honest with me, Brom, for once," I say, running my hands through my hair and tugging. "Please."

"I see why you like it when I say please," he eventually says. He looks away, rubbing his lips together. "I don't know what to say. I don't know what you want to hear."

"The truth," I plead. "All I care about is the truth."

"Even when it hurts?"

"*Especially* when it hurts," I tell him. "Because that means it's real."

"Fine," he says in a clipped voice. He walks over to me and places his hands on my shoulders, and for a moment, a brief moment, I'm afraid he means to hurt me.

But instead, he gives my shoulders a tight squeeze and looks me dead in the eyes.

"I killed the constable," he says flatly. "I told the horseman to do it, and I saw it happen through my own eyes."

I feel faint, but his hands keep me in place. "Why?"

"Because," he says. "I didn't like what the constable said to me. I didn't like how he was treating you and Kat. I didn't like him, period. And the horseman demanded a sacrifice, and that's who I chose, Crane. That's how this works. That's how I'm able to keep him from hurting the ones I love."

"You *can* control him," I whisper, though my heart is stumbling over the fact that he used the word *love*.

He wiggles his jaw, hedging that. "I'm trying to. This is what I have so far."

"Oh, Brom," I say, my heart sinking. "You poor boy."

"Don't give me your pity," he snaps. "I don't deserve it, and I don't want it. This is what has to be done. You want to exorcise him from me, but until that happens, I have to learn to live with him inside me. Sacrifices must be made, and I will do everything I can to never let it be either of you."

I nod, putting my hand behind his head, the other on his neck. "I understand. All right? I understand. You did what you had to do."

"I did," he says. "And I don't regret it. If someone had to die, I'm glad it was the constable. I have a black heart, Crane. I'm the devil's pawn, a chess piece in his game. Nothing good has ever come from me, and nothing good ever will." He gives his head a shake. "And now you're looking at me as if you're any different."

I blink at him, my hands dropping away. "What are you talking about?"

"You think you get to take the moral high ground because you're so composed, so in control, because your emotions could never get away from you like they do with me."

"I—"

"You know my truth, Crane. But I know yours too."

My molars press together, jaw flexing. "What truth?" I grind out.

He takes a step toward me, heat rolling off him, his face inches from mine, black eyes reflecting my anguished face. "You're so used to your own ghosts, you don't even see them anymore," he says. "Vivienne Henry isn't the only thing that haunts you. Your late wife does too. And in the middle of the night, she has a lot of interesting things to say about what you did."

I suck in my breath, feeling the ground crumble beneath me.

"Namely," he goes on, "that you murdered her."

# 23

===

## Crane

I come home after class to a dark house. It's four in the afternoon, but the fog outside the windows, coupled with all the
shutters being closed and not a single candle lit, means that
it's hard to see my hand in front of my face.

*Marie must have a headache again*, I think as I climb the
stairs to the bedroom. I have other thoughts, but I do my best to
keep them at bay. I try not to feel anything. Not resentment. Not
pity. Not anger. I aim to keep my temperament neutral.

I walk down the cramped hall and pause in the doorway of
the bedroom. She's lying on the bed, her back to me, fully clothed.
I don't want to disturb her. I don't want to have to deal with her
anger, or worse, her indifference.

It's been like this for as long as I can remember, though now
my memory seems too fluid. Has it been months? Years? Our
whole marriage? Has she always been this unhappy with me?
Had she ever loved me? For a while there, when we were trying

for a baby, it seemed she did. But when time and time again it wouldn't stick, the blame would turn to me.

Then the malaise came. The melancholy. The headaches.

She started flinching at my touch. She started leaving the house at night, going for walks that I wasn't allowed to go on. Day by day any control, any hold I had on my marriage, slipped through my fingers.

Now we're just two passing ships in the night. I go to work at the academy, I come home. She's in bed, she gets up, she leaves. Sometimes it's not a walk, sometimes it's dinner with friends, sometimes she says she's seeing her uncle.

I haven't let myself entertain the thought of what she could really be doing.

I don't want to feel the shame.

I don't want to feel even more helpless than I already do.

But . . . I'm curious.

I slowly take off my coat, damp with the San Francisco fog, and drape it over the armchair, then quietly walk over to her. I pause by the bed and stare down at her. Her chest is rising and falling, and I watch it for at least a minute. Sometimes she pretends to be asleep when she's not. I should know, sometimes I do the same.

When I'm sure she's truly asleep, I take my hand and I gently place it against her cheek, palm barely pressed against her skin.

I close my eyes.

I travel through the void.

Through her skin, into her mind.

I break all trust between us, commit the deepest invasion of privacy.

Because I need to know.

I need to know.

I step through the darkness, so many doors in front of me, and I pick the one she's laughing behind. I haven't heard her laugh in years.

I open the door and step inside her memories.

She's walking down the street, somewhere I don't recognize at first, then I realize it's a gambling hall, not far from us in the Mission District. She has her arm hooked around the arm of a tall, handsome man with a mustache. He's not just any man.

He's Raymond De Haro, a neighbor from across the street by the baseball stadium.

He's staring down at her, smiling, radiant white teeth, tanned skin, and the sight of him does something to me, something I haven't felt in a long time. I've always felt a strange connection to Ray, but I never knew how to put those feelings into words.

Now I know the word.

Desire.

I desire this man, and I desire the way she's looking at him, wishing it was me.

My wife has been having an affair.

This confirms it.

I should stop watching the world through her eyes.

I should leave the memory, leave her mind, leave the room.

But I don't.

I continue watching, and then things skip and then I see it, I see them outside his yellow house, the lanterns flickering on the red-roofed stucco. Beside them is the Recreation Grounds base-ball stadium, the sounds of a cheering crowd filling the summer air. They disappear inside his house.

I want to see more.

I want to see what he does with her.

I want to see how he fucks her.

I want to see what makes him a better lover than I am.

I want to watch it all.

But her memories skip again, flashing faces, flashing bodies, and I'm starting to get dizzy, as if the nausea she gets with her headaches is seeping into me.

I withdraw.

Back, back, further back.

Until I'm standing in our bedroom and taking my hand off her face.

She stirs below me, and I hold my breath, waiting for her to wake.

She doesn't. She continues to sleep, not knowing all that I've seen.

I've seen too much and not enough.

I vow to never do that again, never read anyone's memories without their permission.

Because now I know the truth.

And now I have to fix this.

I quietly back away from her, let her sleep away her headache, lost in her memories.

I grab my coat.

I head downstairs and out the door.

The cool fog meets my face as I cross Mission Street, the day already sliding into night as it does so quickly here in November. I don't know what my plan is, I just know I have to talk to Ray. The man who stole my wife.

On the other side of the street is a row of houses, including the yellow stucco one from Marie's memory, just a little out of sight from our house, just enough so that I wouldn't see her enter during all those nights with her "friends," with her "uncle." She had her affair in the open for anyone else to see but me.

I haven't thought about what I'm going to say. It's not enough to yell at this man, to strike him, reprimand him. I'm not here to make him pay, I'm not here to ask him why.

I'm here to *know* why.

I stride over to the door and knock on it.

A tanned man with dark chestnut hair opens the door.

His face falls once he sees me.

"Expecting someone else?" I ask him pointedly.

He frowns at me, thick dark brows furrowed together. God, he's handsome. The thought strikes me like God is smiting me from above.

"Mr. Crane," Ray says uneasily. "Can I help you?"

"You can," I say, surprised at how even my voice is. "Can I come in? I'd like to discuss my wife with you."

Ray's golden face pales. He stands there, hand on the door, like he's unsure if he wants to close it in my face. He glances down at me, checking if I have a gun. He thinks I'm here to murder him.

I should be there to murder him.

But the shame I feel over Marie isn't because she's broken my heart.

She hasn't.

I stopped loving Marie months ago, probably around the same time she stopped loving me. I stopped when I realized she had no room in her stone-cold heart for mine anymore.

I'm here because I need to know what kind of man I should be.

I'm here because I need to know what kind of man Ray really is.

"I'm sorry," he says, fumbling for the words. "This is a bad time . . ."

I put my hand on the door and push it open, my height coming to my advantage and intimidating him. "I would like to talk to you," I tell him calmly, removing my hat and holding it in my hands. "I'm not here to cause trouble. I just want to talk. Please," I add.

He takes in a sharp breath, his eyes wild, trying to calculate what I really want, but he still opens the door.

I step inside his house. I'd never been in here before. It's smaller than mine, so it can't be a money thing. And though he's dressed in neat clothing, nothing about what he's wearing says that he's more sophisticated or smarter than I am. I admit I don't know much about my neighbor, but this isn't giving me any clues.

"We've never really had a chance to talk, have we?" I ask as I eye the small living room, the roaring fire, the loom rug on the hardwood floor. "Do you prefer Ray or Raymond?"

"Ray," he says uneasily. "And you?"

"Call me Ichabod," I tell him, turning my hat around in my hands. "That's what Marie calls me."

He blanches. "Of course. Look, Ichabod, I know you say you

don't mean to bring me any trouble, but I can't . . . can't imagine that you won't. If you want to strike me, beat me, go ahead. Just get it over with."

I frown at him. "What kind of man do you think I am?"

"One that's found out his wife has been cheating on him."

I give him an acidic smile. "That I am."

He gulps, his eyes darting around the room. They're a beautiful shade of green, like spring moss. His mouth twists into a grimace and his lips are beautiful too, wide but full. I can see why Marie wanted this man. He is warm while I am cool. He is the sun, where I am the fog. He is soft where I am hard.

And from the pressure building in my cock, I *am* hard.

Shame hits me for a moment.

I'm a sinner for even having these thoughts.

I'm a deviant for wanting them.

If my father only knew his son was fantasizing about another man, he would condemn me straight to hell. But he knew I was going there anyway, didn't he? I had already been too different from him, from everyone, right from day one, and no amount of church would change that. There would never be any salvation for Ichabod Crane.

"What do you want from me?" Ray says.

I step toward him, slowly, and he backs up until I have him cornered against the wall. The wallpaper is peeling in places, a painting of a bull hangs askew.

"I want . . . ," I begin, breathing hard. I lick my lips as I stare at him. "I want to know what you have that I don't." My gaze drops to his mouth. "And I want to have it."

I place my hand on his throat and give it a squeeze.

Ray's pretty eyes bulge, his fingers wrapping around mine to pry me off, but I'm not applying much pressure. I'm just trying to hold him still.

Because I want to take from him.

I lean in and I kiss him.

He doesn't kiss me back, but it doesn't matter.

His lips are surprisingly cool to touch, but still soft, and the scratch of his mustache against my bare upper lip sends a lightning bolt direct to my cock, my balls rising up, a fire stoked inside me.

Ray sputters against my lips, one hand trying to pry my grip off his throat, the other on my chest, trying to push me off him.

I relinquish. Drop my hand and stand back.

"What is wrong with you?" Ray says to me, his eyes wild, mouth parted, panting, and fuck if that doesn't arouse me like nothing else. "Is this my punishment?"

I give him a faint smile. I can still feel his mustache against my skin.

"If you want it to be," I say. "I—"

But before I can finish my sentence he reaches forward and grabs my face.

He kisses *me*.

And I feel the air leave my lungs.

I whimper against him, the feel of his tongue against mine, the opening of himself to me, like a blooming flower, and I realize if this is sinning, then I'll gladly be called a sinner.

He moans, his sounds a tonic to my soul, and then he's

dropping to his knees in front of me. His movements are unsure and frantic, and my heart is galloping like a stallion and I can't believe my eyes, can't believe what's happening, what's about to happen.

He reaches up and stares at me with those pretty eyes.

"Please," he says through a gasp, reaching up for my trousers, and it rattles me to my core.

*Please* is such a simple word until someone says it on their knees.

It feels like a whole new world has opened up to me.

I help him out, undoing the buttons of my fly, and take my cock out. The sight of it, long and rigid, thick-veined and molten-hot in my palm, with this man's handsome face beneath it, makes me feel like I'm going to release right here and now. Already I can see the pearls of my arousal on the flared tip and I swallow hard, wanting to rub it on his tongue, wanting him to taste it, to taste me.

I don't know if Ray has any experience with this, with men. I don't even know if he truly wants this, if he's giving me what he thinks I want in order to avoid further punishment, but I don't care.

I don't care.

"Open up, handsome," I say to him, making a fist in his soft hair.

Ray's mouth parts just in time as I shove his head forward. He makes a choking sound, but I keep him in place with a firm grip. His bottom teeth graze over my frenulum, and I hiss at the bracing mix of pleasure and pain, but then he starts to suck and lick and my eyes roll back in my head.

"Fuck, your mouth is hot, so wet," I swear. "Keep going, don't you dare stop. Don't you dare stop."

I keep Ray's head moving, and he's reaching up, grabbing the base of my cock, tugging gently at my sack and I'm dying on my feet. This is heaven and hell all wrapped up into one.

"You're doing so well, Ray," I encourage him, my voice hoarse, sounding like it belongs to someone else. Even Marie never did this with me, said it was *unclean*.

To hell with clean; I aspire to be filthy.

"Yes," I hiss as he works me deeper into his throat. "*Yes*, suck me dry until you're drowning in it."

His response is muffled, and I stand there, hips thrusting, and I watch as he takes me and I've never felt more powerful in all my life. It doesn't matter what happened in the minutes before this or what happens in the minutes after this, I . . .

My orgasm takes me by surprise, without warning.

"Jesus!" I swear through a clenched jaw as my balls draw up, thighs so tense that the muscles ache, and I'm letting out a low guttural moan that echoes throughout the house. I come, pulsing, jerking inside Ray's mouth, and I open my eyes to watch his Adam's apple move as he swallows me, the most beautiful sight.

Then, when I'm finally finished, I release my cramped hand from his hair and he wipes his mouth, panting for breath.

And then he looks toward the door.

And with a chilling sensation I realize we aren't alone.

I follow his line of sight.

Marie is standing by the door, staring at us with an open mouth.

She must have walked in and we had been so lost to our lust that we hadn't even noticed.

For a moment I think maybe I don't have to leave her. Maybe we don't have to get divorced. Maybe we can just become *this*, three of us learning to share, taking turns.

But then she screams.

Her eyes ablaze with horror and indignation and disgust.

She marches toward us with boiling anger, arms thrown out, yelling at us, calling us immoral, sinners, devils, heathens, as if she hadn't committed adultery first, as if all those terms don't apply to her.

By now Ray is on his feet, my cock quickly tucked away in my trousers, and it seems all her fury is directed at me. Her finger is in my face, her eyes wild like an animal in a cage.

"I knew you were like this," Marie says, seething, breathing hard. "I knew you were one of them. A defective sinner going straight to hell!"

I throw my hands up, trying to stay calm but failing. "You were cheating on me, Marie! I know you were. You can't hide it, can't deny it."

But I don't dare tell her how I found out.

"I was cheating on you because you're a sodomite!" she screeches. "Because I knew your true nature, I saw the evil, the darkness that dwells there. I knew I married a man without scruples and I needed my body to be cleansed of you, my soul freed from the mire that is your own!"

I point at Ray, who remains silent and scared. "By fucking another sodomite?" I exclaim.

"You coerced this man," Marie says, going to Ray and grabbing his bicep. "You forced him to do such a foul, immoral deed. Your true nature is no more than an animal's, Ichabod. But you won't get away with this, you'll pay for this."

"I'm leaving you," I grind out at her. "That's how I'll pay. I'm divorcing *you*, you adulteress tramp."

"You aren't leaving me!" she screams, and before I know what's happening, she's slapping me across the face, the pain like sparks. "You can't! I won't allow it!"

I press my palm against my cheek, trying to rein in my temper. I never let it out, I never let it get the best of me, but now she's provoking me.

Now I'm the animal in the trap.

"I don't care what you allow," I tell her, the rage building inside me, my skin feeling too hot, too tight. "I'm divorcing you, and you can't do a single thing about it."

"Oh, but I can." She bares her teeth. "I'm getting you fired!" she yells, and when she sees the horror in my eyes, she grins. "Yes, I'm telling the world what I saw here. Ray will cooperate, won't you, Ray? The school board will be the first to know, Ichabod. You're about to lose everything, everything, your job, your house, your wife, all because you're a sinner, a bloody sinner, I—"

"You will not!" I scream at her, marching forward and shoving her against her shoulders.

Except I push her harder than I meant to. Marie yelps and goes flying backward, her feet twisting and scrambling in an attempt to keep her footing, but she's falling back toward the ground.

The back of her head smacks the wooden floor with a sickening *crack*, having just missed the rug by inches. The sound of that crack shoots right through me, yanks at my heart, at my soul, filling me from top to bottom with ice-cold dread.

Blood starts to pool from under her hair, her eyes are open and focused on the ceiling.

Everything slows down.

I let out a strangled cry.

Run toward her, knees slamming on the floor, pleading for her to be all right.

"No, no, no, no, no," I cry. "No, Marie. Marie."

I gingerly touch her face, trying to get her eyes to look at me, and my hands are shaking.

She blinks slowly, her eyes open again, staring at nothing.

The blood spreads.

Ray remains where he is behind me, hyperventilating.

"Marie!" I cry, pressing my trembling fingers to the side of her neck, feeling for a pulse.

There is none.

I stare at her chest, it doesn't move; her mouth, there is no breath; her eyes are still as death.

"No," I say again. "You're not dead. You can't be dead."

I look over my shoulder at Ray, who looks close to fainting. "We have to do something. Ray! We have to do something!"

But Ray doesn't move. He's in shock.

So am I. I'm in shock, and yet there's something I can do.

There's something I can do.

I remember medical school, how the cadavers came to life when I touched them.

I look back at Marie's lifeless face, and I know she's dead. She's dead.

But she doesn't have to stay dead.

I put my hands on her cheeks and close my eyes, trying to conjure up whatever energy I have left in my weary, war-torn heart, and once I feel it moving through me, I try to push it through my hands into Marie.

*Please work, please work.*

She twitches under my hands.

I open my eyes to see her open hers.

She stares right at me. Pupils like a black moon.

But there's no gratitude on her face. No relief to be alive.

There's nothing but horror and shock, betrayal and a sense of looking beyond the veil, looking at something no one should ever look at.

I brought someone dead back into this world.

Perhaps that's the biggest sin of all.

Marie opens her mouth in a silent scream, wider, wider, and now she's shaking, convulsing.

"What is happening to her?" Ray finally whimpers, coming closer. "What are you doing to her?"

"I'm not . . . ," I begin, trying to hold her down, panic clawing through me that I've made a huge mistake in attempting this. "I'm trying to bring her back to life."

But I shouldn't have said that. I shouldn't have said anything.

Because now Ray knows, he really knows what's wrong with me.

"Let me die," Marie croaks, the sound coming not from her but from around us, filling the room. "Let me die, Ichabod."

I remove my hands, static shocking my palms, and I watch as she abruptly goes still.

Dead again.

Dead forever.

Dead because I killed her.

"You're . . . ," Ray begins, and I don't have the strength to look at him. "You're a demon."

"I'm not a demon," I whisper to him, running my fingers down Marie's lifeless arm. "I'm just damned."

# 24

## Kat

I feel awful.

I've never dealt with my monthly bleeding alone before. Normally I have Famke, who would sew together the rags and cloth pads that she would then button onto the soft belt I wear under my drawers. And while she had the foresight to pack the belt and pads with the rest of my clothes, I feel embarrassed that I don't have that many pads, which means I have to go use the communal sink on my floor to wash them. I know all the girls in my dorm have to deal with a similar situation, but even so, it seems like something that should stay very private.

In addition to that, I get cramps during menstruation, which in the past I've been able to mitigate with raspberry leaf and willow bark tea, but I'm not sure where to find that here. I suppose I could go out to the herb garden and forage for some, but I never saw any raspberries there, and it's been raining steadily all afternoon, ever since I left Brom and Crane out on the grass as they were about to hunt down the history teacher.

I sigh, trying to ignore the discomfort and my general sense of malaise, and I sit down at my desk, unwrapping the *banketstaaf* that Famke had made me. They're my favorite Dutch pastry and I'd been trying to save them for when I really needed it, but a healthy dose of sugar might do me a world of good right now.

I try and savor the first one, but my stomach growls hungrily, and I end up devouring it, the almond paste from inside sticking to my fingers, leaving flakes of pastry on my desk. I decide to slow down and take my time with the second one, that way I'll still have two to give to Brom and Crane.

But when I pick up the second one, it comes apart in my hands like it's been halved in two, and I realize that there's something inside it. I reach in and pull out a sticky folded-up note wrapped around something hard and silver: a chain necklace. Hanging from it is a small Byzantine cross accented with a black stone, maybe onyx or obsidian, with a crescent moon overhead.

I rub the pastry off until the silver shines, then I pick up the note with shaking hands.

> *Dearest Katrina,*
> *This has kept me safe all these years.*
> *It's time for it to keep you safe.*
> *Your father would want you to have it.*
>    *Famke.*

Famke buried the note and necklace in the pastry for me to find without my mother knowing. Now that I know, I must go back to the house, and soon. I need to speak to her. She knows far too much and I far too little, even at this point.

In any event, I have to tell Crane and Brom.

I grab the note and necklace, gather up the rest of the pastries, slip on my boots and coat, and hurry out into the rain. Darkness will be falling soon, and I know Crane won't want me anywhere near Brom at this hour, but I'm willing to take the chance. At the very least, Crane could put a circle of salt around his room as an extra precaution.

Though I'm starting to doubt that does anything. Constable Kirkbride was beheaded last night by the headless horseman, and I know Brom had something to do with it. He may have protested that it was out of his control, and maybe that's true, but I saw the way Brom was staring at the constable after our meeting. He was looking through that window as if he was plotting to kill him.

But while that should scare me, the thought of Brom being responsible for the murder, it doesn't. I don't know if that means my morals have sunk to new lows, or that the blood ritual cemented us together in ways that defy convention, but I feel myself having empathy for him instead.

By the time I get to the faculty dorm, my hair and coat are soaked, and I'm chilled to the bone. I go through the front doors, the building only a little warmer than outside, and head up the stairs, but once I'm at the top, about to silently creep to Crane's side, I stop. Another cramp flutters inside me, and I remember Ms. Peek. Surely she might have some sort of tea for this kind of thing.

So I head down toward the women's wing and knock on her door, hoping she's not teaching a later class.

She opens it right away.

"Kat," she says quietly. "My goodness, you're a drowned rat. Come in."

I step inside as she closes the door behind me. It's warm and cozy in here, her incense filling the room in a cloud of sweet-smelling smoke.

"Let me take your coat," she says, looking at the cloth in my hands. "And what is this?"

"*Banketstaaf*," I tell her. "I was bringing them for a friend of mine. You're welcome to have one." I'm sure neither of the boys will mind.

"That's kind of you, but I haven't had an appetite lately," she says, placing the pastries on the coffee table and hanging my coat on the hook behind the door. "Have a seat. Make yourself comfortable."

I sit down on the desk chair, but I don't get too comfortable, knowing I won't be staying long.

"How are you doing?" she says, sitting on the bed across from me. "You must be having a rough go. I was there when Lotte fell from the roof, I saw you there too. Horrible thing to witness."

"Fell?" I repeat. "I'm certain she jumped."

She gives me a quick smile. "Yes, well, as you know that's not the official statement that the sisters have put out."

I frown. "It's not?"

"I take it you weren't at the assembly in the cathedral?"

"No."

"I see," she says slowly. "Well, the sisters have declared her death an accident. She didn't kill herself, she didn't mean to fall. She went up to the roof to do some sort of elemental spell and she slipped."

I shake my head, nearly laughing at how incredulous this sounds. "But you know that's not true. You saw her. I saw her too. That was no accident."

Ms. Peek rubs her lips together and looks out the window at the rain spattering on the pane.

"I don't know what I saw except a girl that fell to her death. Tragic."

I frown at her. "I may be a Van Tassel, but I am not on my aunts' side. I'm not telling them anything. You can tell me what you really think," I say to her, though I'm lowering my voice. "They aren't watching you."

Ms. Peek swallows audibly and looks over my shoulder with a fearful expression.

I twist around and look to see a painting on the wall. One of a raven perched in a tree, a full moon behind it. Its eyes are black and shiny and lifelike.

Fear trickles down my spine.

It's almost as if the raven is real and staring right at me.

"What?" I ask, looking back at her.

She clears her throat. "I'm sure it was an accident," she says in a clipped voice. "Poor girl, she should have never been up there."

And now I'm noticing something different about her.

The Ms. Peek of last week had smooth skin, bright eyes, shiny hair.

This version of her has dry, sallow-looking skin, hollows under her cheekbones that weren't there before, and black circles under her eyes. Her hair is dull and peppered with gray.

"Are you all right?" I ask her, leaning in closer.

She gives me a faint smile and nods. "Mmm-hmm. I'm fine,"

she says, rubbing at her thumb. "So, what can I do for you? I feel you came here wanting something."

*What have they done to you?* I want to ask.

Something is terribly wrong here.

"My apologies," she adds, dropping her head slightly and pressing her thumb into her forehead. "I've not been feeling well lately. I think I got a terrible illness over the weekend, and it still hasn't left me. I can barely remember the last few days."

*And you barely remember what happened to Lotte.*

"That's all right," I tell her, wondering if perhaps she's telling the truth. She does look sick. "I came here because I, well, I'm having my monthly bleeds and the cramps that come along with it. Do you perchance have any sort of herbal tea or medicine for it? I suppose I could go to the nurse . . ."

She raises her head and blinks at me. "I have just the thing."

She gets up and goes into her bathroom, coming out holding a small reddish-brown bottle with a faded label on it. "Here. This is laudanum. It's an opium tincture. Better than any herbal or witch's medicine, believe me. I've been taking a lot of it lately. Really does make the pain go away."

At those last words she gets a dreamy look in her eyes.

"Thank you," I tell her, getting to my feet and taking the bottle from her. "How much do I take?"

"Start with a few drops into water and see where it takes you. Avoid alcohol if you can, it will make you extra sleepy. Unless that's what you want." She goes to the door and grabs my coat. "Some nights the nightmares are so terrifying and feel so real, I take more than I should, just to get a good night's sleep."

"What do you have nightmares about?" I ask as I drape my

coat over my arm, slipping the laudanum in my pocket next to the note and the necklace, then gather the *banketstaaf.*

Her face falls in such a way that I immediately regret asking the question.

"It just started a few days ago, but it's almost always the same," she says, her voice a whisper. "I'm on the altar in the cathedral. Completely nude. Four cloaked figures stand around me, chanting. One of them reaches out with a bone, it looks like a human bone, a femur, except the end is carved into a knifelike point. They take the bone and slice open my stomach and remove something. The first time I think it was my appendix. Then my gallbladder. A kidney. Each time they take something different."

It feels like a cold hand is wrapping around my heart. "Then what happens?"

She shrugs. "I wake up." She runs her hand over her stomach. "I'm always so certain I'll see a suture or some sign that something was done to me, but there's nothing ever there. It's just a dream."

I think about that for a moment. "You said that Sister Leona had asked you to bring back a lot of opium for them," I say. "Do you know what they do with it?"

She stares at me blankly. "I'm sorry, Katrina, I don't know what you're talking about."

I'm about to tell her that the last time we talked, she mentioned that Leona had asked her to bring back opium. But I decide the best thing for me to do would be to just leave at this point.

"It's nothing," I say. "It's best I go now. Thank you for the medicine. I'll bring it back when I've taken some."

"Keep the bottle, I have more," she says to me as I exit her room and start walking down the hall. "Be careful," she whispers.

I nod, giving her a quick smile, then hurry around the corner, through the mezzanine and down Crane's wing. The hallway is quiet, and at first, I think perhaps they aren't in his room at all, maybe they're at the library, or went to the dining hall early.

But I knock on the door with bated breath and wait.

It opens slowly, Crane's gray eye peering at me through the crack.

"Kat!" he exclaims once he sees me and throws the door open. "What are you doing here?"

He pokes his head out into the hall to make sure no one has seen me, then puts his arm around me and ushers me inside, locking the door behind him.

I have to admit, I'm surprised that the both of them are fully clothed, Brom just stepping out of the bathroom and rubbing a washcloth at the back of his neck.

"I'm sorry to just come over like this," I tell them. "I know you have to keep our relationship a secret from the sisters, and this is risky."

"Kat," Crane says deeply, coming over to me and cupping my face in his large, warm hands. "I'm ever so glad that you're here." He looks down at the cloth in my hands. "Is this what Famke made for you?"

"Yes, I brought it for you," I tell him. "But that's not the real reason why I'm here."

"What happened?" Brom asks, his brow creasing as he comes over to me. "Are you all right?"

"I'm fine, really," I assure him as Crane lets go of my face and steps back. He takes the bundle of pastries over to his desk and sets them down. "I just found something interesting. Including something I forgot to tell you before."

"What is it?" Crane asks, biting into a pastry already. He closes his eyes and moans. "My goodness, this is tasty. Compliments to Famke."

"Speaking of Famke," I say, and then I begin to tell them everything. I show them the necklace and the note, then I tell them about visiting Ms. Peek and everything she told me: that she looked sick, that she was adamant that Lotte slipped, that she was having bad nightmares, that she seemed to think the painting on the wall was watching her. I finish by talking about Leona putting in orders for opium, orders that Ms. Peek suddenly doesn't remember, then I take the bottle of laudanum out of my pocket and show it to them.

Both of their eyes go wide at the sight.

"May I?" Crane asks, delicately snatching the bottle from me before I have a chance to tell him anything. He turns it over in his palm. "This could come in handy."

"Please don't tell me you're going to start using it like opium," I say.

He gives me a steady look. "As much as I would love to get back on the pipe and smoke my problems away, right now I need to be as sharp as a knife." He jerks his head over at Brom. "This man, however, could probably use some sedation from time to time."

"Is this how it's going to go from now on?" Brom glowers at him. "The chains weren't enough, now you're going to drug me?"

"With your consent, of course," Crane says with a dashing smile, placing the bottle on the desk.

"What happened earlier, with the history teacher?" I ask. "Did you talk to her?"

Crane shakes his head, licking his fingers in such a way that I feel a flare of heat at my core. Not helpful given the circumstances. "No," he says. "She's nowhere to be found." He eyes Brom. "I hope she's not about to get in trouble for teaching you what she did."

"Why would she?" Brom asks. "None of the sisters were there. Just the students."

"Do you have any artwork on the walls of that classroom?" Crane asks. "I'm just thinking about the painting in Ms. Peek's room. Is it entirely unreasonable to think that they can spy on people through the eyes of others?"

"I don't want to think about that," I say anxiously, sitting down on the bed. "There's already too much happening, my brain can't even take it all."

Crane sits down next to me, then Brom sits on the other side. It feels nice to be sandwiched between them, even in a nonsexual way. It feels like we're stronger like this, like a unit.

"One thing at a time, Kat," Crane says to me, and I rest my head on his shoulder while Brom takes my hand in his and squeezes. I squeeze it back. "That's all we can do. But there are three of us, so that means three things at a time, really."

"All I know is that I'm going to that supper with my mother on the weekend," I say.

"What?" Crane says stiffly. "You are not."

"I am," I tell him, lifting my head to meet his indignant eyes. "And Brom is coming with me."

Those eyes widen. "He is not."

"Crane," Brom warns.

"He is," I tell Crane. "I need to talk to Famke, now more than ever. And it's supper. Three o'clock, she said. It's early enough that we'll get back before nightfall."

"I'm going with you," he huffs.

"No," I tell him adamantly. "You're not. My mother said she'd shoot you, and I believe her and, despite my feelings about her, I don't want you to get into some standoff. You're staying here. I'll go with Brom. I'll talk to Famke. While we're at supper I'll try to get some information out of my mother, then we'll come back. Even if it means we have to leave abruptly, we will."

Crane leans over me to look at Brom. "That means I have to trust this fellow over here with your life. That means you'll have to trust him with your life."

"Are you saying you don't trust me?" Brom counters darkly.

"To be honest, *Brom*, you're making it a lot harder these days," Crane says.

At that, Brom drops my hand and gets to his feet, staring down at us. "Why don't you tell her what you really want to tell her, Crane? I know you're waiting for the right time to throw me under the cart. Why don't you tell Kat the truth? Both of our truths."

My stomach twists and I hold my breath. "What truth?" I manage to say.

Crane gives Brom a look that could incinerate someone on the spot.

Then Crane looks away, running a hand through his hair, and lets out a heavy, despondent sigh that I feel in my bones.

"There's something I need to tell you, Kat," Crane says in a gravelly voice, towering over me as he gets to his feet. "Something I've been meaning to tell you but . . . it's gotten away on me."

"All right," I say, trying to keep my voice from shaking, wondering what awful thing this is going to be. "Do tell."

"When your aunt Leona called me into her office, she warned me to stay away from you," he says, pacing back and forth across the room, hands behind his back. "As you know, idle threats don't do much for me. She said I would lose my job as a professor here at the school, but that didn't seem worth holding on to if I couldn't have you."

I'm touched at his devotion to me, but . . .

"I knew I could quit at any time, until she told me she had something on me that would prevent me from quitting. Something she's always had on me. And I knew it too, I knew that she was aware of it, but I never thought she would throw it in my face."

"Marie," I say softly, my eyes going to the floor in thought. "She has something on you about Marie's death." I swallow and look up at him. "What does she have on you, Crane?"

*What did you do?*

His face pales, that downturned mouth twisting in grief. "She knew that I killed my wife."

I feel the air knocked out of me. "Oh."

Then Crane is dropping to his knees in front of me, holding on to my hand. "You have to listen to me, Kat, you have to listen to me and believe me. Please." He takes my hands and brings them to his lips, leaving a desperate kiss. I so rarely see Crane in this sort of anguish, let alone on his knees in such a submissive way.

"Okay," I say softly, feeling any resolve I may have had melt already.

"It was an accident," he says, and with the way he says it, with his whole heart, I know it was. I know Crane isn't a killer. "I had done so many wrong things that evening, but killing her was an accident."

"What happened?" I ask, squeezing his hand, and even that gesture makes his expression crumble with relief.

"I suspected she was having an affair," he says, clearing his throat, emotions swirling in his stormy eyes. "For months, I suspected. There was no love left in our marriage at all, and I knew, I had a feeling. So I did something I shouldn't have. I read her memories while she was sleeping, without her permission. And I discovered she was having an affair with our neighbor, Ray. So . . ."

He closes his eyes and takes a deep breath, holding my hand against his forehead, as if in prayer. "So I paid Ray a visit. I didn't know . . . I didn't know when I went to see him how I would feel. I was so . . . disoriented and confused. I didn't know if I should kill him or . . . fuck him."

My eyes widen and even Brom inhales sharply from beside me.

"I chose to fuck him," Crane says, lowering my hand to look at me, his jaw flexing. "And in that moment, I chose to embrace who I was. Every dark, deviant part of me. There was no turning back. And while Ray and I were in the middle of it, the first I had ever been with a man, Marie walked into his house and saw us. I threatened to divorce her for her adultery, but my own adultery was thrown back in my face. She called me a sodomite, a heathen, and said that she would tell the school board, get me fired, tell the world. So I was angry, I was so angry, and I scared her and she . . . fell."

He trails off, looking away, brows knitted together as if reliving the scene. "And she fell hard. Hit her head on the wood floor. Blood began to pool and I fell to my knees and I panicked. I panicked. I tried to bring her back to life . . ."

"Jesus, Crane," Brom says.

"Jesus wasn't listening," Crane says in a faraway voice. "He was absent in that moment. Because she came back. Just for a moment. Just to let me know how awful I was, and that I had done something no one should ever do. Bring someone back to life. Then she died, again. For good."

He closes his eyes, bringing my hand to his mouth and kissing it. "Oh, and then my troubles really began," he says against my skin. "Ray had seen what I'd done. Called me a demon. It was only because of his participation earlier that I was able to keep him from reporting me. He knew I would turn him in too. Two men in a relationship, a dead woman. It would be easy to spin it any way. In the end we had to pretend we were having an evening in, the three of us friends, and that she had slipped and fallen and that was that. Naturally, I didn't move on in a healthy way. I quit my job. Moved across the country. Discovered opium."

"Discovered me," Brom says quietly.

"Discovered you," Crane says, gazing up at him fiercely. Then he fixes his eyes on me. "And found you, Kat. The only things in this life that have kept me from total damnation."

The room falls silent with the weight of his words.

"But," I begin after a minute, sucking on my lip, "but if that's what happened, then what does Leona have on you?"

He sighs tiredly. "She can plant false memories in my mind, for one. Make me believe that I did it on purpose. And she said she could falsify the original police report in some way. I have no idea how, she'd have to get out to San Francisco, I guess. But I do believe her, I believe in her power. And I do believe she'd stop at nothing to ensure I was out of the picture, so that you and Brom can fulfill your prophecy."

"We have to kill her," Brom says suddenly, staring at nothing. His voice is so raw, so strange, that both Crane and I look at him in surprise.

"We what?" I ask.

He swings his dark eyes over to us. "We have to kill her. We have to kill all of them. That's the only way we get out of this alive."

"Brom," I admonish him. "We don't even truly know what's happening here with my aunts, what the coven stands for, what our union even means. And even if we did know, we are not murderers. Crane may have killed his wife, but not on purpose, and you . . ."

His brows rise, his forehead lined. "And me? I'm a murderer, Daffy. I know you know that too."

"You are *not* the horseman," I tell him.

"I *am* the horseman," he says simply, his eyes so black. "And he is me. And I killed Constable Kirkbride. I told the Hessian to do it, simply because I wanted him dead. What do you make of that now?"

My mouth feels like it's stuffed with cotton balls. I can barely swallow, barely think.

"We are bad men, Kat," Crane whispers, putting his hand on my head. "You deserve better than us."

"No," I tell them, shaking my head. "You're *my* men. The rest doesn't matter."

"Morals don't matter?" Crane asks, his eyes gleaming.

"*My* morals matter," I say adamantly, feeling it burn in my chest. "And your morals matter. That's all. The three of us, we've been put on a raft and set adrift by the rest of the world. We found each other, and we must cling to each other. If that means we have to develop our own set of morals to survive, so be it. I'm not sacrificing any of that, and I'm not sacrificing either of you to fit into someone else's standards of what it means to be *good*." I pause, taking in a deep breath. "They can all fuck right off."

Crane's eyes go wide in shock, and Brom bursts out laughing, throwing his arm around me and holding me close.

"That's a good girl," Crane says, shaking his head through a smile, his eyes dancing with pride. "That's our sweet witch."

I smile right back.

But I meant what I said.

# 25

## Crane

I've fallen deeper in love with her," I tell Brom, placing a drop, just a drop, of the laudanum on my tongue. "I didn't think that was possible, but it is."

Brom chuckles, sitting on the floor and leaning against the side of my bed on which I'm lying in a state of well-earned stupor. "You told her you needed to stay sharp, Crane."

"And in the moment, I meant it," I tell him, passing the bottle down to him. "But it's the middle of the night, and I should be asleep. You should be asleep. Is it so wrong to have a little assistance?"

"She needed the drug for her own pain," Brom points out as he takes it from me, his finger brushing against mine, holding on for just a moment.

"I filled up a vial for her," I remind him. "It's very dangerous to give a young woman that much opium when she's never had it before. Ms. Peek should know that."

"Sounds like Ms. Peek had other things to worry about," he

comments gruffly, putting a drop on his tongue. He coughs, making a face. "Do you really think that the sisters can spy on us through paintings?"

"Let's just assume that they can," I tell him. "Let's assume everything. Let's assume the worst even. That Ms. Peek's nightmares are real. That she's being drugged, perhaps with the opium she smuggled in for Leona, and is being taken to the cathedral in the night, her organs removed while she's still alive, then sewn back up and healed through magic. Let's pretend that's what's happening."

"Fuck," he swears, bringing the bottle back to me.

I take it and put it on the desk, then lie back on the bed again.

"Then I shall stick to my original feelings on the matter," he says. "That we kill them all."

I stare at him, unable to stop from smiling. "You really went from feeling guilty that the horseman was killing people based on your feelings to just wanting to massacre every witch you see."

He shrugs. "I'm already damned, aren't I?" He rolls his head to the side to look at me. "I'm serious. Give me the word, Crane, and I'll get the horseman to do it."

The drug wants my mind to slow down, to relax, to submit, but I can't, not yet.

"Brom," I say, blinking hard at him in order to force my brain to work. "I know you feel connected to this evil spirit inside you, and you think that's a good thing, but it really isn't. The horseman is letting you think he's on your side. He's not. No matter what, he was summoned by the coven, and he belongs to the coven. At any moment they can recall him and order him to do their bidding. He's not going to pick you when the time comes.

And he's certainly not going to kill the coven when they're the ones controlling him."

He exhales heavily. "Then why let my emotions influence him at all? Why let me have some control over what he does and who he kills?"

"Because he's an extension of you. Because the end goal is *you*, Brom. They can't control you, but they can control the horseman, and that means they control you by default. You know what they want. You know they want you to fuck Kat, get her pregnant. They want you to father her child." I swallow down the hurt in those words. "The marriage is for show. If what your history teacher said is true, this is a union between two covens who are promised immortality. You are a bargaining chip. So is Kat. The horseman is a means to an end."

He falls silent at that, his chin dipping down, his dark hair falling forward.

"The two of us," I begin, "we're simple in many ways. Me and Kat? We're also simple. You and Kat . . . you should be the most solid line in this triangle, but you're the most complicated piece of the puzzle. Twisted in on itself and over again."

He snorts. "You don't even want us together."

"I love her," I tell him, sitting up. "And I love you. I don't care how many times I say it to you and you don't say it back, but I love *you*. And all my jealousy and possessiveness put to the side, I want the two of you to love each other. The three of us are one. We don't work without the others."

He gives me a sidelong glance. "Right. And if I stepped out of the picture, you wouldn't take Kat for yourself?"

"I didn't say I wouldn't," I say with a crooked smile. "She's mine to the end, pretty boy. But my life wouldn't be as sweet if you weren't in it."

He frowns at me with a mocking look in his eyes. "What happened to Crane? Who is this man?" He lifts up the end of the covers and pretends to look under the bed.

"This man is high right now," I tell him. "Why don't you take off your clothes and come to bed?"

"Ah," he says with a nod. "There he is."

I grin. "It sounded like a question, but it was a statement."

"Of course," Brom says. He gets to his feet and starts unbuttoning his shirt, knowing what I like to see, the peek of his taut, tanned skin underneath the white fabric, the slow reveal as he pulls it over his head.

I take my time gazing at his upper body, never getting tired of it. His veined, thick arms, the wide expanse of his shoulders, the dusting of dark hair across the chiseled planes of his hard chest, the way the hair leads down over the furrows of his etched abdomen, down farther past the sharp V of his hips.

His trousers come off next. His cock already at attention, a dark and formidable seven inches against his muscular thighs, his balls heavy underneath, swinging as he takes two steps toward me.

"Where do you want me?" he asks. His lids are heavy from the drug, maybe from desire.

"Where do you want me, sir?" I correct him, just for fun.

"Where do you want me, *sir*?"

I watch him for a moment, the petulance in the way he holds his mouth, the defiance and lust in his dark eyes, the furrow in his brow. God, I love this man.

I want him to love me too. That might be my darkest secret—

not what happened to Marie, but that I want this wild, contemptuous young man to love me the way that I love him.

"I want you to undress me, slowly, using your hands, using your tongue. I want you to take your time. Then I want you to take that oil in the drawer and put it on your cock. Then put it on me. I want you to lie on top of me and fuck me."

He stares at me, his mouth parting and wet. "When you say you want me to fuck you . . ."

"I'm saying come inside me. I submit to you for tonight, Brom. I am yours."

He swallows hard, his cock visibly twitching in response. "You really are high," he whispers, practically salivating.

Maybe I am. Maybe this isn't what I would normally do.

But I've thought about it.

I've thought about it with him, wanting to know what his cock would feel like inside me. I've thought about submitting to him for once, just to know what it feels like.

"I'm curious," I tell him, "to see what I'm missing out on."

"Aren't you worried?" he asks, reaching down and undoing my trousers and freeing my cock, which springs to full height. "About the horseman?"

"Not for tonight," I tell him truthfully. "I trust that you can keep him at bay."

He doesn't need to know that while he was in the bathroom earlier, I very liberally sprinkled salt all around the room and placed some obsidian and black tourmaline towers at certain spots for good measure. He might not be in chains, and I might be high, but that doesn't mean I trust the horseman not to show up announced.

He nods at that, and then he gets to work. He slowly undresses me until I'm nude, then takes his time sliding his hands all over my body, running his rough beard along my skin, leaving a trail of kisses in his wake. He does this until my whole body feels alive and my nerves are dancing, begging for more.

Then he takes the oil out of the desk and slides it over his cock. I watch for a perfect minute as his eyes close, and it's just him and his beautiful body, his hands working himself with expert precision, bringing himself close to the edge but never over.

Then his eyes fix on me and he shoves my knees up, making my legs part further, ensuring my hips roll back to give him the best access.

I've never felt more open and vulnerable in my life.

"Am I the first man to fuck you here?" he whispers, circling my hole with his oiled finger. The sensation is so strange and so good, and his gaze keeps coming to mine. His expression is so studious and so earnest as he tries to make sure I'm enjoying it.

"No," I say, feeling breathless already. "I had a tryst with a vampire once."

"A . . . vampire?" Brom says, pausing.

"Don't you dare stop," I warn him, and he goes back to rimming me with his fingertip. I suppose I'm still in control after all. "Yes, a vampire. They exist. I had a very brief relationship with one while he was visiting New York. Which is also rare since witches and vampires are natural enemies."

"And you let this vampire dominate you?"

I chuckle. "He was a lot older than me, by several hundred

years, and he was a *vampire*. Yes, you let them dominate you. You don't get a choice in the matter. They are very persuasive."

"Did you enjoy it?"

"Yes. Very much so. But I dare say I'll enjoy you far more."

*Because I love you.*

The corner of his mouth lifts. "I've never done this before," he says. "I want to do it right."

I laugh and lie back. "Oh, pretty boy. You're already doing everything right. Now hurry up and fuck me before I get too impatient."

Slowly, Brom slides his finger inside me to the knuckle and I instinctively clench around it. My cock is so hard and stiff and weeping onto my stomach and this is already pushing me to the edge. How will I survive him, let alone another finger?

"How is it?" he whispers, staring up at me through his lashes. "Does that feel good? Can I make you feel better?"

I groan as he pushes another finger in, this time farther, and he knows all the places to hit, knows the spot inside where it feels full, where it makes me gasp, my body tight and burning for release.

"Give me your cock, pretty boy. That's how you can make me feel better."

"Yes, sir," he says gruffly. He gets up, the backs of my thighs against the fronts of his, and the sight of him there, this virile young man between my legs, with his feral stare and dark hair, his taut, flexing stomach and the darkened tip of his cock pressed against a place that had been forbidden to him, it's enough to make me want to be a better man for him.

With a shaking breath he steadies his oiled cock against my hole and presses the tip in. It's only an inch, but my entire body wants to protest, and I have to remind myself that this is what happened with the vampire. So I close my eyes and relax. I bear down instead of tense up.

I submit.

It's so damn hard to submit, but I do.

"Fuck," Brom hisses as he pushes in farther. "Fuck, you're burning inside, Crane. It's so damn hot."

I grunt and arch my back, my body wanting more of him, and I look up to see him staring down at where his cock is stretching me, mesmerized. He pushes my knees up farther to get a better look and I gasp, the angle changing everything.

"Fuck me," I swear.

He laughs, breathless and light. "I'm trying. You're so fucking tight."

"Maybe you're too fucking big."

And at that Brom shoves in the rest of the way, knocking the air clear out of my lungs, my hands making fists on the sheets. He's so large, so full, and there's this balance of pleasure and just a kiss of pain that breaks through the thin haze of the drug, of feeling too much and not enough, and at the root of it all is the fact that Brom, my pretty boy, has his cock wedged deep inside me for the first time.

Tears spring to my eyes, taking me by surprise, but I manage to keep them at bay. The last thing he needs is to hear me harp on about how much I love him.

Which is why I'm submitting this way. Why I'm letting him in a place I've never let him in before. Because maybe he doesn't want to hear that I love him, but maybe it's different when I show him. Even if I show him in the dirtiest, most depraved and deviant way.

"That's right, pretty boy," I whisper, my voice choked. "Fuck me like it's our last night together. Make us come."

His breath hitches, and then he starts pumping in and out of me, and I watch in awe as his mouth hangs open, the way his cheeks darken, the sweat beading on his forehead, making his hair stick to his skin.

Then he leans down and kisses me, drawing my tongue up against his, and I wrap my hand around his throat, holding him there. He's shivering with lust now, and his body is moving on top of mine, each thrust, each vibration rubbing along my own cock. There's no sensation like this, the feeling of having your ass and your dick worked at once, and I know I'm not going to last much longer, even though I want to do this all night.

"Keep fucking me," I whisper against his lips. "Keep going until there's nothing left in you."

He slides his arm underneath me, pulling my body against his, my cock effectively pinned, and starts riding me harder, faster, and then I fully let go.

I come with a snarl, with a strangled cry that comes from some other part of me, some other realm where I don't even know my own name. I am out of my head, propelled by the drug and by Brom and my vision blurs and goes dark and I'm gone, terribly gone. But then the feeling of my hot seed spurting long ropes across my stomach, smearing between our bellies, brings me back in enough to open my eyes and watch as Brom releases into my ass.

His head goes back, his thick neck arched, stomach tense, muscles shaking, and I can feel the heat of his seed as it shoots inside me, the pulse of his cock as he empties out. He lets out a series of staccato grunts, each louder than the next.

With a low moan he lowers his chin to look at me, this raw expression of wonderment and something else. Something tender and soft, not the adjectives I usually use to describe him, but still something that feels like it comes from somewhere honest.

Or drug induced.

He collapses against me, gasping for breath, burying his head at the crook of my neck while I put an arm around him.

"You did so well, Brom," I whisper to him. "And even when you're on top of me, you're still so pretty when you come."

He exhales heavily, and I can feel his heart beating against mine, just as erratic as he is.

Then he lifts his head, his elbows planted on either side of my shoulders, and grabs my face in his hands. He proceeds to stare at me, just stares at me until I feel it in my soul.

"What?" I whisper as I search his onyx eyes, not wanting to break the spell, this moment that feels deep and poignant, something real pushing through the haze.

"Love is involuntary," he says, his voice quiet and harsh. "I love you, Ichabod Crane. I love you against my own will."

I go still, unable to believe my own ears.

"It's not the drug," he continues, running his thumb over my lip as I stare at him, frozen. "I know that's what you're going to say, but it's not that. The feeling was there before. It's always been there. I love you because that's just how it is. It's as automatic as taking my next breath."

My heart soars, thumping against my ribs. "Would you rather not love me?"

He gives me a rare, sweet smile. "It would be so much easier if I didn't." He leans in and presses a kiss to my lips, his beard scratching my chin. "But I do."

*We fall asleep* in each other's arms, a deep, blissful drug- and sex-induced sleep that the both of us have sorely needed. By the time I open my eyes, the gray light from outside is bright enough to illuminate the room. If I had an early class this morning, I surely would have missed it.

"Good morning," I whisper to Brom, who grunts into the pillow. "I have a feeling you may have missed your first class. We slept in."

"Who cares?" he grumbles, still face down. "None of it matters anyway."

He has a point there.

"Fair point," I say, lifting his arm off me and getting to my feet and stretching. "But we need to keep up appearances for now."

I walk over to the window, twisting at my waist, trying to wake up, when I freeze.

My hair stands on end.

On the desk, on top of a torn white cloth, is another dead snake with sewing needles stuck through it, pinning it in place, shaped like an S.

There are no words this time, no warning written in blood.

But underneath it, just like the emblem at the gates of Sleepy Hollow Institute, there is a single long key.

# 26

## Kat

"A re you ready?" Brom asks me, bringing Daredevil over to where I'm mounted atop Snowdrop.

I pat the necklace that I have safely tucked away in the small pocket on my dress and nod. "As I'll ever be."

The last few days I've been wearing the cross-and-moon pendant around my neck, believing in what Famke said about its protection, but since she went to the trouble to sneak it out to me in a piece of pastry, I figure that it's best I keep it on me but out of sight. I don't want Famke to suffer if my mother sees it.

"Return as soon as your supper is over," Crane barks at us as he leans against the stable door. "I want you both back here before dark."

I roll my eyes at that, while Brom twists in the saddle to face Crane. "Yes, *Daddy.*"

I burst out laughing. The flustered expression on Crane's face is priceless.

"You deserve a spanking for that, pretty boy," Crane growls. "You also need to be spanked, Kat."

"I didn't even say anything!" I protest.

"And I didn't say you deserved it," he says.

I shake my head. *Any excuse for you to bring out your ruler.*

Then I coax Snowdrop to follow Daredevil down the path and through the center courtyard. For a Saturday, it's awfully quiet, not a soul about the campus, despite the weather being mild, the gray clouds higher than they usually are, and the air calm.

But things seem to have shifted in the last week, since both Lotte's and the constable's deaths. The classes are more subdued, the students seeming to shrink in on themselves. Some of them look just as sick as Ms. Peek, all gaunt and pale with darkened eyes and bruises, and I wonder if her illness (if you can call it that) is spreading. It's enough that only about half the students are even showing up for class.

I voiced this to Crane and Brom the other day, and of course Crane thinks it's all connected. He's probably right too, though we can't figure out how or why. But they've been wrapped up in the bigger mystery of who left the dead snake and key on Crane's desk in the middle of the night. That key goes somewhere, and we've tried it on every door we've come across, to no avail.

"I really hope my . . . ," Brom begins as the gates swing open to let us through. He trails off as we go through the wards, the pressure in my ears ringing until they finally stop. "My parents," he continues, giving his head a shake, "for lack of a better word, aren't there for dinner."

"For lack of a better word?" I question.

He gives me a cold look as we ride side by side down the trail. We're a little early for supper, so there's no use rushing.

"You know my parents aren't who they say they are," he says matter-of-factly. "They aren't my parents at all. Sister Sophie told you I was related to her."

"But that doesn't mean your parents aren't your parents," I point out.

"Nah," he says, looking ahead. "I know they aren't. Ever since I was a child, I knew they were only minders of mine. Think about it, Kat. Think of how they'd always act around me, from day one."

I fall silent, mulling that over as we ride through the autumnal woods, the horses' hooves rhythmically plodding over the damp ground. Brom's parents were always indifferent and distant, yes, but I figured that was how they were. I never for a moment thought that they weren't his actual biological parents.

Then again, I had felt like they acted more like cousins toward him at times. Maybe everything that was once far-fetched is now a distinct possibility. Everything I once thought and feared as being impossible might very well be real.

Even the things I've been too afraid to think about.

Like what really happened to my father.

"Maybe you're right," I say quietly. "But then who are your real parents?"

He shrugs. "Does it matter? They aren't here. All this time I was afraid I never had a real family, and it turns out that I was right. I never did. I never will."

"You know I'm your family, Brom," I tell him, my chest aching at the tired acceptance on his brow. "Crane and I, we're your family now."

He glances at me, longing in his gaze, but doesn't say anything.

"This kind of family is the one that counts," I tell him. "This is the one that's chosen. Not by blood, though I reckon we're bonded by blood now anyway, but by choice and with purpose. The three of us, we have chosen each other, and that counts for everything."

"I want to believe you," he says quietly.

"Then believe me," I tell him. "You can choose to believe me."

He opens his mouth slightly, wanting to say something, then closes it.

We keep riding, and all I can think about is how Brom's inability to believe he's worthy of family and love might be the biggest obstacle of all. How do you get through that? How do you convince someone that they're worth everything?

It's not long before we're crossing over Hollow Creek and nearing Mary's farmhouse, when I decide to bring the horses down her lane.

"Where are we going?" Brom asks.

"I wanted to talk to Mary," I tell him. "It's been so long since I've seen her, and she's the only friend I have left on this side of the gates."

By luck, Mary is outside in her front yard, riffling through the pumpkin patch.

"Kat?" she asks once she spots us. She wipes her hands on her apron and comes running over, a piece of hay in her messy updo.

"What a pleasant surprise!" she exclaims. She looks at Brom and gives him a hesitant smile before facing me again. "What are you doing here?"

"It's Saturday, I was invited down for supper," I tell her. "It's been ages since we talked. Would you like to come?"

"Come to supper?" she asks, surprised.

"What are you doing?" Brom says under his breath.

"Yes," I tell her, ignoring him. "It wouldn't be a problem at all. My mother loves to have company. Brom is coming with me right now, we would love to catch up with you."

She weighs that for a moment, then looks at Brom. "I suppose this would be the time to introduce myself. My name is Mary Wilson," she says, giving him a slight bow. "And you must be the infamous Brom Bones."

"Pleasure," Brom says stiffly. He's never been very affable when it comes to meeting new people, and he's not turning a new leaf with Mary.

"And you don't mind if I come for supper?" Mary asks him. "I wouldn't want to intrude on you young lovers."

"Mary," I chide her with a potent look. "Don't be silly."

She laughs. "All right, let me go ask my mother."

She turns and runs into her house, the front door closing behind her. In some ways it feels like a lifetime ago that I was knocking on that door and pleading for someone to save me from the very person I'm riding next to.

"Why did you invite her?" Brom asks me while she's inside.

"I need time to talk to Famke alone, and I don't think you'll be able to distract my mother long enough," I tell him. "I wouldn't put that burden all on you, and I don't trust her around you either. I also haven't seen Mary in a while. It would be good for me to hang on to the few friends I have."

He nods. "Your mother won't be happy about this."

"Well, it's a damn good thing I don't care."

Finally, I see a ghost of a smile on his lips.

Mary comes running back out of the house. "I can come for an hour or two," she says, taking off her apron and leaving it on the fence post. "I'll skip dessert, if that's all right. I have to help Mathias with his homework after."

She walks over to us, and I pat Snowdrop's back behind me. "Want a leg up?"

She shakes her head. "No, I'm used to walking. I had to lend my brother my horse for the last few weeks. His mare went missing for a bit, she's back now, though."

My stomach churns. Oh no.

"Missing?" I ask, trying to sound calm and not at all like I had stolen her brother's horse in the middle of the night when I was trying to escape the horseman.

"Yes. The sweet little roan? She went missing the night of the bonfire. Which was so odd because after we came back, I checked on the stables and she was there, snug as a bug. Someone must have taken her in the night or freed her. I don't know how else she could have gotten loose."

"Don't you think you would have heard that?" I ask warily.

She laughs. "Oh no. Not our family. We all sleep like the dead. Doesn't help that my father snores so loud he drowns out all noise for acres."

I force a laugh at that. That explains why she never heard me banging on the door that night.

"Well, I'm glad the horse returned," I tell her as we continue down the road.

Mary, meanwhile, has lost interest in the horse and starts peppering Brom with all sorts of questions, telling him she's heard so much about him. She asks him about his parents, about what I was like as a kid, about New York, to which he gives one-word answers.

Finally, she says, "And since you're at the school, I take it that you're a witch too? Don't worry, Kat told me everything."

I give him a cautious look, so that he knows I've told her some things, not *everything*.

"Actually, I'm not a witch," he admits, and for the first time I really hear the resentment in his voice and realize how much that must bother him. "I'm only there because my parents were able to pull a few strings."

"Oh," she says, staring up at him curiously. "So you go to class to learn magic and you just . . ."

"Sit there and look like a fool," he says. "It's fine, I'm used to it."

Oh, Brom. He says that with a faint smile, trying to play it off, but I can tell he means what he says.

As he predicted, when we arrive at my house, my mother is displeased that Mary is there. She doesn't show it, of course—that would be rude and my mother has always tried to uphold her gracious, if reserved, reputation with the town—but I can tell she's upset. She wanted Brom and me alone at supper for who knows what, and I've completely foiled her plan.

So we all gather around the fire in the sitting room that I grew up in, which now feels like foreign territory. I take it upon myself to help Famke and serve tea and cookies. My mother tries to get up and tell me that she'll handle that, but I refuse her, and Brom, knowing what I need to do, ropes her into another conversation.

"Katrina," Famke says in a low voice as I return to the kitchen after I've served them tea. "You know you shouldn't be here."

"You knew I would come back," I tell her, setting down the empty tray and leaning against the counter. "You couldn't expect me to find the necklace and the note and never see you again."

"Yes," she says sharply, wiping her forehead with her flour-covered arm. "I did expect that. That's why I gave you the necklace." She looks over at the door, worry creasing her brow.

"Brom and Mary are in there occupying her," I assure her. "He knows what to do."

"And you trust him?" Famke says.

I frown. "Brom? Of course I do." I grab her arm, firm but gentle. "Famke. You said you want to protect me. You can protect me by telling me everything you know. Please. I feel . . . I feel I'm running out of time up there, and I don't have any answers for any of the questions I have."

She breathes in sharply through her nose, her eyes darting to the door again.

"Please, tell me why you gave me the necklace."

She looks up to the ceiling for a moment, as if having a word with God, then sighs.

"The necklace belongs to my family," she says with a rueful smile. "My grandparents in Holland were religious and also pagan. An odd pairing, yes, but it worked. That necklace was always a melding of both sides, meant to protect oneself from those who wish them harm. The onyx stone is for extra protection."

I pat the necklace in my pocket.

Her gaze follows. "Your father knew that one day he would be gone and only you would remain. He trusted me to look after you. When Brom left Sleepy Hollow . . ." She looks away, shaking her head. "You don't know how happy I was. I knew your father would have been joyous to know you had been freed from him."

I wince. "Did he really hate Brom that much?"

"He hated what he represented," she whispers harshly, her eyes blazing. "The lack of your free will. As long as Brom was in the picture, it meant that your future was determined for you. And he knew that your mother's plan for your future never had your best interests in mind."

I nod, rubbing my lips together, trying to gather all my questions in the short time I have.

"Brom's parents aren't his real parents, are they?"

"No."

"Who are?"

She shrugs and goes back to rolling the dough. "I don't know."

"What are you trying to protect me against?" I ask her pointedly. "What was my father so scared of? What are you so scared of?"

She gives me a dark, cagey look. "Your mother," she whispers. "That she'll do to you what she did to your father."

I reach out and grab her arm, harder than I meant to. "What did she do to my father? Last time you just told me she *took* from him. What does she take? How does she take it?"

"She takes *you*," she hisses at me. "She takes what you're made of and uses it for herself until there's nothing left of you. She siphons, Katrina. She siphons your soul."

I try to swallow but can't. I can barely breathe.

"I met your father when he was twenty years old," she goes on, "hiring me even before he got married. Then your mother came along. She looked the same age that she does now. Oh, she was frail, she was always sick, she was too skinny, except for those few days around the full moon when she seemed to glow with health before she plummeted again. Your mother hasn't aged a single day since the day you were born."

I stare at her blankly, my mind tripping over itself.

"Is she a . . . a vampire?" I manage to ask, my voice barely audible, my head swimming.

Famke cracks a wry smile. "A vampire? No. She's a witch, Katrina. She's a witch from a very powerful coven, and you were always the key to her existence."

Those words float over me like ashes.

"So then why don't you quit?" I ask, trying to keep my voice steady. "Why put yourself at risk by staying here? Doesn't she take from you?"

"I'm not a witch," she says, rolling the dough again. "I don't have any magic or power to offer her. But you, Katrina, you do. There's a reason why your father made you promise to never show your magic around your mother, because he knew it would only tempt her to take it all for herself. And I made a promise to your father. As long as you are in Sleepy Hollow or at the school, I would be here, watching over you. I don't trust you up there with those witches. Your mother is your mother, but her sisters? They are so much worse."

I fall silent. It all feels so impossible to manage.

"Is Mary still someone you can trust?" Famke asks me.

"Yes," I say absently, trying to come to terms with it all. "Of course."

"Good. You will need friends, Katrina."

"And you can trust her too," I tell her. "If something . . . happens to me. Up there, with them. If something goes wrong. If you don't hear from me, please know you can trust her. She will help you when my mother won't."

"*Ja.*" Famke nods, looking grim. "Okay."

I look around the kitchen, trying to think. "How . . . how old is my mother?"

"I don't know, child," she says to me. "But whatever they have planned for you and Brom, the best thing you can do is get on your horses and head to Tarrytown. You could go tonight. Escape now, while you can."

"I can't," I say pitifully. "I can't leave Crane."

She lets out a heavy sigh. "Then go and get him, then leave."

"That's not the only problem," I tell her, debating whether I should tell her the whole truth. Then I figure I don't have much to lose. "Brom's possessed by the headless horseman."

Famke drops the rolling pin and it clatters noisily to the floor. "What?" she asks.

Suddenly my mom bustles into the kitchen. "Katrina," she says. "Stop pestering Famke, and go entertain your company. It's very rude to invite a guest over like that and then completely neglect her."

I hold Famke's wild gaze for a moment before I turn around.

"Of course, my apologies," I tell my mother, walking into the sitting room. In the background I can hear my mother asking Famke what we were talking about. I can't hear her answer.

I give Mary a shaky, apologetic smile and sit down next to Brom on the love seat. He reaches over, taking hold of my hand, and I've never appreciated such a simple gesture so much in my life. It's like his hand grounds me, gives me all the strength and courage I thought I lost. He may be possessed, but at the moment he is still mine.

"I've got you, Daffodil," he whispers in my ear, his breath tickling me, and I know in my gut that it's true. "I will protect you. I will do things, things you won't like, in order to protect you."

I pull back and see his eyes burning with determination, and my heart skips a beat.

But the moment vanishes when my mother comes back into the room and dominates the conversation. All through the rest of the tea, then the supper (after which Mary left), then the dessert, all I could think about was what Famke had said.

My mother hasn't aged a day.

She hasn't aged a day.

I thought back over the years and she's always looked the same to me, even as a child, but that's normal, and memories aren't to be trusted. You see things differently when you're young. We don't even have any photographs in the house. I remember that my father was interested in the new medium, wanting a family portrait done, but my mother was very against it. She had said it was too expensive.

I guess I understand why now.

It would have been proof.

Being watchful of the time, Brom and I eat our dessert

quickly, armed with excuses as to why we need to get back early. I'm sure she knows exactly why too.

We say goodbye to my mother, and there's so much more that I want to say to Famke, but I don't get another chance alone with her. All I get is a quick glance full of warning.

Brom and I head out the door into the cool afternoon, getting on our horses, but then instead of turning to the road, Brom brings Daredevil to one of the fallow fields behind the house. The sun is low in the sky, another hour until it's dark, and fog has started to creep in off the Hudson, infiltrating the last of the cornstalks and dead wheat.

"Where are we going?" I ask him. "We should be heading back to the school now."

"I know," he says, glancing at me over his shoulder, heading into the low sun. "I just wanted to take you to the barn. To the past. I want to get things right."

# 27

## Brom

Kat stares at me from Snowdrop, the golden sun reflecting on her face and making her look like she did in the glen, like a goddess coming into her own power. There's apprehension in her eyes, but it's been there all day, not that I can blame her. She's worried that I'm going to turn into the horseman once it gets dark, even though we will be back at the school by then. She's also worried about whatever Famke had told her in the kitchen, information she hasn't had a chance to share with me yet.

And she's also worried about where I'm leading her.

To the barn.

Because I want another chance to set things right.

Because for the last four years, all I've wanted with her was a chance to set things right.

She doesn't say anything as we ride, and I'm not sure if this is her putting her trust in me or not, but I want that trust more than anything. Earlier she had said that she was my family, I just had to choose to believe it, but it's hard to believe when someone doesn't have faith in you.

And one of the reasons she doesn't trust me, besides the obvious, is because of what happened here four years ago.

We dismount outside the old barn, leave the horses' reins long so that they can munch on the damp grass, knowing they won't go anywhere. Snowdrop does whatever Kat asks of her, and Daredevil, well, I'm still unsure where this horse came from, unsure if he's truly connected to the Hessian's original horse or not, but I know that horse won't leave my side, whether I want him to or not. I just hope he can behave himself around Kat's mare, being a stallion and all.

Then again, he might take after me.

I grab Kat's hand, small and soft against my palm, and lead her into the barn. Just like that night four years ago, I'm nervous. And when I glance down at Kat as she steps into the shadows of the building, I can see she's nervous too.

"When was the last time you were in here?" I ask her as I walk over to the ladder to the hay loft, clearing cobwebs out of the way.

"Not since . . . ," she says, and then doesn't finish her sentence. She doesn't need to.

I test my foot on the bottom rung. It's a little softer than before but should hopefully hold us. I climb up to the top first and then look over the edge, waving for her to follow.

"It's safe." I look around the loft. Nothing has changed at all, though parts of it seem rotted directly below the hole in the roof. But there's still the hay bales we used to sit on, the apple crate with an old tea set. Memories flutter toward me like ghosts, the past coming alive, and once again I feel the shame of that night, the shame that's led me here and now.

Kat slowly comes up the ladder, and once she's at the top, I grab her arms and pull her up the rest of the way.

"Wow," she says, looking around, blowing a loose strand of hair from her face as she sits on her side. "Nothing has changed."

"We've changed," I tell her.

"And I wonder if it's for the better or for the worse?" she muses, a darkness coming over her delicate features.

Her question sinks in. Am I any better than I was at eighteen, before I fled into the night, like a coward who had stolen something he had no intention of giving back? Am I better now that I am possessed by the spirit of a bloodthirsty soldier? Am I better now that I know what's truly at stake and the sacrifices I have to make?

"I guess it depends," I say, settling down in the hay and patting the space beside me. "Are you better off with your innocence taken?"

She gives me a wry smile and crawls over to me. Her proximity causes me to lean in and breathe in her wildflower scent, the smell of her causing my heart to tighten, my cock to harden. How can I love someone so much and desire her so equally? How can I want to lavish her with tender affection yet want to choke her, spit on her, make her writhe beneath me in total depravity? How can those two halves coexist? It's as if there's light inside me that corrupts the darkness, leaving me to live in shades of gray.

"Innocence never did anyone any good," Kat says. "I may have lost my innocence to you, but in its place, I gained power."

The fierceness in her eyes only arouses me more, a deep and chaotic longing that's clawing its way to the surface.

"Kat," I whisper to her, and then I'm grabbing her face in my hands, holding her in place, kissing her deeply, feeling every inch of her mouth with my tongue, wanting more, so much more.

I place one hand on her skirt, making a fist in the fabric, trying to hold myself back, and then she pulls her head away, breathing hard.

"Brom," she says, her mouth wet and open, and God, I want her so badly it's killing me.

"Yes?" I manage to say, removing my hand from her skirt, and trying to remain in control of my emotions and urges that threaten to overwhelm me.

"I . . . ," she begins, picking up the stiff hay between her fingers, the light coming through the hole in the roof illuminating a faint flush on her cheeks. "I'm still menstruating," she says, stumbling over the word. "It's near the end, I think, but it's still . . . I'm not . . ."

"If you don't want to be with me," I tell her, placing my fingers under her chin and forcing her to meet my eyes, "then you don't have to be. I might like things rough, but I'm not about to force myself on you if this isn't what you want. I *love* you, Kat. But if you're worried about blood, then you're worrying for no reason. I want to be with you, just like this. I want to be inside you like I was four years ago." My voice lowers. "I want to come inside you, spread my seed inside your cunt, make you scream my name until all of Sleepy Hollow knows who you belong to."

She gives me a fearful look. "Crane will kill you."

I raise a brow and lean in to her, still holding her head in place. "Is that the only reason I shouldn't? Because Crane will kill me? And what about you?"

She licks her lips, and I want to do the same to her. "I don't want to end up pregnant with your baby, Brom."

Lord, how that stings. It fucking *stings.*

"I'm not saying never," she goes on quickly, reading my face. "I'm not . . ." She closes her eyes. "I don't know, Brom. I want to be with you. Just like this. Now and in the future, in all my futures . . ."

"But the horseman . . ."

"It's not the horseman," she says, looking at me with pain in her eyes. "It's not *just* the horseman," she corrects herself. "It's that our union, our baby, is supposed to be a sacrifice to a demon. You said yourself, the anti-Christ. I'm not about to birth the anti-Christ. You can understand that, can't you?"

Despite the seriousness of the situation, I can't help but smile at how ridiculous we sound. "Oh, I understand," I say, letting go of her. "I'm not too keen on fathering the anti-Christ myself, and that's a phrase I never thought I would utter. But you're still taking that tea and if you're menstruating, it's unlikely you'll get pregnant. That's nature." I pause, feeling the heady, possessive want for her flare through me. "And what else is nature is the need to take what's mine. And you're still mine, Kat, no matter what anyone else says. You're mine, aren't you?"

She nods.

"Then lie back on that hay, hike up your dress, and spread your legs."

Her blue eyes widen a little as she stares at me, and I'm not sure how she'll take to me ordering her around. She liked it once. She likes it with Crane.

And with a shaking exhale, she leans back on the hay.

She obeys me.

A wicked thrill runs through me, the sense of power I've craved. Having the horseman at my disposal is one thing, having Kat obey me, and only me, is another.

She is submitting.

I am taking.

I get on my knees and come around her. "You said your innocence never did you any good. Show me, then, how bad you can be." I place my hands on her calves, spreading her legs. "Lift up your skirt," I tell her. "Or I'll do it for you."

"There's blood," she protests, as if I wasn't aware of that.

"There was blood four years ago too," I point out, putting my hands under her hem and running them up the cool skin of her calves. She doesn't have stockings on, and even that feels illicit.

"I'm not even wearing . . . ," she begins, putting her forearm across her eyes as if she can't bear to watch me. "I ran out of cloth, so I don't . . . It's just . . ."

I have to admit, I've never been with a woman while she's having her monthly bleeds, so part of me is drawn to the forbidden notion of it, of witnessing something so private and secret and raw. It gets me harder than anything.

But Kat is too shy to do anything, so I push her skirt up around her hips.

She's not wearing any drawers at all, and there's just a hint of red around her opening, faint smears along the inside of her soft thighs, and it's a damn beautiful sight.

"You're barely bleeding," I assure her, my voice sounding thick with want. "This is nothing compared to the ritual."

"I don't want you to think of me as dirty and unclean," she protests. "I took a bath this morning, I—"

Before she can finish her sentence, I shove my face between her legs.

"Brom!" she gasps, but I just grab hold of her thighs and hold her open for me. The taste of blood hits my tongue, mixed with the scent of soap and the essence of what's undeniably *her*. It acts like an elixir, like magic, a fever spreading through me, making my skin hot, making my cock so hard and hungry.

I am completely feral for this woman.

And she loves it.

Her hands go to my hair, grabbing on tight, her hips rocking up to meet my lips and my tongue as I ravage her, and I know that deep down, she's no different than I am. That she enjoys sinking into the mire, to the depths of our savagery, our primal instincts taking over until we're just animals fucking because we don't know what else there is.

She is my equal.

We are one and the same.

"Don't stop," she cries out, her back bowing against the hay, and I nip her clit between my teeth until she bucks and squirms, panting for breath, moaning, and I feel as if I'm the one submitting here, submitting to this dark desire that has me in a choke hold.

I eat her out, wet and messy, swallowing down her blood and

arousal, and then she tenses, and I can feel her teetering at the edge before she goes over, letting out a string of expletives that make me smile against her.

She comes hard and loud, her thighs shaking and squeezing the sides of my head, her body convulsing beneath me, and I've never seen such a raw and primitive sight before.

She's so fucking beautiful.

And I am so fucking hard.

"Oh God," she whimpers as I pull back. "If there was any innocence left in me . . ."

"There's no innocence left in you, Kat," I rasp, pulling down my trousers and taking out my cock as I cover her with my body, one hand holding her hands pinned over her head. "I made sure to wring out every last bit."

She stares up at me with wild eyes, hungry eyes.

"You like that, don't you?" I grind out, as she raises her hips, and I position the head of my cock at her cunt, my teeth gritting as I hold myself back. "You like that you're filthy, deviant, unclean. A heathen like me."

She swallows hard, nodding, moving her hips again, my crown just stroking her now.

"You like it when I call you a whore, when I think of you as bad, as dirty? You'll get no praise from me, little slut."

Her expression turns molten, a hint of a smile on her lips that makes her look like she's happily sinning.

"You talk too much," she says.

My eyes go wide with surprise before I release her hands and let out a low growl, shoving the full length of my cock into her in a brutal, savage manner.

She cries out, sounding like she's choking, her fingernails digging into my shoulders, then my back, but I give no quarter. I pump mercilessly into her, rutting her hard into the hay, and she meets me on every bruising thrust with the raise of her hips. I could get carried away, I could come right here, and it would be over in an instant.

But I don't want that. I don't want to burn through this.

The reason I brought Kat here wasn't just so I could relive what happened four years ago.

It was so that we could come full circle.

Because I don't know what the future holds for me anymore.

But I fear this might be the only chance I'll get to be with her like this.

I take in a deep breath and slow down, my muscles shaking.

"I did a bad thing four years ago," I tell her, angling my hips to push into her even farther, my eyes fluttering closed for a moment. "At the time I thought the bad thing was what I had done with Pastor Ross." I bring my mouth to her neck, kissing her, breathing her in. "I thought that was the biggest sin, so big that I was forced to leave town. But even though I came here that night thinking that I had done something awful, the worst thing was yet to follow."

I slowly drag my cock out of her and lift my head, my hands going to either side of her face as she stares up at me with a mix of lust and wonder. "The worst thing I did was take your virginity and leave you. I shouldn't have done either. And for that, I am deeply sorry."

My hips roll back into her, my cock thrusting in to the hilt, and I groan as a breathless sound escapes from her lips.

"I don't regret losing it to you," she whispers, her neck arching. "I only wish you had stayed and told me the truth. But you will always be the man who first claimed me. That will never be taken away, Brom. It will always be you."

Her words do something to me, like there's a loose thread that's finally pulled, finally unraveling the binds around me.

And I decide I can't waste time at all.

I start fucking her faster, each thrust going deeper and deeper, and suddenly I'm fantasizing that Crane is here too. I want to come inside her and watch my seed trickle out of her legs, mixing with the blood, and then I want Crane to shove me aside and do the same. I want to see him fucking her just like this, coming hard so that our semen is mixing together inside the same woman.

Our woman.

When I'm gone, it's Crane who will have to take care of her in my place.

She belongs to him as equally as she belongs to me.

"I'm coming," I grunt, my eyes pinching shut. I slip my hand between her legs, rubbing her clit until she's coming too, and the two of us fill the barn with our rapturous noise, our shaking breath, our shuddering bodies.

I empty into her, filling her with my seed, wishing that someday I could give her a baby for real, that I could become a father, that I would have that life with her that I was once promised. She doesn't owe it to me, to marry me, to carry my children, but I still dream of it just the same, born out of love and lust, and not something outside our control.

Though perhaps love is always outside our control.

When I'm finally done, I stay inside her. I don't pull out. I lie against her, careful not to crush her completely, and I stare at her face, taking in every detail. I see our youth and our history together: the smattering of faint freckles on her nose, what I used to call pollen dust, the faint scar on her chin that she got when we were trying to cross the creek and she slipped on a wet rock. The distinctive shape of her lips, the very lips I used to fantasize about kissing when we were merely the best of friends, and all of this was nothing more than a dream.

"I love you," I tell her, and even though I've told her before, it burns inside me, a furnace that can't be caged. "Don't you ever forget that, Kat. I *love* you and I always have. I always will."

I watch as her eyes grow wet, and she reaches up to touch my cheek.

"I love you too, Brom," she whispers, giving me a mournful smile as her words pierce my heart. "I always have and I always will."

Something inside me breaks. That thread doesn't just come loose, it *snaps*.

And I can't help the tears that spill from my eyes and onto her cheeks.

"Daffy," I murmur, shaking with emotion, and I kiss the tears off her, hers and mine. "Please know, please know that no matter what happens, no matter what happens to me, I am choosing you. I am choosing this. Us."

"Nothing is going to happen to you, Brom," she says. "I promise. We're going to help you. Crane and I. We have the full moon ritual coming up, and it will work. It *will* work. You can't give up hope yet. We won't let you."

But I haven't given up hope. I know the day is coming soon when I'll have to make a choice, a sacrifice, in order to save them. I also know if I voice this to her, she and Crane will do everything they can to stop me.

So I keep that inside.

"You know Crane really loves you," she says after a moment, her fingers trailing over my drying tears.

The smile on my face is instant. "I know."

"Do you love him?"

"I do."

"You should let him know."

"I have."

She bursts into a grin. "He knows? Oh, thank goodness. I know Crane is Crane, and he doesn't really seem to show his emotions, he just states them, but I can see how much he loves you and that all he's wanted is for you to love him."

"What about you?" I ask. "He loves you. Do you love him?"

She rubs her lips together. "I think so."

"Kat," I warn her. "I know you do. And you haven't told him."

She shakes her head. "No. I think I'm afraid to."

"Why?" I frown.

"Because then he'll ask me to marry him."

I stiffen at that, a stab of jealousy between my ribs.

"And you don't want that . . . ," I say carefully.

She licks her lips. "Actually," she says. "I do want that."

I close my eyes in pain and she presses her palm to my cheek. "And I want that from you too. I want you both. And I don't know how I can have you both. If Crane asks me to marry him, I will say yes."

"And if I ask you first?" I open my eyes.

She stares at me and exhales.

"You'll have to say no," I answer my own question.

"You know why, Brom," she says imploringly.

Because of the horseman, the coven, the bargain.

"I know why," I tell her.

And it doesn't matter in the end anyway.

She belongs to us both, but in the end, there will only be Crane.

"Oh, look," Kat says, gazing past me at the roof.

I glance over my shoulder to see a swarm of blue and black butterflies flying just above the hole in the barn and watch as they slowly start to fly down inside toward us.

To my surprise they start landing on Kat's limbs, her hair, her face, then they do the same to me. She laughs, pure joy, and I join in too.

I make a promise to myself to never forget this.

*We took a* little more time in the barn then we should have, so once we got on our horses, we galloped the rest of the way back to the school. It was a freeing sort of ride, cool wind in my hair, the scent of fresh earth and bonfires and fallen leaves, the thunder of Daredevil's hooves underneath me, trying to beat the setting sun.

But I wasn't worried for a moment. With each day I am learning how to barter with the horseman more and more. Kat would be safe after sundown. Crane would be too. The horseman knows how important they are to me. He knows they are off-limits.

I drop Kat off at her dorm room, and then I hurry over through the mist to Crane's. At this point I don't care if anyone finds it suspicious how I head into the faculty dorm every night, then again, I feel everything about the school is in a slow collapse. Perhaps we're the least of its problems.

I get to his floor and Crane opens his door, stares at me in horror. "What happened?"

I frown and walk in his room. "Nothing. Sorry if I'm a few minutes late."

"No," he says, slamming the door shut and then grabbing me by the neck. "You have blood on your face." His eyes drift down. "On your clothes too. What did you do?" he growls, squeezing my neck tighter.

I have to try and think.

*Oh.*

Then I grin at him. "Nothing for you to worry about, Crane."

"Nothing for me to worry about? Whose blood is that?"

I'm smirking now. "Whose do you think?"

He narrows his eyes at me, and then it dawns on him.

"Fuck you," he snarls, pushing me over. "Can't keep your damn dick in your pants, can you?"

"You should talk."

"You know how dangerous this is," he snaps.

"This has nothing to do with some sacrifice or me knocking her up on behalf of a demon. You just don't want me inside her when you're not around."

"And so what of it?" he asks, throwing his arms out. "I told you I'd remain jealous and possessive through it all. The fact that you got to fuck her, lick her bloody cunt when she's at her most primal and powerful, yes, I'm damn jealous that it wasn't me."

I walk over to him and put my hands on his shoulders. "You want to kiss me now? You can probably still taste the blood."

"Fuck off," he sneers. But then that indignation in his eyes burns away to lust, just like I knew it would.

His eyes fall closed, and he leans in and captures my mouth in his, moaning slightly as his tongue licks the rim of my lips, slips past my tongue, and my toes are already bunching up in my boots.

Before we can get too carried away, he breaks the kiss and pulls back.

"I'm mad at you," he scowls.

But I know he can never stay mad for long.

# 28

## Crane

One week until the full moon," Kat says quietly as she places a stack of books on the desk that Brom and I have taken over in the library.

Brom grunts as his eyes flick over her, pausing at her chest and her lips. "Is this your way of saying you want to practice beforehand?"

I kick Brom under the desk, but he ignores it.

"Actually," she says, sitting down across from us, "as much as I enjoyed what we, uh, did in the woods during the dark moon, I think I would rather save myself for the next ritual. There's something about it, about the way the energy gathers, that I feel will be more powerful if we let it build up for a while. Like filling a reservoir."

"I'm inclined to agree with you," I say, tapping my fingers on the desk. "We should save ourselves."

Both she and Brom raise their brows and give me an incredulous look. "*You* think we should save ourselves?" Kat says.

I grin. "I mean, if you were adamant that you wanted to get under this desk and suck both our cocks at once, I wouldn't say no."

"Crane," she hisses, looking around her. "Keep your voice down."

"This might be one of those times you should use your *inside* voice, Crane," Brom suggests. "For the record, I also wouldn't say no."

"No one is paying us any attention," I assure them. And it's true. Though there aren't many students in the library, they're all staring listlessly at their books, some of them even asleep with their heads on the desks. Being a teacher, I'm used to seeing students studying until the point of exhaustion. In fact, that kind of devotion to academics usually warms my heart.

But this is different. This has nothing to do with studying. Something else is ailing these students, something linked to the sisters. But no matter how hard I think about it, I can't figure out *why* this might be happening.

"Crane!" I hear a deep voice yell, and I look over to see Daniels marching into the library, obviously agitated. He comes straight over to us, barely acknowledging either Brom or Kat. "Crane, I need to speak with you."

"Daniels, is everything all right?"

"No," he says. "I need to speak with you. Alone."

I shake my head. "Whatever you have to say to me you can say in front of them."

Daniels looks at Brom and Kat, as if for the first time. He frowns, and I know he's trying to figure out why these two are so special to me. But if he comes across the answer, it doesn't show on his rattled face.

"Last week you were asking after the history teacher, Ms. Wiltern. Why?"

I blink at him calmly. "Because she was teaching some things to her students that seemed off the books, so to speak, and I wanted to get some more information about it. I was merely curious, that's all."

"Well, she's gone," he says brusquely.

"Gone?" I say, sitting up straighter. "What do you mean?"

"I mean she's disappeared," he says, leaning on the desk and breathing hard, like he ran all the way over here. "And Ms. Peek too. Both are gone."

"Ms. Peek?" Kat says with a gasp, jolting in her seat. "What happened to her? I was just in her class the other day."

He takes his hat off his head and starts turning it around and around in his hands. "I don't know. I just don't know. But don't you see how strange this is? First Desi disappears. Then the girl jumps off the roof—"

"Jumped or fell?" Kat says, testing him.

"Jumped. I saw it. We all saw it. She jumped. Then the sisters tried lying to us all, the entire school, to pass it off as if it was an accident. No, ma'am. I know what happened. Now Ms. Wiltern and Ms. Peek are gone. Their rooms are untouched, all their belongings are there, but they're nowhere to be found."

"Do you know if Ms. Wiltern was feeling sick lately?" Brom asks.

Daniels shakes his head. "I have no idea. I barely talked to the woman. She always rebuked me when I did, but I certainly meant her no harm. So where did she go? Leaving all her papers here, not telling a soul?"

I bite my lower lip for a moment. "Have you told the sisters about your concerns?"

"Not yet, but I will," he says.

"Mmm, maybe think twice before doing that," I advise him.

"Why?"

I give him a steady look and lower my voice. "I don't think they're on our side, Daniels."

His chin jerks inward. "You mean to tell me that you think they have something to do with all of this?"

"And you don't?" I counter gently.

He grumbles, moving his mustache back and forth, and straightens up. "I'll tell you who I will talk to. The constable. The new one, who isn't missing a head."

"There's a new one already?" I ask.

"I'm sure there is," he says. "Someone has to protect Sleepy Hollow."

Then he turns around and marches out of the library in the same harried way he came in.

Someone has to protect Sleepy Hollow. But who is there to protect the school?

I sigh and lean back in my chair, running my hand over my face.

It's going to have to be me, isn't it?

*That night Kat* sneaks into my bedroom so the three of us can discuss our plan. With the full moon ritual a week away, we have to do everything we can to make sure it goes off without a hitch. The horseman must be expelled, and I know that with every day that passes, Brom becomes more and more attached to the spirit. Sometimes Brom goes completely silent and drifts off, but it's not his normal brooding way, it's like he's having a conversation inside his head and I have no clue what the horseman is saying to him. But I do know he'll lie to Brom to get what he wants, whatever that is.

"Kat," I say gently. "You said something the other day when you told us what Famke shared about your mother. You used the word 'siphoning.'"

It's a delicate subject because I believe Famke used it with regard to her father, so I don't want to say any more if it's going to make Kat uncomfortable.

Kat's sitting on the bed and leaning against the wall, an open book on her lap that's slowly sliding off. Her eyes have been closed for most of the last hour. It's getting late.

"Yes," she says, sitting up straighter. "She said, 'She takes what you're made of and uses it for herself until there's nothing left of you. She siphons your soul.' And somehow that's linked to her never seeming to age."

Brom grunts at that, and Kat looks down beside her where he's sprawled, face down on the pillow. "It's true," he says, lifting his head slightly. "The more I look back, the more I realize that Sarah has always looked exactly the same. When I was young I always thought she looked tired, but it was more than that."

I tap my fingers on the desk rapidly, urging my exhausted mind to be more useful.

"She's not a vampire," I say. "Female vampires all turn at age twenty-one and stay that way for life, and none of them look *tired*. So she must have some sort of immortality? But no, that doesn't make sense. From what Ms. Wiltern said, and what Leona said herself, immortality seemed something they were striving for. A part of the bargain. Goruun wouldn't give them that before he was given what they promised him."

"She's stealing other people's magic," Kat says. "She took my father's, and she wanted to take mine. I don't think she's immortal, but I think she's able to extend her life from the magic she takes. Maybe the sisters are the same way."

"The sisters are absolutely the same," Brom mumbles.

"How does one . . . siphon?" I ponder.

Kat shrugs, expression strained. "My father seemed to die of a heart attack. If she physically did anything to him, I couldn't see it."

I know it's hard for her to talk about it, so I try to change the subject off her father. "Have you ever felt strange around your mother?"

She lets out a caustic laugh. "Only all the time."

"You've never felt her try and take your magic before?"

"I've never shown her my magic . . ." She trails off, deep in thought. "Only once. The day she helped me move in. I was so exhausted after that, but I had every reason to be."

"Hmm," I mutter. I wonder if it's like the opposite of bestowal. Or what I taught in class the day that Lotte died. Like energy augmentation but different. Energy conversion?

"Kat, can you hand me that book?" I ask.

She picks up the one on her lap, and I lean over, taking it from her, and sit back in my seat, flipping through the pages, trying to find a section on energy.

Meanwhile, Brom adjusts himself on the bed, lifting his arm and hooking it over Kat's thigh, and slowly starts gathering up the hem of her dress.

I watch this from my seat at the desk, wanting to call out to him to stop distracting us like this, but I don't say anything. I just watch as he's gathered up enough fabric, and then slides his hand up her inner thigh.

Kat's gaze drops to where his hand has disappeared, his head still face down on the pillow. She swallows hard and shifts her hips just a little, opening her legs to him.

Fuck.

Now I don't want to watch anymore. Now I want to take part. I just don't know what part to fuck, Kat's mouth or Brom's ass.

I reach down over my crotch, my erection stiff and throbbing needlessly and—

*Thump.*

*Thump.*

*Thump.*

"Jesus," I swear under my breath. "Vivienne Henry, you have immaculate timing."

Brom immediately removes his hand and sits up, eyes wide with fear. Kat presses her hand to her chest. "That's *her*?" she whispers.

*Thump.*

*Thump.*

*Thump.*

Right outside the damn door.

I get up and grab the candlestick.

"You two stay here," I say, heading toward the door.

"And let you go out there alone?" Kat says, getting to her feet alongside Brom.

"I don't want to put you in any danger," I tell her.

"Your late wife tried to drown me in the bathtub," she points out. "I think I can manage."

I nod, feeling a little guilty over that, then I open the door to the hall.

"Wait," Brom whispers, and he runs over to the desk, coming back with the key brandished in his hand, the one that had been left behind with the dead snake. "We might need this."

"Good thinking," I tell him.

I poke my head out and look.

There's the trail of blood as usual, going past my door, and then the sight of Vivienne's feet being dragged around the corner.

"Oh my goodness," Kat gasps, her head below mine. "That's really . . . that's a ghost."

I step out into the hall, only then realizing I disturbed the line of salt I put around the room to keep the horseman contained.

"Do I need to keep you in chains?" I say to Brom.

He stares down at the salt and shakes his head. "He won't be a problem."

"You know I'm trusting you with our lives," I tell him grimly.

He swallows and gives me a single nod as he holds my gaze. "I know."

I believe him. I truly do.

But I don't trust the horseman.

I'll just have to keep a close eye on him. Part of me wants to run back into the room and grab the gun, but I'm afraid that will hurt Brom's own trust in me. So I don't.

I lock the door behind us, and then the three of us walk down the hall after the ghost, following the trail of blood. My heart is already racing and from the shallow, anxious breaths that Kat is taking, I know she's feeling the same. I reach down and grab her hand while I hold the candlestick with the other, perhaps more for my comfort than hers.

But this time the trail of blood doesn't lead to the women's wing.

Instead it goes down the stairs to the first floor.

And with a horribly uneasy feeling that makes my scalp prickle, I'm getting the sense that I've done this before.

We slowly go down the stairs, careful not to slip on the blood, and then follow the trail and the faint *thump*s as they go down a wing that holds a few classrooms.

One of the doors is wide open, the crimson path leading inside it.

"Where does that door go?" Kat whispers. "I thought that was just a closet. For the custodian."

I stop moving, the two of them running into my back.

"What is it?" Brom growls.

I shake my head, closing my eyes as I try to remember something.

"I think I've been here before," I say faintly. "I think I've done this before."

Was it a dream? Did I imagine it? Or did it actually happen?

"Well, if you did, nothing obviously happened to you," Kat says. "I think we should follow her."

I open my eyes and glance down at her in surprise. "If I didn't know any better, Kat, I'd think you were trying to paint me as a coward."

"It's just a ghost," she says with a frown, nodding toward the closet. "Come on."

"Gets haunted once, now she thinks she's an expert," I mutter to Brom, but he's already following Kat as they go after the bloody trail.

I exhale noisily and hurry after them.

They've stopped inside the barren closet, looking down a set of narrow stone stairs, the red glistening under the candlelight.

Yes. I have been here before.

I put my arm out, pushing them both behind me, the candle-stick shaking slightly in my grasp, and I carefully make my way down the steps, with Kat behind me and Brom bringing up the rear. By now I don't hear any more thumps from Ms. Henry, and I can't tell whether it's a good thing or a bad thing.

The staircase seems to twist and turn for a while, the air getting colder and more damp the farther we go down, the smell of sulfur and decaying vegetation and sage filling my nose, until finally my boots meet a floor made of hard-packed dirt.

"What is this?" Kat says as she and Brom fan out beside me.

We're in a tunnel, the candlelight casting flickering shadows on the dirt walls. They seem to glow red, as if soaked in blood, and the tunnel curves ahead, leading somewhere else.

I swallow uneasily.

"Yes," I say softly. "I've been here. There's a door around the corner."

"A door?" Brom asks, holding out the key. "Then Vivienne brought us here for a reason. What else do you remember?"

"I don't know. I never went in the door," I tell him. There's something else there too, but it's hidden somewhere in my mind.

"You didn't have the key," Brom says. "But you do now."

I nod, gathering up my courage, and start walking down the hall. It's narrow enough that the two of them follow me single file, and we round the corner to see a large iron door at the end. The dirt on the ground at the front of the door has been disturbed, indicating it opens outward, and perhaps recently, but it's hard to tell. If Vivienne came this way, her blood has already been absorbed by the ground.

I pause and press my ear to the cold metal, the stench of sulfur growing stronger. I feel like I had heard something when I was here before, someone inside wailing, crying out for me, but now I don't hear anything at all. I suppose that's a good thing.

Brom holds out the key and I take it from him.

Slip it into the old lock.

And turn.

With a heavy *click*, the key finds purchase, and the door unlocks.

"It worked," Kat gasps.

I was kind of hoping it wouldn't.

I leave the key in the hole and pull open the door. It's heavy, and it takes all my strength, plus Brom helping, for me to pull it open, the hinges groaning loudly.

The scent of decay wafts out of the darkness, causing all of us to cough.

"It smells like death," I manage to say, my eyes watering as I cover my nose with my forearm. "Let me guess, you still want to go inside?"

"Yes," Kat says, but her voice trembles.

Brom grabs the candle from me and steps forward.

Kat and I follow and look around.

The light doesn't go very far, but it doesn't need to.

I've seen enough.

We're in a long, oval-shaped room. Giant spiderwebs cover the walls, coming down from the ceiling and anchoring to the middle of the room. Though each web is empty, the strands look thick enough, and the webs are large enough, to support a spider the size of a pony.

And though there isn't much else in the room, there remain a few bones stuck to the strands. A rib here, a pelvis there, a shattered femur, a broken clavicle.

All human.

Dear God.

"What is this place?" Kat whispers.

I put my hand on her back in a vain attempt to comfort her, but I have no answers.

"I think we should leave," I say. "Right now. Before that door closes on us and locks us in here and whatever it is that is kept in this room comes out."

This time, no one wants to be the hero. All three of us turn and hurry out of the room and into the damp air of the tunnel.

Brom and I push against the door until it closes, and I quickly lock it, shoving the key into my pocket.

Then, without wasting any time, we leave the tunnel, go up the stairs, out of the custodian's closet and back into the hall, hoping the nightmare stays in the basement.

# 29

## Kat

None of us slept. After what we discovered in the basement of the building, the three of us went back to Crane's bedroom, locked the door, sprinkled more salt around the perimeter, and then waited for daylight. There was no chance that I would go back to my dorm room alone, not after that, so we did what we could to be comfortable. Crane gallantly gave me the bed and laid out his coat and towels on the floor for himself. Brom gladly took the bed with me, enjoying the sight of Crane beneath him.

But other than Brom holding me through the night, which I appreciated, we kept our hands to ourselves and talked the whole night through, trying to make sense of what we saw and why Vivienne Henry showed it to us.

We came to the same conclusion.

There's something awful in the basement.

Something that's been eating humans.

Those humans may or may not be the teachers that have gone

missing. They might be people procured from town, drifters in the area, or they might be students too, perhaps the ones who were sent home early on because they weren't cut out for the academics of the school, or so the sisters said.

Either way, the basement is a place you don't want to end up.

"And Simon," I say, my mouth tasting sour at the thought. "He said his mother lived in the basement. Do you think she was . . . in that room? Or are there other rooms, other basements? Did he have to visit his mother while she was hanging from a giant spiderweb?"

"For the sake of our sanity," Crane says, getting to his feet and peering out the window. "Let's assume there are other basements, ones that don't have giant spiders in them. The sun is almost up."

I groan, relieved that the day is breaking, but I'm so dizzyingly tired that I just want to sleep for days and days.

"Promise me," I say, leaning my head against the wall. "When Brom is free from the horseman and we leave this place, that we find an inn somewhere with the largest bed in the world, and we proceed to stay on that bed and sleep and have sex for days on end?"

Crane lets out a groan as he fixes his eyes on me. "That is music to my ears, sweet witch."

Brom, however, doesn't say anything. I turn my head to look at him beside me on the bed, and he's staring straight up at the ceiling. A cold finger of panic works its way down my spine. He hasn't been all right for a while now, and it's not just the horseman. Ever since our tryst in the barn he's been quieter and more despondent than usual.

Or maybe it is the horseman. Brom has always been mercurial, but who knows what it's truly like to live with someone else inside you?

"What do you say, Brom?" I ask, tapping his leg with mine.

"Mmm?" he says, blinking. "That sounds like heaven. As long as we can eat on the bed too."

"No crumbs," Crane grumbles as he stares down at Brom. "The only thing we'll be eating is Kat, and possibly my—"

A bloodcurdling scream fills the air, coming from outside.

Crane presses himself against the window as Brom and I spring out of bed.

"What is it?" I ask.

"I don't know," Crane says, eyes darting around the landscape.

He shoves away from the window, grabs his coat, and pulls out his boots, as Brom and I do the same. Then we hurry out of the room and into the hall. As we go down the wing toward the mezzanine, Crane pauses by an open door.

"Daniels?" Crane asks as he peers inside Professor Daniels's room. There doesn't seem to be anyone in there.

"I have a bad feeling about this," Crane mutters, and then quickens his pace as he strides to the mezzanine and down the stairs.

We burst outside into a dark gray mist and out into the courtyard where a couple of students have gathered.

There, in the middle of it, surrounded by a pool of blood, is a man in his pajamas.

Missing a head.

"Oh hell," I swear, covering my mouth in case I vomit, and turn around into Crane's chest. For all that the horseman has done, this is the first time I've actually seen one of his victims after they've been killed, and I don't think I have the stomach for it.

Crane puts an arm around me, holding me tight. "It's Daniels. It's Daniels," he says over again, sounding as if he's in shock. "The horseman killed Daniels."

I raise my head to look up at Crane, thinking the same thing he is, and then we both look over at Brom.

"I didn't do it," Brom says, raising his hands, shaking his head vigorously. "I swear to God, I swear, I didn't do it."

"The horseman did," Crane growls at him. "And you knew."

"No!" Brom says adamantly. "I did not. The whole night you were with me, you saw me, I didn't know what the horseman was doing, I don't know where he went." He gestures to Daniels's lifeless body. "This is not my doing. I had nothing to do with this."

The two other students nearby give Brom a curious look.

"Keep your voice down," I hiss at him.

"You have to believe me," Brom says, the anguish clearly visible in his dark eyes as he presses his palms together as if in prayer. "I didn't know anything about this. This wasn't me and I didn't know. I didn't know!"

Crane is breathing in deep through his nostrils, and I see the corner of his jaw flex, his pulse pounding at his throat, and I'm suddenly fearful of what he might do.

Then he lets go of me and marches toward Brom, whose fists clench in response.

Then Crane goes past Brom.

Heading in the direction of the cathedral.

"Where are you going?" I call out after Crane, gathering up my skirt and quickly running after him.

"I'm going to talk to the sisters," Crane yells over his shoulder. "This has gone on long enough. I should have done this a long time ago."

"Crane!" Brom calls out, running alongside me. "Don't draw attention to yourself!"

But it's too late because as we pass the classroom building beside the herb garden, Sister Sophie suddenly steps out in front of us.

"Mr. Crane," Sister Sophie says in a commanding voice, her hood down. "May I have a word with you?"

"No, I believe I'm going to have a word with you," he says, pivoting toward her.

Sister Sophie nods and looks around her, then motions with her hand for us to follow her as she disappears into one of the stone buildings that house the classrooms.

We go inside the front doors, the hallway dark except for the faint morning light coming in through the windows, and Crane springs into action, grabbing Sister Sophie by the throat and slamming her back against the wall.

"Crane!" I yell at him to stop, but Sophie just gives him a faint smile.

"I understand your frustration, Mr. Crane," she says, her voice sounding completely normal despite the fact that he's strangling her. "And to see your anger come out is a beautiful thing indeed. But I don't think you should kill me. I'm on your side, after all."

"Crane, let her go," Brom says in a gruff voice.

There's fire in Crane's eyes, not the usual inferno that I see in Brom's black depths, but something that's both white-hot and ice-cold. I don't think I've ever seen him this way. It's almost as if he's impossible to reach.

But then Crane's grip relaxes, and he lets go of Sophie. Her feet touch the floor, and it's only then that I realize he had her dangling in the air.

She clears her throat and adjusts her cloak at the collar.

"Do you feel better now?" she asks him in a clipped voice. "Was it helpful to get out your rage without killing another?"

"Go to hell," he says, spitting on the floor in front of her, his hair wild across his face.

"Charming," she comments with a curl of her upper lip. Then she looks at me. "And here we have Katrina." Then she looks at Brom, and her face visibly softens. "And, of course, our dear Abraham."

"I'm not your anything," Brom sneers at her.

"Hmm," she muses, her eyes flicking over us. "A den of vipers. I can't say I blame you for all that you've been through. Though I must let you know that you have been spared *so* much."

"What happened to Daniels?" Crane says, his eyes still flickering with anger. "What happened to Desi and Ms. Peek and Ms. Wiltern? To Vivienne Henry?"

"You're asking all the wrong questions, Mr. Crane," she says. "It's not about what happened to them. It's about what will happen to *you*. You, if you don't put your head down and continue doing what you were hired to do. To teach."

"And us," I say to her, pointing at Brom. "What is supposed to happen to us?"

She gives me a tight smile. "You know what will happen to you, Katrina. It's written in the stars. Your fate was decided a long time ago. In 1695, to be specific."

"You were part of the original coven," Brom says to her. "You made the deal with the demon. You were there."

"My dear Abraham," she says, walking toward him. He stands his ground as she puts the back of her hand against his cheek. "I never wanted this. I never wanted any of this. I hated Leona and Ana with a passion. It was Margaret who agreed to the bargain with them. I never would have sacrificed one of my sons if I had the choice. But I had no choice. I am no match for a demon. For a god."

"One of your . . . ," Crane begins. "Are you Brom's real mother?"

She gives Crane a tired look. "I have had many sons, Mr. Crane." Then she sighs and gazes at Brom. "And Abraham is my last one. *No longer shall your name be called Abram, but your name shall be Abraham, for I have made you the father of a multitude of nations*," she quotes.

"You're quoting the Bible now?" Crane asks with a shake of his head.

She shrugs with one shoulder. "I thought it was a fitting name, given that he was the coven's last chance to sire our immortality, the nations of witches."

"Just wait a minute," Brom says. "Are you saying that my father is actually my brother?"

Sister Sophie's eyes dance. "Your father is your cousin. He is

Margaret's son. And you wouldn't even be in this predicament had Sarah married Liam like she was supposed to."

"Technically he wouldn't have been born," Crane points out.

"So my mother was supposed to marry Liam, and they were supposed to have the child given to Goruun," I say. "Is that correct?"

"Yes," she says flatly. "But your mother is selfish. She chose your father because she wanted to use his energy to keep herself alive. Liam and your mother should have birthed the child, it should have been Liam who was disposed of after the sacrifice, not my dear Abraham."

I inhale sharply, and Brom's eyes widen. "You're planning to dispose of me?" he asks, as if he's taking it personally.

"I'm not," she says in a rush, her hands pressed against his chest. "I am trying to help you. You don't have much time left before they put their plan into action. It's imperative that you leave now while you still can. Leave the school, and leave Sleepy Hollow."

"We can't," Crane says grimly. "Not with the horseman attached to him. The minute we're gone, they'd know. We wouldn't get very far, would we?"

She presses her pinched mouth together and shakes her head. "No, you wouldn't."

"I didn't kill Daniels," Brom protests.

"I know you didn't," she says. "They called on the horseman last night to do their bidding, to get rid of Daniels for what he was about to do. They can call on the Hessian at any time. And until he is exorcised from you, he can call on you. You must complete a ritual to drive him from your soul."

"We've been trying," I tell her. "It didn't work."

"Blood magic and sex magic," Crane divulges.

She thinks that over for a moment. "It needs to be under the full moon. In a body of water, so that at least part of you is submerged. The lake is a particularly potent nexus, and blood and sex magic are particularly good anchors. You might want an elixir of the veil to help open yourself to the spirits."

Crane's face is going red with restraint. I can tell he's trying to hold himself back so he doesn't interrupt Sister Sophie and tell her that he already knows everything she's saying.

"And you must bring someone to the brink of death," she adds. "The one you have chosen as a vessel."

Crane's face goes slack. "Brink of death?"

Brink of death, and I'm the vessel.

She nods and looks at me. "It will be you, Katrina, I'm sure. You won't die, of course. That would be counteractive. But by going to the edge of death and back, you are flirting with the veil. You are drawing power not just from your men but directly from the veil itself. You are bringing that light at the end of the tunnel directly to you."

She clears her throat and raises her chin. "Now, I'm not one to advise how one's sexual activities must commence. But if I were you, I think strangulation would be your best option. Of course, you have to know what you're doing." She looks at Crane as she says that. "And you, of course, do. Your talent for control might come in very handy."

Suddenly, movement outside the windows catches Sophie's attention, and she moves to them.

"The other sisters are out there now," she says, looking outside. "Soon they will wonder where I am. I must go."

"Wait," I say, reaching out and putting my hand on her arm. "What are we supposed to do until the ritual?"

"Lie low," she says, looking each of us in the eyes. "Stay out of trouble. Hide away when you can. They will continue to plan your binding ritual—"

"What binding ritual?" Crane interjects, anger flaring in his eyes again.

"The one between Abraham and Katrina," she says patiently. "They know by now that these two aren't falling for each other, not in the way they want. And they know you've inserted yourself into the picture, Mr. Crane, further complicating things. On Samhain, they plan to drug Katrina and use the horseman to take over Abraham fully. I don't need to tell you what will happen next."

A sickly feeling spreads across my stomach as I eye Brom briefly. Thankfully he looks as appalled as I do.

"And after the child is born, well, Katrina, you'll be joining our dear Abraham in death. Which is why your ritual is so important," she says. "Now if you'll excuse me, I am sure this is the last time I'll get to talk to you three." Her jaw flexes and the smallest hint of emotion comes into her strange, ancient eyes. "Please, just complete the ritual and expel the horseman. I will do what I can on my end to protect you and help in the matter, but I'm afraid it might not be enough. The power of one is nothing compared to the power of three."

Then she turns and walks toward the doors, her cloak flowing behind her.

"Sister Sophie!" I cry out, and she pauses and turns, her hand on the knob. "We went into the basement, under the faculty dorm. What happens in the basement?"

She gives me a sour smile. "It's where we keep our most promising candidates."

Then she opens the door and steps out into the morning.

I look at Brom and Crane, and both of them start to blur. "I think I'm going to faint," I mumble.

They both come over and wrap their arms around me, Brom from behind, Crane from the front. I bury my head in Crane's chest and let them hold me.

"We've got you," Crane whispers against my head. "We won't let anything happen to you. You know we won't."

"We'll die before that happens," Brom says hoarsely, and I hate how much he sounds like he means it.

"I'm scared," I mumble into Crane. "I'm so scared."

"I'd be lying if I said I wasn't too," Crane admits. "But fear is just something else we have to live with right now. Just like jealousy, just like rage, it's another figure in our lives that we'll get used to. The best part about fear though? It keeps you alive."

The three of us stand in the hall for a while, all of us trying to make sense of what Sophie told us, what we have to prepare for. We hold on to each other, seeking comfort, and the sound of three hearts beating is like a balm for all the fear.

Finally, we break apart and Crane grabs both of our hands. "We need to go out there," he says. "I know Sophie said to stay low, but it would look odd if we, the nosiest people on campus, weren't out there and gawking at a dead body."

I nod. "Perhaps we should go into town after and raise the

alarm with the new constable. Or try the police in Pleasantville again. Maybe even Tarrytown."

"That sounds like an excellent plan," Crane concedes, to my relief. "It's possible that if we can prove enough to have the school under suspicion, maybe we can have the sisters detained, or at least investigated. That will buy us some more time."

He doesn't have to say the next part.

It will buy us more time in case the next ritual fails.

But I can't think about that, not now, not if I want to get through the day.

Buoyed by the idea of going straight to the police, the three of us leave the building together and walk across the courtyard to where the headless Daniels is lying in a pool of blood that reflects the hazy morning sun. By now a crowd has formed around him, many students and teachers crying and holding on to each other, like a repeat of when Lotte killed herself. Except now it feels different. Now among the tears, there is terror. People are terrified that this is going to happen to them next.

They're starting to fear the school.

Sister Leona stands at the base of Daniels's body, with Ana and Margaret right behind her. Sophie is there too, but off to the side a little, as if she doesn't want to be associated with them, her hood pulled tightly.

"I know you're all worried about what has happened here," Leona says, her voice projecting. "But I can assure you that no matter what, we will get to the bottom of this travesty."

"It's the headless horseman!" someone in the crowd cries out. "He's been killing everyone."

"There is a vengeful spirit known as the Hessian soldier,"

Leona concedes with a nod. "And we are aware of what he is capable of. The horseman should not be able to get through our wards, however, so it is hard to say who exactly has committed this crime."

So many lies.

"What about the other missing teachers?" someone else says.

"We are still investigating what has happened to them," Leona goes on. "It is too early to tell. But for now, I can promise you that we will solve these mysteries, and we will do our best to keep you all safe."

She looks around at everyone in the crowd, then focuses on me, on Brom, on Crane.

"As of this moment forward, the wards have been activated to full power, and the school is on lockdown," she announces. "Until we solve this, no one is coming in. And no one is going out."

# 30

## Kat

We've been under lockdown for nearly one week so far and, surprisingly, the school doesn't feel that different from normal, other than the tension that seems to wrap around the campus and the fear and strain on everyone's faces. Those things were always there, I just don't think anyone was aware of it until now.

Normally I wouldn't have felt the urge to leave at all—I wasn't about to have supper at my mother's again—but I had wanted to head into Sleepy Hollow, Pleasantville, and Tarrytown to talk to the police. I think Leona suspected that was what Daniels had wanted to do (and anyone else who started to think that there was more to the institute than what meets the eye).

But even if the students and teachers could leave, they wouldn't remember why they were fleeing from the school. They wouldn't remember any of the deaths, or the missing teachers, or strange goings-on. Though I suppose the sisters don't want to take that chance. If Brom, Crane, and I can recall, there's a chance others can too.

"Are you all right? Have you eaten?" Crane asks, putting his hand on my cheek. Despite the lockdown, service at the dining hall has remained the same, and the school's food supplies haven't been cut off—yet.

I close my eyes and press against his palm for comfort. "I haven't been hungry," I tell him. "And I have a feeling that I shouldn't eat before the ritual."

It's the late afternoon on the day of the full moon, and we're sitting in the library with Brom, trying to do some last-minute preparations. We're the only ones in here. Even the librarian is gone, though we don't know if she's disappeared or if she's just given up. Everyone is acting like they're walking on a tightrope. I'm amazed that classes are still in session during the lockdown, especially as no one is paying attention in them.

Unless they're in Crane's class, of course. This last week he has been turning every one of his classes into seminars on self-defense. All of us students have learned how to take someone else's power from them and use it for our own, how to block our magic and energy from being used by others, and how to deepen the skills we already have.

For me, I was able to dive deeper into shadow magic, rendering myself invisible when in the dark, and I was also able to turn my ability to conjure flames into a weapon I can throw, which was quite fun, and resulted in setting one student's homework on fire. Even Brom, with his lack of magical ability, was able to borrow Crane's voice, just for a moment.

But despite all the work spent on mastering our magic in the name of self-defense, I still feel woefully unprepared for tonight.

Brom looks up from his book and stares out the large windows. "Sun will set in an hour. When should we head to the lake?"

My nerves dance inside my chest, my pulse quickening at the thought. I need to be able to keep it together or I'll be a complete wreck by the time the moon comes out.

"As soon as it gets dark," Crane says. "Dark enough that we can't see anything—and others can't see us. We'll go to the lakeside and set up. As soon as the moon rises enough that it's reflected on the lake's surface, then we start."

Crane then gives me a long, searching look, rubbing his lips together, and I can tell what he wants to ask me. He wants to ask me if I want to go through with it again, he wants to tell me it's not too late to back out. But he can't bring himself to say it because it *is* too late to back out.

If I don't do this, we lose Brom to the horseman.

If I don't do this, we all lose our lives.

So I just give him a nod, letting him know that I'm in it until the end.

We stay in the library for another hour, until the sun turns gold, choked out by the mist, and twilight descends. Then we gather up our books and swing by Crane's room, where he grabs the sterile knives; the vials of sunflower oil, healing poultice, and the elixirs; a dozen crystal towers; plus the bottle of laudanum. I shouldn't be shocked that the bottle is half-finished already.

"You should take a bath," Crane says to me.

I frown and press my nose to my shoulder, inhaling. I had taken one this morning. "Why, do I stink?"

He gives me an adorable grin. "No. But I think a clarifying bath might help prep your body for the ritual. Allow me."

He goes into the washroom and starts drawing a bath. He brings out a couple of jars filled with salt and dried herbs and flower petals and dumps them in the water, then gathers up a few quartz and tourmaline palm stones and tosses them in the water too, where they land with a splash.

I want to conserve my energy so I don't heat the bath further with my magic, so I take off my clothes and step into the luke-warm water. It still feels like heaven, the salt invigorating me, the floating rose and hydrangea petals and various herbs swirling around me like a watercolor painting.

Brom and Crane are staring at me with desire burning in their eyes. They're already in their robes, naked underneath, and I can see how visibly aroused they are, even though both of them know they can't touch me until the ceremony. But I won't let them leave the bathroom since I don't want to be alone in here, not after what Marie did.

"You do enjoy torturing us," Crane murmurs as I seductively run the soap over my breasts, my nipples hardening under my touch and under their gaze.

I grin at him, teasing, and for a moment it feels like it's just me and the two people most important to me, that there's nothing outside these walls, that there's no ritual to perform, no co-ven of witches who want to use and destroy us, no imminent threat of death.

But I can't pretend for long. Once I feel cleansed and invigorated, I get out of the bath, both men toweling me off like I'm some goddess or queen in the ancient times, and I step into the robe.

We all look at each other and nod.

It is time.

Crane grabs his kit, and we head out into the hall and into the night, the grass cool on our bare feet.

The moon hasn't risen above the trees yet, but there's still enough light for our eyes to adjust as we make our way down to the edge of the lake. Crane had already scouted the perfect spot the other day, near where the wall leads from the shore to the front gates. We're still in the school's perimeter, but we're at the farthest point away from prying eyes and as far as possible from the cathedral. It helps that the shore is softer here, dirt and mud instead of pebbles.

"We obviously can't do a circle of salt if we're going to be in the water," Crane says as he puts down the bag on the shore and surveys the area. "But I will create a pentangle using the crystals, pushing them down into the mud. That should help with some protection."

"Maybe the circle was what prevented it from working last time," I say to Crane. "Maybe we need those from the veil to step inside the circle and come closer."

He gives me a sharp look. "Be careful what you ask for, sweet witch."

Then he drops the robe so that he's completely naked, shivering slightly from the cold, and goes about gathering his quartz towers from his bag, wading ankle-deep into the water, and pushing the sharp ends into the bottom at five points.

"Sister Sophie said to have parts of us submerged, but I don't think we need to go any deeper than this," he says, turning around to face us when he's done. His erection is impressive despite how cold the night is.

"Always ready to go," Brom comments under his breath.

"Enough talking from you, pretty boy," Crane says. "Strip."

Brom dutifully drops his robe, and I do the same, knowing that Crane was going to tell me next. The air really is cold, goose bumps covering my skin, the kind of chill that comes with a partially clear sky in late autumn, the first hint of the winter to come.

I find myself wondering if it's going to be a cold, hard winter this year like it was last year. Then I have to stop myself because I don't even know if I'll be here in the winter, in any winter. What happens if the ritual doesn't work and I'm captured on Samhain? What if they force Brom to impregnate me? Where will they keep me while I'm pregnant? In the basement? Will I have what it takes to fight against it, even if it means ending my own life?

"Kat," Crane says quietly, and I look over to see Brom beside him, naked, standing ankle-deep in the water. "Would you mind grabbing the elixirs and the knives?"

I nod, trying to take in a deep, steadying breath, then go over to his kit and grab them. I walk into the lake, the water's chill biting my ankles, and then stop beside them in the middle of the crystal pentangle.

"Better to do this right away," Crane says, taking the vial from me. We all pop the corks off them and pour the potion down our throats. Like before, it tastes awful, making me shudder.

"How do you want us to do this?" Brom asks Crane after

we've tossed the vials back on shore and they take the knives from me. He eyes me. "Do you want us to warm up Kat first?"

"Why don't we switch it around this time," I tell them as I drop down to my knees in the water. I reach for their cocks with both hands, staring up at them just as the big orange moon begins to rise over the treetops. The way the moon shines on me, their manhood in my hands, makes me feel utterly sensual and terribly powerful.

"Careful, my *vlinder*," Crane says, gritting his teeth together as he stares down at me. "As if your teasing earlier wasn't enough."

"Who says I'm teasing this time?" I ask before I part my lips and slide Crane's cock through my lips, gripping him firmly, while in my other hand I glide my fingers over the pearls of arousal at Brom's tip, spreading it down his length.

Both men groan in unison, Crane's sounding like a hiss through his teeth, Brom's low and guttural, and the sound shoots waves of pleasure through me, and suddenly I don't even feel cold anymore.

"Fuck," Crane swears, his hand in my hair as I suck and lick and do everything he likes, enough so that he keeps thrusting his cock further down my throat. "You take me so well, sweet witch." His fist tightens in my hair. "I don't feel right not sharing it."

Crane pulls my head away from his cock, a line of saliva connecting my lips to his flat crown, then brings me over to Brom's. Always in control, to the end.

Brom thrusts his cock into my mouth, and they take turns, back and forth, thrusting into my mouth, the wet sounds of both cocks sliding against my tongue mixing with their heavy breathing, the weight of their intense gaze.

"I don't know if I can hold on much longer," Brom grunts, his hand in my hair, pumping deep inside my throat, and I know if I don't slow them down, they'll both come here and now.

"Kat," Crane groans. "As much as I hate telling you to stop, go and grab the oil, sweet girl. We'll need it."

I have just enough sense to do as he says, letting go of their cocks and going back on shore to get the sunflower oil. When I turn around to face them, their gazes on me feel like being pinned in place by two top predators whose only instincts are to eat and to mate.

I go back into the lake, and already things are different from last time. I don't know if the elixir is working faster or if it's the full moon or the lake itself speeding things up, but when I look past them, I see dark, gruesome figures hovering in the water.

No, not just hovering.

Coming closer.

No salt circle to stop them.

"Uh," I say, nodding past them, trying to ignore the fear prickling my skin. "It seems we have visitors already."

Crane tears his eyes away from me and looks at the shadows approaching us.

"Ignore them," Crane says. "Even if you feel them touch you."

"They're able to touch me?" I exclaim in horror.

"They can't hurt you," he says, his eyes gleaming as he takes the oil and pours it all over Brom's twitching erection. Brom lets out a gasp that turns into a groan.

"Turn around," Crane says to me next. "Bend over." His voice is calm but clinical, and yet, somehow, that helps with the fear and absurdity of all of this.

I do as he says, and he puts one hand on my hip, the other going between the cheeks of my rear, liberally applying the oil there.

"Where's the romance, Crane?" I ask him, my body shuddering at the press of his slick finger.

"You'll feel it when you come with both of our cocks inside you," he says, then lays a large slap across my bottom, making me almost topple over in the water. "Now drop to your knees again and hold still. This is going to hurt."

I go to my knees, the water splashing around us, doing my best to ignore the approaching ghosts, keeping my focus on the surface of the lake and the reflected orange moon.

Crane holds one of my arms and brings his knife down over the fattest part at the back of my bicep. I want to cry out, to scream at the pain as the cut opens and blood runs down my arm, but I know it would only draw attention to us. Then Brom grabs my other arm and makes a cut in the same place, then they use their knives on themselves, cutting open their palms like before, though they do it to each hand now.

"One more, sweet witch," Crane says to me, his voice low and grave. "Then the pain will end. There will only be pleasure."

I suck in a breath, tears burning the corners of my eyes as I try to hold back my cries, try to handle the pain that's coursing through me. Crane tips my head back with his fingers and then takes his knife and makes two quick slashes across the tops of my breasts. There's no careful precision this time, and though his movements are skilled and confident, they speak to what's happening right now.

The desperation in the ritual.

The fact that we're running out of time.

And how everything, *everything*, rides on this.

He brings his fingers away from my chin, and I glance down at my chest as the blood runs over my breasts in rivulets, dripping into the dark lake.

"Brom," Crane says, and his voice doesn't sound as steady as it normally does. "Lie down on your back in the water. As shallow as possible so that no one is drowning."

I look up to see Brom's jaw clench, but he does what Crane says, lying back in only a couple of inches of water. Beyond Brom, the dark creatures lurk closer, their hands outstretched toward us, and I don't know how I'm going to survive this without dying of fright.

"Close your eyes, Kat," Crane tells me in a deep voice. "You don't have to watch this, you only have to feel it." He reaches down and places his hand at my waist. "Lie down with your back on top of Brom. Spread your legs like a good witch."

I swallow hard and do what he says, even though it feels immeasurably awkward until my back is flush against Brom's hot, firm chest, his hair tickling me. Brom reaches down, his hand sliding under my rear until he's grabbing hold of his cock and pushing it up toward me.

"He's going to enter you from behind," Crane says as he gets down with us, straddling our hips. "I'm going to claim your cunt," he says, his voice a throaty whisper now. "I'll control when we all come. I'll begin chanting the spell, then I'll start applying pressure to your neck."

My eyes widen. I had forgotten that part.

"Wait, the pressure, you're still—you're going to try and kill me?"

"Bring you to the edge of death," he says gravely, his eyes dark and hard. "I won't push you over, Kat, you know I won't. I'll apply just enough pressure on the sides of your windpipe, but the moment I feel you start to go limp, I'll let go and you'll breathe again."

I'm terrified.

"Okay," I say quietly, having to put all my trust, my life, into Crane's hands. And I do trust him, with everything, but it doesn't stop the fear from snaking through me, making my heart run a mile a minute.

And that fear quickly turns to pain as Brom starts pushing the head of his cock against my entrance at the back, the thick head of him oiled and shoving inside me in the most slow and agonizing way. I start squirming on top of him, trying to escape the pressure, but he grabs my arms, the blood from his palms mixing with mine, and holds me in place.

Then Crane's long lean body looms over me, positioning the lewd, long length of his cock between my legs, and he starts pushing into my cunt.

I cry out, my back arching, trying to move, but with Brom holding me in place from behind and Crane pressing down on me from the front, I'm trapped between them like a firefly in a jar.

"Stay still, my *vlinder*," Crane says through a stifled groan as he pushes inside. "Stay still." His head drops down, the muscles in his arms straining. "Oh, fuck, Brom, I can feel you inside her. She's so tight."

Brom grunts in my ear, then runs his lips down the rim. "Relax, Daffy," he says breathlessly. "You can take us both. Relax. We've got you."

Brom then brings his mouth to my neck and starts to suck and bite at my skin, his beard scratching me, his hands moving down from my arms and to my waist, taking a hold of me there. "That's it, Kat. Oh, sweetheart, you feel so good," he whispers hoarsely. "Fuck, I love you. I love you so much."

That's enough for Crane to raise his head and spear Brom with his gaze as he pushes in to the hilt. I gasp, the air pushed out of my throat, while Brom whimpers with need.

"Why do you sound like you're saying goodbye, Brom?" Crane warns him. "Stay with me, pretty boy. You stay with us. Keep fucking our sweet witch, yes, just like that."

Crane starts to move deeper and harder inside me, and Brom starts thrusting up my ass in unison, and I let myself go. I let go of the fear, of the terror of the shadowed faces that have gathered around us, of the idea that this might not work, of the horror that I might lose these men, of the panic that lies in bringing me so close to death that I'll be able to taste it.

"That's it," Brom rasps against me, kissing my shoulder, my neck, the side of my cheek. "Yes, oh fuck. Kat, Kat, you're doing so good."

"Such a good witch," Crane murmurs as he continues to drive his hips against mine, so hard I think he's leaving bruises, his cock going in deeper each time until all I feel is them, all I am is these two feral men inside me, both loving me and fighting over me. Fighting *for* me.

"Not much longer," Crane groans, and he leans in and down, his chest pressed against mine, his mouth crashing over my mouth. He pulls me into a deep, intoxicating kiss that feels like it's infiltrating every part of my body until I'm dying for more, my hunger insatiable now.

Then he pulls away, wet and messy, and brings his head down over my shoulder and starts kissing Brom, just as hard and wild. I hear their shaking exhales, their soft moans, and I bite Crane's shoulder, wanting a piece of him still, my fingernails digging into his smooth, muscular back. The three of us move in unison now, writhing together in the water like the unholiest of creatures.

One body, one beating heart, one damned soul.

"It's time," Crane whispers thickly, pulling back enough to wrap his hand around my neck, squeezing on either side of my throat with his fingers and the heel of his palm. I stare up at him, unable to look away from the fervent storm in his eyes, and while he applies the pressure to my neck, he starts reciting the spell, the same strange low words from the ritual before.

*Stay with me, Kat,* Crane says inside my head, though his lips are still moving, still chanting the foreign incantation. *Stay with me even when it seems like I disappear.*

I try to nod but I can't. I can't breathe. Already my vision is going gray and fuzzy at the corners, dots appearing in the middle between us. I see Crane and then I don't really see him anymore and the world starts to slip away as my lungs burn and I start to panic.

Then the *hands* come.

Dozens of hands.

They reach up over me, cold as sin, and grab my ankles, my calves, my thighs. They dig their long fingers into my hands, my arms, my head.

They are the dead and they want me.

They're going to take me away right when I'm held between the two men that I love.

"Make her come, pretty boy."

The voice sounds far away, it sounds like it belongs to another time, another place. All I feel are the cold hands wanting to drag me down into the grave, the panic of not being able to breathe starting to fade into nothingness and peace.

"She's gone limp, Crane," the other voice cries out. "Save her, save her."

Suddenly I feel a hard slap against me. Then another.

A mix of pleasure and pain.

Someone has slapped my breasts.

I'm still alive.

The hands start to release me.

The cold leaves me.

Death lets go.

Warmth floods back inside my body.

Heat goes right between my legs where Brom is rubbing my clit to the point of no return.

I gasp for air, my chest heaving, my back bowing off Brom, and I'm staring right into Crane's relieved face, all oxygen surging back into my lungs, my veins, my cells, my body ablaze with light, and then I'm coming.

"Oh God!" I cry out, the sound torn out of me, the orgasm hitting me so hard that I fear I might break my bones. The water is sloshing around us as both Crane and Brom pump into me, their movements synced, from their thrusts, to the pulse of their cocks as they spill their seed inside me, to their quick, shallow breaths.

And then it's all over. Brom sinks farther into the lake, while my head falls back, angled over his shoulder so that my hair swirls in the water, and Crane lowers himself on top of us, bracing most of his weight on his elbows in the mud.

We lie there for a minute, maybe more, trying to breathe, and I'm lost to the feeling of their two bodies pressed on either side of me, their two cocks still inside. I can feel their seed leak out between my legs, and as before, in the forest, I feel like I've captured lightning in a bottle. I've never felt more exhilarated. Never felt more alive.

But as much as I feel our collective energy burning inside us like a captured sun ray, I know that this union, this ritual, had a purpose.

"Did it work?" I whisper, staring up at the patches of fog that flirt around the moon.

There is no answer. Crane lifts up his head and meets my eyes with a quizzical expression, then looks past me at Brom.

"Did it work?" Crane asks him, his voice demanding.

Brom tenses beneath me, then moves, his cock sliding out. He stands up, causing water to splash on me as my back hits the bottom.

He stares down at me and Crane.

"No, it didn't," he says bluntly.

Then he starts walking to shore.

Crane eyes me, that cold inferno burning inside him again, and he gets to his feet, following Brom. I sit up in the water, trying to ignore all the shadowy figures around us still, to see Crane grabbing Brom's arm and pulling him to a vicious stop.

"What do you mean it didn't work?"

"I said it didn't work," Brom says through a scowl.

"Why not?" Crane cries out, throwing his arms up, practically whining. "Why the hell not, we did everything right this time!"

"Maybe because I don't want it to," Brom says, and he grabs his robe, pulling it on.

"You don't want it to!" I exclaim, staggering to my feet and sloshing through the water toward them. "What are you talking about? Brom, you know we need to do this. We need to save you."

"And maybe you can't save me!" Brom yells. "Did you ever think of that? Did you ever think that maybe you couldn't even save me to begin with, that this was out of your so-called expertise?"

I glance at Crane. I don't think I've ever seen him look so hurt.

"Why would you think that?" Crane says softly.

"Because it's true!" Brom roars, the vein on his forehead protruding. "This is beyond what you can do, Ichabod Crane. I have a damn spirit attached to me, and the reason he won't let go is because I've never been more than the devil's spawn! Don't you see? Don't you understand? I'm the product of evil, and we finally have the proof. I was born to be a soldier in a demon's war."

"Brom," I say, my heart breaking at his words. I put my hands on his arms but he just yanks them up, knocking me away.

"You know it," he says, panting. "You know I'm a hopeless cause. I always have been. But the horseman, I know I can get through to him. I have evil in my veins, but I have no power. I am a product of ancient witches, but I have no magic. But he does. He can protect me, and he can protect *you*."

Crane tries to get closer to him, his palms splayed as if trying to calm a skittish horse. "He tells you lies, Brom. Whatever the Hessian is making you believe, it isn't true. This is what they want. The coven wants you, and they're using the horseman to control you. Nothing you do or say will be enough to convince the spirit to go to your side. He's bound to them, not you."

"And for once," Brom says with a bitter laugh, shaking his head. "For once, Crane, you know nothing! But it doesn't matter, it truly doesn't. Because I'll prove you wrong. I'll prove the both of you wrong. You want the horseman expelled from my body because you fear who I'll become once I finally have power. Once I'm finally equal with the both of you. You like keeping me beneath you, under your fucking thumb!" He yells that last part, jabbing his finger into Crane's chest, his eyes so black and wild. "You know it's true."

Crane is speechless. He swallows hard as he searches Brom's face. "You've always had power, Brom. Over Kat, over me. You hold our hearts in your hand. What more power do you want?"

"The power to protect you," he growls, looking to me now. "The power to actually fight back. I'm not going to let go of that, not now with our lives on the line. You can yell at me, you can feel betrayed, you can call me whatever fucking name you want, but the truth is, I am better off with the horseman inside me. And you're better off too."

"Brom," Crane says, trying to grab him, but Brom shrugs him off.

"Leave me alone," he growls, storming toward the buildings.

Crane makes a move to go after him but I run over and grab his arm, pulling him back.

"Let him go," I tell him.

Crane gives me an incredulous look, his mouth parted in disbelief. "I can't let him go."

"I know you can't," I tell him, holding him harder. "And I'm not letting go of him either. But for tonight, I think we must. We have to let him have time to think."

"We can't afford to give him time to think," he says, brow crinkled. "Kat, we need to do the ritual again. You heard what Sister Sophie said."

"I did. And you know you can't force him. You can tie him up, gagged and bound in chains, but you can't force Brom to do anything he doesn't want to do. That's how you approach things, Crane. With force and control, but not everything works like that. Brom has to be allowed to come to this decision on his own."

He stares at me, blinking. "You're taking his side."

"I'm not taking his side. There are no sides here. I just know Brom better than you do, sorry to say, but it's true. And the more you corner him, the more you push him, the further he will run. Running away is his default, don't you see that now? And, right now, he's trying to do his best by us and for us, even though it doesn't seem like it. He wants to protect us because he loves us and thinks the horseman gives him the best shot."

"But he's wrong," Crane says despondently, looking out at the darkness where Brom disappeared.

"And maybe he is wrong," I say. "But as much as we both hate it, he has to find that out for himself." I pause. "There's also a slight possibility that *you're* wrong."

Crane looks at me as if I slapped him.

I shrug and let go of his arm, gathering up my robe as the cold starts to creep in. "I'm sure it happens to you from time to time."

He presses his lips together, the wheels turning in his head, and then he looks back out over the lake. "Well, it feels a little embarrassing to have had this failed ritual and lover's spat in front of all these dead people."

I follow his gaze. The shadowy figures are only a few feet away, staring at us with ravenous eyes and gaping mouths, and I have to immediately look back at Crane. "How long until the elixir wears off?"

He reaches down and grabs my hand. "Not soon enough."

# 31

Crane

I quickly gather up all the items I brought out for the ritual, stuff them back inside my satchel, and then pull Kat up toward the faculty dorms. The elixir will take time to wear off but I can put a circle of salt inside my room, ensuring it's a dead-person-free zone. It will at least prevent us from seeing the shapes beyond the veil until the drug fades.

As we walk into the building, I'm so angry I'm beside myself with it. But it's not the usual anger that leads to rage and unwanted consequences. It's a different kind of anger. It's not directed just at Brom, it's also directed at myself, as well as the coven. It's a helpless anger, the kind where you know that letting it out won't make a lick of difference, and that there's nothing you can do to prevent it. It just exists, it just is what it is.

I just feel like such a bloody fool. I should have seen this coming, should have picked up on the many, many times that Brom hinted that he liked the horseman, that he thought he had a special bond with him, that he thought he could control him. I never actually thought he would find himself so attached that he wouldn't want to expel him at all, especially when he knew, he *knew*, exactly what was at stake.

His own life and Kat's.

"He's playing with fire," I mutter as I unlock the door to my room and usher Kat inside. "He doesn't know what he's doing."

"He'll come around," Kat says simply, and it's enough to make me slam the door so hard it nearly comes off the hinges.

"Come around!" I yell at her, unable to keep my fear at bay. "There is no time, Kat! The coven is going to drug you, they're going to take over Brom with the horseman, and that's it. There's no time for Brom to figure this out on his own."

"I know!" she yells back, her eyes blazing, wet hair hanging around her shoulders. "I know there's no time, but what do you want me to do? What do you want me to say?"

I shake my head, my chest feeling like it's caving in on itself. "We're going to lose him, sweet witch," I whisper, the realization eating me alive. "We're going to lose him."

Her jaw goes tight, her eyes widening. "No. We won't. I won't stop believing in him, even if you do."

I stare at her for a moment, at how much she's changed in such a short time. Though her face is still round, sweet, and angelic, she's no longer delicate. There's a toughness in her blue eyes, there's a ferocity in the way she holds her mouth, there's resolve in the set of her jaw. She's no longer just a student of mine, she's my equal and more. She can teach *me*. I used to think she was more powerful than she ever knew, but I'm starting to suspect she finally knows it.

"I won't stop believing in him," I say, coming over to her and putting her beautiful face in my hands. "Because you won't. But until he comes around, I can't take any chances. I am going to have to do everything I can to protect you, and I mean everything."

She goes still at that, frowning with a faraway look in her eyes, as if she's remembering something.

"Brom said something like that to me too," she says.

I ignore the petulant flare of anger inside me. "I'm sure he did, but now I'm talking about me and I'm talking about you." I kiss her hard and fast, stealing her breath, reminding her of who she's in front of. "I'm not going to let them get away with what they're planning," I whisper to her, my forehead pressed against hers. "You're mine to protect until the end."

"What are you going to do?" she asks, breathing hard.

I run my hand down her face, my thumb over her lips, and so many emotions are battling inside me for dominance, I don't know which one to let through.

"I want to make a baby with you," I whisper to her point-blank, staring intensely into her eyes.

They widen in shock. "Wh-what?"

I lean down and kiss her open mouth, drawing her lips against mine for a moment, then pull back and smooth her wet hair off her face. My cock is already hard, already wanting her, wanting this. It always has. "I want to father your children," I tell her. "I want to breed you."

She blinks wildly, and I have to smile at how innocent she looks, knowing she's anything but.

"Crane," she whispers, placing her hands on my chest.

I bite my lip. "Let me be the one to get you pregnant, sweet witch. Even if this is something you don't feel ready for, even if it's something you never thought about with me, let me be the one to do it."

"Now?" she asks incredulously, searching my eyes.

I smile and press my lips against her cheeks. "Yes, now. Obviously there's a chance you might already be pregnant after earlier, but I want to do this with purpose. And I normally wouldn't be in such a rush, but considering current circumstances, the sooner I can get you with child, the better it will be. Think of the worst-case scenario here. Think about what could happen."

I don't want to think about it, but I need her to.

She pulls back with a gasp, looking fearful. "You think that would work?"

"If I get you pregnant before Brom does, then yes. Then their plan is foiled."

"If they find out, they'll . . ."

"They won't find out. They can't know. I'll do everything in my power to stop them from taking you, but in the event the worst happens, this is insurance that you won't birth the damn anti-Christ and bring about the end of the world. I think it's worth a shot, don't you?"

"So you're only doing this to save the world?"

I can't help but laugh, holding her bewildered face in my hands. "The world? You are my world, Kat. You're my everything. And I want you to be the mother of my children. That's plural, sweet witch. More than one. I want to have many beautiful babies with you. It's all I've wanted from the moment I first saw you. I'm starting to think you don't realize what exactly you mean to me."

She swallows hard. "I guess I'm too afraid to see it. In case it isn't true."

"It's true, Kat," I say, kissing her forehead. "I love you to death."

"And Brom," she says warily, searching my eyes.

"If all goes well, if he comes around, like you said, and we all get out of this alive, he's going to be there too. He's part of my world, right alongside you, and I'm not forgetting him in this. Whether that grump wants to be there or not."

She finally smiles at that and looks away for a moment before she slowly nods. "Okay," she whispers.

"Okay?" I ask, my heart lodged in my chest, afraid of the hope of it all.

She nods. "Okay," she says, taking my hand and pressing her lips against it. "Put a baby in me."

"I thought you'd never ask," I growl. I walk her backward across the room, tugging at her robe until it falls loose, then push her gently down on the bed. She lies beneath me, naked in the moonlight that beams through the window, and I have to remind myself to take it slow with her, slow and easy. She just had both our cocks inside her, and I haven't even had the time to apply the healing oil to the cuts on her arms and her chest. For all I know she's still high on the elixir too.

"You're so beautiful," I tell her as I discard my robe at my feet and prowl over her. "So beautiful it hurts to look at you sometimes," I admit. "As if just gazing upon you is a gift, one that you know can be taken away."

Her throat moves as she swallows and stares up at me. "Then don't let me be taken away."

My possession over her, my protectiveness, it roars inside me like a caged animal, infiltrating my veins, making my blood run hot. I pounce, pinning her arms above her head while I slip my hand between her eager thighs. She raises her hips to meet my fingers, and it's so natural, like instinct, like breathing.

A soft flutter falls from her lips as her legs spread for me and I find purchase in her wet cunt, feeling her desire and my seed from earlier.

I stroke her with gentle touches, soft strokes that give more than they take, letting her wetness build all around my fingers until her lower belly trembles and her breath comes out in pants.

Her eyes shine as she stares up at me, half-lidded and hazy.

In my mind I see the seed I'm about to plant, the seed of our future life, and I feel my cock pulsing even harder in anticipation.

I've never wanted anything more.

"I love you," I whisper as I spread her legs wider, pushing my fingers in deeper. She's soaked, and I run my tongue along her collarbone before pressing my body against hers. She moans as she feels the full weight of my body press her into the bedding beneath us, and I watch as her eyes go heavy and soft, her lips parting as my cock presses against her belly.

"I love you so damn much," I murmur again as I adjust my cock at her entrance, kissing her again, our tongues dancing with each other, deeper, messier. She gasps when I enter her, when I spread her open and push my cock into her waiting cunt. She arches her back to me, her breasts taut and her nipples hard as I draw out and push back in, all the way inside her, her body shivering under the moonlight. It's like fucking her for the first time, like being reunited with a part of myself I thought I had lost forever.

I drive into her, watching her eyes flicker, seeing her lips open in pleasure and feeling her legs wrap around me as I grind into her.

When I feel myself rising up, getting too close, I pull back, trying to regain my control, trying to give her this time, this moment. This moment where I mark her as mine.

"I want a baby with you," I whisper. "I want that, Kat. I want you."

I kiss her forehead, her nose, her cheeks, her lips, before I roll my hips, grinding into her with the barest of thrusts. I trail my fingertips over her, reading her skin like a treasure map. I memorize every inch of her as I press my cock inside her, letting it pulse hot and heavy and desperate in her cunt.

I'm so close to losing it that I have to pull out, roll her to her side and push back in from behind. I bury my face in her neck, hold her hip in my hand and try to concentrate on anything else but the feel of her, the feel of this, but I know there's no use.

She's all I feel.

She's all I know.

And as I bury my cock inside her, thrusting into her over and over, I feel her clenching around me.

I groan into her shoulder as she tightens around my cock, her breath sharper now. I pull back and push in again, giving her more of myself, a part of myself that I want her to keep forever. A part of myself that is hers now.

And beyond the bedroom, the clock is ticking.

Goose bumps race over her skin, her nipples hardening as I run my fingers over them, and her hips tense under my touch, almost ticklish. The noises she makes, they drown out all the thoughts in my head and set my soul on fire. I close my eyes as I press myself deeper, trying to get even closer, trying to get even more of her. I wrap my arms around her waist, pressing her back against my chest as I thrust into her.

I kiss her shoulder and feel her shiver in response. Her cunt flutters against me like a butterfly.

My *vlinder*.

"Oh God, Crane," she calls out, her body stiffening, and that's all it takes to almost push me over the edge.

I quickly draw out of her and turn her to her back again, my cock standing stiff and strong, pointing up at the dark ceiling. She wraps her legs around my waist and I enter her with one smooth push.

With a rough growl, I pound into her, fucking her with abandon, not holding anything back. I pull her legs up around me and hold her knees against her chest as I drive into her, this beautiful woman, this beautiful witch, and I feel my orgasm building, ready to claim me as it did earlier.

I drop my head into the crook of her neck and pant against her skin as I thrust into her. Her nails bite into my back, and I feel the hot slickness of her body around my cock, sweat pooling between us.

"I'm going to come," I say through a groan, my muscles seizing as my orgasm comes for me.

I slam into her, and the noisy wet sound of our bodies coming together is almost too much to bear. It's like a drug, better than an opium high, and I'm past the point of being addicted to my sweet witch.

I roll my hips hard as I spill my seed inside her and she cries out, her nails raking down my back as my body lets loose and I'm coming again and again.

I kiss her, hard, and breathe her in as my cock pulses and I pour inside her in hot, life-giving streams that don't seem to end. I rock into her a few more times, my head light, my vision blurry at the edges.

My heart aches for her love.

I pull my lips away from hers and look deep into her eyes, her cheeks rosy pink with pleasure. I can hear her heart beating, can feel it racing in her chest, and it's beating for me.

Beating for our family.

"If that didn't do the job, I'm happy to try again," I say with a delirious smile.

She lets out a breathless laugh and places her hand on my cheek, gazing into my eyes.

"I don't doubt you are," she says, and she's smiling too.

But it's a soft smile, a fragile one, one that holds the weight of the world in it.

In the back of my mind I'm aware of the dangers outside this room, I know that we have to go after Brom in the morning and do what we can to convince him to not hand himself over to the Hessian, and I know that there's so much we have to get through to get to our happily-ever-after, the one that includes the three of us and Kat pregnant with my child, and yet I want to cling to this moment with her for as long as I can.

"Kat," I say to her, reaching down and gathering her hands in mine, my palms stinging slightly from the cuts. "My beautiful witch. I don't know what the future holds in the morning, but I do know this. I want to be a father, and I want to be the father of *your* children. I want the house somewhere far, far away from here, where we can live, with Brom a part of this as much as you are, and I want it as soon as I can."

I pause, taking in a shaky breath. "I want to marry you."

She looks less surprised by this than she did about the baby. Her eyes soften at the corners, her sweet mouth lifting. "Are you asking?" she says, her tone both coy and shy.

I smile and press her hands against my lips. "Marry me, Kat."

And it's only then, after the question has been laid out in the open, raw and vulnerable, that I realize I've proposed to a woman who has never even said she loves me.

My jaw clenches as I prepare for the rejection.

But then she squeezes my hands.

"You know I love you, don't you, Ichabod Crane?" she says.

I nearly collapse on top of her.

I shake my head, too afraid to let my heart swallow her words, so greedy for her love and affection. "I wouldn't be going mad and losing my mind over you if I had that bit of information," I admit. "But you could easily put me out of my misery."

She lets out a light laugh, the kind of laugh that fools you into thinking everything will be okay. "I suppose that's my fault, isn't it? My brain has taken far too long to catch up to how my heart was already feeling."

I raise my brows expectantly, waiting for her to say it.

"I love you," she says earnestly. "I'm quite terribly in love with you."

I exhale in relief and rest my head on her shoulder. She lets go of my hands and starts sweeping them down my back. "Even Brom knew," she says.

I lift my head to peer at her, my heart skipping again and again. "Brom knew you were in love with me?"

She nods. "He did. And I told him I was afraid to tell you."

"Why?"

"Because I thought you would ask me to marry you. Little did I know that you would do it anyway, on top of telling me that you want to get me pregnant."

"You were afraid I was going to ask you to marry me?" I repeat.

Jesus, am I that predictable?

"Yes. Because I knew I'd say yes."

"Well, that sounds terrible, saying yes to me."

She grins at me. "You have no idea how consuming you are, Crane. Everything revolves around you, and I'm not even sure you realize it. Me, Brom, we're caught in your orbit, no different from the stars in the sky. It's impossible to stay away. It's impossible to say no to you."

"Do you want to say no to me?"

Kat shakes her head, sucking on her lower lip for a moment. "Never."

"So if I lie down beside you and make you climb on my face while I eat your cunt, you won't say no?"

She laughs. "I won't say no. But if you're still looking to get me with child, then I hate to break it to you, but that's not the way to do it."

"No, but it's still a lovely appetizer," I tell her.

Then I roll over on the bed, grab her by the hips, and have my way with her into the depths of the night.

# 32

## Kat

*T*hump.
*Thump.*
*Thump.*

I sit up with a start, my heart pounding in my chest. The room is dark, except for the slice of moonlight coming in through the window, and beside me Crane snores softly in a deep sleep.

How long have I been asleep for? Can't have been more than an hour.

"Crane?" I whisper, putting my hand on his forehead. His skin is hot to the touch and he doesn't stir, his eyelashes fluttering in dreams. "Crane?" I say again.

*Did I just hear the ghost of Vivienne Henry outside the door?*

But he sleeps on, and I don't have the heart to wake him. I eye the bottle of laudanum on the desk and wonder if he took some when I was already asleep. Then again, after the night we had, the ritual, the blood play, the sex, the emotions, I wouldn't be surprised if he's truly that exhausted.

I'm tired too, but I still could barely sleep. All I could think about was the fact that Crane proposed to me and I said yes. That we're engaged. And I'm possibly pregnant with his child.

And all I could think about was Brom. I know he's angry, I know Crane said some fairly cruel things to him out of fear, but if I could talk to Brom, maybe I could get through to him. I saw the pain and anguish in his eyes when he said he was a stronger person with the horseman inside him, and I know why he thinks he can cling on. But the horseman will never help Brom the way he thinks he will. In the end, the Hessian will only divide us.

I swing my legs out of the bed, wondering how angry Crane would be if I snuck on over to Brom's dorm to check on him, when the thumps sound again, just outside the door.

"What do you want, Vivienne Henry?" I say into the air.

Silence.

I get up, glancing back at Crane, hoping he'll wake, but he's still snoring away, his mouth open. I'm surprised he's not drooling.

I grab the candlestick and conjure a flame with my finger, lighting the wick. Even that act of magic drains me a little, but I need to be able to see. I grab Crane's coat and slip it on against the chill, then cross to the door and open it, peering down the hallway. The trail of blood goes past and around the corner, just like last time.

I glance back at Crane and then softly close the door. I want to know what Vivienne has to show me this time, but I'm not about to head into the basement alone if that's where she's leading me.

With the candle slightly shaking in my hand, I creep down

the hallway. It's so quiet now, especially knowing that the teachers Desi and Daniels are gone, and even though Crane has mentioned that the custodian lives here too, I wouldn't be surprised if he's disappeared.

I go around the corner, expecting to see the path of blood leading down the stairs, in which case I planned to turn around and go back to Crane's room, but instead the blood continues across the mezzanine and turns the corner into the women's wing.

I quicken my pace after her, careful not to get my bare feet in the blood, then slow down as I'm about to turn down the other wing.

I go around the corner . . .

And let out a soundless scream.

Vivienne Henry is standing a foot away from me.

The woman stares at me with her empty white eyes, her mouth a black open hole, as if she's swallowing my screams, as if she's going to swallow me whole.

Then she suddenly moves backward and to the side, out of my way, and points down the hall with a crooked bony finger.

I can't even breathe, my lungs are gasping for air, and my heart feels like it might quit on me. I clutch my hands to my chest, and my gaze follows where she's pointing.

She's pointing at Ms. Peek's room, the door closed.

I look back at Vivienne. She's a rotting, festering corpse, with a giant gaping hole in the middle of her, staining her torn nightgown with crimson. It looks like all her organs have been removed and she's bleeding profusely onto the floor.

And yet, even in those white eyes, I don't sense anything malicious or evil. I think she's trying to help me, not lead me into a trap.

Goodness, I hope I'm not being naïve.

"You want me to go inside there?" I whisper to her.

Vivienne raises a finger to her nonexistent lips and nods once.

I gulp down my fear and start toward Ms. Peek's room. It feels wrong to turn my back on Vivienne, but I do.

Then, when my hand is on the doorknob, I stop and look back at her over my shoulder.

The hall is empty.

There's no blood either.

Vivienne Henry is gone.

I take in a deep breath and open the door, finding it unlocked.

Ms. Peek's room is dark save for the moonlight. It looks exactly like it did when I was last here, and though there is no lit incense or cigarettes, the room smells of it anyway.

I step farther inside, leaving the door wide open, and look around. The painting of the raven has been slashed, the raven cut right out of the canvas, sending chills down my spine. Her bed is unmade, and a few drawers of her dresser are open, undergarments spilling out.

A small bottle lies toppled over on her desk, the cork beside it. I pick it up and hold it to the moonlight, seeing just a little bit of black liquid inside. I sniff it, a licorice scent, and then look at the label, which is handwritten in ink: *Carbones Corrumpebant.* Something with charcoal.

I put the cork back in and slip the bottle in my pocket, thinking Crane might find it useful for something.

Then I hear a splash from the bathroom.

My heart stills.

Oh God.

*Leave the room*, the voice inside me says. *Leave the room and run to Crane.*

But what if it's Ms. Peek? What if she's alive still?

Vivienne Henry told me to come in here, didn't she? Isn't she trying to help?

I try to steady my breath and I slowly, silently, creep toward to the open door of the bathroom.

I step inside and gasp, dropping the candle, the flame going out.

The bathtub is filled to the rim with blood, the full moon from outside reflecting on the surface.

And as I stand there, staring at it, the blood starts to ripple and move.

A head starts to rise out of the liquid.

At first I don't know who it is, if it's Ms. Peek, if it's Vivienne, or maybe even Marie.

Then the head fully emerges, dark hair plastered down the sides of the face, rivers of blood falling away from its features. The eyes open and stare directly at me, fully black.

And familiar.

It's my *mother*.

"Mother?" I squeak, frozen in shock. I don't dare get any closer to her, but I couldn't move even if I tried.

"Katrina," she says, and despite the fact that her eyes look so inhuman, the fact that she's bathing in a bathtub full of blood, she sounds normal. "You shouldn't be here."

I shake my head violently. "No. I . . . I don't understand. Why are you here? What is this?"

Her black eyes hold my gaze steadily, and I can feel power in them that she's using to pin me in place, like a butterfly on the wall. "I don't think I'm supposed to be here either," she says, looking around, mercifully breaking her stare. "I had a hard time getting through the wards. What has happened to this place?"

"Why are you in a bathtub of blood in Ms. Peek's bathroom?" I ask sharply, surprised at the strength of my voice.

She stares at me for a moment before she sits up in the bath, draping her arms over the sides, blood splattering to the floor. "This is my replenishing. I do this every full moon. Though it seems this time they wanted to keep me out. Thought the wards would discourage me, did they?"

"We're on lockdown," I tell her. "The sisters strengthened the wards a week ago so no one could come in or out. Didn't you know that?"

She shakes her head. "No. You know I only come here once a month. I suppose I'm lucky they made an exception for me. Or maybe this place just knows me so well. They may have kicked me out of their coven, but it doesn't mean the school has done the same. It's probably why you've been able to recall what you learn here; your bloodlines are entangled with this place just as mine are."

I blink at her, trying to understand the horror of it all. "And you come here to sit in a bathtub of blood? Is this what you've been doing every month? Whose blood is this?"

She shrugs. "I don't know. After the sisters are done with the candidates, done with their organs, it's hard to know what the person originally looked like. I took whoever was left downstairs and brought them to the first empty room. All I need is their blood."

Left downstairs?

Dear God.

"From the web room?" I ask, feeling sick.

"From Goruun's den," she says darkly.

Oh, goodness. I stumble backward until I hit the wall, needing something to keep me upright. "This building sits on top of a demon's den?" I gasp.

"Most of the buildings are built on top of something," she explains. "This land held magic long before the first settlers arrived, even before the covens. What my sisters did was build the school directly on top, all the better to draw up the ancient energy into the teachers and students and then back into us."

"You mean siphon," I say bitterly. "Just like you did to my father."

She narrows her eyes at me, and I feel it inside my brain, like I'm being poked with a hot iron. "Your father served his purpose. He provided me with the energy and magic I needed to stay alive. It was a transaction, nothing more."

"And you also had me to use as your pawn."

"Better you than me," she says coldly. "I would have had to marry Liam Van Brunt. Awful man. Your father was at least kind and entertaining."

"So then I would be the sacrifice instead of you."

She blinks at me, drops of blood flecking on the water. "Sacrifice? You would have had Brom's baby, it's what you always wanted anyway. I hardly call that a sacrifice."

"But you would have taken the baby and then killed me and Brom."

"Don't be absurd," she says, as if all of this isn't already absurd. "I wouldn't kill my own daughter, and Brom would at least be useful if he were to sire another heir with you."

"You wouldn't kill your own daughter, yet you wanted to siphon my magic from me?" I cry out. "You wouldn't kill your own daughter, yet you would have given me over to your sisters, and *they* would have killed me?"

"I never had any intention of taking all your power, Katrina," she says indignantly. "I only needed some here and there. I've been taking from you your whole life, and you haven't even noticed."

My eyes widen. "*What?*"

"It's a mother's prerogative. I gave birth to you. I gave you the gift of life. In exchange you owe me your soul. Motherhood is a transaction the same as marriage is. But I didn't want to kill you, dear daughter. I only wanted the best for you. When you give birth to Brom's baby, you'll see what I mean. You'll want the best for that child too."

"That child is owed to the demon!"

"And what an honor that is." She raises her chin. "Your child will usher in a new age. Goruun's promises will all come true. Witches will inherit the earth, and it will all be because of you. You will be royalty, you the queen and Brom the king, and you will rule alongside your child. You will have eternal life."

I shake my head. "No. No, that's not what Sister Sophie told us."

"What did Sister Sophie tell you?" she asks, tensing up.

"That they plan to kill us both. That when Samhain comes, they will fully take over Brom using the horseman, and they'll drug me, and they'll force him to impregnate me. And after that, Brom will be killed, and the same will happen to me once I've given birth."

She frowns, sitting up straighter, the bloody water spilling over. "No," she says. "That's not right. That's not true at all. Sister Sophie is lying to you."

"I don't think she is. She's on my side, she says."

"And I am on your side too, Katrina!" my mother exclaims.

I laugh bitterly, not sure who to believe anymore. "I can't trust anyone," I tell her. "The only ones I can trust are Crane and Brom. And we're going to get out of here as soon as we can, as soon as we can get rid of the horseman from Brom. Then we'll leave and we're never coming back."

My mother opens her mouth to say something, but then goes still, as if she senses something.

"Who goes there?" Leona's powerful voice comes from the other room where I hear her enter.

My mother looks to me in horror and mouths the word: *Hide.*

There's only one place to hide, only one thing I can do.

I quickly move along the wall until I'm in the shadows of the bathroom and I close my eyes, conjuring shadow magic through my veins, until I've blended in with the dark, until I'm sure that no one can see me.

Oh heavens, I hope no one can see me.

I watch my mother in the tub, but she's not looking in my direction. Instead, she's watching the doorway as Leona's cloaked silhouette appears, with Ana right behind her.

"Sarah," Leona says, her voice chastising. "What are you doing here?"

I hold my breath, terrified that my mother will purposely give me away, or perhaps do it by accident.

"You know why I'm here," my mother says, her tone firm and cold. "Did you think I would forget it was a full moon? Not when I'm barely hanging on, not when I'm losing fingernails."

"But we have strengthened the wards," Leona says, lowering her hood.

I nearly cry out but manage to smother the noise.

Leona's face is devoid of skin and fat, composed of slimy grayish brown muscle and sinew, her eyeballs nearly hanging out of black sockets.

This is what they look like underneath the magic.

Monsters.

"How did you get in?" Ana asks her, mercifully keeping her hood on, her face in shadow.

"You always underestimate me, don't you?" my mother says snidely. "Think my power amounts to nothing just because I'm no longer part of the coven."

"We are on lockdown," Leona says. "The students and staff are getting restless. We've managed to make them think the Hessian is behind all of it, so they understand that the extra wards are up for their own safety."

"And so, what is your plan?" my mother asks pointedly. "In all these years I've never seen such sloppy, careless work. People are losing their heads every other day it seems, not to mention the rumors have even slipped into town. Normal folk discussing what's happening up here, talking about missing teachers, and students committing suicide in front of an audience."

"That's your daughter's fault!" Leona snaps. "Your daughter and that damn professor!"

"And then there's Brom, whom you've had no problem manipulating for your own gains," my mother counters.

"You're using him too!" Leona says. "Our gains are your gains. Our goals are one and the same."

"Then why did Katrina tell me that you are planning to kill Brom after he impregnates her? And that you plan to kill her once the child is born? Did you think I would idly sit by and let you kill my only daughter?"

Oh no. No. No. Why is she telling them this?

"Who told Katrina that?" Leona sneers with her lipless mouth. "When did she tell you that?"

My mother lifts her chin. "When she and Brom were over for supper last weekend. She knows the truth. I don't know how she knows, but she does."

"Sophie," Ana mutters, and Leona looks to her and nods.

"Yes," Leona muses. "Yes, Sophie. As I've always suspected she might. She cares too much for her son."

"As I care for my daughter," my mother says. "Why is this a shock to you? Are you not used to mothers caring for their children?"

Leona lets out a sour laugh. "Oh yes, Sarah, you are the portrait of a perfect mother. Look at you, bathing in blood so that you can carve out your meager existence for another month. You know, had you not chosen Baltus and married Liam instead, we would have never expelled you from the coven. You could be feasting on the magic-filled parts of these witches, instead of bathing in their leftover blood. But you seem to love scraps. That's all you deserve, after all."

My mother leans forward in the tub, glaring at them. "I need you to promise me that you won't harm Katrina. I understand if you want to kill Brom, but you are not to harm my daughter in any way. She belongs to me, not to you."

Leona scoffs. "You belong to us, Sarah, and by default, your child does too. If Katrina plays her cards right, then perhaps we can make an exception. But if she doesn't, she's as good as dead, and feasting on a witch of her power? Nothing will taste so sweet."

"So sweet," Ana chimes in, and I have to suppress a shiver at her ravenous tone.

"We just need that child, Sarah," Leona goes on. "That's all we need. And we need it soon. I don't mind if the world outside the gates falls apart a little, because give us three months, and as soon as that child is born, then that world is over as they know it. Maybe Goruun will help speed up the process even more. Perhaps one month instead of three, and all of our troubles will go away."

"You seem overconfident," my mother says grimly. "All this talk of her giving birth in three months and she's not even pregnant yet."

"Oh but you see, the plan is already in motion," Leona says

with a wicked smile. "The ceremony can commence as soon as tonight."

"I thought you were waiting for Samhain?" my mother says uneasily.

"The harvest moon works just as well," Leona says. "We already have Brom in the cathedral. The horseman was very adept in handing him over."

No.

*No.*

My eyes go wide, my stomach twisting, and it takes all my energy to keep the shadow magic going, to keep myself hidden in the dark.

"You already have Brom?" my mother asks warily.

"Yes. His body, anyway. His seed. That's what counts. I'm afraid the horseman has fully possessed him at this point, and there will be no going back. Once we find Katrina, our ritual will commence, with Goruun's presence to bless the whole thing." She pauses. "You haven't seen Katrina, have you?"

My mother shakes her head. "No."

"Why do I feel like you're lying?" Leona says, stepping forward.

"I'm not lying."

"You wouldn't be lying to try and save your own daughter, would you?"

"No. I'm not . . . I . . . Have you checked Professor Crane's room? I'm sure she's with him."

"We just came from there," Ana says, and my heart drops. "There was no sign of either of them."

Oh thank goodness.

"I see," my mother says, averting her eyes.

"You told them," Leona says, seething, leaning in across the tub. "You told them to run and hide, didn't you?"

"I didn't," my mother says, shaking her head. "I didn't." Then she meets Leona's awful gaze. "But I wish I did."

Leona straightens up, a smirk on her fleshless mouth. "Hmmph. Thank you for being honest, Sarah. At least we know now that we can't trust you."

And at that, Leona puts her hand out and lights the bloody bathwater on fire.

"You should have burned like your ancestors did, my dear daughter," Leona says to her as my mother screams and tries to crawl out of the bathtub. The flames catch, burning higher, and the heat fills the room, and it's only by sheer luck that where I'm standing is still in shadow.

"No!" my mother cries out, the agony going straight to my heart, and the fire engulfs her head, the blood burning like she's been doused in oil. She screams again, and I am certain any teachers left in this building will hear it.

But where will they go?

Where can they go when the coven will find them anyway?

Leona and Ana turn around, their cloaks swishing around them as they leave the room, and I am left alone with my dying mother as she burns and drowns in the bathtub.

And I can't even save her. I want to. Despite all she's done to me, I want to save her. I want to try and redeem her, as if that will spare me some awful fate. Blood runs deep, and it holds tight, and I want to spare her from this horror, solely based on the fact that I think she would have spared me.

But I can't. I just stand there in the shadows, and I watch as she's burned to a crisp, until the flames go out, plunging us back into moonlight, and her charred body sinks beneath the surface.

Until it looks like it did when I first came into the room.

As if nothing had happened at all.

# 33

## Brom

The day the horseman caught up with me I was in Manhattan, standing outside a laborers' union, looking to see if I could find some work. I had this awful feeling that I was being watched, which normally wouldn't have felt unusual. After all, for those four damn years I had run away from Sleepy Hollow, I thought I was being watched everywhere I went.

But this was different. This was a sense of being watched from inside.

The feeling that there was someone else, not just inside my mind, but inside my body.

I had never known fear like that before.

To know my soul was halved and quartered. Compromised beyond my own hand.

After that everything went black, a blur, until I found myself in Sleepy Hollow again.

But tonight, now, I'm already in Sleepy Hollow.

I just know I'm about to find myself somewhere else.

I can feel that darkness, that blackness, that blur, waiting to take me there.

There's a knock at my dorm door and with it I sense death. I almost laugh. I know it's not Crane. I want it to be Crane. I want it to be Crane and Kat, I want to tell them I'm sorry.

But it's not them.

It's my destiny.

I get up from my bed and walk over and open it. It's just a formality anyway. He would have axed open the door and let himself in.

On the other side is the horseman himself.

Eight feet tall, no head, cloaked in black.

I stare at him, at where his head should be, and I resolve to not show any fear.

That isn't how a hero should die.

"You're here," I say to the monster.

*You called for me*, the Hessian says inside my head. *You know what you must do.*

I nod, swallowing hard. "I know. Give up my soul."

The Hessian walks into the room, sucking in all the air and energy, his ax dragging behind him. He spins around to face me, darkness hanging off his cape like growing shadows, waiting to smother me.

"But we have a deal," I tell him, squaring my shoulders. "And you must keep this deal. It's the only thing that will redeem your own soul by the end of it."

The Hessian laughs. *You know nothing of my soul.*

"No. But I know mine. And ours will be one and the same."

I stick out my hand, as if shaking hands with an evil spirit is

a normal, polite thing to do. I hadn't ever cared about being polite, about formalities, until this last moment. How fitting.

*You have my word, then,* the horseman says.

Then the Hessian reaches out and shakes my hand.

And then I feel him from the inside again.

I feel the world go black.

# 34

## Kat

I don't know how long I stand there in Ms. Peek's bathroom, staring at the bathtub of blood with my mother's corpse submerged, but it's enough that I'm sure Leona and Ana must be out of the building by now. Perhaps they've gone down to the basement—to Goruun's den. I can't help but shudder at that thought.

But I can't wait any longer. There's no time to grieve the complicated loss of my mother. There's only enough time to find Crane and retrieve Brom from their grasp.

I run out into the hall, forgetting my candlestick behind, but there's enough light to see from the moon as it slices through the windows. I run all the way to Crane's room, even though I don't expect to find him there, not after Leona and Ana already paid him a visit.

Still, the door is open and I walk over the line of salt and into the middle of his room, looking around frantically for any signs of him. At the very least, maybe I can use his gun. The witches aren't immortal yet. They won't survive a bullet to the head, I'm sure of it.

"Kat," I hear Crane whisper, and I whirl around to see a shadow moving off the wall, looking exactly like the shadow version of himself in the glen that first ritual night. I almost scream until the shadow dissolves and turns into Crane.

"How did you do that?" I exclaim. "When did you learn shadow magic?"

He grabs me, pulling me into his arms, holding me so tight that I can't breathe. "I didn't. I borrowed it from you. Oh, thank God you're all right."

"But I just used the magic myself. I thought when you borrowed it, you took it from the person."

He pulls back, his gaze flicking anxiously over my face. "I suppose when it comes to us, from the way we're bonded or perhaps by the rituals, we naturally bestow it on each other." Then he gives his head a shake. "What happened to you? I woke up just as I heard Leona and Ana outside the door. Managed to get my body into the shadows under the bed. They searched under there but they didn't see me."

"They have Brom," I cry out softly.

His eyes nearly bulge out. "What?" he hisses, squeezing my shoulders. "How do you know?"

"I was in Ms. Peek's bathroom. My mother was there, she was bathing in blood. That's what she does under the full moon. Bathes in the blood of those they sacrifice so that she can stay alive."

"Did she hurt you?" he asks, grinding his teeth.

"No, she's dead," I spit out. "She's dead. I hid in the shadows, using the magic, and Leona and Ana came in the room. They said they had Brom, that they were going to find me and do the ritual tonight, not wait for Samhain. And when my mother told them she didn't want me hurt, they killed her. Right in front of me. Burned her alive. And on top of it, I think Leona is actually my grandmother."

Crane just nods, his gaze intense as he tries to process what he's hearing. "Where is Brom? Do you know?"

"In the cathedral," I tell him.

He lets go of me and I feel unsteady on my feet. He strides over to his desk and pulls out the gun.

"But they said he's gone. That the horseman has fully taken over now," I add, on the verge of tears. "He's completely possessed and not coming back."

"As far as they know," Crane says, putting his gun in the back of his pants. "They don't know what we've accomplished with those rituals of ours. We may not have expelled the horseman from Brom, but that's only because Brom was holding on to him out of fear. We are still bonded, still united and tethered to each other. There will be no room for the horseman because he would have to possess us too. Now come on, get on your shoes."

"Are we going to get him back?" I ask hopefully as I slip my boots on, even though terror has a hand over my heart.

"We're getting our man back," he says to me with pure determination. He comes over and grabs my face in his hands and kisses me deeply before he lets go and grabs my hand, pulling me to the door.

"Oh, I found this in Ms. Peek's room," I say as we go down the stairs quickly, pulling out the strange bottle from my coat pocket. "Maybe this will come in handy for something?"

Crane takes it from me, pausing in a patch of moonlight to read it clearly.

"Ah," he says appreciatively. "This comes in handy indeed." He passes it back to me. "Quick, drink what's left of it. It should still work."

"What is it?" I ask, taking out the cork, the metallic licorice smell wafting out.

"In the event that something goes terribly wrong tonight and they drug you, this will prevent the drug from taking hold. It's a charcoal neutralizer. Drink up."

I nod and swallow the contents of the bottle. I don't want to think about what will happen if things go terribly wrong, but I need to be prepared for the worst, especially if Crane is.

We burst outside the doors of the building and together we use our shadow magic in sync, sticking to the darkness where no one can see us, while we make our way over to the cathedral. The building is dark except for a soft flickering glow coming through the upper stained-glass windows. No doubt the ceremony is already underway, but they won't get far without me.

We creep alongside the stone building, trying to look in, but it's hard to see past the colors on the glass, and we also don't want to risk being seen outside the shadows.

"You know, I think I know what they did during our tests," I whisper to him, my voice shaking. "When we were first admitted to the school."

"What?" he asks as we stop beside a holly hedge, trying to see in through the next set of windows, though we can't see much through these either.

"I think they opened us up the same way that they opened up Ms. Peek," I say quietly, trying to press my face against the stained glass. "Her nightmare was real, and they really did cut her open and take from her, one piece at a time, the way I'm sure they did to Vivienne Henry and the others."

I pause, trying to push past the sickly feeling in my gut. "I think when we were first admitted and they did the tests, they weren't sifting through our minds—they were sifting through our bodies. The sisters opened us up and took a look at our insides. I think they were able to gauge how much magic we contained, how much we would be able to give them. So they could build us up with the classes, increase our capacity for magic, creating reserves they could eventually siphon from us."

When Crane doesn't say anything to that, I glance over at him behind me, and though he's still partially hidden in shadow, I can see he's staring at me with absolute disgust, his lip curled. "I choose to believe that's not true," he grimaces.

But he knows, as well as I do, that it is the truth. I don't know what else the sisters did to us, but there's a damn good reason why none of us can remember our tests. They drugged us all with opium, literally sliced us open and prodded around, making sure we would be fruitful enough for them to eventually consume.

Like my mother had said, fruit ripe for the picking.

I fight a shudder, feeling simultaneously angry and awful over my mother dying in such a way. The terrible realization that I'm now an orphan. But that is something I'll have to deal with another time, if there is another time after this.

I'm about to turn to Crane and ask him if we should try going through the front door or if there's a back exit into the cathedral, perhaps another way through the offices underground, when I turn my head and . . .

Crane is gone.

I stare openly, blink, look around. There's only darkness. Did he become an even deeper shadow?

"Crane?" I whisper, reaching out with my hand, hoping I'll touch him.

And then I do touch something.

Something hard and cold.

Something *not* Crane.

I gasp, withdrawing my hand as the headless horseman steps out into the light, his ax raised above his head.

# 35

## Kat

The moon shines on the blade of the horseman's ax as it hangs above me and a scream escapes my lips.

But instead of bringing it down on me, his hand shoots forward and he grabs me by the throat, lifting me up in the air. I've never seen him this close before, never felt his hands on me, the immense power, the horrible stink of evil that rolls off him in dark waves.

I try to breathe, to speak, but I can't. My fingers go to his gloved hand in vain, trying to pry him off, but he holds me there, my feet dangling above the ground, and I feel him watching me despite not having eyes.

Why is he staring at me like this?

"Are you just going to stand there like an idiot?" Leona's clipped voice says, and the horseman swings around toward her. Leona is standing by a wilting dahlia bush near the back of the cathedral, Ana on one side of her, Margaret on the other. No Sophie.

She motions to the horseman with her bony hand and the

Hessian starts marching toward her, dragging me along. The sisters go through a back door into the cathedral, and the thing with no head follows.

Before I know what's happening, the horseman is placing me on a table, no, an altar, and Ana and Margaret go to my arms, holding them down above my head. The horseman keeps a firm grip around my throat, preventing me from screaming, just allowing me enough oxygen to breathe, while Leona goes to my legs, parting them wide and strapping them down to the table before I can kick free.

Then Leona does the same to my hands before she grabs a bottle of laudanum from underneath the altar. The horseman forces my mouth open with his foul-smelling gloves and Leona pours the poison down my throat.

It stings and burns and as the fear and panic take hold of me, threatening to obliterate me, I can only hope and pray that what was in the charcoal neutralizer is enough to work through this because they just gave me enough to knock out a horse.

Then the Hessian releases me and I open my mouth to scream but I stop myself. Leona, Ana, and Margaret are staring down at me, their faces now monstrous, like I saw in Ms. Peek's bathroom, and they're all looking at me expectantly.

They're waiting for the drug to work.

This is the only defense I have.

I have to pretend.

I close my mouth and blink at them slowly, as if I can't keep my eyes open any longer, and let my limbs go limp under the restraints, let my head loll to the side. With half-closed eyes I try to survey the scene inside of the rest of the cathedral.

And my heart drops.

I see Brom standing in the middle of the aisle, inside a pentangle lit by clumps of melting black candles. He's completely nude, his cock stiff, and he's staring straight at me with his dark and intense eyes.

*This is the Brom that the horseman is controlling*, I think to myself. *This is really going to happen to me, isn't it? They're going to force him on me.*

But where is Crane in all of this? I don't see him in the room anywhere. Is he being held elsewhere, perhaps with Sophie? Or did they already kill him? Is he being sorted and sifted and siphoned right now, somewhere in the depths beneath the cathedral?

My heart feels stuck in my chest, the pain immense, and I can't bear to think those thoughts without giving myself away, can't bear to think about losing Crane.

But I still have to think.

I have to do something, don't I?

I think about my power, my magic, and if only my hands weren't restrained, then I could at least try to light the sisters on fire. The bigger problem is the fact that I *wouldn't* light Brom on fire, and he's currently the biggest threat.

"She's ready for you, Abraham," Leona calls out to him. "Don't be afraid, dear boy. Come and take what is rightfully yours. Come and sire your heir."

Brom nods stiffly and starts walking down the aisle toward me, the weapon bobbing between his legs. I keep my eyes half-open, feigning drowsiness, hoping I can still reach through to him somehow. Isn't there some small part of him that recognizes what's happening?

But his black eyes show me nothing. They are cold and damned and there is no love for me in them anymore. I'm just a vessel.

The sisters step away from the altar, the physical horseman doing the same, as Brom approaches. He stops right beside me, his empty gaze coasting over my body, and it takes all my strength not to react, to pretend to be drugged and helpless. I must fool him, I must fool everyone.

"Part her legs, shove up that nightgown," Leona barks. "Get on top of that table and penetrate her."

Brom does as he is told, climbing up onto the table with ease, going between my legs. He reaches forward with his hand and roughly moves my nightgown up to my waist, so I'm bare and defenseless below.

Then his cold gaze finds the corner of my eye for a second.

*Daffodil*, Brom's voice comes inside my head.

I nearly open my eyes wide but he quickly hushes me. *Don't react. Lie still.*

*Brom?* I think. *Is it really you?*

*I borrowed Crane's voice*, he says, and I'm unsure if he actually heard me or not. *They don't know I'm in complete control. They think I'm being controlled by the horseman, but I have control of him too.*

He has control of the horseman? No wonder he knew how to choke me without doing any harm.

*But we still have to go through with this*, he goes on. *I'm sorry.*

I gulp and feel his cock as he pushes against my entrance. No surprise, I'm not wet in the slightest. I can't help but resist him.

*I don't want to hurt you, Daffy*, he says mournfully.

Then he spits into his hand and brings it between my legs, pushing his spit inside me.

"How crude," I hear Sister Margaret sniff.

*Just relax if you can*, Brom continues, sliding his fingers in and out. *I love you. I don't want to hurt you. Please.*

I take in a deep breath and try to relax even further, try to open up myself to his hand. I force myself to pretend that we aren't here, that we're together somewhere alone, the barn, and that this is my Brom, my Brom who I love so dearly, and it's only for us.

He spits into his hand again, bringing more of the moisture inside me, and I find myself relaxing into his familiar touch, let myself believe in the illusion.

*That's it. Good girl*, he whispers. *I'm going to push inside you now, okay? I'm not going to come. We're going to act this out, but I'm not coming. Don't worry.*

He adjusts himself above, reaching back for his cock. Slowly, he pushes his cock in and I wince at the sharp pain, but I quickly turn my face blank again, grateful that the sisters can't see my expressions clearly. The farther he pushes in, the more I relax, and it almost feels good, and I'm focusing on the fact that it's my beloved Brom inside me.

*Oh, Kat*, he murmurs, his words pained. *I will get us out of this. Just a little bit more. Just hang on.*

"That's the spirit," Leona says. "That's how fornication should be done." Then she claps her hands together, the sound echoing across the cathedral. "I think it's time we bring out Goruun. He would want to see conception take place. He will want to be the first to eat Abraham Van Brunt when he's spent his seed. It's an awful shame that Sister Sophie isn't alive to watch her son's gruesome demise."

Oh God.

*Don't worry*, Brom says, still pumping inside me. *Don't worry.*

How am I not supposed to worry?

How is *he* not supposed to worry?

Then there's a terrible noise from the other end of the cathedral. I open my eyes enough to see a giant creature coming into view, coming down from above. Like it's been in the rafters of the church this whole time and is slowly descending.

I whimper, unable to help myself, and Brom grunts loudly, purposefully burying my noise with his.

The creature, meanwhile, rights itself.

It's as black as night and at first I think it's Daredevil; it's about the same size as the stallion.

Until it moves forward.

It has eight spindly legs, but the front of it looks like a human draped in black sinewy muscle, and it moves toward us slowly, the legs making a tapping sound on the stone floor.

Despite all that's happened, all that's currently happening, I have never been so terrified in all my life.

Goruun is a demon and a giant spider centaur.

And we are so utterly damned.

*Try not to look at it*, Brom says, still fucking me. *I saw it earlier. Sister Sophie had led it out of the basement below the cathedral. Then it proceeded to tear her limb from limb and eat her alive at Leona's command.*

This isn't helping.

*We are waiting until the right moment*, Brom says, his breath becoming raspy with exertion as he thrusts into me. *I have been speaking to Crane inside his head and he's inside mine. He's moving around in the shadows. He's waiting.*

*Oh thank God*, I think, my heart skipping, but the relief is short-lived when I hear the *click-click-click* of those spider legs coming toward us.

*It won't be hard to kill the sisters*, Brom says. *You have your fire magic, magic that Crane can borrow too. You can incinerate them. And I have the horseman. He will do my bidding now until the end, as long as I uphold my end of the deal.*

*What deal?* I think with a stab of panic.

*The demon will be hardest to kill*, he goes on, thrusting slower now. *But we're going to give it all that we've got. Isn't that right, Daffy?*

I meet his eyes for a moment, his troubled, sweet, dark eyes.

*That's right*, I think.

Or we'll die trying.

*I'm going to pretend to come now. You'll know what to do. Just wait until I free you.*

He quickens his pace, making his breath sound shorter and more labored, throwing a few more loud groans in there, and it's hard to know what he's faking and what he's not.

"Oh, Goruun, come see this up close," Leona says, clapping her hands together. "Come see the point of conception for the new age."

The spider centaur comes closer.

I can barely breathe, I'm so terrified.

Brom cries out, a strangled yell, pretending to come inside me, his body shuddering. For a moment I believe it until I don't feel his cock release, until he remains just as hard inside me.

"Oh, how wonderful," Leona says. "Isn't this wonderful, to witness such a thing?"

I feel the spider stop a foot away, the smell of sulfur and rotting flowers and death overpowering me. I open one eye, just a little, to see the waxy hide of the spider's chest where four needle-like cocks protrude, fighting for dominance, blood dripping from them, and it takes everything not to vomit in my mouth.

The horror might kill me in the end.

*He didn't release,* Goruun says with a deep, craggy metallic voice, so inhuman that it makes my skin crawl, makes panic thrum through my veins, and I feel the urge to run away screaming.

But I am still in restraints.

And Brom is still inside me.

*He didn't release his seed!* Goruun yells.

"What?" Leona says.

*Now!* Brom's voice booms inside my head.

The Hessian soldier springs forward, ax raised, and brings it down over the spider's head, slicing it clean off. It rolls on the floor, stopping just below me, its beady red eyes staring up at me, looking both human and not.

Then Brom pulls out of me, jumps off the altar, and starts undoing the straps that are keeping me down. Once I'm freed he picks me up off the table and places me on the ground behind him, putting himself between me and the sisters.

They're screaming, trying to attack the horseman. The Hessian lops off Ana's head, an arc of blood spraying in the air, and it goes thumping across the floor, causing Leona to shriek. She retaliates by pointing at the Hessian, lightning coming out of her fingers and zapping him.

He shakes uncontrollably, the air filled with the scent of fried leather, then Brom reaches for the wall, pulling a long broadsword away from the stone where it was mounted.

"Kat, stay back," he says, holding the sword out.

I'm about to tell him that he doesn't know how to use a sword when Sister Margaret comes flying through the air at him, her hair turned into writhing snakes, her eyes bulging out, her tongue long and flicking like a serpent's.

I conjure flames to my fingertips, ready to throw a fireball at her.

But Brom stands in my way as he takes the heavy sword and raises it like it weighs nothing at all, waiting until the last moment before swinging it, slicing it below Margaret's awful face, cutting her head clean off.

Brom can control the horseman.

Brom *is* the horseman.

He looks at me over his shoulder with an expression of shaky pride as her head bounces to the floor, but that look on his face quickly turns to horror as his gaze goes behind me.

Because eight giant spider legs wrap around my stomach from behind, pinning my arms to the side, before I'm suddenly yanked high into the air.

# 36

===

## Crane

When I first saw the horseman silently approach us from outside the cathedral, I immediately pulled myself deeper into the shadows, wanting to wait until he was almost at Kat before I roasted him in flames.

But then Brom's voice came inside my head.

I'd never been so overjoyed to hear him in all my life.

Never felt so proud as a teacher either.

He quickly filled me in on the plan. For the time being, he had complete control of the horseman. He was able to control the Hessian's physical form, and he was able to take the Hessian's strength and use it for himself. The coven didn't know he had already made a bargain with the horseman, for what I'm not sure, but we'll have to cross that bridge when we come to it. So the coven was intent on using the horseman to capture Brom and bring him to them, which he did.

With Brom controlling both the Hessian's physical body and

his own, he was able to do some acting, pretending that he was possessed and ready to do their bidding.

Their bidding, of course, involved capturing Kat, drugging her with laudanum, and then having Brom essentially rape her, spreading his demon spawn inside.

He told me all of this as he captured Kat, holding her safely by the throat in a way that I know was modeled after me, and then brought her over to the sisters, acting like the dutiful soldier in their control.

I was delighted to find that I could still use my voice too, which meant I could use it inside other people's minds. I wanted more than anything to tell Kat what was really happening, but instead I trusted her with Brom. I trusted her life in his hands. And I sank back into the shadows, and started running around the campus and projecting my voice into everyone who could hear me.

I told them all that their magic was needed. That they had a chance to fight back against the powers that held them at the school. And I told them that if they didn't do this, they'd all flunk my class.

I don't know if anything will come from that. I didn't have time to wait around and see if some student was going to come out waving elemental magic. Even if they're too scared to do anything, I at least let them know what the dangers really were, and what they were up against.

I just wish I had done that a long time ago.

But now I'm running back inside the cathedral, wondering what scene I'm going to find.

Sheer chaos.

The physical horseman is being fried by lightning that's coming out of Leona's palms, Sister Ana is missing a head, and Sister Margaret is flying through the air at Brom.

Brom, who is naked, with a broadsword raised, looks every inch the glorious warrior, making my blood run hot despite the circumstances, while Kat is being kept back behind him. She looks ready to use her own magic on Margaret, but Brom beats her to it, slicing off Margaret's head with the sword.

I plan to slink through the shadows until I'm close enough to Leona to set her ablaze without her seeing me, or perhaps I have enough time to load my gun, but then I realize that there's a huge bloody mess on the floor by the altar, and what looks like the decapitated head of some humanoid creature. My eyes follow a wide smear of blackish blood over to the wall, just behind Kat, then up the wall and . . .

Before I can yell, a horse-sized spider descends from the rafters of the cathedral, right behind Kat, eight spindly legs shooting out and wrapping around her.

She screams as it yanks her up into the air.

I shout, running forward, my palms raised, ready to ignite the thing, but I can't do that without setting Kat on fire too.

"Ichabod Crane!" Leona yells at me now, having defeated the Hessian soldier who lies in an electrocuted heap beside her, his body twitching. She comes at me, hands out, flying through the air toward me until Brom takes his sword back behind his head and whips it forward at her.

The sword goes flying through the air, doing several rotations, until it strikes her in the back and she lets out a bloodcurdling screech as it pins her to the ground.

*Get Kat*, Brom says to me, running over to Leona to finish the job.

I'm already sprinting toward the opposite wall, staring up at the rafters where that beast has Kat in its grasp, wondering how I'm going to get up there.

Then I notice the thick string of a spiderweb dangling in front of me, leading up the way the spider went.

I take in a deep breath and put my hands around the sticky string and shudder profusely.

*Hold on, sweet witch*, I project into her head. *I'm coming for you.*

I start climbing up the sticky silk strand, the disgust turning into anger the farther up I go.

They won't take her from me, no one is taking her from me.

*Almost there, Kat*, I cry out, hoping she's still alive. From the quick glances up above, her feet are dangling, seemingly lifeless in the spider's bloody grasp.

Finally, I reach the bottom of the spider, a disgusting hole where the silk web comes out, and I reach out for Kat's foot to let her know it's me. She jerks it from my grasp involuntarily and I breathe a sigh of relief.

Until the spider throws back one of its legs, spearing me through my shoulder with a burst of blinding pain, pinning me against the wall.

The air leaves my lungs, the agony immense, and I'm trapped.

*Who goes there?* the spider without a head says in an inhuman voice. *Who disturbs Goruun?*

Jesus. This thing is Goruun?

But the thought starts to fade as pain begins to overtake me, blood running from the hole in my shoulder and dripping down, down into the cathedral below with sickening splats.

*Hold on, Crane,* Brom's voice comes from somewhere, and I'm starting to feel delirious. Where is he?

*Save Kat,* I plead with him tiredly. *Forget about me.*

*Like I ever could,* he says.

Suddenly there's a thump from the roof above, and I look up to see fragments of it falling on top of us, and then the edge of an ax breaks through. Another swing and then Brom's face appears above us.

"Remember me?" Brom says to the demon.

Then he crawls through the hole and lands on one of the wooden rafters, brandishing the ax and coming toward Goruun. Because the spider can't see him, it flails around trying to face its attacker, and for a moment Kat comes closer to me.

She meets my eyes, looking dazed but all right otherwise.

*Kat,* I tell her. *On the count of three we'll light him up. He'll let go of you before you catch fire.*

She nods.

*You hear that too, pretty boy?* I say to Brom.

*Loud and clear, sir,* he says, and I can't help but smile.

*One,* I count down.

*Two.*

*Three.*

With all the strength I have, I coax the fiery energy through me and set the bottom of the spider on fire, flames catching, and Kat moves around enough in its grasp to do the same to where the missing head should be.

Goruun screeches, letting go of Kat enough for her to wriggle out of his grasp, though at the same time he's yanking his spider leg out from my wound, leaving both of us about to fall to our death. At the last minute I reach for the rafter, wrapping my good arm around it, and grabbing Kat before she falls.

I groan, pulling her up to me so she can hold on, the pain in my shoulder making me feel faint, and we watch as Goruun starts coming after Brom along the wooden rafter, its body on fire. Brom takes his ax, and as he balances on the beam, moving backward, he starts slicing into the spider with merciless hacks of the blade.

The spider cries out, falling in bloody chunks onto the altar and the dead bodies below, but now the fire that was burning him is burning along the rafter, the flames coming toward us.

"Shit," I swear, and look up above at the hole Brom made in the roof. "That's our only shot."

I carefully lift Kat up to her feet on the beam, and I go to the hole, pulling myself out and onto the roof, then reaching back down and grabbing Kat and pulling her up alongside me.

"Brom!" I yell toward the hole. "Get out of there!"

But Brom doesn't answer.

"Brom!" I scream again, Kat screaming along with me, and I lie flat on the roof, looking over the side into the burning cathedral. Brom is standing on the rafter as the flames creep toward him, cornered.

*Damn you, pretty boy!* I yell inside my head. *Run through the fire and get out of there, now!*

But Brom just shakes his head.

Holds my eyes for an agonizing moment.

Just as the rafter crumbles beneath him.

He falls through the flames, disappearing to the cathedral below.

"Brom!" I scream so loud that my eyes feel like they're bleeding.

Kat is crying and sobbing beside me. "No, no, please no!"

And in the distance I hear people yelling.

"Professor Crane, Professor Crane!"

In a daze I get up and look over the edge of the roof to see the students gathered below, dawn beginning to rise from the east.

"The building is going to collapse!" Paul yells up at me. "You need to get down from there!"

"Brom is inside the building!" I yell back. "You must save him!"

"We can do both!" yells Josephine, and she runs inside the cathedral with a few other students.

"Jump off the roof, Professor Crane!" Paul yells up at us. "I have you. I have this. You taught me well!"

I don't know what the hell I taught Paul at this point, and I can't seem to move, I can't seem to meet my fate, but Kat grabs my hand, gives me a small smile, despite the tears running down her face, and says, "You at least have to trust your own students. You're the one who taught them."

I nod, swallowing hard, and look over the edge again.

The vision of my tarot card comes into my head.

The Tower.

It was like this, but it wasn't.

I saw the future, but I also didn't.

So much of our destiny is in our hands.

"Jump?" I say to Paul.

"Leap of faith!" he yells. "Learn to let go and trust."

I sigh heavily. Of course there's a lesson in this for me.

"Oh, to hell with it."

With Kat's hand in mine, the both of us jump off the edge of the cathedral.

But instead of falling to our death the way that Lotte did, we descend slowly, as if being lowered on an invisible hand, until both our feet are gently placed on the ground.

"What on earth was that?" I ask Paul, relieved and terribly impressed.

"I can control gravity," he says with a shrug, shaking out his hands. "I've never done it with an object as tall as you, but I'm happy to say that it worked."

I pat him on the arm, then wince as my shoulder explodes in pain.

"We've got him," Josephine yells, coming out of the cathedral with a couple of students, an unconscious, soot-covered Brom in their arms, his nudity covered by one of their coats.

"Oh thank God, Brom," I say, and Kat and I run over to him as he's lowered to the ground.

"Brom, wake up, Brom," I say, dropping to my knees beside him, tapping his cheeks, checking for a pulse and not finding one. He has some burns on his arms and the side of his handsome face, but otherwise he looks unharmed.

Kat goes to the other side of him, holding on to his hand and squeezing it, tears rolling over her cheeks. "Come on, Brom, please," she whimpers.

*Brom*, I say inside his head. *I know you did a brave and noble thing back there, I know sacrifice was always on your mind, but this isn't where your story ends. You story begins here. It begins with a life with us.*

I slap him again lightly on the cheek but he doesn't stir.

Then I do something I swore I would never do.

I put my hands on him and close my eyes and I push all the energy I have left into him. He can't be dead, he can't be that far past the veil, he—

Suddenly he gasps, his eyes going wide. They turn to look at me and for a moment I think I've made that same horrible mistake again, brought someone back from the dead, broken a cardinal rule.

But then his eyes soften and he smiles at me, chest rising as he gasps.

"I saw inside your mind for a moment," he manages to say through a cough, his voice hoarse. "I must say, you are even more complicated than I thought. And you think about sex far more often than any man should."

I laugh at that, pure joy spreading through me.

"Yes, well, it's hard not to with the two of you around," I tell him, smiling at Kat, who is grinning ear-to-ear.

Paul clears his throat from beside me and I look up at him.

"Yes, Paul?"

He just shakes his head, biting back a knowing smile.

"Professor Crane." Martha comes over to me. "I can help too. I've learned how to heal. I can fix your shoulder and I can fix Brom's burns. I can at least try."

I nod at her, feeling even more proud of my students. If she can at least heal me enough, then I can heal Brom. "I have a healing poultice in my room," I tell her. "It's in my bag on the desk. Third door on the left, men's wing."

She nods determinedly and then runs off.

"And I helped take down the rest of the wards," Mark speaks up. "I sent a raven into town to tell them what happened. I'm sure the police will be here soon."

"They're already here," Brom says with a cough.

I follow his gaze to see Famke, Kat's friend Mary, and several constables on horseback riding toward us across the courtyard.

"How the hell?" I mutter to myself.

"Famke, Mary!" Kat yells, getting to her feet and sprinting toward them.

I get up and reach down and help Brom up to his feet, quickly adjusting the coat around him so that he's not being indecent in front of the authorities.

They stop a few yards away, in front of Kat.

"Oh, thank goodness we got here in time," Famke says on top of Sarah's chestnut horse. "I had come here twice over the last week. I knew something had gone wrong, I could just feel it. Each time the wards wouldn't let me in, but they'd done so before. Then Sarah said she was coming here for the full moon, and I knew, I just knew you were in danger, Katrina."

Mary nods from on top of her horse. "Famke came to my house last night and told me what she feared. I told my parents, thinking they would laugh and ignore me, but they said we had to at least tell the police what was going on."

"We rode into town and talked to the new constable," Famke says, jerking her head toward the three officers behind her.

"Interrupted my supper," one of them says, a man with muttonchops and a mustache, who I assume is the new constable. "But I can see now that this might have been worth it. We've been outside those damn gates for the past few hours, we've been all along the property trying to find our way in to no avail."

The police continue to describe their efforts, but my attention is stolen by Brom, who leans into me.

"So now what?" Brom says in a low voice.

"What do you mean, now what?" And then I realize the price he must have paid to still be here, talking to me. "Don't you have some bargain to uphold with the horseman?"

He gives me a small smile, shakes his head. "The Hessian is dead now. That's all he wanted in the end."

I blink at him. "How can he die if he was already dead?"

"There is more than one death, Crane. You should know that. He's been used and abused by the coven for decades now. He's never known peace, only vengeance, usually on behalf of someone else. He's been made to kill, made to retrieve, a puppet on a string. A soldier with no escape. All he truly wanted was to die a real death on his own terms, and with sacrifice, and never be used for anything ever again."

"It sounds like you knew him on a personal level," I comment.

He shrugs. "I do. And by the end, I think he knew me."

I grin at him, the elated feeling in my chest slowly expanding. "So you're free now?"

"I'm absolutely free," he says, leaning his head against my shoulder briefly, and I have to fight the strong urge to reach down and kiss him. "But I'll tell you what, the minute we get out of here, we're going straight to Manhattan and we're getting the biggest fucking bed we've ever seen. And you're not going to care if I get crumbs all over it. Got it?"

"Sir, yes, sir," I tell him, biting back a smile. "Of course, those things cost money."

He raises his head and his lips twist into a sly smile.

"What?" I ask.

"Well, you know all those gemstones inside the glass cases of the cathedral are worth a pretty penny," he says. "Would be a shame if they were to all disappear with the fire. Never to be seen again."

For a moment I'm not sure what he's getting at.

But then I know.

"Brom, you sneaky bastard," I say to him.

The both of us turn and run back into the building, everyone yelling at us in shock as we go, wondering why we're running back into the flames.

Luckily the fire hasn't spread far yet, and the glass cases that display crystals, gemstones, and other esoteric relics are untouched. I take my gun from my back pocket, happy that it's finally useful for something other than shooting Brom, and start smashing the glass.

Then we pocket as much of the stuff as we can before running back outside.

Naturally, everyone is staring at us.

"You fellas all right?" one of the officers asks us.

"Never been better," we both say in unison, patting our pockets and making sure the gems are hidden.

"Are you sure?" he asks with a squint. "Because you seem to

be burned, and I think your shoulder is about to fall off, and you both just ran back into a burning building, so I'm thinking mentally you aren't very sound either."

Brom and I look at each other, quickly remembering we're dealing with the world outside witchcraft.

"You're right, we should go get this all checked out," I tell him with a firm nod. "Where's our school nurse? Josephine? Might as well have them check you over too, Kat."

Kat comes over and I put my good arm around her as Josephine leads us away from the cathedral and around the corner and out of the prying eyes of the police, just as I see Martha running toward us with the healing poultice.

"I'll tell you what, I'll be glad to leave this place," Josephine says under her breath, then looks to us. "Are the three of you going to stick around Sleepy Hollow?"

I laugh. "After we're healed, we're going to get on our horses and ride out of here and never ever return."

"Farewell to Sleepy Hollow," Kat says. "May you never look back."

And isn't that a fact.

# 37

---

## Brom

Last night when I made the bargain with the horseman, I wasn't sure if he was truly going to go through with it. It is one thing to assume a handshake is binding between two morally upstanding individuals and another when you expect an evil spirit to actually uphold the deal.

But as I found out, the Hessian wasn't an evil spirit at all. He was just a soldier who had died a long time ago in a horrific manner and had wanted peace ever since. Peace he could never find, roaming the veil in search of something—someone—that would ease his plight, never realizing that acceptance was the only escape.

And so the coven used him, used his tortured spirit and made him their puppet to do their bidding. He's been used to retrieve wayward souls such as myself, he's been used to murder and enact revenge. All has been done for the cruelty of the coven, never for his own gains.

When you've been controlled by someone for so long, you forget what freedom even looks like.

When the horseman found himself bound to me, he saw something in me, similar to how I found something in him. He was attached to my humanity. I was attached to his monstrous side. I liked the power he gave me. He liked the love I received.

We saw freedom in each other.

We each gave what the other needed.

And with Kat's and Crane's energy inside me, the bond among us unbreakable, I had the upper edge in our symbiotic relationship. Three is more powerful than one.

So I told the Hessian that if he came into my body and gave me strength, I would go into his and control the both of us. I would ensure that a sacrifice would be made so that I would be free of him and he would be free of me.

I would give him the noble, final death he so desperately craved.

Still, I wasn't sure it would work. Even when I was operating the horseman and myself at the same time, I wasn't sure if I would lose myself to his strength and power. Swinging that ax and that sword with ease was the closest I'd ever felt to being a god.

But then when I saw Kat taken by Goruun and saw Crane pierced by the spider's leg, and I already started to feel the Hessian's power slip away as he sank toward death, I realized that it didn't matter if I felt like a god or felt like the devil; none of that compared to the love that I felt for them.

They were everything to me.

My true power.

And worth every sacrifice.

I was going to do all I could to live, because I wasn't about to leave them behind.

Ironically, the Hessian ended up saving my life as his final deed.

When I fell from the rafters, I ended up landing directly on top of his body. He broke my fall, and I would have walked away had I not inhaled so much smoke.

But after Josephine, the student healer, helped heal my burns with her hands and some of Crane's poultice, I ended up walking away from Sleepy Hollow Institute feeling better than when I had walked in.

Of course, Crane is a little worse off than I am. I joke that it's what he deserves for shooting me, since it's in the same spot as the bullet wound, but I think in a few days he'll be fine. Hasn't stopped him from complaining for the last several hours, though, as the three of us ride toward Manhattan, following the Hudson.

"Do you think we'll make it all the way into Manhattan by nightfall?" Kat asks with an awed smile. She's on top of Snowdrop, whom they collected from the stables before stopping by Kat's house where she left Famke—for now.

"If not, we'll find a nice inn close by," Crane says, sitting on the buggy that had belonged to Sarah, with Gunpowder pulling it. We needed someplace to store all of our belongings, though we didn't grab much when we left the school. All of us were too eager to get out of there, especially as more police showed up from Tarrytown and Pleasantville and started poking around. I was certain that they would soon be suspicious of us and want to talk about all the occult paraphernalia, let alone all the dead bodies, so we left before they could.

"With a big bed," Kat notes.

"The biggest bed," I confirm.

"Oh, by the way, Brom," Crane speaks up. "Did I tell you I'm getting married?"

My heart lurches in my chest and I swivel on Daredevil to look at him. Of course he's grinning like a fool.

"To Kat," he goes on. "In case that wasn't clear. Don't worry, pretty boy, you're invited to the wedding."

My fists automatically clench and I glare at him. "I could kill you."

It's not even that I'm mad he asked her—I knew he would. It's that he did it when I wasn't there. I would have liked to see that moment.

"Boys," Kat says loudly. "Let's not fight over me, we still have a long ways to go."

"Who says we're fighting over *you*?" I tell her, trying not to smile. "Perhaps I wanted Crane to marry *me*."

Crane laughs. "Be careful what you wish for, Brom. If you ever find yourself married to me, just know that I'll never let you go."

Despite the smile on my face, my heart pinches for a moment, because in some other world, some other lifetime, I would hope to marry Crane. I would hope a marriage between us would be as legally binding as the one he'll have with Kat.

But though I'm sure that day will never come, in the end it doesn't matter.

Because they belong to each other and they also belong to me.

And nothing will ever break that bond.

No witches, no demon, not even death.

# EPILOGUE

## Kat

*Three months later*

re you nervous?" Crane asks me as he pulls at the laces of my corset, tightening it around my ribs.

"No, but I can't breathe," I tell him, looking back at him from the corner of my eye.

He grins at me and places a kiss on my shoulder. "Sorry," he tells me, finishing tying me up. "You know it's good luck to have a little bit of pain on your wedding day."

"Is that so?" I say coyly, turning around and reaching up, hooking my wrists behind his neck. He ducks his head a little since I can barely reach. "I don't recall you causing me any pain on our wedding day."

He places his hands on my waist. "I figured you were in such shock at having to marry me to begin with, no additional pain was needed. Though I wouldn't say there wasn't any pain on our wedding night."

I close my eyes to the memory of the three of us on a king-sized bed in our fancy hotel room, my wedding dress torn in half by two very impatient and demanding men.

"But," Crane goes on with a heated smirk, "since this is Brom you're marrying now, well, perhaps I'm just a little jealous."

I laugh, leaning to the side as the ship lists and Crane's steady hands keep me up. "How can you be jealous? We've been legally married for two months now. You're my husband. How do you think Brom has felt being on the sidelines?"

"You know he's never on the sidelines. He's always at the forefront, right alongside you," he says. Then his hands drop to my belly and he holds them there gently. "Though I suppose soon you shouldn't be wearing any corsets at all. You have to give the baby space to breathe."

I bring my hands over his and squeeze, so much love fluttering up through me I don't know what to do with it. I'm three months into my pregnancy with Crane's child, my husband's child, and in a couple of minutes I'm supposed to meet with the captain of this ship, where he will marry me to Brom. There's been so much change since we escaped from Sleepy Hollow, but it's all been for the better.

It's been better than I could have ever dreamed of.

A clock chimes from the wall of our double cabin, and Crane pulls away. "Time to get you dressed." He goes over to the wardrobe and brings out my other wedding gown. This one is simpler than the one before, mainly because I know both Brom and Crane will be tearing it off me later with impatience, or at the very least getting it stained.

Also, we have to be more frugal with our money. Crane

walked away from the cathedral with thousands of dollars' worth of rare gems, but that won't last us forever. We spent a lot on our tickets for this ship across the Atlantic, and the rest of the money will go to buying a house in London, England. After that, Crane will get a teaching job somewhere prestigious, while Brom says he wants more of an industrial job, and I'll be taking care of the baby.

A knock at the door sounds just as Crane has finished buttoning up the back of the dress.

"Come in," he says.

The door opens and Famke pokes her head inside. "Your witness is here," she says. "Reporting for duty." She always jokes this way around Crane. I suppose his bossy personality rubs off on everyone.

"I'm ready," I tell her, sitting on the bed while Crane slips on my shoes. Of course, I won't be alone in raising our child. Even with Brom and Crane off working, Famke will be there to help me every step of the way.

"You look lovely, dear," she says to me when I get up, taking my hands in hers.

"Thank you," I tell her. "I wanted something more simple with Brom, being on a ship and all."

"And Brom's a much more simple man," Crane comments.

"Oh, you," Famke chides him. "Bristling with jealousy because your best friend is marrying your wife."

Crane laughs. "Well, when you put it that way."

Once Famke was able to leave Sleepy Hollow and join us in Manhattan, she quickly realized how special the relationship between the three of us was. I think she always suspected, but being with us she was exposed to it openly. There would be no hiding with us, no pretending that Brom was just a good friend of ours and that's it. And she went along with it. She protected our relationship from the outside world, telling people what they wanted to hear, while she knew how deep our feelings for each other went.

Which is why when I asked her to be my maid of honor for my wedding to Crane, she was happy to take part, and when I asked her to be a witness to my marriage with Brom, she wanted to be a part of that too.

Of course, legally I can't be married to two men at once, but we figured since my marriage to Crane took place in the state of New York, and this marriage to Brom will take place on international waters, it will still be honored. If not by the world, then by us, and that's what really counts.

"Let's go," Crane says, putting his hand on my lower back.

We step out into the hall of the great ship, Famke's room right across the way, and head through the corridors until we end up near the top deck beside the navigation bridge. I get a few appreciative nods as I go past some of the passengers, some of whom I've already seen a few times during the last week at sea. They probably don't know who I'm marrying at this point since I've been seen around Brom and Crane equally.

Crane and I haven't been wearing our wedding rings during the crossing, but I've been keeping mine on a necklace chain, right next to the protective amulet Famke gave me, which is hanging in our cabin.

We enter the captain's stateroom right beside the bridge, a small space lined with maps and books and teak furniture and, standing right beside the captain with a large window overlooking the gray Atlantic is Brom.

He's never looked more handsome. His beard is neatly trimmed, his dark eyes seeming brighter and lighter than they've ever been, and he's wearing a dark tailored suit that fits him perfectly. He grins at me, dimples flashing, and I've never felt more in love.

Even Crane's breath hitches from beside me. "Jesus, he's pretty."

Famke takes my arm and leads me toward them as Crane goes and stands to the side of Brom, acting as his best man, which he well and truly is.

"I have to admit," says the captain, a grizzled older gentleman with a kind smile. "I don't get asked to officiate many weddings. I hope you know you will still have to file all the paperwork when you arrive in England."

"That won't be an issue," Crane says, and the captain gives him a queer look, wondering why he's speaking for us.

"Well, with that said, let's get this started," the captain says, and gestures for me to stand beside Brom, which I do, the two of us turning to face the captain.

Brom clasps his hands at his front, gives me a sidelong glance and a quick smile, checking in on me, and I can't help but beam up at him in return.

It's been a long time coming.

The captain clears his throat. "We are gathered here, near the end of our Atlantic crossing, on this beautiful winter day of January 30th, 1876, to celebrate and bring together the lives of these two people who are very much in love, Abraham Van Brunt and Katrina Van Tassel, into holy wedded matrimony."

He turns to Brom. "Now, repeat after me: I, Abraham Van Brunt, take thee, Katrina Van Tassel, to be my wedded wife," the captain says, and my heart twists at the mention of my maiden name. I've been known as Mrs. Katrina Crane for the past two months, the first woman in my family to take a man's name. As complicated as it's been to grieve the loss of my mother, I was happy to leave my family name behind.

Brom squeezes my hands, staring into my eyes so deeply that it makes my knees want to buckle. "I, Abraham Van Brunt, take thee, Katrina Van Tassel, to be my wedded wife."

"To have and to hold from this day forward," the captain goes on, "for better, for worse, for richer, for poorer, in sickness and in health, to love and to cherish, till death do us part, according to God's holy ordinance; and thereto I pledge thee my faith."

Brom repeats it all, each word burning with intention.

"Now, Katrina, it's your turn," the captain says, and he walks me through the vows again, having me repeat them the same way Brom did.

I say every word.

I mean every word.

"I pledge thee my faith," I say to Brom, feeling that golden coil of energy inside me. My faith is for him, to him, for us.

"Now, the ring," the captain says.

Crane comes forward, a sheepish look in his eyes as he holds the ring out for Brom. "Sorry, I probably should have given this to you earlier. I thought I lost it in the room."

I roll my eyes. Some things never change.

Brom laughs and takes the ring from Crane's fingers, and I can't help but notice the way their fingers brush against each other, the way Crane's gaze burns on his, the smallest details that warm my heart.

God, how I love these men; my chest could just burst with it, like the sun is caged inside me.

"Now repeat after me, Brom," the captain says. "I give you this ring as a symbol of my love; and with all that I am and all that I have, I honor you, in the name of the Father, and of the Son, and of the Holy Spirit."

Brom holds out the ring with a trembling hand while he grasps my left hand with the other. "I give you, Kat," he says, his voice shaking too, "this ring as a symbol of my love; and with all that I am and all that I have, I honor you, in the name of the Father, and of the Son, and of the Holy Spirit."

"I now pronounce you man and wife," the captain says with a great big smile. "You may now kiss the bride."

Brom breaks into a grin and then grabs my face in his hands, holding me tight as he presses his lips to mine. "I love you, my wife," he whispers against my mouth.

"I love you too, my husband," I say, smiling so hard that it hurts.

Suddenly Crane starts clapping loudly, and Famke joins in with a little cheer. I pull away from Brom and look at Crane, my other husband now, and his eyes are wet with emotion, his mouth firm, as if trying to hold it together.

"Come here," I say to Crane, opening my arm for him, not caring what the captain thinks. We're just all good friends who are celebrating this joyous occasion together.

Crane comes right in, not between us, but surrounding us, one of his long arms over me, the other hooked over Brom's neck, holding us together. "Congratulations, you kids," he whispers to us before placing a fierce kiss against the top of my head, then bringing down Brom's head and doing the same to him.

I let his arms press me against Brom, and I'm engulfed by my two husbands, my two lovers, my two soulmates, with a baby deep in my womb, and I don't think I could feel more whole than this.

But though I want to stay in that embrace forever, the captain needs to get back to work, so we leave the stateroom and go back to our cabin. Famke tries to get us to come up to the bar deck and have celebratory champagne with her, but we promise we'll meet up with her later.

Right now, all three of us want to be as selfish as possible.

We go to our cabin, Brom scooping me up into his arms just as Crane kicks open the door. I'm brought over the threshold and right over to the bed, Brom dropping me on it so that I bounce and then both men attack me, two sets of mouths devouring me, four hands tearing off my dress, taking off their own clothes.

I'm swept away in their current, letting myself go, letting them take the lead.

My dress is removed, and Crane practically rips the corset off, grumbling that he was a fool for putting it on in the first place, and then the three of us are naked.

They cover me with their bodies, taking turns. One of them will kiss me deeply while the other will go between my legs and lick me out. Then the other will suck and kiss at my breasts, while the other fingers me deeply. I come over and over again, lost to these two dark-haired men with their deviant but wonderful souls, feeling utterly loved and cherished.

And they whisper and murmur to me too, they tell me that I'm such a good girl, such a good *wife*, that I belong to them and only them, that they love me more than they can bear, that they are my husbands and they will always take care of me.

Then they start fucking me, Crane taking me from behind while Brom takes me from the front and the three of us come in unison, our souls uniting in fire and lust, these two hard, masculine bodies using me up until I'm screaming both their names.

Just when I think I can't take anymore, when I feel boneless, nothing more than hot blood and a beating heart, breathless and raw, Brom leans back against the wall and Crane takes me and pins me there, my chest against Brom's, while Brom takes his cock and pushes it inside me, the sensation making me shiver. But when Crane goes behind me, I don't feel any oil and he doesn't go for my rear. Instead he kneels down and positions himself against my cunt, where Brom's cock is already shoved inside.

"I'm going to fuck his cock inside you," Crane says hoarsely. "Something I've always wanted to do. I want to spill my seed at the same time he spills his, I want it to mix together, messy and ours."

My eyes widen as I stare at Brom, but Brom holds the back of my neck. "Just relax, Mrs. Van Brunt," he says, and the use of that name makes me feel delirious in the best way. "You can take us."

"Surely I can't," I say, then I feel Crane's fingers pushing inside me, sliding along Brom's cock, stretching me.

"Oh God," I cry out, the pain already intense.

"That's my good girl," Crane murmurs. "Easy does it."

Brom wraps his arms around me, holding me tight to him, as if to prevent me from escaping, and I'm overwhelmed by his bonfire scent, by the soft texture of his chest hair, the hot, taut planes of his muscles. I press my forehead against his shoulder and try to breathe through the intrusion. Crane keeps adding more fingers, pushing them deep inside until I start to squirm.

"I love you, my beautiful wife," Brom coos, kissing the top of my head, though he too is starting to shake, his heart becoming louder through his chest.

"I love you," I whisper.

Then Crane removes his fingers and I feel his cock press against me now.

"This will hurt," Crane says. "But it won't hurt for long. Just relax."

"Deep breaths," Brom murmurs against my head.

Crane starts to push inside now, just the head, and I yelp, trying to buck my hips away, to escape the pain.

"You can tell us to stop," Crane says gently, though his breath is shaking, his cock paused halfway inside me, halfway against Brom. "And we'll stop."

I shake my head, my eyes pinching shut. "No. I want this. I want you, I want both of my husbands inside me like this. I want both your seed where it counts."

Brom swallows audibly. "As if I wasn't already this close to losing it," he says gruffly.

"Stay the course," Crane says, and then he puts his hand against the wall behind Brom, bracing himself as he shoves himself inside me with one brutal thrust.

I open my mouth to scream but then remember where I am

and I bite down on Brom's shoulder instead. He hisses, but whether it's from how mind-numbingly tight I am with Crane wedged inside me, or from the pain of my bite, I don't know.

"Just breathe," Brom says to me, holding me tighter as I try to squirm and move away from the invasion.

"That's it, sweet witch," Crane rasps, kissing the back of my neck. "Stay still so we can both fuck you. I promise this will feel good soon."

*How the hell do you know?* I want to yell at him. *You're not the one being split in two!*

But as Crane pulls out and pushes back in, as I force myself to just succumb to the pain instead of fighting against it, I let everything go and collapse into their arms.

And as always, when I let go, I find myself coming alive.

Brom and Crane start moving in tandem now, and I can not only feel their cocks inside me, but feel as they slide along each other's, and I'm lost to their ragged breaths, their beating hearts, the sweet words they whisper to me, the hard words they whisper to each other. I am pinned between them like a butterfly, I am soaring higher and higher as my body is pushed to the edge of everything.

Then I come, biting Brom's shoulder again so as not to scream, my body convulsing and shaking, my heart feeling as if it will punch right out and into the world.

My men. My husbands.

They come together, Crane biting my neck, grunting hoarsely as he shoots inside me, cursing up a storm, while Brom's hips thrust up violently, his arms around me shaking as he tells me loves me over and over again.

*My wife, my wife, my wife.*

Then I am just a doll in their arms, their semen spilling out of me before their cocks do.

"Jesus," Crane groans as he pulls out and then brings me down into the bed beside him. I slide away from Brom and he joins us on the other side, and the three of us lie there, crammed on a bed that's just a little too small for three people.

Eventually, when my heart returns to normal but that utterly joyous feeling still remains, I turn over on my stomach and look at them. They're both gazing at each other, matching satisfied smiles.

And I wish more than anything that they could be united in the same way that I'm tied to both of them.

"I think I should marry the two of you," I whisper.

They both blink at me in surprise.

"You know that's not possible," Crane says, though the hope in his voice is unmistakable.

"Maybe not legally," I say. "Maybe not in the eyes of God. But in our hearts, in our souls, it's more than possible. And it counts for more."

Crane's optimistic gray gaze fixes on Brom. "Well? What do you say, pretty boy? Will you marry me?"

"I'll have to think about it," Brom says, his face serious. Then that dimple appears and he laughs. "Yes, of course. Even if I said no you'd still order me to do it."

Crane grins boyishly at him. "You know me so well."

I straighten up on my elbows, taking hold of both their hands. "Then do you both promise to love and cherish and honor and obey each other, for as long as you both shall live?"

Crane's smile widens at the mention of *obey*.

"Crane," I chide him.

"Yes," he says, squeezing my hand. "Yes I promise to love and cherish and honor and obey my Brom."

"And, Brom, you'll do the same?"

"I do," he says with a solemn nod.

"Say it," Crane coaxes. "Say it, pretty boy."

Brom gives him a wry look. "I promise to love, cherish, honor, and . . . obey."

Crane gives him a smug smile in return.

I clear my throat. "Then by the power vested in me, by the universe and the gods unknown, I now pronounce you man and man. You may now kiss the groom."

Crane's smile morphs into something reverent as he reaches forward and grabs Brom's face, pulling him in for a kiss, while Brom's fingers run through Crane's hair. I watch as their kiss deepens, their tongues meeting each other, mouths open in longing, their brows furrowed in their utter desire and love for each other.

And even though this is one of the most romantic things I have ever witnessed, I am still a witch with a deviant appetite, and I feel heat begin to pulse between my legs despite how sore my body already is.

I slide back along the bed, watching as their kiss intensifies, knowing what will happen next. Crane breaks the kiss, his eyes heavy with lust, and grabs Brom by the back of the neck, pulling him over, making him lie flat, and then Crane starts kissing him down the length of his body, both cocks standing at attention.

I watch this, watch as Crane takes Brom's cock into his

mouth, as Brom starts making fists in Crane's hair, and then when I feel like they might forget I'm even here, I crawl forward and make myself known. They pull me down into their embrace with strong, greedy hands and the three of us are swept away together again, finally united as one.

# Crane

"W hy do you have to leave?" Baltus whines, dropping to his knees and wrapping his arms around my leg as Kat and I are about to descend down the stairs to the front door.

"Goodness, Baltus," I tell him, placing my hand on top of his head. "It's only for a few hours."

"But why can't we go?" Johnathan asks in a small voice from behind him. He seems to hesitate a moment before following his brother's example and throws himself around Kat's leg instead.

"Boys," Famke chides them, swooping in to pull Baltus off me, while Brom runs up the stairs two at a time to grab Johnathan and bring him off Kat's leg.

"We won't be gone long," Brom says to Johnathan, holding him at an angle so that Johnathan can pretend he's flying. He jogs down the hallway to the boys' bedroom, making whooshing sounds as he goes. Meanwhile Famke pries Baltus away and takes him down the hall after them.

"We'll bring you back a present," I shout after them, feeling bad that I can't take our children to this dinner party, though the invitation specifically said that minors were not allowed.

My wife gives me a look, elbowing me in the side. "We will not. Crane, you're the one who said we need to stop spoiling them."

"Well, Mrs. Crane, I meant that *you* should stop spoiling them. Being the man of the house, I believe it's my duty to lay down the double standards."

Brom scoffs as he approaches us, adjusting his bow tie for the umpteenth time. "There he goes with the man-of-the-house business."

"Sorry, Brom, it's only fair since I'm the father of the brood and you're the fun uncle."

He gives me a loaded look, telling me to tread easily.

When Kat gave birth five years ago, the last thing we expected to see were twins. Two beautiful healthy twin boys, whom we named Baltus, after her father, and Johnathan, after the old spiritual Indigenous man who first showed me what I was capable of when I was young. We were overjoyed and at that point had already settled here in London, having bought this house on Baker Street. To the outside world, I was married to Kat, with Famke as our housekeeper, and Brom as my "brother."

But as the boys grew older, we realized they were fraternal twins and didn't look as alike as we initially thought. Johnathan was born hours earlier, is taller and leaner, and has my gray eyes, petulant mouth, thick black hair, and high cheekbones. But Baltus . . . Baltus was born looking slightly premature and is the spitting image of Brom. The darkest brown eyes, low thick brows, strong wide jaw, and built shorter and stockier than Johnathan.

It seemed the impossible had happened, though not that impossible, if you look at the breeding of cows, which Brom was quick to tell us about, how often in the bovine world a cow can give birth to twins with each one sired by a different bull. Once a farm boy, always a farm boy.

While we have no proof that this has happened, and we often joke about Baltus being the evil twin and possible anti-Christ (a joke that Brom and Kat rarely laugh at but I find to be quite funny), I have taken to the notion that Brom is Baltus's biological father in a miraculous way, and I think Brom feels that way too.

Granted, to the outside world he must still remain their uncle and I don't think the children will know until they're older that Brom isn't their uncle at all, but until then, we must keep up appearances. The boys love Brom to death anyway. He gets to have all their love without laying down any rules.

I reach out and grab Brom by the back of the neck, pulling him in for a kiss. "My apologies, pretty boy," I say, pressing my mouth against his. "Let's enjoy this evening."

The three of us leave the house and step out into the awaiting carriage, the spring evening air fresh enough to dilute the smoke from the factories across the Thames. The driver takes us past the prim white houses along Baker Street until we are pulling up to a sprawling mansion at the edge of Grosvenor Square.

"Whose party is this again?" Kat asks as I grab her arm and help her down from the carriage.

"Dorian Gray," I tell her. "He's formed a society for mystics."

"So he's a witch?" Brom asks.

"Not quite," I tell him as we walk up to the door of the mansion. "I'm honestly not sure what he is."

I ring the doorbell, hearing laughter and piano from inside, and the door swings open, held by a pretty-looking maid.

"Are you expected?" she asks sweetly, and I can tell from her aura that she's a witch.

"Yes," I say with a nod, taking off my hat. "Ichabod Crane, Katrina Crane, and Brom Bones."

She raises her brow over Brom's last name. Legally he's still Van Brunt, but he long ago decided to shun his familial name as much as possible since it reminds him of his heritage, his ties to the Erusian coven.

"There you are," Dorian says from the end of the grand hall, striding toward us in his tuxedo.

"He looks like Brom," Kat whispers to me. "If Brom were to ever shave."

Dorian does look similar, though he has both a jovial nature and a snobbishness that Brom could never possess.

"So glad that you could make it," Dorian says to us. He shakes Brom's hand and then takes Kat's and kisses the back of hers. "Brom Bones and Katrina Crane, I take it. I am Dorian Gray."

"She prefers to be called Kat," I tell him, putting my hand on my wife's lower back in a possessive manner, lest she be charmed by this man. Three's not a crowd, but four certainly is.

"Of course, Kat," he says to her, bowing. Then he straightens up and waves us over. "Come along, let me introduce you to the rest of the mystics."

We follow him into a grand parlor with about a dozen or so people, everyone around the same age as us, if not younger, dressed well in their tuxedos and gowns, waiters walking around with trays of champagne and canapés.

My senses go wild and I know Kat feels it too. There are witches here, and if I'm not mistaken, a vampire or two, which immediately gets my hair standing on end. I have to remember the tryst I had with my vampire in order to recall that they aren't *all* bad.

Dorian takes us around to everyone, where we meet Dr. Henry Jekyll, an affable, if reserved, scientist. Then his scientist friend, the much more buoyant, and potentially drunk, Dr. Victor Frankenstein, and his sister Elizabeth. There are also a few society people, like a beautiful young opera singer from Sweden by the name of Christine Daaé, and chatting in the corner are the two vampires I sensed when I walked in.

They both look up at me, one darkly handsome with a scowl on his face that would rival Brom's, the other an elegant redhead wearing spectacles, sipping a glass of red wine. I recognize this man. He was with my vampire when I met him in New York.

"Yes, I thought it was you," the redheaded vampire says, getting to his feet. "Ichabod Crane, isn't it? We've met before. I'm Dr. Abraham Van Helsing."

"Nice to see you again," I tell him, staring down at his hand. I wouldn't normally shake a vampire's hand, but I know this one means me no harm. I clasp his, expecting him to compel me, but Van Helsing does nothing of the sort.

"This is a friend of mine, Heathcliff," Van Helsing says, gesturing to the surly vampire.

"Heathcliff . . . ?" I prod for a last name.

"Just Heathcliff," the vampire grumbles. Thankfully he doesn't offer to shake hands because I don't think I'd take him up on it. Van Helsing I trust, but this vampire seems to have all his demons along for the ride.

"Heathcliff with no first name and no last name, I understand," I say, flashing him a smile that only seems to anger him, before Kat and Brom introduce themselves.

We don't hang out in the vampires' corner very long; in fact, with most people at this party being witches, the blood-suckers are given a wide berth, and soon we're all taking our places at the dinner table, waiters bringing out enough food and drink to serve an entire village.

"I'd like to propose a toast," Dorian says, standing at the head of the table and raising his glass. "To the newest members of the mystic society: Ichabod Crane, Katrina Crane, and Brom Bones. May you always feel welcome in this house, may it be your shelter against the world that can't even begin to understand you. But here, in the mystic society, we do."

"Hear hear," people cheer, tapping their knives on their glasses before we all take our drink.

The bubbles feel warm going down and I glance at my lovers on either side of me, putting one of my hands on top of Kat's leg and the other going on top of Brom's, anchoring us together.

Dorian Gray might think his society is a shelter from the world at large, but I have my own shelter right here. I have my pretty boy and my sweet witch, and it's in loving them both that I truly know I'm home.

And I'm finally safe.

**THE END**

# Acknowledgments

I'm not sure how many people read the acknowledgments of the books they read, but if you do, and you have happened to read mine before, you'll see a familiar theme.

Mainly that I often say, "This was the hardest book I ever had to write," and I'm being honest every time.

Now, *Legend* was one of the hardest books I've ever had to write, but it was in the same way that *Hollow* was. Meaning it was all external circumstances, including travel, mental health struggles, world events, et cetera.

All of that said, the writing of *Legend* itself was an absolute delight and I am *so* sad that my time with Kat, Brom, and Crane is over. I already miss them so much. These characters told me a lot about myself, and I didn't even realize at the time that I was writing a story about generational trauma, but there you go! Hopefully none of you have been coerced to birth the anti-Christ though.

Must thank my usual suspects: first and foremost, *you*, the reader! Thank you for taking a chance on this duet, I know it's a departure for me with a poly/M/M/F relationship, so thank you for trusting me with this.

Thanks to Laura Helseth for her edits on the go for the original self-pubbed version, and Sarah Blumenstock for her help with this version for Penguin Random House, and of course, as always, Scott—my pretty boy. ;)

DON'T MISS

# REALM OF THIEVES

*on sale now from ACE*

# Brynla

This is as far as I'll take you," the man says. His voice is as gnarled and rough as his hands that grip the oars.

I stare at his pockmarked face for a moment, my stomach pinching with unease at the thought of this mission going even remotely wrong.

"This wasn't what we agreed upon," I say. Beside me Lemi shifts on his haunches, casting a wary eye at the boatsman.

"I said I'd take you to Fjallen Rock," the man says, and nods past me at the hazy shape of land shrouded by smoke in the distance, backlit by the orange glow of the Midland volcanoes. "That's it right there."

I give him a tight smile. I don't want to start arguing with my only ride back to Esland and a stranger at that. "You know I meant past the wards."

"You should have been more specific, then, girl," he says, eyes narrowing. "Because that's not what you said. There's no law against coming this far. There is a law against going through the wards and to the Midlands."

"The last boatsman—" I begin.

"Your last boatsman is no more," he says, flashing me a smile of missing teeth. "Otherwise you wouldn't be using me now, would ya?" His salt-crusted lips curl into a smirk.

*I live more in each second of the day than you'll ever live in your lifetime*, I think as I try not to scowl at him. It's hard for me to rein in my temper, but tonight I don't have the luxury of letting it loose. I'm about to be dropped off at the most dangerous place in the world and I'm counting on this asshole here to pick me up. If he doesn't, my dog and I are as good as dead.

"Also, most boatsmen wouldn't allow a hound on the vessel," he says, eyeing Lemi, who eyes him right back. "You're fortunate I'm such an animal lover."

I roll my eyes at that. On the two-hour boat journey he's done nothing but try to spear every turtle, dolphin, and whale that's come in passing distance.

I take in a deep breath to quell my mounting frustration, hoping I can reason with him. "But if you don't go through the wards and bring the boat to shore, how am I supposed to come back with the egg?"

"That sounds like a you problem, not a me problem," he huffs and sits back, crossing his arms until I get the point.

I sigh. It *is* my problem, and I don't have the luxury of trying to figure out a solution with him. My plan was to be dropped off at the rock and, if I was lucky, I'd find an elderdrage nest. If not I'd head farther in to the other islands. But elderdrage eggs are at least three feet tall and they weigh a ton. It's hard enough to carry them back across the rugged land and then swim them over to the boat, even with Lemi's help.

Which means that now I'll have to find either sycledrage or blooddrage eggs, and both are significantly smaller and harder to find in an unattended nest, let alone any nest at all.

But going back to the Banished Land empty-handed isn't an option either. I need to come back home with something or I might be paying for it with my own blood. I've been too sick over the last few moons to come to the Midlands, so I already owe Sorland's syndikat, and they aren't the types to let a few absences go. Not only that, but the faster I get my coin, the faster I can hire a healer so that my monthly pains don't continue to take me out of the game. I swear every month, every year, the pain gets worse, like it's some punishment for being both a woman and alive. Even surgery from the discredited doctors in the Dark City costs more than I have saved so far.

Lemi lets out a *whumpf* of air through his nose, bringing my focus back to him. Of course more money would pay for more food for him and for my aunt Ellestra.

Staying alive is infinitely expensive.

"Fine," I say to the boatsman, hating how right he is. My last boatsman disappeared while I'd been recuperating. People disappear all the time in Esland, especially those who have dealings with the Freelanders—the exiled such as myself—and the more likely you are to visit the Banished Land, the more likely it is that you are an unsavory character to begin with. My last boatsman might have been knifed during a card game gone wrong, or he might have been captured by the Black Guard and taken to the capital for execution. If it was the latter, they would know he'd been helping a Freelander steal dragon eggs to sell to House Dalgaard, Sorland's syndikat, which means they'd be looking for me.

But they've been looking for me for the last nine years, ever since I escaped the convent. And, somehow, I'm still here.

"Promise me you'll be here when I get back," I implore the new boatsman. It's awful having to put your trust in someone you don't even know.

"I'll have to be if I want my egg," he says casually, splaying his calloused hands.

I swallow hard, still unsure if I'm making the right choice. I'm always paid handsomely for the services I render, often based on what eggs I end up stealing. If I don't, I'll be left behind. Another reason I can't come back to the mainland empty-handed tonight.

"I don't know how long I'll be," I tell him, glancing up at the dark sky. It's the cycle of the pink moon, the crescent shape barely visible through the smoke from the volcanoes. Pink moon dragon eggs are mellower than the others, much like humans born under it, but beggars can't be choosers in this case. Some people prefer the softer side effects that come with consumption of pink moon eggs, though the Sjef, the head of the syndikat, Ruunon Dalgaard, would scoff at that. The syndikat is the opposite of soft.

"You bring me the finest and the strongest eggs," Ruunon had said to me the one and only time I'd met him. It had been a heavily guarded clandestine meeting on the blackened lava fields outside the Dark City. "You do this consistently, and we will have a fine partnership."

So much was implied with what he didn't say. That if I didn't, then he'd kill me, Lemi, my aunt, and anyone else I knew. That was the way the syndikats worked. I had never met any of the other houses from Vesland or Norland and their crime families, despite how regularly their hired thieves pilfered the Midlands, but I imagined they all operated in the same way. With ruthlessness and violence and aversion to mercy.

But at that moment, when Ruunon offered me the job, I felt the first taste of hope since my father had died. It was dangerous to work for such men, but the promise that came along with it, the promise of a better life, sealed the deal.

"I'll leave at dawn," the boatsman says gruffly. "I'll be here until then. You don't show, I'll assume you're dead and you'll be left in my wake. And no, I won't give the dog a ride back even if he makes it."

I try not to narrow my eyes at him. "I'll see you before dawn," I tell him before I say the wrong thing. Then I look to Lemi. "You okay with a night swim?" I ask him as I gather my empty bags and tie them to the holsters and straps around my leathered armor.

Lemi just wags his tail eagerly, knowing his fun is about to begin.

"Now don't go disappearing on me. You'll be towing me to shore," I warn my dog, adjusting my two swords on my back, thankful that they're made from ash glass forged in the depths of the Banished Land, weapons as light as they are strong.

Lemi seems to frown at that, his fluffy brows furrowing over his warm brown eyes.

I stand up, the boat rocking back and forth from my weight, and give the man one last glance, willing him to be here until dawn and not either chicken out or sell me out. Then I take a deep breath, preparing myself for the half-mile swim, and swan dive overboard.

Despite my armor and swords, I barely make a splash, the dark, frigid water engulfing me. I take in a harsh gasp of air as I surface, just as Lemi lands in the water beside me. Shivering already, I manage to swim over to him, grabbing ahold of his harness with stiff fingers. I hear the man on the boat chuckle behind me but I don't bother paying him any attention now. All I can do is hope he'll be there when I get back. Focus on getting the goods and getting back before the sun rises.

Lemi pulls me through the water with ease, though I can tell he just wants to shift himself onto the shore already. "Easy, boy," I warn him. He's shifted before while I've been holding on to him and it's most unpleasant. Even though I don't end up traveling with him, there is a bone-rattling shock as I'm left behind and he shifts elsewhere.

Thankfully the wards are close now. They're nearly invisible to the naked eye, save for the faint glimmer of rainbows when you look at them from your peripheral vision. In the dark they're harder to see but you still feel them, the faint hum and vibration of energy they give off, eons of magic condensed, a warning to those who may have strayed off path. A warning that would work on anyone else except for me and any other egg thieves.

The wards are magicked walls that extend to the bottom of the ocean and high into the farthest reaches of the sky. In the Old Text of Dragemor, the First Sorcerer—Magni—said it was akin to a dome, one that would prevent any dragon from escaping, whether they swam to the inky depths or tried to soar into the stars above.

The dragons can't get out, but *we* can go in.

And, with any luck, come back out again.

I instinctively hold my breath as Lemi swims through the wards. They're about as thick as a window pane and my skin prickles with heat as we push to the other side. The water is as warm as the air on this side of the barrier, the atmosphere heavy with smoke. There are three active volcanoes along the Red Rift that snakes across the belly of the Midlands like a gaping wound, and depending on which way the winds are blowing, your visibility can be close to zero. At the moment the wind is pushing the volcanic fumes my way, so as soon as we reach shore I'll have to wear a mask in order to breathe properly. Just another punishing feature of this forsaken land for those who dare to tread it.

The shore feels far away this time, the craggy features of the small island of Fjallen Rock hidden in the grimy haze. There are times I think the Midlands and its austere and terrifying geography can be quite beautiful, in the same way a dragon can be beautiful. But you're always aware of the danger. Of how feeble and useless you are in comparison. The Midlands and the beasts that fly above it dole out death without second thought.

But that's why I have Lemi. I couldn't do this without him. The other thieves who pilfer the Midlands have heightened abilities and powers thanks to their egg consumption, senses that may help them find the precious commodities and fight back against dragon attacks. I have no powers except my dog and years of training with the best fighters of the Banished Land.

Now as we're getting close to shore, Lemi swims faster. While the eggs—and more specifically, the suen compound that's extracted from them—don't work on me for reasons I still don't understand, they do work on Lemi. He's stronger and faster than any dog ought to be, plus he has the ability to shift through time and space, as long as it's to a place he can see or a place he's already been to. The moment my boots reach the sharp rocks of the seafloor I let go of his harness and he immediately disappears in front of me. One moment he's here, the next he's vanished into thin air, with only a faint whiff of his warm doggy smell left behind.

He quickly reappears farther down the coast, his giant black body blending in with the lava-sculpted shoreline, his head down to the ground, sniffing for our prize. I let out a sigh of quiet relief and keep my eyes on him as I stagger out of the water and onto land. I should have stopped worrying about him years ago after he proved no dragon could catch him, but even so, I watch him like a hawk.

It's only for a little while, I tell myself, though I feel the bitterness on my tongue. All those *one more time*s and *soon I can stop*s and *almost there*s and *not long now*s have melted into chains of hope that keep me fastened to this trade.

The existence of tomorrow is more intoxicating than any drug.

I want to call out to Lemi so that he doesn't go too far, but now that I'm on land, I don't want to attract any attention to myself. Instead I pull up my mask from around my neck so that it covers my nose and mouth. It's wet but that makes it easier to breathe, and in no time I'll be completely dry, with the heat and the winds the way they are.

I start walking along the coast, the seawater squishing in my boots, keeping an eye on Lemi while minding my step among the sharp rocks. Occasionally a rock will move and charred legs will appear—a lava crab that scatters back into the dark sea. If I felt more optimistic about tonight's hunt, I'd spear the crab and take it back home with me because they're my aunt's favorite dish and she's been doing all the cooking as of late. But now that my plan has changed, the less I have to carry with me, the better.

Lemi is still visible, though he's getting farther and farther away. I've always had unnaturally good eyesight, and the constant eruptions from the distant volcanos of the Midlands illuminate the sky in an orange glow, but even so he's getting harder to spot.

An image of my mother flashes across my mind, as it always does whenever I step foot in these dragon lands. The scene is of the last time I saw her, at the front of the square ship, the lone person at the helm with five hundred rockdeer packed behind her. Though I grew up in the capital I had never seen what happened every moon at Sacrifice Bay on the outskirts of the city of Lerick. I always thought the deer would be bleating, terrified at being herded onto the long, wide boat, but what struck me was the silence. It's like they knew their only purpose in life was to end up as dragon food.

The silence extended to my mother. She had the same look in her eyes as the sacrificial deer, as if she always knew her purpose would come to this, to be used as a pawn for a religion of sycophants and hypocrites. She stared directly at me while the Black Guard held me in place at the front of the crowd, forced to watch, just as they forced me to watch my father's execution, and then with a lingering look that I still can't seem to decipher to this day, she turned around and steered the boat toward the very land I'm standing on now.

Both of my parents were so elegant and poised when facing their death. I fear that when my time comes, their composure will not have been passed on to me.

I sigh and shake my head, clearing the memory before my attention goes to Lemi again.

I freeze.

My heart thundering in my throat.

Lemi is gone.

And in his place is a dark-cloaked figure standing at the end of the shore.

I'm not alone here.

**Karina Halle** is a screenwriter, a former music and travel journalist, and the *New York Times* bestselling author of *Realm of Thieves*, *River of Shadows*, and *The Royals Next Door* as well as eighty other romances across all subgenres, ranging from spicy rom-coms to gothic horror and dark fantasy. Needless to say, whatever you're into, she's probably written an HEA for it. When she's not traveling, she, her husband, and their pup, Perry, split their time between a possibly haunted 120-year-old house in Victoria, British Columbia, and their not-haunted condo in Los Angeles.

### Visit Karina Halle Online

AuthorKarinaHalle.com

 AuthorKarinaHalle

 AuthorHalle

 AuthorHalle

 AuthorKarinaHalle.Bsky.Social

Ready to find
your next great read?

Let us help.

**Visit prh.com/nextread**

Penguin
Random
House